Provided

by

Measure B

which was approved

by the voters in

November, 1998

IRREPARABLE DAMAGE

also by joseph t. klempner

Flat Lake in Winter
Change of Course
Shoot the Moon
Felony Murder

IRREPARABLE

joseph t. klempner

DAMAGE

THOMAS DUNNE BOOKS

ST. MARTIN'S PRESS

NEW YORK

THOMAS DUNNE BOOKS.
An imprint of St. Martin's Press.

www.stmartins.com

Library of Congress Cataloging-in-Publication Data

Klempner, Joseph T.
    Irreparable damage / Joseph T. Klempner. — 1st ed.
      p. cm.
    ISBN 0-312-28303-2
    1. Divorced fathers—Fiction. 2. Custody of children—Fiction. 3. Fathers and daughters—Fiction. 4. Photography of children—Fiction. I. Title.

PS3561 L3866 I77 2002
813'.54—dc21

                                                        2001058486

First Edition: June 2002

10 9 8 7 6 5 4 3 2 1

This book is for J.

AUTHOR'S NOTE

Out of a concern for the privacy rights of certain individuals, I have taken the liberty of changing names and locations, and even modifying some of the less important details of the story that follows.

But it happened, it really did.

As the old saying goes, you just can't make up stuff like this.

IRREPARABLE
DAMAGE

ONE

The boxer tapped the speed bag softly with a left, just hard enough to get it moving, before following up with a right, then another left, followed by another right. The idea was to catch the bag with the next punch at the precise moment it swung back through the bottom of its arc and began to rise toward you. If you did it right, you quickly fell into a rhythm, making contact with each punch and producing a pleasing *rat-tat-tat, rat-tat-tat* sound that echoed through the gym. It was a lot like jumping rope: It was all in the timing. Someone good at it could do it for minutes at a time, *hours* at a time, if it weren't for the fatigue that would eventually set in.

The boxer working at the speed bag was good, but not *that* good. Before long, one blow caught the bag just an inch off to the side, sending it slightly to the left, instead of straight back. Somebody really good—a professional, say—might have been able to make the necessary correction. But the boxer was only an amateur, and something of a novice at that, and the correction turned out to be an overcorrection, and before long the pleasing *rat-tat-tat* had disintegrated into a *rat-tat-tat . . . tat . . . tat,* before ceasing altogether.

"Okay, Mulholland," the trainer called out. The trainer was a squat fireplug of a man, who couldn't have been more than five foot three, but who must've weighed in at 220, 230 easy. Everyone called him Tony. It was entirely possible that he had no last name. "Okay," he called out again. "Gimme ten minutes on the heavy bag. And *work it!*"

The boxer moved over to the heavy bag, leaning into it with one shoulder before starting to throw short jabs at it. Here it was much harder to develop any kind of a rhythm at all. The heavy bag was simply too heavy: Unlike the speed bag, which would go whichever way you hit it, the heavy bag had a tendency to stay put. But that was okay. Here you weren't working on timing so much; you were working on strength. And your reward came not from any pleasing rhythm or sound, but from a drenching sweat and a pair of arms that after five minutes felt like they had lead in their veins.

"C'mon, Red!" yelled Tony. "*Hit* the sonofabitch, willya?"

The boxer responded by lashing out harder, tiny droplets of sweat flying with each blow, until the leaded arms simply became too heavy, first dropping down after each punch, then skipping a punch, then finally hanging down lifelessly, as though the gloved hands at the ends of them might have been carrying invisible pails of water.

"Okay, okay," said Tony. "Good workout, kid. Go get yourself a shower."

But there was no going anywhere, not just yet. It took a full three minutes just to peel the drenched gloves off, another three to unwrap the yards of soggy tape beneath them. Even then, there were fingers that needed to be flexed and rubbed and kneaded, before the circulation gradually returned to them and they were supple enough to work properly once again. Only then did the boxer finally reach up to unsnap the chin strap of the protective leather helmet and, using both hands, lift it off. Then two good sideways shakes of the head, first to the left, then to the right, causing long red hair to spill down onto her narrow shoulders.

Twenty miles to the east, Stephen Barrow held the inside of his wrist under the spigot to test the temperature of the water, the exact same way they'd showed him how to do it at the hospital, almost seven years ago. "If you use the palm of your hand," the nurse had told them, "you're liable to end up scalding baby." *Baby,* she'd said, instead of referring to their daughter by her name. "Baby's skin is much more sensitive than yours, but she has no way of telling you that the water's too hot or too cold, until it's too late." Stephen had listened to every word, memorizing each bit of wisdom as though his daughter's very life depended upon his ability to do so. He'd even taken notes at times, so struck had he been by the awesome responsibility that fatherhood had suddenly thrust upon him. He'd marveled back then at his wife's nonchalance, her confidence that everything would be all right, even as he'd secretly wondered if perhaps she loved their new child less than he did. Even then, even in those first terrifying days, he'd wondered.

Now, more than six years later, bath time was still a special time for father and daughter. Gone was the fear that he'd scald Penny with water that was too hot, or induce instant frostbite with liquid ice. Gone was the need to hold her tiny head above the waterline, or to keep the shampoo from burning her sensitive eyes, the "No Tears" assurance on its label notwithstanding. And though he no longer felt the need to stay in the bathroom for the entire time she was in the tub, he never strayed far, and not a minute went by that he didn't call out her name to make certain she was still okay.

"I'm *fine,* Daddy," she'd call back. And she always was.

Bath time was unwinding time. It was that period of transition at the end of the day, that shifting-of-gears process designed to slow Penny down from full speed ahead to something approaching calm, something that would allow her to sit still for a bedtime story, curl up beside one stuffed animal or another, and eventually let go of the day and slip into sleep.

"Look at me," he heard her calling to him—or perhaps to no one in particular. "I'm a *unicord!*"

He put down whatever he was doing (later he'd be unable to remember just what it had been) and went to her to investigate. It wasn't every day, after all, that your only child was transformed into a unicord.

When he poked his head into the bathroom, there was Penny, her long hair piled on top of her head with the assistance of what must have been half a bottle of shampoo and an equal measure of bubble bath. And, true to her description—give or take a letter—she'd somehow managed to create a spike at the very top of her head that pointed straight up, in absolute defiance of the laws of gravity.

His reaction was to laugh out loud. His daughter did that to him at least once a day, and often more. Even in the first early weeks of the separation, even during the divorce proceedings and the custody battle that followed, even when there was precious little to feel good about, she'd never lost her ability to make him laugh.

"*I* wanna see!" she said now, lifting her arms for him to pluck her up and hold her in front of the mirror.

"No," he said, "you stay put. I'll be right back." And he'd gone into his bedroom to find a hand mirror, the one he used periodically to check on that tiny bald spot threatening to spread across the top of his head.

And had the mirror been there on his dresser, where it was supposed to be, that would have been that: He would have picked it up, brought it into the bathroom, handed it to his daughter, and let her see for herself how funny she looked.

But the mirror *wasn't* there, where it was supposed to be. Instead, it was down in the kitchen, where he'd left it the night before, after trimming Penny's bangs. But there was something else on the dresser that caught his eye: his camera. A 35mm Nikon that had seen better days, but still worked well enough. He picked it up, checked to see if it was loaded, and saw it had seven exposures left on a roll that had once contained twenty-four, or maybe thirty-six; he couldn't remember.

Back in the bathroom, he set the camera down so that he could pick Penny up and—being careful not to let her soapy body slip through his hands—held her in front of the medicine cabinet mirror, so that she could see her reflection and share his laughter. Then he set her back in the bathtub. He expected her knees to bend, which would have returned her to the sitting position she'd been in before, but she stiffened them—much the same way a cat will stiffen its legs to avoid being placed in water—and ended up standing.

"Show me again!" she laughed, but by that time he'd already reached for the camera. With a certain measure of tolerance, she indulged him as he snapped away. He took three shots of her from the shoulders up, paying little attention to her expression, concentrating instead on the absurd hairdo she'd created. It was only when he went to put the camera down on the sink that he became aware of her exaggerated pout.

"Show me again," she repeated, this time in mock seriousness.

And it was a combination of that pout and that seriousness on the one hand, and her vulnerable, skinny nakedness on the other, that struck him so, that filled him with a tenderness he could not have put into words. He picked the camera back up, and, pressing the button that pulled her image away from him in the viewfinder, he clicked away, taking full body shots of her standing in the tub, *unicord* hairdo, bubble bath and all.

Her reaction, though not immediate—he managed to get three or four shots first—was to turn away from him. This, too, he saw through the viewfinder. And as he watched the tiny image, she bent over so that her head suddenly appeared upside down between her legs, grabbed the cheeks of her tiny butt with either hand, and made a noise that could best be described as a Bronx cheer by one on a diet of baked beans.

He snapped the shutter one last time.

"Dadd*eeee*!" she protested.

"You're just lucky," he told her, "that I was out of film."

They both laughed.

―――――

It took Theresa Mulholland twenty-two minutes to drive from the gym to work. Anyone else, it might have taken half an hour. But Theresa Mulholland had what is commonly referred to as a heavy foot. Beyond that, she knew the back roads of Columbia County as well as anyone. She'd grown up in Chatham, and—except for four years of college spent over in Boston—she had lived her whole life in the area. And as areas went, it was pretty, and she liked it okay. But there tended to be a lot of time left over for getting to know the back roads.

Work, for Theresa, was at the offices of the *Hudson Valley Herald,* a regional newspaper that came out twice a week and served New York's Dutchess and Columbia Counties, as well as southern Vermont and the northern Berkshires of Massachusetts, to the east.

Theresa Mulholland was a reporter.

And though it was after nine o'clock at night when she arrived at the *Herald* office, working an occasional evening shift wasn't all that out of the ordinary. *Evening shift,* they always called it; call it a *night shift* and suddenly extra pay would be required, union organizers would be coming over from Pittsfield, there'd be dues and lockouts and strikes, jobs would be lost, God knows what else would happen. So to play it safe, they sent you home around one or two in the morning, before their idea of *evening* ended, and actual *night* began. It was a once-a-month thing, maybe, something that only happened when some real news came along just when they were about to put an issue to bed. *Real news* in the tricounty area being a relative term: some teenage vandalism in Chatham, perhaps, or the sudden cancellation of an auction down in Copake. Today's event had been the unexpected announcement that the Columbia County Board of Assessors was thinking about reappraising all the homes in Hudson. News like that certainly couldn't wait till the next issue.

But for Theresa, it was no big deal. It wasn't as if she'd made previous plans for the evening. Theresa—or Terry, as most everyone called her, the principal exception being Tony the

Trainer, who referred to her as Mulholland, Red, Kid, Hey Youse, Yo, and an assortment of other things—was pretty, and at thirty-one she was not only unmarried but, as they like to say, *uninvolved*. Which was, surprisingly or not, a fairly common state of affairs for college-educated young women living in the area. There were lots of young men around, to be sure. But they all seemed to have grown up right there in town after struggling to make it through high school, or not quite. Now they worked at contracting jobs by day, drank beer by night, and saved their deepest commitment for deer hunting and snowmobile maintenance. And though Theresa didn't like to think of herself as a snob, she nonetheless had her standards. And those standards tended to result in a number of free evenings.

The bedtime story Penny had picked out was the Maurice Sendak classic *Where the Wild Things Are*. With its elaborate illustrations of fanciful monsters, it had long been one of her favorites. Early on, even before she herself had begun to read, Penny had committed many of the passages to memory. Stephen had paused each time he'd come to the end of a sentence, pointing at some item in one of the drawings to cue Penny, who dutifully supplied the missing word. So thoroughly had she memorized the story that when Stephen would slip in a wrong word here or an extra phrase there, she'd instantly correct him. And now that she could actually read many of the words herself, Stephen would require her to do so, even if it meant covering up the illustration that would otherwise provide her a clue.

They read for twenty minutes like that, Penny propped up against her pillow, a stuffed animal flanking her on either side, while Stephen sat on the edge of her bed, his back wedged against the headboard. If the position caused him physical discomfort (and it did, owing in no small part to a motorcycle accident dating back to earlier, more reckless years), it was a small price to pay. This quiet time—this period at the end of the day when Penny, at last wearied by the day's frantic adventures and soothed by her bath—brought inexplicable joy to Stephen Barrow. It wasn't a matter of having the rest of the evening to himself to get back to his writing, or open a book, or even catch part of a ball game on the TV. Working out of his own home gave him plenty of free time during the day, when his daughter was off at school. No, it was more than that. It was a special time because it was quiet, unhurried, safe.

When his marriage to Ada had come apart, Stephen had fought hard for custody of his only child, hard but fair. He'd had his lawyer stress his parenting skills, his obvious closeness with Penny (who was only four when the battle came to a head), and the fact that his writing gave him the advantage of being home full-time to care for her. At the same time, over his lawyer's considerable protests, he'd forbidden any mention to be made of Ada's own shortcomings, including her sometimes erratic behavior and her affinity for the three-martini nightcap. But in the end, the judge—herself a mother—had pretty much figured things out on her own.

In the two years since, father and daughter had forged a relationship that eventually astounded even Stephen. At the age of six, Penny was more than his daughter; she was his friend, his companion, his approving audience, his sometimes critic, his doting parent. She provided him with nonstop conversation, much of it surprisingly intelligent. She helped him with chores, reminded him of things he might otherwise have forgotten (like her gymnastics lessons or soccer practice), shared cooking responsibilities (she was a leading authority on the grilled cheese sandwich), mastered electronic devices that were total mysteries to him (had it not been for Penny, their VCR would still be nothing but a clock, perpetually flashing *12:12*), and kept her own room, well, reasonably neat. Her occasional outbursts and rarer tantrums he viewed as the stuff of a normal six-year-old. Never did he cease to marvel at her overall resiliency, her amazing adjustment to life without a mother.

For even as the two of them grew closer, Ada receded farther and farther into the distance. In the months following the judge's decision, she'd done her share of coparenting, taking Penny one night a week and every other weekend. But as time went by, her work increasingly got in the way, or her image of herself as a mother who didn't have custody of her own child became too difficult for her to bear; or perhaps it was a combination of those things and more. At first, her last-minute cancellations totally unhinged Penny and infuriated Stephen. But in time they came to expect and accept them, and finally to count on them. There was never a formal end to Ada's participation in the raising of her daughter; it just seemed to gradually dwindle to a point where it simply no longer existed. Now there was a man in her life, a live-in boyfriend Stephen had met once or twice. He seemed a decent enough guy who made her happy, which was nice for Ada, and nicer still for Stephen and Penny.

"One more story," Penny begged.

"Not for me," Stephen said, straightening his back with difficulty. "I'm all storied out. But you can read to yourself, if you like."

"Thanks, Stephen."

She had this habit of calling him by his first name. Not always—only when she wanted to seem like an adult. It had totally unsettled him at first. After all, how were you supposed to maintain parental authority over a person who addressed you as *Stephen*? He briefly considered discouraging the practice, or even outright forbidding it. But he didn't, and he got over it soon enough, coming to realize that if he was to earn his daughter's respect, he was going to have to do so on grounds more significant than the mere accident of being her biological father.

He bent down to kiss her. "Goodnight, kiddo," he said. "I love you."

"Goodnight, Daddy. I love you, too."

"Hey, Terry, thanks for coming in."

The voice belonged to Neil Witt, the managing editor and Theresa's boss.

"No problem."

"Hope you didn't have plans."

"Luckily," said Theresa, "I have no life."

"Listen," Witt said. "Grady's out again."

Tom Grady had been a reporter for the *Herald* for thirteen years—a record, so far as anyone could figure out. He'd been in the business for fifty. You found that out anew each time he confided in you, "I began as a copy boy for the *Daily Mirror*," and launched into his life story. Sober, Grady was a good reporter—a capable investigator and a decent writer. But his periods of sobriety were decidedly finite, and Neil Witt's announcement suggested that the latest such period had come to an end.

"Can you pick up 'Coming Events' for the time being?" he asked Theresa.

"Sure." "Coming Events" was a royal pain in the butt. You left out some meeting of Gardeners' Anonymous, and you'd never hear the end of it. Grady would owe her big-time when he got back.

"Thanks," said Witt. "And—"

"*And?*"

" 'From the Police Blotter.' "

"From the Police Blotter" was a list, printed on page 2, of everyone who'd been arrested since the previous issue. You got to read their names, their ages, their home addresses, and what they'd been charged with. Critics assailed it as nothing but gossip, invasion of privacy, and slander. Defenders (Neil Witt among them) countered with claims of free speech, the community's right to know, and the fact that such details were a matter of public record, anyway. Tom Grady, who regularly compiled the list, was a natural for the task. He was a police buff, a cop wannabe who drank with most of the officers and all of the chiefs in the area. They knew to phone him as soon as a new arrest came across their desks; each one was worth a drink or a pack of smokes, not to mention the added ego gratification of seeing their own names in print.

"How'm I supposed to do *that*?" Theresa asked.

"I've got Tom's phone book," Witt explained. The way he said it, it sounded to Theresa like Grady voluntarily surrendered it each time he was about to fall off the wagon. "All you'll have to do is make some calls. Okay?"

"Great," said Theresa, heading for her desk before her boss could come up with yet some other assignment for her.

Tom Grady would owe her *huge*.

Back downstairs in the kitchen, Stephen Barrow sat at the wooden table, a flea-market purchase, twelve dollars, bargained down from twenty. A lot of sanding and a little shoe polish had transformed it from a piece of trash to—well, a piece of furniture. Sure, there'd been those first couple of weeks when everything had a slight taste of cordovan to it, but they'd gotten past that.

The two mismatched chairs he'd found antiquing, over in Great Barrington. Penny had needed a booster seat at first, but she herself had put it away a long time ago, announcing one evening, "I growed up, Stephen." Her little chin resting on the tabletop, she continued to deadpan even as Stephen laughed out loud. It must have been a struggle for her to eat like that, but she stayed with it. On the bright side, a noticeably greater percentage of her food got inadvertently trapped by her mouth, instead of completing its inexorable journey to the floor, than had previously been the case.

He toyed with the idea of doing an hour of writing. He was maybe seventy pages into a new manuscript, a story about a miracle diet drug that turns out to be so effective its users can't stop losing weight, even after they've stopped taking it. He wasn't sure about the whole idea. There were times when he thought it could be the next big disaster book, soon to become a major motion picture. There were other times when he felt like he was selling out, writing a script for some made-for-TV summer-schedule filler.

He'd had four novels published over a span of six years—not too shabby a track record for someone who'd been at it for such a short time. But in those same six years, there'd been four other books that *hadn't* made it, that at this very moment existed only as boxed manuscripts stacked in his closet as though in a mausoleum, waiting there in suspended animation for some prince of a publisher to awaken them with a kiss or, even better, a contract.

On top of his uncertainty about the out-of-control-diet-drug idea, there was another problem. He was at the end of a chapter—Chapter 2, to be precise, where the pretty young research assistant discovers that her laboratory mice are losing weight—and he had no clue how to begin Chapter 3. So he found himself stuck with a minor case of writer's block.

He'd once read something Ernest Hemingway had said, or supposedly said. Always stop writing in the middle of a sentence, or at some other place where you know exactly what's supposed to come next. That way you'll never have any trouble picking up where you left off.

He should have listened.

Then again, who was to say? Maybe Hemingway forgot to follow his own advice at the end.

He decided against bringing his manuscript up on the computer, in favor of spending a few minutes straightening up the kitchen. He put away the dishes that had been in the drying rack—they had a dishwasher, but seldom used it—filled and set the coffee machine so it would be ready to turn on in the morning, and looked through a small pile of papers on the counter. There were some unpaid bills, a letter from his editor, a few notes he'd written to himself, a newspaper item or two he'd clipped out for future reference, and a square red envelope he didn't recognize. Looking inside, he found a sheet of lined paper that had been folded over twice, until it roughly resembled the shape and size of a greeting card. With no less certainty than a mother seal identifying her pup by its scent, he recognized his daughter's artwork. On the front was the figure of a person, probably male, wearing what could have been a coat or a bathrobe or a cape of some sort. It was carefully crayoned in red (or perhaps magenta or vermillion or one of those other exotic shades that seem to exist only in the world according to Crayola), except that on the figure's chest was printed a large letter D in bright blue. He opened it to the centerfold. Right away he could see that she'd gotten some help with the spelling (though apparently not too much), but the sentiment was clearly hers.

> HAPPY VALENTIMES DAY, DADDYMAN.
> I LOVE YOU.
> PENNY

He sat there and smiled for a very long time, before finally folding the card back up and returning it to its envelope. Then he checked his watch. It was a calendar watch, sort of: It had a little box with a number in it, which told you the date, so long as you remembered to advance it manually following any month that had fewer than 31 days. As far as what month it actually was—or what year or day of the week, for that matter—you were left to figure that out for yourself. Right now the number in the little box was 10. Four days (really three, now that today was all but over) till Valentine's Day. Or Valentimes Day, if you were six. Once again Penny had come to the rescue and reminded him of something, if only inadvertently.

He made a mental note to go to the Drug Mart in South Chatham the following day so that he could buy her a card of his own, and perhaps a little present of some sort. He'd mail her the card: She absolutely *loved* getting her own mail. Then he locked the door, turned down the heat, flicked off the lights, and headed upstairs. He made a stop at Penny's door, saw she'd fallen asleep with the book spread across her chest, the Wild Things dancing on its cover. He marveled that she didn't get nightmares from them. As he tucked her in and kissed her softly on the forehead, she shook her head, but never quite opened her eyes.

"Am I safe?" she asked, her voice thick with sleep. Maybe she *did* get nightmares.

"Yes," he told her. "You're safe."

And he realized in that moment that if he accomplished nothing else in his life, if he never made another nickel or got another book published as long as he lived, he could point to one unqualified success: He'd somehow managed to make things safe for his daughter.

It might not earn him a place in history, let alone pay the bills, but it certainly had to count for something.

TWO

Theresa Mulholland was a creature of habit, and even on four hours of sleep, she awoke promptly at 7:00. They'd put the paper to bed just after 1:00, bumping a story about a mountain lion sighting from page 1 in order to make room for the big item about the Columbia County Board of Assessors. Mountain lions were one thing, but real estate taxes—now *there* was news.

She remembered her new assignments, "Coming Events" and "From the Police Blotter," but decided to try not to think about them, let alone *do* anything about them. She had three full days before she had to get her work in for the next issue; so there was no sense making calls yet, since things were bound to change before press time. Besides which, even thinking about it made her pissed off at Tom Grady all over again.

Today was Friday. No deadline, no workout at the gym with Tony the Trainer. She knew she ought to get the oil changed on her Honda, but that was a pain. She'd have to wait at Jensen's while they did it, and it was always cold in there and boring, unless your idea of a good time was reading back issues of *Car and Driver*, or looking at old pinup calendars from the '80s. She also needed to go food shopping—she was out of just about everything—but that meant driving over to Pittsfield, to the Stop-and-Shop and Guido's. You went to the local Grand Union, and they never had what you wanted, no matter what it was.

She pulled the curtains back and looked outside. It had snowed overnight, sometime after she'd gotten home. Just a dusting, though; not enough to shovel. The winter had been pretty dealable so far: only two snowstorms that had amounted to anything, and a few subzero nights, but only a few. There'd been a good deal of talk about global warming, but Theresa never added her voice to those of the believers. She knew how quickly the temperature could drop in Columbia County, and she wasn't about to jinx things.

She even thought about putting her skis on top of her car and heading over to Jiminy Peak, or down to Catamount. But it was Friday, and that meant the weekenders would already be beginning their invasion.

No, she'd take a shower, have some breakfast (though she was pretty much down to Fig Newtons and Rice-a-Roni), and then head over to the Drug Mart. She was out of toothpaste and dangerously low on tampons, and she'd been shaving her legs with the same disposable razor for two weeks now. Besides which, they had two whole aisles of food there. Good things like chips and salsa, M&M's, marshmallows, cookies, crackers, and Cheez Whiz. All of the essential food groups invariably overlooked by the Department of Agriculture, but definitely on Satan's recommended list.

Stephen and Penny Barrow shared a breakfast of scrambled eggs and toast. The eggs had to be scrambled and well done; that was the only way Penny would eat them. With any other kind of eggs, the white was identifiable, whether *yucky* if fried, poached, or soft-boiled, or *truly disgusting* if hard-boiled. Then, while Stephen did the dishes, Penny got ready for school.

School was the Hillsdale Day Center, and a thirty-five minute drive. But it was the best school in the area and, as far as Stephen was concerned, worth both the private tuition and the trip, which he made each morning and again each afternoon. Penny was good company in the car, keenly alert to sights along the way, and always ready to talk about *stuff*.

"So, Stephen," she'd asked him out of the blue just last week, as they headed down the Taconic Parkway, "how's the writing coming?"

His initial response at moments like that had been to laugh at how precocious she was, even as he'd dismiss the notion that she was really interested. But soon enough he came to realize she wasn't just being cute or showing off—*she really wanted to know how the writing was coming*. So he began to tell her. And though he didn't yet rank her up there with his literary agent or early draft readers, he knew better than to ignore her comments on his choice of names, occasional attempts at humor, and plot development. Just last week, for example, he'd run his out-of-control-diet-drug idea past her.

"Is it a pill?" she asked.

"Pill, capsule, whatever." It didn't seem to make much a difference, at least as far as he was concerned.

"Why don'tcha make it a *drink*?" she suggested. "You know, like an Ultra Slim-Fast shake. They come in three delicious flavors. That would be much more realistic, don'tcha think?"

And he'd been forced to agree with her. The pill was transformed to a shake, and from there to an herbal tea. And all of a sudden, his worries about how the lab would get FDA approval were eased. Not that it had done much to solve the rest of the problems of the book. But no doubt they'd eventually get around to discussing those, and she'd have some suggestions for them as well.

The drive back north was a different experience, to be sure, but Stephen enjoyed it, too. He seldom turned the radio on—his Jeep had no tape deck or CD player, but he wouldn't have played music even if it did. In his daughter's absence, he simply preferred the silence, using it to think about his writing or something else, or often nothing at all. The upper stretches of the Taconic were beautiful—long, rolling hills with views of the Berkshires to the east and the Catskills to the west—and on this particular morning the bright sunlight fairly dazzled on the fresh snow.

Right before the parkway ended, he exited onto Route 203 and turned left, toward South Chatham. He slowed down dutifully just outside of the village, where the speed limit dropped without warning from fifty-five to thirty, and where most days a white police cruiser would be waiting for the unwary out-of-town motorist. He gassed up at the BP station, astonished to note that the price of a gallon had climbed to nearly a dollar and a half.

Back in his car, he drove the two blocks to the Drug Mart, found a spot right in front, and went inside. He spent ten minutes picking out three Valentine's Day cards and a Safari Barbie. He wanted to introduce Penny to camping out that summer, and he figured it would be as good a way as any to bring up the subject. When succumbing to the temptation of spending nineteen dollars on a Barbie doll, it always helped Stephen to have an adult rationalization handy.

At the checkout counter, Stephen waited patiently while the clerk, an elderly man, struggled with the keys of the cash register.

Theresa Mulholland tossed her final purchase, a jumbo-sized bag of pretzels, into her shopping cart, and aimed it for the checkout counter. She was a little embarrassed that she'd needed a cart in the first place (this was a *drugstore,* for God's sake, not a supermarket), so she'd actually spent a few moments arranging her purchases so that the particularly flagrant ones were hidden by the more sociably acceptable ones. The pretzels, for example, bragged in big letters that they were only one gram of fat per serving; little could be said in defense of the family-sized Mallomars.

There was only one register open, and she got on line behind the man buying a Safari Barbie. Just the doll—no Jeep, no tent, no mosquito netting. He probably didn't get it, that it was supposed to be, like, a *set*. But he was handsome, tall and kind of rumpled looking, but not in a *dumb* way, like the men she was always meeting. She wanted to say something to him, make some silly stab at contact, before he paid, got his change, and walked through the door and out of her nonlife. Still, what was there to say about Safari Barbie? It wasn't really her place to take him to task on how cheap he was being to refuse to spring for the whole set, was it?

"Going to Africa?" she asked him.

He swung around and looked at her. From the serious expression on his face, it was clear that he didn't understand she was joking, trying her hand at *small talk*. But he sure was nice to look at, with good cheekbones and dark eyes that promised, what? Intelligence? Kindness? Sensitivity?

She had a full head of red hair, which she wore in ringlets. He wondered if all she had to do was towel-dry it after she got out of the shower. Or maybe she had to spend half an hour with scary-looking electrical appliances to get it to look natural, the way Ada used to do. He never knew about those things.

"It's for my daughter," he explained.

"Really," said the woman.

What a jerk, he thought. *Of course* it was for his daughter; he needn't have said *that*. It was little wonder he hadn't had a date in two years.

"That'll be twenty-six fifty," said the clerk.

He reached into his pocket for his wallet, locating it and an unfamiliar object as well. He brought both of them out.

"Oh, yes," he remembered. "I need to drop this roll of film off, too. Sorry," he said to the woman behind him.

"No problem," she assured him.

The clerk slid him a form and a pen to fill it out with. He wrote down his name and phone number, and checked the box that said he wanted only one set of exposures, even though checking a much larger red box would have gotten him a second set at half price. He gave the form back to the clerk, who tore off the stub and handed it back to him, along with his change.

And then he was out the door, just like that, just as she'd known would happen, without another word between them.

Going to Africa? God almighty. If that was all she'd been able to come up with, her best line in a no-pressure setting, it was easy to understand why she had no life.

Jim Hall got to his office a little before ten. It was one of the perks of seniority, of being the boss. Although in Jim Hall's case, both *seniority* and *the boss* were relative terms. At forty-two, he was indeed the senior member of the staff, in terms of both age and longevity of service; and as the District Attorney of Columbia County, it was his office to run. But the truth was there were only three lawyers in the entire office—Jim and his two assistant DAs, who were both recent law-school graduates still in their late twenties. As for his *support team,* as he referred to them, they consisted of a single investigator (a former deputy sheriff who'd developed a heart murmur and had to be reassigned to modified duty), an administrative aide (something they used to call a secretary), and a part-time book-keeper. Columbia County had far less crime—and therefore far less in the way of a budget—than its sister counties to the north, Rensselaer and Albany. With no big city to mix unemployment and low-income housing into its demographic profile, Columbia County couldn't quite make the boast that it was crime-free. But what crime there was was pretty much restricted to a steady trickle of minor drug sales, possessions, and petty thefts right there in Hudson; after that, you were talking about driving under the influence, taking a buck out of season, and the occasional outburst of teenage vandalism. There hadn't been a nondrug felony trial in over a year; the county jail had a dozen cells, but a current population of only five; and if anyone was thinking of mounting a campaign against the incumbent in the upcoming election, they'd kept their plans to themselves. So, all things considered, getting to the office a little before ten was actually an act of considerable civic responsibility on the part of Jim Hall.

"Good morning, Mr. Hall."

"Morning, Miranda."

Miranda Concepcion was Jim's administrative aide. If her skills were modest, her disposition was certainly bright. And she brought with her the added bonus of a federal grant that reimbursed the county for 90 percent of her salary. As a qualifying "Hispanic," Miranda single-handedly fulfilled the United States government's incentive award program under Title XII, accounting as she did for a minority presence of one-fifth of the office's full-time staff. All this she accomplished without being Puerto Rican or Mexican or Jamaican or Dominican — or Latin American at all, for that matter. Miranda's father came from a wealthy family of olive oil exporters in southern Spain. But under the government's liberal interpretation of the term Hispanic, that was good enough.

"Que pasa?" Jim asked her, pretty much exhausting his familiarity with the Spanish language. Miranda opened the office at 9:00; by the time Jim arrived, she'd already played the phone messages, checked the faxes (E-mail was still a thing of the future for the office), and made coffee.

"Not much," she said. "Troopers picked up an underage driver over in Austerlitz. Had to keep him, 'cause his folks were out of town."

"That's it?"

"That's it."

For this he'd spent three years in law school and $2500 of his own money on party fund-raisers, just so he could win a token primary and an uncontested election.

"Coffee?" she asked him, though she knew he always said yes.

"Sure," he said. "Why not?"

From South Chatham, Stephen Barrow drove home, stopping only to pick up his mail. He could have arranged to have it delivered; in fact it would have saved him the $12 a year it cost him to rent a box at the post office. But he rather liked the idea of having a box number for an address: It gave him a feeling of insulation from the credit-card companies, the catalog purveyors, and the disseminators of bulk-rate advertising. Lori the postmistress, was a willing accomplice to those who shared this sentiment: she provided a large trash bin by the door, so folks could discard unwanted junk mail right on the spot. He enjoyed his daily visit with her much the same way he enjoyed buying his *New York Times* and quart of milk from Joe and Gail over at the general store in Queechy Lake, where there was always somebody willing to discuss the weather if he was so inclined, or just nod hello to if he wasn't.

Today he lingered long enough to address his Valentine's Day cards to his daughter and drop them in the slot to make sure they'd arrive on Monday. "To the love of my life," he inscribed one of them, thinking how very true the words were. As an afterthought, he signed it, "Love, Stephen." He smiled, knowing Penny would get a kick out of that.

Then he headed home to spend a couple of hours wrestling with his miracle diet drug—or shake, or herbal supplement, or whatever it was going to be, if ever it was going to be anything at all.

Just before noon that same Friday, as Stephen Barrow sat in front of his computer, as his daughter Penny and the rest of her first-grade class learned the names of different geometric shapes, as Theresa Mulholland snacked on pretzels and diet

Sprite, and as Jim Hall stared out the window of his office and sipped his fourth cup of coffee, a woman named Emma Priestley turned on the switch of the ColorMaster 3000 in the back room of the South Chatham Drug Mart. The ColorMaster 3000 was a relatively new arrival at the store. For as long as anyone could remember, when a customer had dropped a roll of exposed film off at the counter, you'd toss it into a wire bin marked TILLMANS. Each day, around 2:00 or so, a driver from Tillman's Photo Processing would show up to collect whatever was in the bin. At the same time, he'd deliver a big paper sack. In the sack were envelopes containing the prints ordered by customers from the day before.

Six months ago, Tillman's had raised their rates, virtually doubling what they'd previously charged to process film. For a while, Drug Mart absorbed part of the increased cost and passed the remainder on to the customer. That made absolutely no one happy: the store saw the small profit margin it made by handling film dry up and disappear; the customers noticed the difference, and either grumbled about the new higher prices or took their film elsewhere.

Then one day in November, a salesman had showed up from an outfit called Rochester Enterprises. He told Ernie, the day manager, that Rochester was a division of Eastman Kodak. That had made sense to Ernie, who seemed to remember hearing that Kodak was to the city of Rochester what DuPont was to the state of Delaware. Within a week, the salesman had "placed" a ColorMaster 3000 in the back room of the Drug Mart, on something he described as a "no-lose six-month trial lease with an option to buy." For Emma—who didn't much care if customers dropped their film off for processing in the first place—the whole thing had been pretty unsettling. To begin with, the machine was as big as she was, and no doubt weighed considerably more. It came with all sorts of switches and lights, and even when it was supposed to be in something called REST MODE, it made noises that were downright scary. But the worst news of all came several days later, when Ernie announced that all of the employees would have to learn how to use the thing.

The way Emma had understood it at the time, they were supposed to be sent to a special three-day school up in Schenectady, where they'd be put up at a nice hotel, fed free restaurant meals, and continue to get paid just the same as if they'd been working the whole time. But that hadn't worked out. Instead, this pimply-faced kid who couldn't have been more than sixteen had shown up one afternoon with an instruction manual to, in his words, "walk you through this one time."

Now, three months later, Emma hated the thing as much as she had the first time she'd set eyes on it. She could work it—though it had taken her a full two weeks just to be able to say that—but she'd developed no comfort level with it whatsoever. Instead, she sat in front of it this Friday afternoon as she always did, with her eyes squinted and her arms stretched out in front of her, as though the contraption might suddenly explode without warning at any given moment. She winced each time another colored bulb lit up unexpectedly, and jumped at every hiss and clank that came from inside the angry belly of the thing. It would be the death of her, she knew. If it didn't blow up on her, it would surely cripple her with carpal tunnel syndrome, or give her bone cancer from its radiation. Already she'd begun to inquire about other job openings in town. But if the rest of the nation was riding the crest of an economic boom, things were pretty slow in South Chatham. And for a sixty-three-year-old store clerk who couldn't drive and therefore had to find work within walking distance of her home, there simply weren't a lot of opportunities.

The first set of exposures were of the Andersons' vacation in Disney World. She recognized Darcy and little Katie. For Emma, the only *good* thing about working the ColorMaster 3000 was that you got to look at the snapshots customers had taken, as they came out of the machine. In a small town, you often knew the customers personally, which meant you got to see where they'd been and what they'd been doing. Emma liked to play a little game with herself: she'd look at the snapshots *before* reading the customer's name on the envelope, see if she could figure out whose film it was on her own. Sometimes it was easy: The Andersons at Disney World was a perfect example. Other times it was harder, like when somebody had taken pictures of *things* instead of people. But even in those cases, she'd gotten pretty good at picking up on clues. For instance, if you saw a lot of shots of antiques, that was likely to be the pretty woman over in East Chatham who called herself the Wood Witch of the East; houses meant it was Jean, the real estate broker from down in Red Rock; and dogs were usually Flaky Annie, who worked over at the pet shelter.

The day's second set of photos puzzled her for a moment, but not for long: halfway through the roll she recognized Maude Shoemaker's barn, a dead giveaway. Maude's granddaughter Tracy fancied herself a photographer, and was trying to get herself set up with a scholarship down to New York City. But Emma knew better. If Tracy was ever going to get anywhere, she'd better stop taking all these pictures of dead trees and old barns and woodpiles and get busy with something pretty, something folks wanted to look at, like vases of flowers or smiling faces.

The third set stumped her. It was a man and his little daughter, that much you could see, but no one she knew. On a couple of the shots, the man must have set the timer on the camera and then run back around to get into the picture: the shots were slanted, and the man and the girl were laughing a lot, waiting for the shutter to click. There were a lot of just the girl, hiking through the snow, standing next to a snowman they'd built, throwing a snowball—stuff like that. She was pretty. Then one or two of a sunset, again slanted and slightly out of focus. The man had probably let the girl take those; men didn't take pictures of sunsets all that much.

Then they were indoors, the girl bathing, with shampoo in her hair. Several showing her from the neck up. One of her completely naked, except for a few soapsuds, standing in the bathtub, facing the camera. Emma Priestley drew back from the developer. *What kind of a man takes pictures of his daughter like this?* She looked at the envelope, saw the name printed on it, *S. Barrow,* and felt *relieved* she didn't know these people.

And it might have ended right there. Emma was a God-fearing woman who said her prayers each evening and went to church every Sunday morning, but she'd never thought of herself as a *prude.* If this man *S. Barrow* wanted to expose his little girl for the rest of the world to see, that was his business, Emma figured. She stared at the image of the little girl, standing there in the bathtub. You could see both her nipples, just like that; thank God she was too young to have breasts. Her . . . her area *down there* was partially hidden by bubbles, but only partially.

Whatever had this man been thinking?

Still, it might have ended there, but for the very last photo. Emma's reaction upon seeing it was a physical one: The sight of it actually caused her to recoil, to literally slide her chair away from the machine, until a good six feet separated her from it. But even *that* wasn't far enough, and she was forced to stand, to retreat to the far wall of the room, until she could feel the door pressed hard against her back.

It was a full minute, a very long time under the circumstances, before Emma Priestley could get herself to approach the machine, and without sitting back down—she never did get herself to sit back down—to look at the last photo. It was numbered twenty-five. The roll was only supposed to have twenty-four exposures, but with those old cameras you sometimes got an extra one or two, especially if you didn't wind it too much when you first loaded the film. The little girl's body was turned away this time, and she was bent over at the waist so that you could see her face, upside down, between her legs. Her rear end was fully visible, along with her *private parts,* in perfect detail. In fact, she'd placed her hands on either side of her rear end and spread herself wide open—no doubt at her father's coaching—so that, like it or not, you were forced to see every minute detail of her anatomy.

As horrified as Emma was, she could not stop herself from staring at the photo. She continued to do so for the next three minutes, and if a minute is a long time in such a context, three minutes is an *eternity*. And the entire time she stared, her mind raced. She thought about bringing the photo to the clerk up front; but that was Max, an old-timer who had his hands full just making change, let alone decisions. She considered calling Ernie, the day manager, at home; but Ernie absolutely *hated it* when you bothered him on his day off. She toyed with the idea of trying to reach Mr. Gentry, the owner; but she didn't have his number there in the back room, or any other way of reaching him. For a moment she even thought of phoning the 24-HOUR TOLL-FREE EMERGENCY HELP LINE number printed on a sticker on the ColorMaster 3000; but she decided this probably wasn't the kind of situation they were there to help with.

Yet she couldn't very well do *nothing* about it; that much was certain. Anyone could see this was pornography. Worse, it was *child* pornography. A little girl was being exposed and abused in the worst way imaginable, and by her own *father*.

Or maybe it *wasn't* her father at all. Maybe it was her uncle, or her stepfather, or someone else in whose care she'd been placed. But whoever it was, it made little difference. You had only to look at the photo to know there was no excusing it. It was what it was: a clear-cut case of abuse. And somebody had to do something about it, and quickly, before the little girl became a runaway, found herself driven into child prostitution, or worse. For Emma Priestley, it didn't take much of an imagination to picture the poor child lying naked and horribly mutilated in a pool of blood, in some dark, garbage-strewn, rat-infested alleyway off Times Square, down in New York City.

In the end, Emma didn't bring the photo up front to show Max, the register clerk; she didn't phone Ernie, the day manager; she didn't try reaching Mr. Gentry, the owner; and she didn't call the 24-HOUR TOLL-FREE EMERGENCY HELP LINE, either.

What she did was pick up the phone and dial 911.

The writing was going surprisingly well. As long as he remembered not to get bogged down in too much scientific detail, Stephen Barrow found that he could keep the reader's attention—at least the *theoretical reader's* attention—in the early part of the story by providing a little more detail into his account of the experiment that somehow went awry and produced the miracle diet drug.

The director of the research lab was running the place on a shoestring, struggling to survive. He was trying to discover a way to keep the sun's ultraviolet rays from burning the skin and causing cancer. Suntan lotions afforded a certain amount of protection, but recent studies showed they didn't do a very good job of preventing malignant melanoma, the most deadly form of skin cancer. Worse yet, sunbathers who used the lotions tended to stay out in the sun longer, confident that those high SPF ratings on the labels would adequately protect them. The result, when combined with the well-documented thinning of the ozone layer, had been an unprecedented increase in melanoma.

The idea, it seemed, was to find some substance that would trigger the body's own natural defenses to UV rays. Unable to afford the prohibitive costs associated with the research and development of a new drug, the lab's director had instead turned to drugs that were already on the market, but were being used for other things. One such drug was already widely in use in emergency rooms for serious burn victims. Administered in a single massive dose, it seemed to arrest the tissue damage sustained in third-degree burns, cases where there was actual charring of the skin.

The drug was known generically as MU-26, and marketed by Pfizer under the brand name RetroChar. (Stephen got a kick out of that; he loved making up names for things.) The lab's pretty young blond research assistant (if you ever wanted movie companies to read the book, you had to have a pretty young blonde somewhere in it) had been testing RetroChar on mice. The mice were genetically engineered—were all identical, virtual clones of one another. They were albinos—meaning they had no pigmentation in their skin—and on top of that, they were completely hairless. The combination of these two traits made them remarkably ugly, with their beady little red eyes and pink skins (pink because their blood showed through their skin). It also made them particularly vulnerable to sunburn.

The mice had been divided into two groups, a test group that was given small daily doses of RetroChar, and a control group given a placebo. Then both groups were bombarded with UV rays.

The research assistant had been following the two groups for several weeks now, and measuring their little sunburned skins with an instrument called the Chromometer 300. (The Chromometer 300 was, of course, another invention of Stephen Barrow's fertile imagination; any similarity between it and the ColorMaster 3000, an actual machine, while perhaps ominously ironic, was nevertheless purely coincidental.) Now, the lab assistant reported sadly to the director, it appeared that the test mice were burning just as badly as the control mice. "Other than that," she added, "there is one peculiar development I've noticed."

"What's that?" the director asked, peering over a stack of bills he couldn't afford to pay.

"For some reason, the mice being given RetroChar are losing weight."

Aha!

From there, they give up on the drug as a sunburn-protector and instead devise an experiment to test it as a diet drug. And, naturally, it works like magic. The good folks at the lab want to write up the results, let the public reap the benefits, and pocket a little change for their efforts. But the Evil Forces of Big Business get wind of the experiment. Records disappear in the middle of the night, the lab is mysteriously burned to the ground, and soon the drug finds its way onto the marketplace—not only renamed, but now disguised as a tasty milkshake (Penny's contribution) or an exotic herbal supplement.

All goes well for a while. The pounds melt away from the nation's obese; the bucks roll in to Big Business's coffers— until the startling revelation comes that once you begin taking the drug you continue to lose weight forever, until you finally waste away and die. Then must we turn back to our noble lab director and his beautiful blond assistant to somehow come to the rescue.

Okay, so it was *trash*.

The fact was, there were a lot of people out there writing trash, and making millions in the process. And if Stephen Barrow happened to have the terrible fortune of seeing one of his books become commercially successful (he didn't dare think in terms of a *bestseller*, lest lightning strike him dead on the spot), wouldn't that in turn give him the luxury of getting back to the kind of writing he *really* wanted to do?

Was that such a terrible fantasy to have?

When you dial 911 in the village of South Chatham, your call is not routed to the local police department. The local police department, you will recall, exists for the sole purpose of entrapping those unwary motorists who are not prescient enough to know that a speed limit can be fifty-five miles an hour one second, and thirty the next.

No, your call is instead routed to the New York State Police barracks down in Claverack, where the officer on duty answers in a businesslike voice, as he did that Friday afternoon, "Troopers. Harrington speaking. What's the nature of your emergency?"

There was a brief silence on the line, followed by the somewhat shaky voice of what sounded like an older woman. "I want to report a, a crime," she said. "To the authorities."

"What sort of crime, ma'am?"

There was another brief silence, during which (at least on a recording of the call) an audible *beep* can be heard, warning the caller that the conversation was being monitored, and perhaps even preserved. The silence suggested that the woman wasn't quite sure what to call the crime she was reporting, what *label* to affix to it. But then she seemed to find the words, and proceeded to answer in a voice that was controlled, if somewhat less than steady.

"A case of child abuse," she said.

"Physical abuse or sexual abuse?" asked Harrington, for whom life seemed to present few gray areas. But the either/or choice he presented apparently created no more difficulty for the caller than it had for Trooper Harrington.

"Sexual abuse," she replied.

When asked about it months later, Emma Priestly would explain her response quite matter-of-factly. "Listen, I knew it was *abuse* the moment I set my eyes on that last photo. But I couldn't really say it was *physical* abuse. I mean, it wasn't like I saw him *beating* her, or noticed *bruises* on her body, or anything like that. On the other hand, you looked at that snapshot, and anyone with a pair of eyes in their head could see it was all about *sex*. So I said, 'Sexual abuse.' I mean, wouldn't you of?"

And thus it was that, from the very beginning, the case against Stephen Barrow became one of abuse, and specifically of sexual abuse. Those were the first two words Trooper Timothy Harrington jotted down on the notepad in front of him as he sat at the duty station. They were the two words he listed in the box marked SUSPECTED OFFENSE on the investigation form he filled out just moments later. They were the two words he used in putting the job out over the air, when he asked the nearest available unit to respond to the Drug Mart in South Chatham and see the lady in the back room. And, for better or for worse, they were the two words that would be forever linked with the entire sordid affair.

THREE

It was nearing two o'clock in the afternoon when Stephen Barrow shut down his computer, stepped outside, and climbed into his Jeep to begin the day's second drive down to Hillsdale and his daughter's school.

Despite the fact that the temperature was still well below freezing, the engine caught on the first try. This was hardly a testament to modern advances in ignition, or recent improvements in engine alloys. The Jeep was a 1983 CJ-7 Renegade, the kind they used to make before Ralph Nader or one of his friends discovered they were prone to roll over when cornering at speeds in excess of sixty-five. As far as Stephen Barrow was concerned, that finding posed no discernable risk for his family of two. While the Jeep's odometer showed only 57,562 miles at the moment, it was the old kind of instrument, without a sixth wheel, so it simply reset after hitting 99,999—something it had already done twice in its seventeen years. And the likelihood of the Jeep's approaching (let alone exceeding) sixty-five miles an hour—while perhaps a theoretical possibility, if one were to simultaneously come upon a long, downhill straightaway and a gale-force tailwind—was so remote as to be safely ignored.

Then again, the fact that the engine caught on the first try was not entirely dumb luck, either. Rather, it was the product of many years of painstaking trial-and-error experimentation. When the mercury dipped below thirty degrees or so, the trick was to shut off any accessories (not that there were that many to shut off), floor the gas pedal once, holding it down for a generous count of "One-Mississippi," release it, close your eyes, hold your breath, turn the key, and pray.

And, more often than not, it worked.

The truth was, Stephen Barrow loved his Jeep, and so did Penny. She loved its high seats, boxy shape, and noisy muffler. She especially loved it in the summer, when they could put the top down. When she'd first begun to read, somewhere around age four, she'd asked him what the long word stenciled on either side of the hood was.

"Renegade," he'd told her.

"What's *renegade*?"

"A renegade's a sort of outlaw," he'd said.

"Like a *bad guy*?" she'd wanted to know.

"Not necessarily. Just someone who's, well, not part of the crowd."

"Are *we* renegades?"

He'd smiled at the time. "Yes," he'd said, "I suppose we're renegades."

And she'd said, "Neato."

Now he pulled out of his driveway and onto the dirt road that would take him down to the county highway, making sure not to take the corner at over sixty-five.

When Trooper Timothy Harrington had depressed the SEND button on his radio and asked the nearest available unit to respond to the Drug Mart in South Chatham and see the lady in the back room, the nearest available unit had been a marked radio car being operated by Gregory Nye. Nye had been over in Ghent, the town just to the west of Chatham, looking at power equipment at Brook Cove Marine. (In an area that was landlocked, places with names like Brook Cove Marine tended to sell much more than boats. Depending on the season, you could find an assortment of lawn tractors, tillers, dirt bikes, snowmobiles, snowblowers, and even an occasional log-splitter. When the call came in, Nye was in the midst of a heated debate with another customer over the relative merits of Husqvarna, McCulloch, and Stihl chainsaws. He declared a timeout, so that he could answer on his portable.)

"Nye here," he told the dispatcher. "I'm headed that way."

"What's your ETA?" Harrington asked. Another unit was calling in, but they were up in Valatie, twelve or fifteen minutes away.

"No more than five minutes."

There is a brief burst of static audible on the tape on which the exchange has been preserved. Then Nye can be heard saying, "Sex abuse, huh? Fuckin' perp better not be there when *I* show up, sonofabitch knows what's good for him."

Two lessons are to be learned from Trooper Nye's remark. First, it reveals a hostility toward sex abusers that is virtually universal, no matter the generic nature of the phrase. Second, absolutely no one—be he president, politician, or police officer—is immune from forgetting from time to time that the tape recorder is running. Though in Nye's case, when his words were later replayed, transcribed and criticized, not only would he stand by his warning, he would wear it like a second badge.

As Gregory Nye drove the five-mile stretch of Route 66 from Ghent to South Chatham, itching for a confrontation with a sexual predator of Hannibal Lecter proportions, Stephen Barrow cruised south on the Taconic, his gaze divided between the roadway ahead of him and the temperature gauge on his dashboard. Of all the Jeep's instruments, it was the most accurate. The speedometer cable was prone to freezing up and emitting a wailing noise of truly frightening proportions; the tachometer had given out a full two years ago; the oil pressure indicator took weeks off at a time for no discernable reason; and the fuel gauge tended to tell him more about the incline of the road at any given moment than the amount of gas left in the tank. But the temperature gauge was accurate, and it was that accuracy that Stephen relied on in making adjustments to the square of carpeting he'd draped over the car's radiator. Without the carpet in place to block out some of the cold, the radiator failed to heat up sufficiently to warm the passenger compartment; with *too much* of the radiator surface covered, the coolant superheated and eventually boiled over.

At the moment, the little needle of the gauge hovered right around the 210-degree mark, just about perfect for both man and machine.

Stephen Barrow smiled—not only because of the small measure of satisfaction he allowed himself for solving one of life's little challenges, but because of the broader realization that although it was cold outside, he was warm and dry and happy, his writing seemed to be going well, and he was on his way to pick up his daughter and spend the weekend with her. No doubt she would have colorful drawings to show him, new stories to amuse him with, important questions to ask him, and interesting sights to point out and share with him on the return trip home. If she wasn't exactly adult company, she was pretty close, and in many ways she was even better.

Of course Stephen Barrow had no inkling of the events that were taking place that moment back in the village of South Chatham. Totally oblivious to the firestorm that was even then being kindled and beginning to smolder, he drove on—silently counting his blessings while marveling at the gentle hills and graceful bends of the parkway spread out in front of him, with no greater concern in life than to glance from time to time at the temperature gauge on his dashboard.

It took Trooper Gregory Nye even less than the five minutes he'd predicted to drive his cruiser from Brook Cove Marine in Ghent to the South Chatham Drug Mart. With dome lights flashing—regulations forbade him from using his siren on a nonpriority call; otherwise he no doubt would have—he passed six cars along the way, striking fear in the hearts of six drivers who'd been reckless enough to exceed the thirty-mile-per-hour speed limit.

A block from the Drug Mart, Nye turned off his dome lights, opting instead for stealth in his final approach. Evidently, it was his expectation to sneak up on the sex abuser and catch him in the act, though just what act he expected to catch him in remains somewhat less than clear.

What *is* clear is that upon his arrival, Trooper Nye entered by the front door and went directly to the checkout counter, where he found a clerk—the same elderly man who'd rung up the purchases of both Stephen Barrow and Theresa Mulholland earlier in the day.

" 'Scuse me," said Nye. "I'm here to see the lady in the back."

The clerk glanced up from his register, then looked the trooper up and down. "You mean Emma?" he asked.

"I mean," said Nye, "whoever the lady in the back is."

"I guess that would have to be Emma."

"Then I'm here to see Emma," Nye deadpanned.

The clerk pointed to the back of the store, where the prescription department was. "You want the door marked 'Office,' " he explained.

The door was actually marked OFFICE—KEEP OUT. Not that the warning deterred Trooper Nye, who was quite accustomed to going where others might hesitate. Still, after knocking once, he used his left hand to turn the doorknob and push the door inward. His right hand he rested on the butt of his holstered weapon, a 9mm Glock semiautomatic pistol capable of discharging sixteen rounds in approximately five seconds.

Because you never knew when a sex abuser might turn violent.

What Nye found, of course, was only Emma Priestley, sitting next to a large machine of some sort (Nye was a stranger to the wonders of the ColorMaster 3000) and chain-smoking while awaiting the arrival of *the authorities,* as she thought of whoever might show up in response to her 911 call. In addition to Emma Priestley, Nye found a photograph, a color photograph of a naked Penny Barrow in a bathtub, mooning the camera.

If Nye was disappointed at the absence of a drooling, leering, violent sexual predator barricaded in the back room, he managed to contain his feelings. He studied the offending photograph, then turned his attention to the others that had come from the same roll of film. Included in those were other images of the same child, some clothed but several naked. And one or two of a man.

"This must be our perp," said Nye.

"Our what?" asked Emma Priestley.

"Our perpetrator," Nye explained. "Our sex abuser. I'm afraid I'm going to have to take these with me. Is that all right?"

"Whatever—" said Emma Priestley. She didn't mean it as a completed thought, the way the younger generation was always using the word nowadays. She meant to follow it up with, "—you have to do," or "—you think is best." Only she hesitated slightly after the *whatever,* and it was as far as she got.

"Thanks," said Nye, scooping the photos into the envelope that lay next to them on the table. " 'S. Barrow,' " he read aloud, noting that there was a phone number written right beneath the name, in the same pen and handwriting. "This is evidence, too," he explained. And with that, he turned, let himself out the door, and walked through the store and back out to his cruiser, leaving Emma Priestley to her chain-smoking.

Stephen Barrow arrived at his daughter's school early, as he always did. He was a firm believer in allowing extra time for unforeseen events—traffic jams, flat tires, mechanical breakdowns, and random acts of God or Nature. It was one of the things that had driven his wife—make that *ex*-wife—crazy. As much as Stephen had always insisted on being on time for things, Ada had been equally devoted to arriving late. She loved the dash down the airport corridor, the grand entrance at the dinner party, the challenge of finding the last two seats in the darkened movie theater. Toward the end of the marriage, things had actually gotten to the point where they'd begun to take separate cabs to the airport. Stephen would arrive at the gate a full hour early, a relaxed smile on his face, a copy of *The New York Times* tucked under his arm, a large container of Pepsi in one hand. He would sip the Pepsi and work his way through the paper, then board the plane as soon as his row was announced. He'd locate his window seat, stow his carry-on luggage, find one of those little pillows, buckle his seat belt, and enjoy the view. There'd be other planes landing or taking off, fuel trucks topping up tanks, and baggage handlers working conveyor-belt loaders. Then, just when he was figuring she'd finally cut things too close, a sweating, out-of-breath Ada would come lurching up the aisle and collapse into the seat beside him, even as the flight attendants secured the doors for takeoff.

He made no apologies for his obsessive behavior. It was simply that he so much preferred doing things in a relaxed way, rather than suffering the anxiety that came with last-minute rushing, that he was willing to pay the small price of waiting once he'd arrived. And that was particularly the case when it came to picking up his daughter, or getting her somewhere she had to be. The last thing he wanted was for her to miss the beginning of some activity, or be sitting forlornly on some stoop, wondering if he'd forgotten all about her.

Today, as always, there were no traffic jams: such things were unheard of in the area, except on summer weekends at county fair times. There were no flat tires, no mechanical breakdowns, no random acts of God or Nature. And a full twenty minutes after he'd parked outside the Hillsdale Day

Center, Stephen heard the sounds of squealing children, looked up from his *New York Times*, and spotted his daughter exchanging desperate good-bye hugs with classmates she wouldn't be seeing again for a full two days. Finally prying herself away from the last clinging embrace, she headed his way. Stephen pushed the passenger door of the Renegade open for her, but he didn't get out to help her in; he'd made the mistake of doing that once, but only once.

"Daddeee," she'd said, "I can get in myself. God, how *embarrassing!*"

She'd been five at the time.

Now he waited while she buckled her seat belt—something else she insisted on doing herself—before pulling out of the parking lot and onto Route 22.

"So," he asked her, "what did you learn today?"

"You're not going to believe this," she said. "But most human beans are made of *water*."

Stephen thought about that for a moment. He knew better than to laugh, as he had, for example, the time she'd confessed she'd dropped a thermometer and all the *Jupiter* had spilled out. Penny had a wonderful sense of humor, but she hadn't yet fully developed the capacity to laugh at her own mistakes.

"Could it be," he asked her gently, "that human beings are *mostly made* of water?"

"Didn't I just say that?" she shot back, already unrolling a painting for his inspection.

"I guess you did."

"I'm afraid you're going to have to learn to pay more attention," she warned him, "if you ever want to make it to second grade. Here's a picture I made for you. It's called 'The Meaning of the Universe.' "

With the evidence from the South Chatham Drug Mart firmly in hand, Trooper Gregory Nye radioed the barracks in Claverack for instructions.

"What have you got?" The voice was that of Timothy Harrington, the same trooper who'd dispatched him on the job half an hour earlier.

"Pornography," Nye replied. "*Child* pornography."

"Stand by," Harrington told him.

Nearly five minutes went by before Harrington came back on the air with instructions. "Lieutenant Coffey says for you to give him a call on the land line."

"Ten-four," Nye acknowledged. "The land line" was police-speak for the telephone. No one knows quite why they don't just call it the telephone, which admittedly takes longer to say, but only by one syllable; were that the extent of the problem, *phone* might be the solution. But police jargon traces many of its terms to the military, a not-so-surprising development, in view of the fact that historically, police departments have drawn heavily upon the military for a variety of things, from infrastructure and tactical planning to recruits.

In any event, Nye soon found a land line and called Lieutenant Coffey, who had apparently deemed the subject matter too delicate to discuss over the air. You never knew who had scanners these days and might be listening in.

"What have you got?" Coffey wanted to know. It was the exact same question Harrington had asked Nye not ten minutes earlier.

"Photographs," Nye told him. "A little girl, looks to be about seven or eight."

"Nude?"

"Ten-four." Even though he was no longer on the radio, Nye tended to use the same phrases designed for it.

"Can you see her *privates*?" Coffey asked.

"That's affirmative," Nye replied. "And then some."

That last remark seemed to give the lieutenant pause. "You mean her, her *rectum*?" Apparently there had been no anatomy questions on the most recent lieutenant's test.

"Affirmative," Nye repeated.

"Tell you what you do," said Coffey. "You run those photos

over to the courthouse right now, see if you can catch Jim Hall before he leaves for the day. We'll see what he wants to do about this."

"Ten-four," said Gregory Nye.

What Jim Hall wanted to *do about this* was simple. As the district attorney, he could barely believe his good fortune. An arrest and prosecution for child pornography: what could possibly look better on his list of accomplishments when campaign time—and especially campaign *contribution* time—came around? But as a lawyer who might end up having to try the case himself, he also knew the difference between having the evidence delivered to his office by a state trooper, and having it seized from the defendant himself.

Because, looking at the envelope that Trooper Nye had brought him, and reading the name printed on it, Hall instantly regarded this 'S. Barrow' as precisely that: a defendant. A defendant in a criminal prosecution. And pulling out his copy of the New York State Penal Law, Hall thumbed through a list of crimes that might or not apply to the situation at hand. He stopped when he came to something called "Possessing a sexual performance by a child." Perfect. But the key word was *possessing*.

"Get these back to the store," Hall instructed Nye. "Have them wrap them up just like any other customer's photos. Only when our Mr. Barrow shows up to pick them up, and actually has them in his hand, you'll be waiting to arrest him. Got it?"

"You mean stake out the store?"

"That's exactly what I mean." Hall smiled broadly.

"But, sir, that could take *days*."

"Well, it doesn't have to be you personally," said Hall. "Any trooper'll do."

"Yes, sir," said Gregory Nye. But he couldn't have been

pleased at the notion. An hour ago, he'd been ready to put his life on the line and engage in hand-to-hand combat against a foaming-at-the-mouth sex abuser; now he was being told it might not even be his arrest to make when the time came, that any old trooper would do.

Had the photographs been on Stephen Barrow's mind that Friday afternoon, he could easily have made a detour into South Chatham on the way back home. The Drug Mart, after all, advertised a two-hour turnaround time on prints, something made possible by the ColorMaster 3000. And it had been more like five hours since Stephen had dropped the roll off to be developed.

But Stephen Barrow either decided there was no rush or forgot about the film altogether; when asked later, he simply couldn't recall which had been the case. In either event, it would seem reasonable to conclude that if the photographs had already become vitally important to five people—those five being Emma Priestley, Troopers Tim Harrington and Gregory Nye, Lieutenant Elmer Coffey, and District Attorney Jim Hall—they were less than a burning issue to the man who'd taken them.

For even as Nye returned to the Drug Mart with the photographs and the envelope that would link them to their creator, Stephen Barrow headed north in his Renegade, his daughter seated next to him. In fact, at the precise moment that Nye was handing the damning evidence over to the store's manager and explaining the necessity of catching the customer in physical possession of them, Stephen and Penny Barrow were singing at the top of their lungs. The song they were singing was a favorite of Penny's, and had been made famous by the recording artist Bobby McFerrin a few years earlier.

Don't worry, be happy!

was about all they knew of the words, so they sang them over and over again, as loudly and as happily and as worry-free as they could, until their voices cracked and threatened to disappear altogether. But if they were hampered by their lack of lyrics, the four-word refrain seemed a perfect fit for a clear, crisp Friday afternoon and the beginning of what promised to be a beautiful weekend.

FOUR

Theresa Mulholland awoke with a hangover. Not an alcohol-induced hangover; she'd had a glass of wine the evening before, but only one, which her Irish heritage could easily absorb. No, the culprit had been marijuana this time.

Not that smoking a joint had been the direct cause of her bloated feeling, or the distinct sensation that there was a small elephant lodged just beneath her breastbone, making it impossible for her to breathe deeply. No, marijuana worked in more devious ways.

What it did, was to give you the *munchies*. A few tokes, and suddenly everything tasted wonderful. Mallomars became delicate truffles, Cheez Whiz turned to Welsh rarebit, and salmon spread took on the properties of Beluga caviar (not that she'd ever had Beluga caviar, but she had no trouble imagining what it was like). Sitting on her sofa, nested in a half-dozen throw pillows, covered with an afghan her mother had knitted long ago, she'd spent the evening watching old movie rentals. After all these years, she'd still cried at the end of *An Officer and a Gentleman* when Richard Gere walked into the cardboard factory to pick up Debra Winger, and at the final number in *Dirty Dancing* when Jennifer Grey successfully executed the steps Patrick Swayze had taught her. Of course, crying had made Theresa hungrier, so she'd eaten a few more Mallomars, a little more Cheez Whiz, and the rest of the salmon spread. Feeling stuffed, she'd relit the joint and taken a couple of hits. Relief had come instantly, almost magically. She'd taken another hit—no sense in letting good grass go to waste, after all. The stuffed feeling had become a thing of the past, all but forgotten. Using a safety pin as a roach clip, she'd finished off the last of the joint, taking care to quit before burning her lips or inadvertently inhaling the lit roach, a practice well worth avoiding. She'd felt absolutely great. A bit *hungry*, in fact. . . .

Now she was paying the price.

A shower and two cups of black coffee helped, but not that much. Part of the problem was that it was the weekend, and as was usually the case, Theresa had no plans. She could go to the gym and work out with Tony the Trainer, but on Saturdays the place was filled with guys, and they'd stand around in small groups and gawk at her in her boxing gear until one of them would get up the courage to wander over and ask what a nice girl like her was doing in a place like this. She didn't need that today, not the way she felt.

She could have read, but she was having trouble getting into *Cold Mountain*, in spite of how good everyone kept telling her it was once you got into it.

She could have made any of a dozen phone calls she had to make, to any of a dozen people who'd left her messages—some multiple—over the last several days. But that would have meant dealing with her mother, who'd want to know if Theresa was *seeing anyone*, and her sister, who could be counted on to share her latest strategies in the ongoing battle to toilet-train her three-year-old.

In the end, she did pick up the telephone. But she opted for making business calls instead of personal ones. Even though it meant she'd have to do follow-ups, she started working on the "Coming Events" column, Tom Grady's assignment. *Her* assignment now, until Tom dried out. As for the other column she'd inherited, "From the Police Blotter," well, that could wait.

———

Stephen Barrow woke up with a sick daughter. Sometime during the night, he'd heard Penny coughing. Not a bad cough, like the croupy ones she used to get as an infant, when he and Ada had taken turns holding her in the bathroom, with the hot water turned on full blast in the shower to create a pretty impressive tropical rain forest. But enough of a cough to keep him awake for an hour, listening to make sure she was okay.

From the moment she'd come home from the hospital as a newborn, Stephen's sleep habits had changed. He'd always been a heavy sleeper, totally impervious to the ringing of a telephone or an alarm clock. "I hear something," Ada would tell him in the first years of their marriage, but neither the noise, her comment about it, or her subsequent shaking of him would rouse Stephen. "The house could burn down," she complained at one point, and no doubt it could have, so soundly did Stephen sleep.

All that changed with the arrival of Penny. Suddenly Stephen was alert to every sound coming from the next room—every sigh, every hiccup, every breath. Noises from downstairs or outside that he'd once been oblivious to now caused him to hold his own breath as he tried to identify them as benign or menacing.

When Penny would wake in the night for her feeding, it was Stephen who'd hear her first whimper, Stephen who'd be at her crib even before her eyes were fully open, Stephen who'd change her and bring her to Ada's breast, Stephen who'd return her to her crib once mother and daughter had fallen back asleep. Had he only had milk of his own, it would no doubt have been Stephen who'd have done the nursing, too.

By morning, Penny's cough had ripened into a bark. "I sound like a seal," she announced, her voice breaking on the word *seal*.

"I'll see if we have any herring in the refrigerator," Stephen told her.

"I don't want *herring*," she said. "I want *Cheracol*."

Cheracol was a cough medicine that was going the way of

the dinosaurs. It was one of those old-fashioned syrups that contained alcohol and cherry flavors and little else. Cough medicines these days came in scary blue shades, were mentholated, had serious names followed by qualifying initials, and tasted bad enough to be effective. Penny hated them all with a passion. Cheracol was the only one she'd tolerate. Concerned about the alcohol content (the original formula had also included codeine, but that had long since been eliminated), Stephen had once sat down and calculated just how much there was in a teaspoon, the recommended dosage for a child under twelve. The answer had turned out to be about a drop and a half.

Cheracol it would be.

The problem was, you couldn't find the stuff anymore. Robitussin, Dimetapp, Vicks: no problem. Cheracol? "Oh, we're out of that." Later, "We don't stock that anymore." Until finally, "They stopped making that." Every once in a while, Stephen would spot a single bottle—he always looked—usually with an expiration date that was history. (What, the alcohol had evaporated? The cherry bark extract had gone bad?) He'd immediately scoop it up. But with coughs and colds a routine thing for school-age children, it never took long for the red liquid to disappear.

"If you want Cheracol," Stephen told Penny now, "we're going have to go out hunting for some."

"Like a search-and-destroy mission?"

"Just the search part. Meanwhile, what do you want for breakfast?"

Penny let out a bark that would have put an adult sea lion to shame. "Cheracol," she said.

For Trooper Gregory Nye, that Saturday was an RDO, a regular day off. Nye had tried to swap shifts with several other troopers, so intent was he on being present at the South

Chatham Drug Mart when Stephen Barrow showed up to claim his pornographic photos. For, thanks to a minimum of effort on the part of the DA's investigator, "S. Barrow" now had a first name. He also had a date of birth, an address, a Social Security number, and a driver's license. That last piece of information meant that he also had a photograph on file, a color photograph that had already been E-mailed to the district attorney's office—well, actually to the county clerk's office next door; the DA's office wasn't on-line yet. It hadn't yet been determined if Stephen Barrow also had a daughter whose age was consistent with that of the child depicted in the pornographic photos; that might have to wait until Monday, when school offices reopened.

But Gregory Nye hadn't been able to find anyone to swap shifts with him. It wasn't that there was a stampede to arrest the Uniphotographer (as one trooper had already dubbed Stephen Barrow); it was simply a matter that troopers got paid overtime rates for working weekends and holidays. Even so, you could generally find someone willing to forego the extra money on Christmas Day, or New Year's Eve, or on a clear summer day, or during hunting season—*especially* in hunting season—or at various, assorted other times. But this was February. Too late for hunting, too early for golf, too cold for relaxing in the hammock with a couple of cold ones, but not enough snow on the ground for getting out the Arctic Cat. A Saturday off could mean having to take the wife food shopping, or the kids to swim lessons, or finally getting around to cleaning out the basement. "Sorry, hon," the sad-faced troopers would tell their wives, "gotta go to work."

The particular sad-faced trooper who drew the assignment of staking out the South Chatham Drug Mart that Saturday morning was a tall, thin veteran of eleven years named Todd Stickley, who, for obvious reasons, everyone called "the Stick." In fact, Stickley was a distant relative of the Stickleys who made fine furniture. Though state troopers tended not to be too knowledgeable when it came to fine furniture; their tastes seemed to run more to pool tables, Formica counters, and La-Z-Boy recliners.

Todd Stickley had been chosen for the assignment for two reasons. First, he was an investigator, a designation roughly equivalent to that of detective in most metropolitan police departments. As such, he worked in plain clothes rather than uniform. Second, his physical appearance was nonthreatening and belied the fact that he was law enforcement. Someone, whether at the DA's office or the state police barracks, felt it was critical that Stephen Barrow not be spooked when he showed up for his photos and make a break for it. By having Investigator Stickley inside the store, mingling with the customers, while his partner waited outside in an unmarked vehicle — a late-model black Ford Crown Victoria being the closest thing available to an unmarked vehicle — the hope was to lull Stephen Barrow into believing that the coast was clear, and that it was safe to transact his dirty little business.

So, beginning at 8:00 that morning, Todd Stickley had been wandering the aisles of the South Chatham Drug Mart, trying his best to look inconspicuous, never straying too far from the checkout counter. His 9mm Glock was holstered, but it was fully loaded, with one round already chambered: although a name-check of Stephen Barrow had revealed no prior record, you never knew when an arrest could turn violent. A radio transmitter was taped to Stickley's chest and concealed by his sweatshirt: His partner out in the parking lot could hear Stickley's every fart and belch. And in Stickley's jacket pocket, where he could slip it out and glance at it from time to time, was the color Motor Vehicle Department photograph of his target, Stephen Barrow.

The Stick was ready.

There were a limited number of places in the area that might stock Cheracol, and Stephen Barrow knew them all. There were the big supermarkets, which these days carried a fairly wide assortment of cold remedies. But they tended to go in for the favorites—the Robitussins, the Vicks, and the NyQuils. At the other end of the spectrum were the independent mom-and-pop drugstores. They occasionally came through with off-brands or hard-to-find items. But they also tended to keep odd hours, were geographically concentrated in hard-to-get-to places like Hudson, Poughkeepsie, and Rhinebeck, and they routinely charged double or triple what you might expect to pay elsewhere. In between the two extremes were the large chain pharmacies—places like Walgreen's, Rite Aid, Eckerd's, and Drug Mart. They usually offered a pretty wide selection, and their prices, though by no means bargain rate, were reasonable. Besides which, there were two of them nearby, one in Chatham and one in South Chatham.

Stephen Barrow decided they were probably his best bet. Scraping his daughter's barely touched French toast into the garbage—they had a disposal in the sink, but Stephen didn't trust it with much beyond crumbs, peelings, and an occasional lemon wedge—he called out to Penny.

"Get dressed, kiddo," he told her. "We'll take a ride into Chatham."

"You mean *Chat ham?*" Ever since she'd first identified the name in print, Penny'd decided it was spelled weirdly. She alternated between calling it "Chat ham," as though it were some kind of talking meat, and "Cha-*tham*," which she pronounced to rhyme with *Shazam*.

"And bundle up. It's cold outside."

"I'm hot," she said.

His hands still wet from doing the dishes, Stephen reached out, caught her by one wrist, and pulled him toward her. She squealed and tried unsuccessfully to wriggle free. He placed his free hand against her forehead.

"Do I have tempature?" she asked.

Stephen removed his hand and studied his palm solemnly. "A hundred and twelve point six," he told her.

"Liar, liar, pants on fire," she said.

"Nose as long as a telephone wire," he dutifully completed the verse.

The truth was, she always felt warm to his touch, and she almost never complained of the cold, even on days that sent chills through Stephen's own adult bones. He attributed it to her youth, to her acceptance of the weather as just another part of her surroundings that, as a child, she couldn't control. He was certain she *felt* the cold every bit as much as he did; it was just that she didn't conceptualize it as something extraordinary that had to be reckoned with, defended against, and endlessly talked about.

Twenty minutes later, more or less dressed appropriately— he more, she less—Stephen and Penny Barrow climbed into the Renegade, fastened their seat belts, and headed for Chatham.

Taking full advantage of the miracle of call forwarding (a technology so far beyond his grasp that he placed it in the category of mysteries that included automatic redial, caller identification, and spontaneous human combustion), District Attorney Jim Hall had set up a *command post* in his living room that Saturday morning. Never much of a fan of spending weekends at the office, Hall had been able to rationalize his decision by pointing out that the county courthouse, which housed his quarters, went unheated from Friday evening to early Monday morning—or at least would be heated only to the point where water pipes wouldn't freeze solid and burst.

Joining Hall in his living-room-turned-office was Hank Bournagan, one of his two assistant district attorneys. The other assistant, Wendy Garafolo, was currently out on her last week of maternity leave, which to Hall was just as well: to his way of thinking, the command post of a sex-abuse investigation was no place for a woman, let alone a new mother. Also present was Hall's investigator, Ed Sprague. Sprague was the former sheriff's deputy who'd developed a heart murmur and been restricted to modified duty ever since a big black bear had chased him clear across Lew Hatch's apple orchard one autumn afternoon. It turned out the bear, a good-sized female, had been gobbling up apples in preparation for hibernating. Only there'd been an early hard frost that year, and thousands of apples had fallen, spoiled, and quickly fermented. The bear had not only been *in estrus*, but she'd been legally drunk—a fact confirmed once she'd been knocked out by a tranquilizer dart, and a blood sample had been taken from her. Her alcohol level tested out at .23, more than twice that required for a DWI conviction. Which was probably a lucky thing for Ed Sprague: sober, the big gal no doubt could have caught him, and might even have killed him, or—as some folks later suggested—even worse than that.

Rounding out the foursome was Captain Henry Coopersmith, the commanding officer of the state police barracks. Coopersmith was a former Marine Corps drill sergeant whose chief claim to fame was that he'd once collected a thousand-dollar wager by performing a hundred pushups with three live howitzer shells strapped to his back. If he'd gained forty pounds since then (pretty much compensating for the removal of the howitzer shells), at fifty-three he still cut an imposing figure, with his ramrod-straight posture and his silver-gray hair.

The command post was connected to the *field operations team* by both two-way radio and land line. The radio was tuned to the same dedicated-frequency channel as the unit worn by Investigator Todd Stickley. The result was that Stickley's transmitter operated as an open mike, sending everything he said, and most of what was audible in his immediate vicinity, not only to his partner in the unmarked car parked outside the South Chatham Drug Mart, but to the command post, as well.

Thus was the foursome able to monitor the situation from a distance, while at the same time being ready to leap into action as soon as any was called for. Or, as Captain Coopersmith put it, "We're loaded for bear!"

A remark that immediately produced a nervous tic in Ed Sprague's facial muscles.

The South Chatham Drug Mart was actually the second stop that Stephen and Penny Barrow made that morning in their hunt for Cheracol. They'd already tried the Eckerd's in nearby Chatham, without luck.

Stephen found a parking spot for the Renegade that turned out to be less than a hundred feet from the unmarked state police car idling in the same lot. But the investigator behind the wheel of that car was busy monitoring the radio, hadn't been provided a description of the Renegade (even though it was available from the same Department of Motor Vehicles that had supplied the photo from Stephen's driver's license), and therefore failed to spot the father and daughter who walked into the store.

Once inside, they wandered around until they found the cold-remedy section, which was toward the pharmacy in the back of the store. At one point, Penny noticed a tall thin man who seemed to be talking to his own chest. Only a week earlier, her teacher had introduced the class to a child's version of *The Legend of Sleepy Hollow*. It was all but required reading for schoolchildren in New York's Hudson Valley region.

"Is that Ichabod Crane?" she asked her father now.

Stephen studied the man, who studiously averted his eyes. "Could be," he said. "Either that, or some *other* kind of crane." Then, realizing the nuance might be lost on a six-year-old, he added, "A crane's a tall, skinny bird."

"Duh," said Penny.

There was, alas, no Cheracol to be found. Penny drifted over to the toy aisles and was about to zero in on the Barbie section, but Stephen steered her back up front. And they'd almost made it out the door when something stopped

Stephen. Although he couldn't later pinpoint exactly what it was, it may have been nothing more than the familiarity of the checkout counter. *I was just here yesterday,* he would remember recalling. And from that thought flowed the next: *I dropped off a roll of film.* The second thought stopped him in his tracks and prompted him to fish into the pockets of his jeans, the same jeans he'd been wearing the day before, and most of the week, for that matter.

Writers are like that.

And sure enough, there it was: the little stub from the envelope, the receipt he'd need to pick up the developed photos.

"Hold up!" he called to his daughter—who was by that time nearly out the door—loudly enough to cause the tall thin man to speak even more excitedly to his chest, and to reach nervously toward his waistband. *What a weirdo,* thought Stephen. He caught Penny's eye and motioned her to come back and get into line with him.

"Bingo!" came the transmission from the Stick to the undercover car in the parking lot outside. *"Bingo!"* heard the fearsome foursome at the command post in Jim Hall's living room. All ears waited for details.

"The subject is on the checkout line," they heard next.

The rest, as they like to say, is history. Stephen and Penny Barrow stood on line until it was their turn at the register. Stephen handed the stub to the clerk, a plump woman with gray hair. She thumbed through the tray of envelopes until she came across the one that matched the number on the stub, noticed the red piece of paper wrapped around it with a rubber band, and remembered the instructions given her by the tall thin man who'd showed her his badge that morning and scared her half to death. She handed the envelope to the customer.

"That'll be twelve-ninety-five," she told him.

She took his twenty-dollar bill, made change, and gave him his copy of the register receipt. Then, just as she'd been instructed to do, she hit the bell on the counter three times. It was one of those old hotel bells they used to use to call bell-hops, something she was old enough to remember.

She need not have rang. As soon as Stephen stepped away from the counter, envelope in his hand, the Stick was on top of him, grasping him firmly just above his right elbow.

"Huh?" said Stephen Barrow. The comment would typify his reaction to a large majority of the events that were about to unfold that morning.

"I'm afraid you'll have to step outside with me," said the tall thin man.

"What for?"

"You're under arrest."

"Huh?" said Stephen Barrow again.

"You're under arrest," the man repeated.

It wasn't that Stephen hadn't heard him the first time; it was just that the remark had been so utterly incomprehensible to him that he had trouble absorbing it. Had he been driving, for example, he could have understood an officer's pulling him over for some violation, real or imagined. Had he pushed ahead in line, or caused some sort of disturbance, or argued over the amount of his change—if any of those things had happened, he could have at least conceived that there was some misunderstanding on the part of the man, whom he was willing to assume was a police officer of some sort. But none of those things had happened: He'd waited his turn in line, caused no disturbance, and accepted his change without even counting it.

Then it occurred to him, and he smiled with relief. "You mean, from when I said, 'Hold up,' right? I'm sorry, I simply meant 'wait up!' The thing is, I just didn't want my daughter here wandering out into the parking lot without me. It wasn't that I was going to hold up the store or anything like that. See?"

But if the man saw, his only reaction was to talk to his chest again. "He's got the girl with him," he said. "Don't start shooting or nuthin.' "

Shooting? Later on, Stephen would remember experiencing the bizarre feeling that he'd somehow been trapped on the set of a movie, a B movie being acted out all around him in slow motion. At one point he actually caught himself thinking, *Who could that guy possibly have hiding down inside his sweatshirt?*

But as disoriented as Stephen Barrow may have felt, it was, of course, no movie scene that was being played out around him. With Investigator Stickley holding him firmly by one arm, and a bewildered Penny in tow, he was led out of the store and into the parking lot. Stickley's partner had by that time climbed out of the Ford Crown Victoria, in time to aim a camera at the three of them and snap away. Although the resulting image would be slanted and slightly out of focus, it would nevertheless accomplish its objective: magnified, it would catch Stephen Barrow still grasping in his right hand the envelope containing the photos he'd just been handed by the clerk at the checkout counter.

Or, as District Attorney Jim Hall would proudly announce to anyone who was willing to listen, "Right there, I got me all I need. *Proof of possession* is what I got."

A remark that may have struck some who didn't know Hall as just a bit personal.

Theresa Mulholland hung up the phone, completing her eleventh conversation in the past hour. "Coming Events" was coming along, but it was proving to be every bit as big a pain in the butt as she'd imagined it would be. The Ladies' Auxiliary—what they were auxiliary *to*, she had absolutely no idea—was holding a tea. The Canaan Volunteer Fire Department was hosting a Sunday breakfast fund-raiser. Auctions were scheduled at Mike Fallon's down in Copake, and Meisner's over in

New Lebanon. The Catamount Ski Resort was having a February Festival.

Theresa was beginning to understand what had driven Tom Grady back to the bottle.

Still, it had only taken her an hour, and she already had enough stuff to fill a column and a half, even more if she fluffed it up a bit. What worried her, though, were all the events she *hadn't* found out about. How could she be sure she wasn't leaving anything out? She thought about calling Neil Witt, the managing editor who'd talked her into taking the assignment. She even thought about trying to reach Tom Grady himself. But for all she knew, he was in rehab somewhere, locked up in a rubber room, folding paper airplanes.

She reached for another Tums—she'd stopped counting at five—and popped it into her mouth. "High in calcium," announced the wrapper. Keep it up, she was going to have the strongest bones in Columbia County. She bit the thing in half, and winced at the bitter, chalky taste.

" 'Chalky' is a *consistency*," she could hear her boss correcting her, "not a *taste*."

Well, fuck you, Neil Witt.

And you, too, Tom Grady.

As far as "From the Police Blotter," was concerned, she could only imagine what a nightmare *that* was going to be.

Over in South Chatham, Stephen Barrow's nightmare was just beginning. As soon as he'd had his photo snapped (he assumed, wrongly, by a newspaper photographer), he heard the arresting officer—the tall thin one who still had him by the upper arm—say something to him.

What he said was this: "The envelope, please."

Which only threw Stephen farther off balance. Having failed to make the connection between the envelope and his arrest, he'd proceeded to forget completely about the envelope, despite the fact that it was still clutched in his hand.

So when the tall thin man said, "The envelope, please," Stephen had no idea what he was talking about. All he *could* think, as a matter of fact, was of the Oscars, when the presenter of an award, having read off the list of nominees, was about to announce the winner.

"The envelope, please," is what they always said.

Which only added further to Stephen's notion that he'd been suddenly and inexplicably transposed into some minor character playing a role in an unfolding movie scene. And now, as if that hadn't been unsettling enough, here he was at the Academy Awards.

For as upset as Stephen Barrow was—after all, he'd just heard the words, "You're under arrest," unmistakably directed at him—he felt no overt panic yet, no sense that his life was about to implode. All that would come later, to be sure. But for the moment, Stephen could only feel as though he were floating, floating through some strange movie he couldn't comprehend. So even when the tall thin one pried the envelope loose from his hand, Stephen stood there dumbly, still failing to make the connection.

And it's likely he would have remained in his fog had he not overheard, as though the words were coming to him from across a great distance, a request the tall thin one made of the other one, the one Stephen had thought was a newspaper photographer, but who was evidently another cop of some sort.

"Find out what we're supposed to do with the little girl, willya?"

Do with the little girl. The *little girl* was his daughter. Slowly it dawned on him that this was about *him*, about *them*, and that it was serious business.

"What do you mean," he heard himself asking, "*do with the little girl?*"

But the tall thin one seemed to look right through Stephen as though he weren't there. "Find out," he instructed the other one again.

A small crowd had by this time begun to gather in the parking lot, and now Stephen found himself—and therefore Penny as well, since he continued to hold her hand—steered over toward the same black car that the photographer cop had gotten back into. They ended up right against the side of the car, so close to it that they could hear the photographer cop speaking into a radio microphone.

"Whaddaya want us to do with the girl?" he was asking. "Keep her separate from him?"

It was right about then that Stephen Barrow found himself yanked back to the present.

District Attorney Jim Hall sat hunched over the Motorola unit they'd set up in his living-room command post, the other three members of his team surrounding him in football-huddle fashion.

"Of *course* I want you to keep her separate," he barked into the microphone. "This is a sex-abuse case, and she's the *victim*."

"Well, whaddawe *do* with her?" the staticky voice in the radio asked. "We didn't bring CPS or anything."

CPS was Child Protective Services, the county agency that took temporary custody of minors when their parents were arrested for abuse or neglect. Apparently no one had had the foresight to alert them ahead of time. Which was an understandable oversight, seeing as the general level of expectation shared by the authorities was that the perp would most likely be keeping the victim chained up in his basement, subsisting on bread and water.

It was around then that Henry Coopersmith reached for the mike. Coopersmith was the commanding officer of K Troop, the regional division of the state police that covered the area.

"This is Captain Coopersmith," he announced. "Did the subject and the girl arrive at the set in a vehicle?" Only he pronounced the last word *vee*-hickle.

There was a pause, followed by another staticky transmission. "Uh, we don't know, sir."

"Why don'tcha *ask* him?" It wasn't for nothing that Coopersmith had risen through the ranks to his present status.

There was another pause, then, "That's affirmative, sir."

"Good. One of you transport Mr. Barrow in the cruiser. The other of you bring the victim in Mr. Barrow's *vee*-hickle. You copy?"

"Ten-four, sir."

"And they call themselves *investigators*," grumbled Coopersmith, handing the microphone back to Hall. "That there pair couldn't investigate a busted taillight."

Standing next to the black car in the parking lot, Stephen Barrow was of course able to hear the entire conversation, spared only Captain Coopersmith's appraisal of his field troops. The phrases he did hear hit him like a series of electric shocks. *Keep her separate. . . . This is a sex-abuse case. . . . She's the victim.* Next the tall thin one was asking Stephen if he'd driven there, and would he kindly point out his car to them, and hand over the keys.

And then they were taking Penny away from him, prying her little fingers from his.

"What's happening, Daddy?" she was asking, looking up into his face and expecting him to be able to explain things, as he always could.

But he couldn't explain things; he had no answer for her; in fact, he had absolutely no idea what was going on, or why. All he could do was kneel down so that he was more or less her height, look her in her eyes, and say, "You do what they say, Cookie. Everything's going to be all right."

"Promise?" Her eyes tearing up.

One of Stephen Barrow's cardinal rules of parenting was to never promise anything unless it was completely within his control to make good on it. As a result, he rarely promised his daughter anything. Stephen was, remember, a believer in the inevitability of traffic jams, flat tires, and random acts of God and Nature. And the last thing he wanted was to promise Penny something and then have it not happen. Yet now Stephen held his daughter's hands with his own (the tall thin man having displayed the good sense to release both father and daughter for this moment of parting), looked into her eyes, and spoke to her in as calm a voice as he could possibly muster.

"Yes," he told her. "I promise."

Then he straightened up and watched as the photographer cop reached for Penny's hand, was firmly rebuffed, and had to settle for placing a hand on her shoulder before leading Stephen Barrow's child away from him.

The next thing Stephen would remember hearing—for tears that had been welling up in his eyes now spilled over, making it difficult for him to see—was a ratcheting noise, a noise that reminded him of the sound made by a fishing reel when something big has suddenly taken the bait and tried to run with it. He felt his arms being moved to his sides, and his hands being pulled together behind his back, and he realized he was being handcuffed. Then he was being bent over forward and helped into the backseat of the car, one hand pushing him forward, another pressing down on the top of his head to keep it from hitting the door frame.

Just like in the movies.

FIVE

Theresa Mulholland decided to let the phone ring. You answered it on a Saturday, you deserved whatever you got. It could be a telemarketer, a crank call, an *insurance salesman*, for God's sake. Worse yet, it could even be her *mother*.

"*So, tell me, Theresa, talk to me. You never talk to me, you know? I mean, I'm only your* mother."

"*That's not true, mother. I talk to you all the time.*"

"*Yes, but only because I call* you."

"*That counts.*"

"*Counts, shmounts. If I didn't call you, for all I know, you could be lying there dead in that, that* apartment *of yours.*"

"*It's not an* apartment, *Mother. It's the entire top floor of a house.*"

"*It's very depressing, is what it is. But look, I don't want to upset you. Why don't we change the subject, okay?*"

"*Okay.*"

"*So, sweetie, what's new? Are you seeing anyone special these days? We're not getting any younger, you know?*"

Which is precisely why God created the answering machine in the first place.

"Hello, Terry, you there?" The voice was decidedly that of a man. No deeper than her mother's, and none of that endearing raspy quality. But definitely a man's. "It's Neil, Neil Witt."

Her boss. Another reason God must have had in mind.

"Pick up if you're there, Terry. There's something important breaking, and I need you to get on it right away."

She picked up.

"Hello, Neil."

"Terry, you're there. Thank God."

Which only suggested that He was playing both sides of the fence today.

"This better be good," she told him.

"It *is* good," he said. "I need you to get over to the town hall in South Chatham right away. The state police have just picked up some guy for *sex abuse*. It seems the victim is his own six-year-old daughter."

"*Sex abuse*? This sounds like a *crime* story to me."

"Okay, it's a crime story. But didn't you tell me you'd do 'From the Police Blotter' until Tom Grady got back?"

"Right," Theresa admitted. "But you said that was just phone calls. Come on, Neil, it's *me* you're talking to, remember? I do garden shows, pet adoptions, antique fairs, human-interest stuff. I don't do *crime*."

"Well, you do until Tom gets back."

If Theresa Mulholland's instructions were to get over to the South Chatham Town Hall right away, the state police had other business with Stephen Barrow before they'd get around to taking him there. Under their procedures, set out in considerable detail in a thick volume (that, despite its catchy title, *The New York State Police Procedure Manual, Revised and Annotated Edition XIV (1994),* is unlikely to make the *New York Times* bestseller list anytime soon), they first had to process their prisoner. This could only be accomplished at their nearest facility, which in this case was the K-Troop barracks, down in Claverack. Which meant that, following his arrest, the first thing Stephen Barrow would be doing was going for a ride. And, sitting in the backseat of the black Crown Victoria, his wrists handcuffed painfully behind him, it promised to be a pretty uncomfortable ride at that.

The tall thin man waited until the other one had strapped Penny into the Renegade, started it, and pulled up behind them. Then, convoy style, they pulled out of the parking lot.

"Can you tell me what I'm being charged with?" Stephen asked.

"Sex abuse of some sort."

"For doing *what*?"

"Better for you, you don't say anything, sir."

"But I have no idea what this is about."

"I'm pretty sure," said the man, "that it's about them *pitchers*."

Pitchers. Stephen tried his best to make sense of that. He pretended it was a crossword-puzzle clue, tried to come up with a synonym. Pitchers, as in *vases*? Madison Avenue *admen*? *Baseball* pitchers?

"Pitchers," he said aloud, hoping the sound of the word might somehow reveal some secret meaning that hadn't yet occurred to him.

"Snapshots," said the man. "The ones you just picked up back there in the store."

"*Pic*tures!" he shouted, and realized immediately that he'd insulted his captor, probably the worst thing he could have done. But his mind was already on the pictures, the photographs. What on earth did they have to do with *sex abuse*? He tried to visualize the prints, tried to remember what they'd be of. They had to be mostly shots of Penny—his photos almost always were—playing, laughing, doing silly stuff, whatever. They'd been out hiking, hadn't they been? Then back home—

Stephen felt his jaw drop open. The bathtub . . . the shampoo . . . the *unicord* hairdo . . . the *mooning*!

"Oh my God," said Stephen Barrow. And laughed out loud. "That's really *it*?"

Much later, Stephen would recall allowing his body to relax

just a bit at that point, to shift his cuffed hands slightly to one side and let his weight slump against the imitation leather seat-back of the Crown Victoria. And the thought he had went something like this: Even though he'd known all along that he hadn't actually *done* anything, it had nevertheless occurred to him that whatever it was they *thought* he'd done—albeit mistakenly—might be so serious that it could take a little time before it got straightened out. But *this*—this was nothing. This was a *joke*.

It would be the last time he would think that way.

The booking process took place in a basement-level set of rooms collectively called the Prisoner Processing Unit, or PPU. Stephen was led, still handcuffed behind his back, to a holding cell, where finally the cuffs were removed. He was patted down by the tall, thin one and told to empty his pockets. His watch was taken from him. His shoelaces were pulled from his shoes. He was locked in a six-foot-square cage with metal bars. There was no window, no chair, no lightbulb. A metal bench protruded from the back wall. That was it.

"What's happening with my daughter?" he asked a gray-uniformed trooper who sat at a desk across the room. He looked like he was still in his teens. *I thought they had to be at least twenty-one*, Stephen caught himself thinking.

"Don't worry," the trooper told him, "she's okay now."

Don't worry, be happy!

Stephen didn't like the way he'd said *now*. "Can I see her?" he asked. There didn't seem to be any harm in asking. What did they say? Nothing ventured, nothing gained. And there didn't seem any downside to it. The worst that could happen was that he'd be told no.

Or so he thought.

"You know what you can do?" the trooper called out to him.

Something in his tone told Stephen that the question was somewhat rhetorical, and that the answer was about to follow.

"You can *shut the fuck up*, is what you can do, you fucking *pre*-vert."

After about forty-five minutes, an older trooper, one with gray hair, came into the processing area and spoke to Stephen through the bars of his cell.

"Mr. Barrow?"

"Yes." Stephen suppressed the urge to make some clever remark about his being the only one in there, not to mention the only one in sight who wasn't wearing a uniform.

"Captain said for me to ask you who you want us to call to come pick up your daughter."

Pick her up?

"Can't she just wait here until we're finished?" Stephen asked. "Until I can take her home?"

The two troopers shared a chuckle.

"How long is processing going to take?" Stephen asked.

"Oh, *processing* isn't going to take long at all," said the gray-haired one. "Hour, hour and a half, tops."

"Well?"

"Well, the thing is, when we're done with you here, we gotta take you back up to South Chatham, bring you before the town judge there."

"You mean they spent half an hour driving me down here," said Stephen, "so you could spend another half an hour driving me back up where we started from?"

"Like they told you, you gotta get processed."

"But after that, I'll be going home, right?"

"Not unless you got the money to make bail," said the young trooper.

Bail?

"What kind of *bail*?"

"Sex abuse?" said the gray-haired one. "Six-year-old girl? If I were a betting man, I'd start at, say, fifty thousand. Whaddaya think, Tommy?"

"Me? I think *any* bail's too low for a *pre*-vert."

"So who do we call to come pick up the girl?"

Stephen tried his best to focus on that. But he was having a hard time getting past the image of standing before a judge and having *bail* set. For the first time, it was beginning to dawn on him that he might not be going home at all that night.

"Captain said if you don't come up with a suitable relative of the child, we'll have to call BCW."

"What's *BCW*?"

"Bureau of Child Welfare," explained Gray-hair. "They'll pick the kid up, put her in a shelter until . . ." His voice drifted off.

"Until *what*?"

"Until they can place her with a foster family."

Foster family?

"You can call her mother, I guess." Stephen couldn't think of anyone else.

"We've been trying that," said Gray-hair. "Haven't been able to reach her. Any other ideas?"

Stephen looked at his watch, remembered they'd taken it from him. "What time is it?" he asked.

"One-thirty."

He had no idea where Ada would be at one-thirty on a Saturday afternoon in the middle of February. Skiing, probably, or shopping. "I've got her cell-phone number," he said. "It's in my wallet."

The young one retrieved Stephen's wallet from on top of his desk. "Does she know about any of this?" he asked.

"Any of what?"

"That she married a pedophile." Only he pronounced it *pee*-dophile, which prompted Stephen to wonder if the trooper might possibly have had his perversions mixed up.

Some of those who later listened to Stephen Barrow's account of the hours following his arrest would remark that they found many of his reactions to the events surprisingly clinical and detached. One observer would be moved to describe his affect as "flat," meaning that, considering the circumstances in which he suddenly found himself, Stephen seemed to lack a level of animation appropriate to the situation. Another evaluator (for in time, there would be many observers, evaluators, and other professionals asked to offer their opinions on the subject, as well as a myriad of other subjects) would go so far as to suggest that Stephen may well have been in a state of shock that first afternoon, so traumatized had he been by the arrest.

Stephen would see things somewhat differently. "Remember," he would tell one interviewer, who had suggested that his early reactions bordered on the bizarre, "I'm a writer by trade. I spend a lot of my time observing, analyzing. My livelihood depends upon my being able to notice things like humor, absurdity, and irony in even the most catastrophic of events.

"I was *off the wall* when they arrested me, just like anyone else would have been. But at first, I had to remain calm for Penny. If she'd seen me freaking out, there's no telling what it might have done to her. So I had to *seem* as though I was in control, even if I wasn't. Then, later on, even as I was going through this truly frightening experience, at the same time there was a *surrealness* to it, a Kafkaesque quality that kept part of me detached from it. Like when the troopers and investigators kept saying things meant to scare me out of my wits. But each time they came to the most menacing part of what they were saying, they'd somehow manage to mispronounce a word, or use the wrong word altogether. And each time that happened, the writer in me couldn't help but notice it. In spite of myself, I kept on seeing the humor, the absurdity of the situation. After a while, I found there was a part of myself that was actually enjoying each new intimidation, just so I could find the silliness in it. You know, sort of the way you listen to a joke, trying to figure out the punch line in advance?

"Who knows? Maybe it was my way of protecting myself from the insanity of it all. I mean, if I'd taken every dire prediction to heart, I'd have ended up believing I was never going to go home, that I was going to spend the rest of my life in prison, and that my daughter was going to become—what do they call it?—a *ward of the state*. That's one of the things they told me. If I'd believed that, *really* believed that, I'd have killed myself right then. With or without my shoelaces."

Whatever it was, Stephen's sense of detachment stayed with him for the duration of his processing. He was taken out of the holding cell so that he could be photographed and finger-printed. He'd always thought that the photographing process was done professionally, that the creation of all those mug shots you saw was performed by trained technicians using sophisticated machinery. Instead, the young trooper handed him a wooden placard with little plastic letters and numbers slid into it, movie-marquee style, and told him to hold it beneath his chin, while the trooper aimed a huge Polaroid camera that looked older than he was. Twice the flash failed; then they ran out of film. Stephen couldn't help wishing he had been so unlucky the day he'd photographed his daughter.

The fingerprinting was accomplished without incident, and while Stephen was trying to wash the ink off his hands, the tall thin man who'd arrested him and later driven him to the bar-racks reappeared.

"When you're finished," he told Stephen, "come on in here and have a seat." With that, he motioned to a door marked INTERVIEW ROOM. Stephen dried his hands; the remaining ink would take the better part of a week to fade.

The interview room was an enclosure, maybe ten by ten, with a table and chairs. Set into one wall was a large mirror, which Stephen right away decided was one of those that allowed people on the other side of it to observe them. Only he couldn't remember the name for it.

"Do you call that a two-way mirror," he asked, "or a one-way mirror?"

"I just call it a mirror," the tall thin one said, in perfect deadpan.

Sure. Or was it possible he really didn't know? Could it be that he'd never been in the adjoining room? That he honestly thought it was *just a mirror*?

"I'm Investigator Stickley," the man said. "I need to ask you some questions. But first I'm going to advise you of your rights." With that, he proceeded to read a list of questions from a piece of paper. Each time he read a question—for example, did Stephen understand that he had a right to remain silent?—he looked up and waited for Stephen to answer "yes" or "no." Each time Stephen answered, Investigator Stickley wrote something on the paper. When he was finished, he slid the paper across the table and asked Stephen to read it and sign it if the inked-in responses were accurate. They were, and Stephen signed it.

The first part of the interview dealt with what Stickley called pedigree questions. How old was Stephen? What was his date of birth? His address? His Social Security number? How tall was he? How much did he weigh? Was he employed? And so forth.

Stephen answered them all, and Stickley noted each of his answers on one or the other of several printed forms. Then, the *pedigree* portion of the interview apparently over, he moved to the next phase. Stephen caught himself wondering what the second part was called, what the opposite of *pedigree* was. *Mixed breed*, perhaps?

"Whose film was that," Stickley began, "that you picked up at the Drug Mart?"

"That actually wasn't film," Stephen explained. "You drop the film *off*. What I was picking up was prints."

"I see," said Stickley. "Whose prints?"

"Mine."

"And who had earlier dropped off the—"

"Film."

"—the film?"

"I had," said Stephen.

"And who had taken the—"

"Pictures?" In spite of everything, there was a part of Stephen that was getting into the absurdity of this.

"Right. The pictures."

"I had, most of them. I think my daughter might have taken a few of them. If you want to show me the prints, I'm pretty sure I can tell you who took which."

"That won't be necessary." Which meant Stickley didn't *have* the prints anymore. "How about the ones of your daughter in the bathtub? Who took those?"

"I did."

"When you took those, were you aware that your daughter was naked?"

"Excuse me?"

"When you took the shots of your daughter standing in the tub and, uh, *bending* over like that, did you know she had no clothes on?"

"Of course I did."

Stickley wrote for several minutes without looking up. Evidently, this was the *essay* part of the exam; the pedigree portion had been the *short-answer* part.

"Okay," he said finally.

"That's *it*?" Didn't he want to know the *circumstances* of why Stephen had taken the bathtub shots, the *context*? Wasn't he interested in whose idea it had been that Penny bend over and stick her tongue out at the camera? Didn't he care that those were no more than three or four isolated shots at the end of an entire roll of film?

"That's it," said Investigator Stickley.

"But don't you want to know what was *going on* when I took the pictures?"

Stickley shook his head slowly, from side to side. "Nope," he said. "Better off saving that kinda stuff for your lawyer."

My lawyer?

Until that moment, until he heard the word spoken aloud by Investigator Stickley, the thought had never occurred to Stephen Barrow that he was going to need a lawyer. So certain had he been that this whole thing was going to simply go away, vanish, as soon as everyone realized their mistake, that he'd not once thought to himself, *I'm going to need to get myself a lawyer*. And as strange as that may sound at first, to hear Stephen explain this lapse makes a certain amount of sense.

"There were at least three separate times that day that I was absolutely convinced that whoever these men were who'd arrested me, they'd made some sort of a mistake, and I'd be let go within the hour, as soon as it was cleared up. I felt that way when I first got arrested inside the Drug Mart; I was sure they had the wrong guy. Then I heard it was for some kind of sex abuse, and I *knew* they had the wrong guy. Finally, when they told me it was about the photographs, I realized it *was* me they were talking about, but I refused to believe they could really be serious about *charging* me with something for that.

"So even when they took Penny from me and drove me to their headquarters, even when they fingerprinted me and photographed me and read me my rights and told me I had a right to a lawyer and would be going before a judge and might go to jail—even then, there was a part of me that couldn't believe it was really happening to me. Notifying friends or family? Thinking about raising money for bail? Getting a lawyer? Those were the furthest things from my mind. I swear, if Stickley hadn't finally mentioned it, I don't know how long it would've taken me to realize I was really going to need a lawyer."

SIX

FLYNT ADAMS, ATTORNEY AT LAW, proclaimed the shingle affixed to the door of the small, brick one-family on Main Street—*Main Street* being a designation that was somewhat redundant, seeing as there *were* no other streets to speak of in the village of South Chatham, just a tangle of interlocking off-shoots, alleys, and driveways.

If Flynt Adams typifies the current generation of the small-town lawyer—and a good case can be made that he does—we've come a long way since Norman Rockwell presented us his version of the balding, bespectacled barrister.

Other than his name—which is actually a combination of his mother's family name and his father's, the latter traceable all the way back to John Quincy (a fact you're unlikely to learn from Adams himself)—there is nothing pretentious about Flynt Adams. He is a trim man who carries himself like the athlete he once was and still is, if only recreationally. He looks far too young for his gray hair, but it's a head of gray hair most men would kill for and plenty of women would die for: a mop that looks almost silver, cut short enough to reveal its owner's conservative nature, yet long enough that it never seems quite under control.

Unless he has a court appearance or a closing, Adams dresses casually, favoring sport jackets and slacks over suits. He prefers open collars to buttoned ones, and keeps several ties in the office to pick from when the occasion arises.

The inside of Flynt Adams's office reflects its owner's informal taste. The waiting room is small and well lit, the receptionist's area tidy but typically empty (Adams cannot, or chooses to not, afford full-time help). To the rear of the office, in what Adams refers to as his work space, the visitor will find no oak or mahogany partner's desk, no leather-covered judge's chair, no wall full of plaques or laminated diplomas intended to impress clients. There is instead a simple pine table, which once served as a teacher's desk and now holds a computer, four more-or-less matched wooden chairs, and a couple of wooden file cabinets that may be antiques, or simply tasteful reproductions. One wall is the original red brick of the building, rough and unadorned; another bears a single large oil painting of an ocean regatta. As a young man, Adams did a lot of sailing, and he has an attic full of trophies. These days he's landlocked, and far too busy trying to support his family to enjoy expensive, time-consuming hobbies.

This particular Saturday found Adams at his computer, drawing up a contract for the sale of a home over in Canaan. He represented the seller, and would make seven hundred dollars for his trouble; the buyer's lawyer was a hotshot from New York City who was charging his client $350 an hour. At those rates, Adams had been surprised the guy didn't want to draw up the contract himself, so he could bill for the hours; but apparently he either didn't know how to do it, or intended to bill for it anyway.

If it wasn't exactly Flynt Adams's favorite way to spend a Saturday, he had little choice in the matter. With a wife and three teenage children to support, he didn't have the luxury of picking and choosing his cases. When he'd made the decision to hang up his shingle in a small town—and South Chatham was about as small as you could get—he'd known he was going to have to do everything he could to build his practice. That meant being in his office long hours, getting to know the townspeople, joining whatever civic groups he could stomach (the local school board and the volunteer fire department were okay, but he drew the line at the Young Republicans), and being willing to handle every type of case imaginable. Wills, closings, accidents, collections, bankruptcies, speeding tickets—you named it, Flynt Adams would do it. He would have loved nothing more than to specialize in some area, say environmental law or criminal defense. But there were few environmental issues to champion in Columbia County, and (except for petty drug dealers over in Hudson) even fewer criminals. You ended up taking whatever came in.

So on this Saturday in February, Adams sat at his computer, filling in the blanks on a form he'd devised and named "Contract.house.sel." Not exactly the sort of work he'd dreamed of back in law school.

The drive back up to South Chatham took the same thirty-five minutes as had the drive down to the K Troop barracks. Stephen Barrow sat alone in the backseat, handcuffed as before. The young trooper did the driving this time, with Investigator Stickley sitting alongside him. The two of them spoke to each other in muffled tones, and didn't include Stephen in their conversation. It was as though, with the processing phase now completed, they were finished with him, except for delivering him to others. Apparently, they no longer felt the need to exchange small talk with him.

He was *cargo*.

He had to interrupt a discussion of snowmobile engines to ask them a question. "Excuse me," he said, "but can you tell me who's looking after my daughter?"

"We left a message on your wife's cell phone," said Stickley.

"Ex-wife."

"Right."

"Did she ever return the message?"

"I honestly don't know."

"So then," Stephen asked, "where *is* my daughter? Who's taking care of her?"

This time the only response he got from the front seat was a matching pair of shrugs. Penny wasn't their daughter, and despite the initial concern they'd shown for her, now she was in someone else's hands. Police work is a terribly fragmented business, in which moving on to the next job is the rule, not the exception, and "Out of sight, out of mind" is a frequently employed defense mechanism to permit the emotional separation needed to concentrate on the next assignment. They weren't bad people, these officers, but at this point they simply couldn't have cared less about Penny. It was the nature of the job, that's all.

The sky was already beginning to get dark—it gets dark early in Columbia County in mid-February—by the time they reached South Chatham and pulled up in front of the town hall. Stephen figured he must have walked or driven by the old red brick building a hundred times, but he'd never once had occasion to go inside. He sent off his taxes to the township of New Lebanon, grieved his property assessment over in Hudson, and had paid the only speeding ticket he'd gotten down in Ghent. So here he was, entering now for the first time, hand-cuffed behind his back and flanked on either side by state troopers. The only saving grace he could think of was that there didn't happen to be anyone standing out in front to recognize him. A young, redheaded woman holding a notepad looked vaguely familiar to him, but he couldn't quite place her.

Theresa Mulholland had fairly rushed over to the South Chatham Town Hall after getting off the phone with Neil Witt. Not being a crime reporter, she had no idea that, before he was ready to go before the town justice, the newly arrested sex abuser would first have to spend three hours being driven around and processed. So when she'd arrived just after one o'clock, notepad in hand, she'd discovered that except for the building's custodian (who happened to be there that Saturday because they'd been having problems with the furnace) she was the only one there, and certainly the only one there who knew anything of a new arrest.

"C'mon in," the custodian had told her. "Might as well stay warm while yer waitin'."

As things turned out, *warm* had been a relative term. Theresa had spent the next two hours shivering, going for coffee, cursing Tom Grady, shivering some more, cursing Neil Witt, going for lunch, and cursing Tom Grady, Neil Witt, and the entire newspaper business, all over again. Finally, a little after three, a sprinkling of other people had begun showing up, though it wouldn't be until later that she found out who they were—the town attorney, the town clerk, a court reporter, a couple of sheriff's deputies, and finally the town justice himself. It was as if they'd all known there was no rush. All of them, that is, except Theresa herself.

A while later, one of the deputies (a young man named Bill Ashworth, whom Theresa had gone to high school with) got a call on his radio. "They're about five minutes away," he told her. "You slip outside, you'll be able to get a shot of them bringing him into the building. You know, a perp walk."

Perp walk? Shot of them? Was Theresa supposed to have brought a *camera* along? She couldn't remember Neil Witt having said anything about that. Evidently she was supposed to have known that on her own, without being told. *Great.* So here she was, her big moment as a crime reporter coming up, and already she'd managed to screw it up.

But she'd put her gloves on, pulled her jacket collar up, and wandered outside anyway, so she'd at least be able to say she'd been there for the *perp walk*, even if the *Hudson Valley Herald* readers would have to settle for her written description of it. For once, a thousand words would simply have to be as powerful as a single photograph.

So she'd been standing out on the sidewalk, shivering in the fading daylight, when the cruiser had at last pulled up and two troopers—she guessed they were both troopers, even though only one was in uniform—opened up the back door and helped their prisoner out.

Until that moment, Theresa hadn't quite known what to expect. She'd known that the man was supposed to have sexually abused his young daughter. She wasn't sure if that meant he'd raped her, or what. *Sodomized* her, perhaps. You were always reading how defendants were charged with raping and *sodomizing* their victims, though it was generally left to the reader's imagination as to just what the particulars of the sodomy were. But this much she'd already decided: You didn't need to know too many of the details of this story to know this guy was a monster.

Only now, looking at the bewildered, compliant man being helped out of the back of the cruiser, Theresa found herself hard-pressed to imagine him raping or sodomizing anyone, let alone his own young daughter. To her, he simply didn't look capable of such an act. The only thing he looked, as a matter of fact, was vaguely familiar.

To Stephen Barrow, the little bald man sitting behind the nameplate that read HOMER J. QUACKENBUSH, TOWN JUSTICE didn't seem much like a judge. He would later learn that not only was Homer J. Quackenbush not a judge, he wasn't even a lawyer. But neither of those facts prevented him from being the town justice for the village of South Chatham. Although New York now required that town justices be lawyers, the law that imposed that requirement had grandfathered in all those holding office at the time of the change. Homer J. Quackenbush had been holding office then, and was still holding on now at the age of eighty-two, and had no intention of letting go until the Good Lord Himself said it was time.

At the moment, however, it was time for him to address the defendant standing before him. "Do you have counsel, young man?" To Quackenbush, anyone under sixty was young.

Counsel? Stephen Barrow stared back at this figure straight out of Dickens and said nothing.

"Counsel," Quackenbush repeated. "A lawyer?"

"Oh," said Stephen. "No, I don't."

"Can you afford a lawyer?"

Stephen had no idea what a lawyer would cost. His divorce lawyer had charged him $150 an hour, and with the custody battle, had run up a bill of close to ten thousand dollars, just about wiping him out. He imagined that a criminal lawyer could be much more expensive. After all, they weren't just talking about dividing up the furniture here, or drawing up a visitation schedule. "I'm not certain," he said.

"Do you have a job?"

"Not really."

"How do you support yourself?"

"I write."

"For the purpose of this appearance," said Justice Quackenbush, "I find the defendant indigent and entitled to have counsel assigned by the court. We'll take a recess while we find you a lawyer, young man. Off the record, somebody call Flynt Adams. I noticed the lights in his office were on when I drove by a while ago. Poor guy probably doesn't know it's Saturday."

Stephen was given a chair to sit in. While he waited, he tried to absorb what he'd just heard. For the first time, he'd heard himself referred to as *the defendant,* and he didn't much like the sound of the phrase. Fragments of movie lines came drifting back to him. *Mr. Foreman, how do you find the defendant? . . . We find the defendant guilty as charged, your honor. . . . Will the defendant please rise? . . . The defendant is ordered hanged by the neck until he shall be dead.*

Next, he'd been found *indigent.* Had the judge asked him if he was *employed,* he could have said yes: self-employed was employed, after all. It was that *job* question that had thrown him. So suddenly he found himself not only a defendant but a *pauper* as well. To everyone else in the room, he was already a man who'd sexually exploited his six-year-old daughter; now on top of that he was an unemployed welfare cheat, a drifter, a homeless person.

And who was this free lawyer they were getting a hold of? Some poor slob who evidently didn't even know what day of the week it was.

Things were not looking up.

Flynt Adams looked up at the first ring of the telephone. It was always an approach-avoidance thing with Adams: He wanted new business—*needed* new business—but at the same time, on this late Saturday afternoon in February, he wanted to be home with his family. Yet that same family—that and Flynt Adams's strong Protestant work ethic—now forced him to reach across his desk and pick up the receiver.

"Law office," he said.

"That you, Flynt?" It was a woman's voice, but one he didn't recognize right away.

"Yes, it's me," he said.

"This is Eleanor Smeal." Eleanor was the town clerk; Flynt had written a new will for her, not four months ago.

"Hi, Eleanor. What's up?"

"What's up is Homer's got a criminal appearance to do. Turns out the man doesn't have a lawyer, or the money to hire one. Homer was wondering if you might like to take it, as eighteen-bee."

It was Article 18-B of the state's County Law that authorized and governed the assignment of counsel. Flynt was no stranger to the system: you got paid forty dollars an hour for in-court time, and twenty-five for out-of-court. At rates like that, you learned to identify with your indigent clients. Still, he knew he couldn't afford to say no.

"What's the charge?" he asked.

"Some kinda sex abuse," said Eleanor. "Something to do with his kid."

"Nice. When's the appearance set for?" He'd now killed half a Saturday, and wasn't much looking forward to working the rest of the weekend as well. Then again, if he could persuade them to schedule it for right after Sunday services, he'd already be dressed in his suit and tie.

"Five minutes ago."

"*Now?*"

"Now."

"I'll be right there."

To Stephen Barrow, who'd been expecting the worst, the man who walked into the courtroom and introduced himself as Flynt Adams was a pleasant surprise. It was hard to tell how old he was, the way his boyish features contrasted with his gray hair. And if his outfit was a bit unusual—the navy blazer, denim shirt, and yellow print tie were okay, but the faded jeans and sneakers struck Stephen as a bit out of place—well, it *was* a Saturday, after all. But by far the best part about Flynt Adams was the way he looked you in the eye when he spoke, and then continued to look you in the eye when *you* spoke.

"Do you understand what they're charging you with?" he asked Stephen. The two of them were sitting off to one side of the room, and their conversation was private, so long as they whispered.

"Sort of."

"Why don't we read this thing together," Adams suggested, unfolding a set of papers he'd been handed a moment earlier. "It says here, according to an Investigator named Todd Stickley, that you've committed a violation of section two-sixty-three point fifteen of the Penal Law, Possessing a Sexual Performance by a Child, in that you, 'knowing the character and content thereof, had in your possession a photograph or photographs displaying a lewd exhibition of the genitals and anal area of a child less than sixteen years of age.' Do you understand that?"

"I guess so," said Stephen.

"So tell me," said Flynt Adams. "What's this all about?"

So Stephen told him, as well as he could, given the constraints of time and circumstances. He described the shampoo-and-bubble-bath hairdo Penny had fashioned, his attempt to record it on film, her unexpectedly mooning him, and his recording that as well. He recounted how he'd dropped the film off at the Drug Mart on Friday, and picked it up this morning, and how they'd suddenly arrested him.

"That's it?" Adams asked.

"That's it," Stephen assured him.

"According to this," said the lawyer, turning the page of what he'd been reading from, "this is your first arrest. Is that accurate?"

Stephen hesitated for a split second, and Adams caught it. "Listen," he said. "I'm your *lawyer*. I've got to know these things. Besides, it's *privileged*. That means I can't mention it, unless you allow me to. Right now, I just need to know."

"I paid a ten-dollar fine once for urinating in public. It was down in New York City. I'd drunk a six-pack of beer, and my bladder was about to explode. So I walked down an alley, and, well, some cop spotted me."

"How long ago was that?"

"I was eighteen."

"Forget about it. Anything else?"

"No, nothing."

"Good," said Adams. "Next question: Can you make any bail?"

"Like how much?"

"Hard to say." For the first time, Adams seemed to avoid making eye contact. Or maybe it was just Stephen's imagination.

"I mean," said Stephen, "how serious can this be?"

"Well," said Adams, looking at the first page again, "it *is* a felony."

"And that means?"

"That means they could indict you. Worst comes to worst, you're looking at four years. But with a clean record, and—"

"Four *years*?"

"You ready, Flynt?" called Homer Quackenbush. "It's gettin' dark out there, and my dinner'll be waitin'."

"Two minutes," said Adams.

"Four *years*?" Stephen repeated. He still couldn't believe it.

"That's what we call the worst-case scenario," Adams explained. "Right now, we've got to talk about bail. Where do you work?"

"I'm a writer," Stephen explained. "I work at home."

"How long have you lived there?"

"Two years."

"Are you married?"

"Divorced."

"How much cash do you have on hand?"

"On hand?"

"In your pocket, for starters."

"Thirty bucks."

"And in the bank?"

"Seven, eight thousand."

"Is there someone who can get at it?"

"Just me, I guess."

"Hmmmm," said Flynt Adams.

"Okay," said Homer Quackenbush. "Let's get this show on the road."

Stephen stood at the front of the room, Adams to his right, and the town attorney to *his* right. All three of them faced the judge, or justice, or whatever he was. The clerk read a bunch of stuff, beginning with the name of the case, *The People of the State of New York versus Stephen Barrow.*

The People of the State of New York? It was a phrase Stephen had heard before but never given any thought to. Now it suddenly struck him that those were the sides: everyone else in the entire state against him. Hadn't it been humiliating enough to be arrested, to be the defendant? Now it seemed that wasn't bad enough; now he was *Public Enemy Number One.*

"Are the People requesting bail?" the judge asked.

"Yes, your honor," said the town attorney.

"Go ahead."

"These are serious felony charges," he began. "I've already spoken with District Attorney Jim Hall, who says he plans on presenting them to a grand jury next week. He says he's got a very strong case, including testimony from several witnesses employed at the Drug Mart here in town, as well as a confession by the defendant himself. Mr. Hall feels there's a significant risk of flight. We're therefore asking for bail in the amount of twenty-five thousand dollars."

"Mr. Adams?"

"This is a case of a man taking family photographs of his daughter. We may not like several of the photographs he took, but there's no suggestion he intended to sell them, publish them, or otherwise exploit the child. Besides that, Mr. Barrow has a clean record. He lives right here, outside of East Chatham. Writes books. He's not going anywhere. I'm asking you to R-O-R him."

The judge turned back to the town attorney. "What makes you think there's a significant risk of flight here?" he asked.

"The seriousness of the case, your honor."

"Anything else?"

"The *strength* of the case?"

"You already told me about those things," said the judge. "Anything else *specific* you got?"

"Uh, no, sir."

"Okay then. The matter will be adjourned till February

twenty-eighth for grand jury action. The defendant is ordered released on his own recognizance. Dinnertime."

Theresa Mulholland had been sitting off to the side, trying to place the defendant, the man called Stephen Barrow. So far, she'd been able to understand about half of the proceedings. She'd been jotting down key phrases on her notepad—things like *serious felony, grand jury,* and *several witnesses*—hoping to get one of the participants to fill her in with more detail afterward, when another phrase suddenly woke her up. That other phrase was *the Drug Mart here in town.*

That's who he was!

The guy in line yesterday, in front of her. The one buying Safari Barbie for his daughter! Only now he stood accused of taking lewd photos of that same daughter. Hadn't he dropped off a roll of film while she waited? *The* roll of film, it had to be. And Barbie—was she some sort of a *prop* he'd used in the photos? No, that couldn't be; he was already dropping the film off when he was buying the doll. So Barbie had to be a *bribe,* a *reward* for posing. Talk about a *creep!*

Theresa tried to picture the man's daughter. She came up with a pretty little girl, seductive beyond her years. A pouty, lipsticked mouth; loose, blonde ringlets for hair; and big, blue eyes with a haunting suggestion of sadness in them.

The picture she'd come up with, of course, was that of Jon-Benet Ramsey.

The guy was a writer, she was hearing now, a local man living somewhere outside of East Chatham. She guessed he was divorced, or at least separated: otherwise, he would have left the Barbie-buying to his wife. Then again, we were dealing with a total *pervert* here. Maybe his wife went off to work in the morning, and he was one of those guys that stayed home and played housewife. Or house*husband,* if you wanted to get technical about it. One of those sensitive, new-age guys. Maybe he was even gay. Sure, he had a kid—like *that* wasn't possible?

Yeah, that was it: He *had* to be gay. When they were *that* good looking, they always turned out to be gay.

And suddenly, it was over. The gay pervert househusband was being released without having to put up any bail at all, simply because it happened to be the judge's *dinnertime*. Theresa looked at her watch. For God's sake, it was barely *four o'clock*. What'd the guy do, live on a *farm* or something?

For once, she was right on the money.

I'm going home.

Stephen heard *nothing* after that, and understood nothing *but* that. But it was enough. Had they told him he'd be executed in a month, it wouldn't have mattered. The only thing he cared about was that he was going home.

Tonight.

Now.

Outside on the sidewalk, he pumped Flynt Adams's hand in thanks until Adams finally had to pull free.

"What happens now?" Stephen asked.

"You go home," said Adams. "And you keep your mouth shut, okay? I'm the only one you talk to. That's important."

"Okay," said Stephen. This wasn't exactly the kind of stuff you ran to tell friends about, anyway. "But what I mean is, where can I get my daughter?"

To his considerable credit, Flynt Adams met Stephen's eyes this time without flinching. "You can't," he said softly.

"I can't?"

"That's right. CPS has her. They're—"

"Who's CPS?"

"Child Protective Services."

"But who *are* they? Do they know what they're *doing*?"

"They're going to turn her over to your ex-wife, as soon as they locate her."

"But I have custody, I, she lives with me."

"Not right now she doesn't. A County Court judge signed

an order an hour ago, transferring custody to your ex-wife. He also signed a temporary order of protection against you."

"What does *that* mean?"

"It means that for now, you can't go anywhere near your daughter. You can't see her, you can't call her, you can't write her. You do any of those things, you'll be arrested."

Stephen suddenly felt as though he'd been enveloped by a thick cloud. He could still hear what Adams was saying, but the words sounded funny, like maybe they were being played too slowly. He fought to understand them, but the cloud grew even thicker. "How long is *for now?*" he managed to ask.

Adams considered that for a moment. "We can't go into court to challenge it until next week," he said. "But . . ."

"But what?"

"Mr. Barrow—"

"Stephen."

"Stephen, think about it for a moment. We're going to be asking a judge to return a six-year-old child to a father who's admitted to taking what may amount to pornographic photos of her. No judge in the world is going to take a chance doing that. Hell, we'll be lucky if they don't set *bail* when we get over to Hudson."

"Judge Quackenbush said—"

"Judge Quackenbush. Homer Quackenbush isn't a *judge*. He's a *goat farmer*. He'll be a town justice till they drop him in the ground and shovel dirt over him. Homer could care less what people think. The rest of them, the *real* judges, the first thing they do when they wake up in the morning is to check the newspaper, see if anyone they cut loose the day before went and shot up the high school basketball game overnight."

"So when can my daughter come back?"

Flynt Adams would remember those words for the rest of his life. Not *when can I get my daughter back*, which was what he might have expected. But *when can my daughter come back?* If the distinction was a subtle one, it wasn't lost on Adams. Even that first day, when Stephen had just heard the news and had barely had time to digest it, his thoughts hadn't been centered on his own loss, as huge as it was; his only concern had been for his daughter, for *her* loss.

"Not till the criminal case is over," said Adams. "Provided we win it, that is."

"Oh, we'll *win* it," Stephen assured him. "Just tell me how long it'll take."

"All told?"

Stephen nodded. He was fully prepared to hear three weeks, a month, two at the outside. It was simply inconceivable it could any longer than that. So when Flynt Adams answered him, it almost knocked him over. It likely *would* have knocked him over, too, but for the fact that the enveloping cloud suddenly thickened even more, and served to protect him from the words.

"Could be six months," is what Adams said. "Could be a year, maybe even more."

"No," said Stephen Barrow. "No, it can't."

SEVEN

It had been cold out there on the sidewalk in front of the town hall, and almost full dark. Flynt Adams had been ready to call it a day.

"Listen," he'd told Stephen. "Go home and get some sleep. What's your schedule like Monday morning? I'd like you to come to my office first thing, so we can start talking strategy."

"Monday," Stephen had mumbled, trying to focus on what seemed like the far-off future. His weekday routine was to get up at 6:30, have breakfast, and do the dishes, so they'd be ready to leave the house by 8:00. By the time he got back from Hillsdale, it would be 9:30, 9:45. Reflexively, he built in an extra fifteen minutes for unforeseen emergencies. "How's ten o'clock?" he'd asked. "I've got to drive my daughter to school first."

For a long and uncomfortable moment, he hadn't been able to understand why Adams was staring at him. Then it had hit him: He wouldn't *be* driving Penny to school. Not Monday, not for weeks, not for months. A *year* was out of the question; he couldn't even begin to deal with that.

He'd smiled nervously and had tried to laugh off his mistake, but it had come out sounding more like a sob. "I guess," he'd finally said, "I can come in anytime you like."

Flynt Adams had reached out and put a hand on Stephen's arm. It was a nice gesture, but it had reminded Stephen of the way Investigator Stickley had led him around by the same arm, earlier in the day. One had been about control, the other about compassion; but to Stephen, they'd ended up feeling remarkably similar.

"Eight o'clock too early?" Adams had asked.

"No," Stephen had said. "Eight'll be fine."

And with that, Flynt Adams had nodded and walked up the block.

Theresa Mulholland had been standing on the sidewalk, off to one side. She'd wanted to ask Flynt Adams a few questions, but had backed off when she'd seen he needed to talk with his client. She'd been almost out of earshot, but not quite, and though she hadn't been able to hear all of their conversation, she'd caught the drift of it, and she'd heard the part about how Stephen Barrow wouldn't be getting his daughter back anytime soon. And she'd heard what sounded like a tiny sob escape from Stephen Barrow's mouth, and she'd seen his lower lip quiver uncontrollably a moment later. Then, when the two men had finally parted, and Flynt Adams had begun walking away, Theresa had found herself inexplicably glued to the sidewalk, unable to follow him.

Later on, she'd try to rationalize her behavior and do her best to convince herself that, since she already knew where Flynt Adams's law office was, she'd be able to find him anytime she wanted to speak with him. On the other hand, this might be her only opportunity to question Stephen Barrow. But Theresa knew better; she knew that really wasn't it at all. What it came down to was this: At that particular moment, it simply wasn't within Theresa's power to turn her back and walk away from that sob, and that quivering lower lip.

And yet, she wasn't just some bystander; she was a reporter. It wasn't like she could just walk over to the man and introduce herself. *Hi, I'm Terry Mulholland from the* Hudson Valley Herald. *Got any choice comments you'd like to share with our readers?*

So she'd ended up just standing there on the sidewalk, her notepad clasped in her hands, her arms crossed tightly in front of her for extra warmth, the collar of her down jacket pulled up to protect the back of her neck from the wind. And she'd watched Stephen Barrow, and waited to see what *he'd* do.

What Stephen Barrow did was to look up and down the block. Anyone watching him—and under the circumstances, *anyone* would have been a designation pretty much limited to the pretty redhead standing by the curb, some twenty-five feet away—might have thought he was confused, disoriented, and trying to get his bearings in an unfamiliar situation.

They would have been only half right.

The other half, the half that troubled Stephen Barrow most immediately at that moment—and prompted him to look up and down Main Street—was that it had suddenly dawned on him that he had no car, and therefore no way of getting home. Sure, there were taxis in Columbia County, but they were pretty much confined to the train station over in Hudson, a good half an hour away. This wasn't New York City, after all, where cabbies cruised around at all hours of day and night, and you simply walked into the street and waved until one stopped or ran you over.

It was only after he'd looked up and down the street three or four times in vain that Stephen finally noticed the redheaded woman standing off to one side of him. With her collar pulled up it was hard for him to be certain, but he was pretty sure she was the same woman who'd been inside the courtroom earlier, the one who'd looked familiar to him but whom he couldn't quite place.

Now he took a tentative step toward her, squinting to get a better look at her. "Can I help you?" he asked.

Her only response was to laugh. It was a *little* laugh, one that struck him as slightly curious, but at the same time was neither condescending nor cruel. It was just enough, in fact, to encourage him to continue walking, until he found himself standing in front of her, looking slightly down into eyes that were teary from the cold, but were at the same time extraordinarily green. The same pair of extraordinary green eyes he was certain he'd seen somewhere, recently.

"Do I know you?" he asked.

"No," she said. "Well, we met once, sort of. I'm Terry Mulholland, from the *Hudson Valley Herald*."

"You're a *reporter*?"

"Yes, but—"

It was as far as she got. Stephen spun around and walked away. It didn't matter that he happened to be walking in the direction completely opposite from his home. It didn't matter, because home was a good twelve miles away, and if he had to go another mile out of his way, he didn't care. At that point, he was resigned to walking home. What was the difference whether it took him three hours or four? Either way, he was going home to an empty house. And he knew this much: The last thing on earth he wanted to do right now was to talk to some *reporter* and end up getting his name in the paper as some kind of *child pornographer*.

His failure to realize that that was going to happen anyway, with or without his cooperation, was a testament to just how poorly his mind was working that evening.

So here's this guy, standing out there on the sidewalk on what's rapidly becoming a seriously cold February night. In the space of the last six hours, he's been arrested on felony sex charges and had his daughter taken away from him, and now he suddenly finds himself alone and stranded. When he finally looks up and notices her standing there, what does he ask her?

Can I help you?

Not *can you help me?* Not *could you possibly give me a lift home?* Not *do you know anyplace where I can call a cab?*

But *can I help you?*

So she laughed—it had simply been too absurd a thing for him to say for her *not* to have laughed. But as crazy as his question had been, it had also been totally disarming, so much so that when she'd introduced herself a moment later, she'd suddenly felt compelled to not only tell him her name, but to confess who she was as well.

And that had been the last of him.

Neil Witt was always telling his writers to get the story, but to be ethical about the way you went about it. Driving home now, she knew it had been the *ethical* thing for her to do, telling Stephen Barrow right up front like that that she was a reporter. *Ethical?* Hell, anything else would have been downright *indecent*.

Still, it had ended up costing her the defense slant. By the time she'd recovered from Stephen Barrow's departure and thought to take a walk over to Flynt Adams's office, the lights were out and the door locked. And tomorrow was Sunday.

Ethics and decency had their own drawbacks, she was learning. She found herself trying to imagine how Tom Grady would have handled things.

Hey, buddy, you look like you could use a drink.

And an hour or so later, after he'd gotten the rest of the story, he might or might not have gotten around to mentioning who he worked for.

Well, she'd never asked to be a crime reporter in the first place. And she still wanted no part of it, not if *that's* what it took. Just the same, it sure would have been interesting to hear what Stephen Barrow had to say.

"SHIT!" is what Stephen Barrow had to say.

He said it as he circled back around the town hall and began his idiotic walk home. He said it again as he realized his moccasins were not exactly the ideal footwear for an extended trek. He said it on at least five more occasions in the first half hour, each time he turned an ankle, stubbed a toe, or just felt like cursing. Still, he was beginning to find a rhythm, and was considering the possibility that he might actually live long enough to make it home when a blue pickup truck with a mismatched white cap roared by him, nearly knocking him into the ditch that ran alongside the road. He watched the brake lights come on as the driver screeched to a stop in a spray of gravel and dirt.

"Steve," the driver called out. "That you?"

Through the darkness, he recognized Louie the plumber, a Brooklyn-born transplant who'd once spent a day and a half up at Stephen's house sweating leaky pipes that had frozen over the winter. When at last he was done, he'd asked for seventy-five dollars for the job. Stephen had given him a hundred, and had still felt guilty about it.

"Yeah," Stephen said. "It's me."

The passenger door swung open, and Stephen accepted the invitation and climbed in.

"Jesus Christ," said Lou. "What the fuck's amatta witchoo, out walkin' on a night like this?"

"Don't ask," said Stephen.

And something about his tone must have told Lou that he meant it. They spent the ten-minute ride talking about the weather, and when they were done talking about the weather, they rode in silence. When Lou turned up Stephen's driveway, he must have noticed that all the lights were out and there was no Jeep Renegade in sight, but if he was curious about what was going on, or where Stephen's little girl was, he kept his thoughts to himself.

"Thanks, Lou," said Stephen.

"Any time, Steve."

Inside, the house was cold and dark. It was Stephen's habit to turn the heat down and the lights off when no one was home. Some of his neighbors considered such behavior foolish and even unwise from a security standpoint, but Stephen had inherited his father's penny-pinching ways and couldn't help himself. And as far as security was concerned, hell, he'd grown up in the South Bronx, where you got robbed once a month, like clockwork. To him, his house in the woods—whether lit up or pitch dark—was the most secure place on earth.

He turned on a single floor lamp and lit a fire in the wood-burning stove. It occurred to him that he'd had nothing to eat since breakfast with his daughter, an event that now seemed days ago, *weeks* ago. It was hard to believe it had been that very morning. Still, he wasn't hungry. In fact, the thought of food sent a wave of nausea through him.

What he was, was tired. *Enormously* tired. Tired beyond words. *This is what they call clinical depression*, he told himself as he sat down on the sofa, *this is* escape. He pulled a comforter around his shoulders, allowed himself to lie down and stretch out. There was no way he could make it up to his bedroom, he knew, no way he *wanted* to be upstairs, up there where his daughter's empty room was. The sofa was fine. He'd just lie there for a few minutes and close his eyes, trying his hardest not to think about anything at all, except maybe to pretend that everything was fine, and that the whole day had never happened.

He was a writer, after all, a writer of fiction. He could make things happen or not happen, as he chose. He could give people cute names, fill their mouths with clever dialogue, and steer them safely through terrible predicaments. He had it within his power to create sad or happy endings. Surely he could exercise that same power in real life, on his own behalf, if only this once. So that when he'd wake up in the morning, he'd find that none of this had happened, that his daughter was right there in her room where she belonged, and that in spite of how real it had all seemed at the time, everything else had just been a dream.

That's all—nothing but a dream.

EIGHT

LOCAL MAN ARRESTED IN CHILD PORNOGRAPHY CASE

By Theresa Mulholland
Special to the *Hudson Valley Herald*

An East Chatham man was arrested early Saturday by state police investigators and charged with Possessing a Sexual Performance of a Child, his own 6-year-old daughter.

Stephen Barrow, a published novelist, was taken into custody as he left the South Chatham Drug Mart, immediately after having picked up photographs that he had dropped off for developing the previous day.

An alert clerk had noticed that among the photos were several of a young girl, in various stages of undress. At least one of the photos lewdly displayed the child's private parts, according to a source close to the investigation.

Barrow appeared Saturday afternoon before South Chatham Town Justice Homer Quackenbush, who released him without bail over the objection of the town attorney. The charge is a felony that carries as much as four years in state prison, according to Columbia County District Attorney Jim Hall, who will present the case to a grand jury in Hudson early next week.

Well, if it wasn't quite Pulitzer Prize material, there it was on the right-hand column of page 1: Her very first crime story, beneath her own byline.

It was Monday morning, and within hours, copies of the edition would be stuffed into thousands of specially marked green-and-white letterboxes throughout the area; stacked up into neat piles in scores of convenience stores, supermarkets, and diners; and on their way by mail to hundreds of readers who lived beyond the immediate delivery area.

Reading the article in its entirety for the tenth time, Theresa decided she liked its compactness, its matter-of-fact tone, its careful attribution of sources. Not that she'd actually spoken to Jim Hall, of course. But she'd paid attention to what the town attorney had said, and one of the things he'd said was that the DA intended to present the case to a grand jury early next week, in Hudson. She'd have liked to include some comment from the defense, and had even toyed with the idea of saying that Stephen Barrow himself had refused to comment on the charges. But that seemed like a stretch, seeing as she'd never had the chance to *ask* him for a comment once he'd turned tail and walked away from her in a huff.

Well, she could always get around to him in a follow-up story, get his side of things or nail him for refusing to talk to her. Assuming, that was, that Neil Witt *wanted* her to do a follow-up. Or would he give it back to Tom Grady, once Tom got back? Though that hardly seemed fair, at this point. After all, here she'd given up an entire Saturday just to get the story in the first place.

Didn't that make it *hers*?

She finished her second cup of coffee, put the dishes in the sink to soak, and looked around for her car keys. She felt full of energy, and it seemed like a good morning to take a drive over to Pittsfield, get a little workout on the bags with Tony the Trainer.

———

Although he was a regular subscriber to the *Hudson Valley Herald*—a year ago, he'd succumbed to a telephone sales pitch from a teenager trying to raise money for a class trip—Stephen Barrow hadn't seen his copy of the paper yet. It waited for him in a green-and-white letter box at the bottom of his driveway, next to where his mailbox would have been if he'd had a mailbox. It would wait there for him for three full days before he finally got around to noticing it.

On this particular Monday morning, Stephen was noticing very little. He'd spent what he considered a lost weekend. He'd collapsed on the downstairs sofa Saturday evening, after Lou the plumber had picked him up on Route 295 and driven him the rest of the way home. He'd awakened in a panic an hour later, realizing he had no idea where his daughter was. For all he knew, she could still be down at the state police barracks in Claverack. He'd gotten on the phone, placing more than a dozen frantic calls to his ex-wife's home, her cell phone, her *mother*, the state police, the county sheriff's office, and anyone else he could think of. Finally, between calls, his own phone had rang, nearly scaring him out of his wits.

"*Hello?*" he'd shouted into the receiver.

"Stop screaming." It was Ada's voice.

"Is Penny with you?" he asked, holding his breath for the answer.

"Yes, she's with me. Where did you *think* she was?"

"I didn't know, I've been calling all over—"

"I *know*," she said. "Your phone's been busy forever. When are you going to get *call waiting*?"

He refused to get call waiting. He hated when people put him on hold while answering another call, and refused to do it to others. But he didn't much feel like arguing with her right now, so he let it go.

"Is she okay?"

"Sure, she's okay. She just *loves* being a child porno star. It was so thoughtful of you to prepare her for a career in—"

"Can I speak to her?"

"No, you can't *speak with her*. I've got a piece of paper right here that says if you even try, I can have you arrested for *contempt*."

That would be the order of protection they'd told him about. He'd completely forgotten about it. "You're sure she's okay?" he asked, but even as he waited for her answer, the feeling of total exhaustion suddenly came over him again and engulfed him, like some huge ocean wave. He pressed the receiver hard against his ear, straining to hear what she was saying, but the noise of the wave drowned out her words. He felt himself losing his footing, falling over, slipping under the wave. . . .

It would be light out when he awakened.

He would spend the next twelve hours going through the motions of his Sunday routine. He would try to eat breakfast. He would walk by the open door of Penny's room a dozen times, on each occasion staring at the neatly made bed and put-away toys. He would wander outside, figuring to take a drive over to Queechy Lake, so that he could buy the *Times* and busy himself with the crossword puzzle—only to discover all over again that he didn't have his car. He would sit in front of the computer for an hour at a time, trying to compose a single sentence. He would stare at images flickering silently on the television set, having earlier turned the volume all the way down because he couldn't stand the babble that poured out of it. He would sit for long stretches watching the phone, waiting in vain for it to ring.

Around eight, the wave would roll over him again, suggesting that there was something tidal about it, something *cyclical*. This time he would make it upstairs, to his bed, where he would bury himself under the covers, press his face into his pillow, and finally cry himself to sleep.

A grown man of forty-two, crying himself to sleep.

And in the morning, when at last he could sleep no more, he forced himself to climb out of bed. It took monumental energy just to shower and dry off, and he didn't have the strength left to shave. Downstairs, he found the phone directory, thumbed through the yellow pages, found the listing for John's Chatham Taxi, and waited to be picked up and driven to his lawyer's office.

He arrived there a full hour and a half late for his appointment, unshaven, his hair uncombed. In spite of the fact that about the only thing he'd done all weekend was to sleep, he looked like he he'd been up for a month. Now, as he sat across the desk from Flynt Adams, waiting for Adams to tell him what their *strategy* would be, he couldn't remember if he'd even brushed his teeth.

"You look terrible," said Adams.

"Thanks."

"I'm not joking," said the lawyer. "You've got to take care of yourself."

Stephen managed a nod.

"You have to understand," Adams said, "this thing could take a long time."

"You already told me that," said Stephen.

They talked for almost an hour, Stephen describing for the first time how he'd meant no harm in taking the photographs of Penny, even the one where she'd mooned him. "I'd completely forgotten about it," he explained.

"Had you ever taken nude photos of your daughter before?" Adams asked.

"Sure," said Stephen. "I mean, doesn't every parent?"

Then again, from the way Adams had stared at him without saying anything, maybe not.

"Have you ever had copies made of any of them?"

"Not that I can recall."

"Put any of them on the Internet?"

"I wouldn't even know how to do that."

"Have you ever developed your own film?"

"No."

"Do you know how to?"

"No."

"Did you pose your daughter?"

"What do you mean?"

"In the one where she's, uh, *bending* over like that. Did you tell her to do that?"

"No, I told you, she mooned me. She'd seen it in a movie."

Adams raised an eyebrow. "What movie?" he asked.

Stephen couldn't remember.

"I've already gotten a call from your ex-wife's lawyer," Adams said. "They're going to go into county court to try to get permanent custody of your daughter."

"Can't we fight them?"

"*You* can. *I* can't."

"Why not? Don't you do that kind of thing?"

"I do," said Adams, who pretty much did everything. "The thing is, the court appointed me only to represent you on the criminal case, because you said you couldn't afford your own lawyer. A custody battle, even though it obviously grows out of the criminal case and is therefore related to it, is a separate matter, in a separate court."

"What does that mean?"

"It means you'd have to *hire* counsel."

"Can't I hire *you*?"

Adams explained that there was a catch-22 to that: If Stephen were to hire him on the custody matter, that would demonstrate that he had money, meaning Adams could no longer represent him for free on the criminal case.

"So," Stephen said, "if I want you, it's double or nothing."

Adams smiled. "Something like that," he said.

"How much are we talking about?"

Adams explained that, assuming he got the court's permission to represent Stephen on a private basis, his fee was a hundred and twenty-five dollars an hour.

"*Jesus,*" said Stephen.

"How about a hundred?"

Stephen closed his eyes, tried to visualize his last monthly bank statement. He was always losing track of his balance, and depended on the bank's figures. The figure $8,000 came back to him, and he was busy dividing it by 100, wondering just how far eighty hours would get him, and deciding not all that far, when Adams spoke first.

"The very best I can do is seventy-five."

Stephen opened his eyes. "Thank you," he said.

They talked a while longer. Adams explained that Stephen had a right to testify before the grand jury, but that he thought it would be a bad idea.

"Why's that?" Stephen asked.

"Because they'd only indict you anyway," Adams explained, "and then you'd be stuck with what you said."

"It's not like my story's going to change, you know."

"Oh, yes it is."

"How's that?"

"It's going to get better," said Adams. "It's going to get so good that no one'll be able to listen to it without breaking into tears."

"And that's what we want?"

"No," said Flynt Adams. "That's what we *need*."

What Jim Hall needed was a grand jury.

Columbia County didn't have enough serious crime to keep a standing grand jury to hear felony cases. In these times of inflation, jurors got paid at the rate of forty dollars a day for their services, in spite of the fact that a *day* was really only *half a day*, either a morning or an afternoon session. Unlike a trial jury, which was made up of twelve jurors plus maybe a couple of alternates, for a grand jury you needed twenty-three people. That meant it cost the county nine hundred and twenty dollars a day for the privilege of having a bunch of folks sitting around, waiting to hear maybe thirty minutes' worth of testimony before calling it a day.

So with a wink from the district attorney and a nod from the judiciary, the county clerk had quietly drawn up a list of forty or fifty volunteers who were only too happy to get an occasional phone call telling them there was about to be a felony presentation, requiring their services for an hour or so the following morning—as long as they had nothing better to do with their time, that was. Never mind that such an arrangement was of dubious constitutional value; with no one ever having raised a voice to challenge it, it had stood the test of time and eventually come to pass for the way things were done.

So on this Monday morning, anxious to press forward with the sex-abuse case they'd sent him over from South Chatham, Jim Hall turned to one of his assistants. "We're going to need us a grand jury for Wednesday morning," he said. "Go see Hanna Lovejoy, down in the clerk's office, willya? Tell her to get on the horn, round up a buncha the usual suspects. And while you're at it—"

The assistant looked up from his notepad, waiting for the rest of his instructions.

"—why don't you get to work on a draft of a search-warrant application. Might be intrestin' to know what else that Barrow creep keeps tucked away in his house. Besides naked pictures of his little girl, that is."

The last thing Stephen Barrow had remembered to ask Flynt Adams was how he was supposed to go about getting his Jeep back.

"Getting it back?"

"Yeah," Stephen had said. "They left it down in, wherever I was—"

"Claverack."

"Claverack, right. How do I get it back?"

"You don't."

Stephen had cocked his head slightly to one side, as though maybe he hadn't heard correctly the first time. "Say that again?"

"You don't get it back," Adams had repeated. "Under New York law, any motor vehicle, vessel, or airplane used in the commission of a crime is subject to civil forfeiture."

"But I didn't use it in the commission of a crime."

"According to the troopers, you drove it to the Drug Mart to pick up the photos. Isn't that true?"

"Well, yes, but—"

"I'm afraid that constitutes use in the commission. See, the crime you're charged with is a *possessory* one—specifically, possession of the photos. Their theory is, you used your car in order to *obtain* that possession."

"And that makes sense to you?"

"It's not a matter of whether or not it makes sense to *me*," Adams had told him. "It'll make sense to the *judge*. That's what counts, I'm afraid."

"Can't we fight it?"

"We can," Adams had said, "but we'd probably lose. It's not like it's a criminal proceeding, where they have to prove things beyond a reasonable doubt. In a civil case, the standard is much less. And remember, you'd be paying me seventy-five bucks an hour. What's the thing worth, anyway?"

Not much, Stephen knew. Still, it was his Jeep, his car, the only car he and Penny had. It didn't seem fair, that they could take it away from him, just like that. Not that *any* of this seemed fair.

"What'll happen to it?" he asked.

"What?"

"My Jeep."

"Sheriff'll sell it at auction a couple months from now. You can always go to the auction, buy it back, if you like."

Now, an hour later, Stephen stood in the parking lot of Jensen's Oil and Tire, kicking the tires of a tiny '83 Ford Fiesta with a cracked windshield and extra rust as a heavyset man who went by the name of Butch stood nearby, scratching the back of his neck.

"Easy on that," said Butch. "You're liable to knock the wheel off."

Stephen laughed; Butch didn't. Evidently, he hadn't been joking.

"How much for this one?" Stephen asked. He'd already given up on a Dodge pickup truck and a Subaru wagon as more than he could afford. Winter was almost over, after all. How much longer would he really need four-wheel drive?

"I can put you in that one for eight hundred," said Butch, scratching his belly now.

"That's it?"

"You can pay me the other eight hundred when you get a chance."

"You're sure it runs?" Stephen asked.

"Had it out myself the other day."

Looking at Butch, Stephen wasn't convinced he could even *fit* in the thing, let alone *drive* it. "Mind if I ask you where you got it from?" he asked.

"Where I get most of 'em," said Butch, scratching yet another part of his anatomy now.

"Where's that?"

"Sheriff's sale."

An hour later and eight hundred dollars poorer, Stephen had coaxed the Fiesta up his driveway, wedged a brick behind one of the tires as an emergency brake, and notified his insurance company of his change in vehicles. "We'll send you out a new card right away," the helpful representative assured him. "As well as a bill for the increase in premium."

"*Increase*? Why should there be an *increase*?"

"The '83 Fiesta is so small, we list it as a sports car."

By the time she got back home from her workout at the gym, Theresa had three messages stored on her answering machine. The first two she ignored, having little desire to speak with either her mother or the MCI representative who promised he could save her fifty percent on her long-distance calls. The third call, the one she returned, was from Neil Witt. No doubt he was phoning to let her know how positive the reaction had been to her crime story. He picked up on the first ring.

"Witt here." Neil was definitely not a graduate of the Lou Grant School for Editorial Charm.

"Hi, Neil. It's Terry."

"Oh, hi, Terry. Lemme think. Why did I call you?"

"The story?"

"Right, the story. 'Coming Events.' Is it done yet?"

" '*Coming Event?*' " He had to be kidding. "I've been working on that child pornography case."

"Still?"

"Yes, *still*. It's not quite *over*, you know."

"Well," Witt asked, "what did you have in mind?"

"A follow-up, *several* follow-ups, maybe. A *series*."

"With what kinda slant?"

"I don't know," she was forced to admit. "But it's an important story. Child abuse, exploitation. A Jekyll-and-Hyde type living right next door. C'mon, I haven't even scratched the surface yet."

"Well, do me a favor, will you? *Scratch out* 'Coming Events' first."

"Can't you give that to someone else?" Theresa asked. "Pretend I'm on special assignment?"

"No way. You know I'm already shorthanded."

Short*sighted* was more like it. Couldn't he see there was a series here? "Good-bye, Neil," she said.

If there was good news, it was that at least he hadn't taken her off the story and given it back to Tom Grady. Not yet, anyway.

But if there was going to be a Part Two, it was going to have to happen pretty soon: the clock was ticking. Reflexively, Theresa looked at her watch. But for some reason, what caught her eye wasn't the time of day, but the date: MON FEB 14, it said. Valentine's Day. Not that anyone had sent her so much as a card.

Speaking of clocks ticking.

With the grand jury presentation scheduled for Wednesday, Jim Hall didn't want to waste any time before executing a search warrant against Stephen Barrow's home. He knew he already had enough to indict Barrow—hell, he could indict *Mother Teresa*, if he put his mind to it—but he didn't want to have to go back into the grand jury to ask for a superseding indictment in the event the sheriff's deputies came up with more evidence that warranted additional charges. Even more important, he didn't want to give Barrow time to dispose of evidence. Bad guys were always flushing drugs down the toilet, tossing incriminating business records into the fireplace, and burying guns in the compost pile. Not that this particular bad guy seemed smart enough to cover his tracks—look at the way he'd dropped his film off at the local drugstore for everybody to see—but still, there was no use giving him time to get rid of anything.

So by noon, Jim Hall had an affidavit that had been drawn up by one of his assistants and signed by Investigator Todd Stickley, a warrant authorizing the search of Stephen Barrow's home and any other structures on his property, and a document called a *return*, on which the searching deputies would inventory anything they seized. Because Hall claimed that it was likely Barrow might attempt to dispose of evidence when the authorities showed up (by trying to flush a camera down the toilet, say, or swallowing a computer), the papers sought permission for a "no-knock" entry, as well as one not limited to daytime hours.

Around 12:30, Hall walked upstairs and found Justice Everett Wainwright in chambers, on the phone with his broker. The NASDAQ was up eighty-three points, it seemed, and Justice Wainwright was in good spirits.

"Hey, Jimbo. What can I do for you?"

"You can put your John Hancock on the dotted line right here, if you don't mind."

Justice Wainwright scanned the affidavit. " 'Sexual paraphernalia,' huh? What are you *really* expecting to find?"

"Tell you the truth," said Hall, "I haven't the foggiest."

"Going fishin', huh?"

"You might say that."

"Well, good luck to you," said the judge. "Any man exploits his own daughter like that oughta have his pecker cut off. Not that I'm *prejudging* the case or anything like that."

"No, sir. I know you wouldn't do that."

"Got a pen handy?" asked Justice Wainwright.

By evening—and in northern Columbia County, February evenings have a habit of setting in around three-thirty in the afternoon—Stephen Barrow needed to get out of the house.

He'd gotten home, courtesy of the Ford Fiesta, around noon. Over the next three hours, he'd dealt with his insurance company, put away the dishes, walked past Penny's room a few times, straightened things up, sat down at the computer and tried to write, walked by Penny's room a couple more times, stood in front of the open refrigerator for a good five minutes, tried to write some more, and checked Penny's room one last time.

All the while, he'd alternated between bursts of activity so intense as to cause him to pace back and forth frantically and even begin hyperventilating once or twice, and waves of exhaustion so profound that there were times he felt he could no longer keep his head up, and was forced to lie down on the sofa just to avoid collapsing on the floor.

Fears—real fears and imagined fears—filled his every thought. Penny was alone and uncared-for. Ada was punishing her, depriving her, beating her. He was never going to see her again. He was going to jail, where she wouldn't be permitted to visit him.

At one point he thought he heard water running in the house, and he ran from room to room trying to locate the source. It turned out to be the refrigerator motor that had kicked on. A little later he became panicked that his manuscript wasn't properly backed up on disks, and decided he couldn't possibly wait another minute to print it out. But the next moment, after noticing that his printer was out of paper, exhaustion overcame him, and he couldn't summon the energy to walk the ten feet to the closet to refill it, and was forced to abandon the idea.

It was going on four o'clock when he decided he had to get out of the house before he went completely crazy. He grabbed the keys to the Fiesta, slammed the door behind him, and literally ran to the driveway, so convinced he was that if he confined himself to a walk, fatigue would set in and he'd never make it.

He headed for East Chatham—it was the only place he could think of going. He'd pick up a *New York Times* at Slattery's and check his mailbox. He panicked only once on the way, when the bizarre notion struck him that the walls of the post office would be plastered with his photograph as the new Number One on the FBI's Most Wanted List. Most wanted *what*, though? What *was* he, after all? A sex abuser? A child pornographer? A pedophile? All he'd done was to snap his daughter's photo the instant she'd mooned him. But already, his entire life was unraveling because of it.

He paid for the *Times* with quarters—they were far enough north of the city that it took four of them. And if Don Elsasser seemed to look at him a little longer than usual, he said nothing. Then again, Don was a guy who'd been through enough troubles of his own, his wife losing a long bout to cancer, his grandson born damaged, his old store up for sale.

"Have a good one," he told Stephen.

Have a good one. That itself was a *good one.* The truth was, there weren't going to *be* any good ones for Stephen, not anymore.

His photo, it turned out, wasn't on display at the post office. He picked up his mail quietly, furtively, afraid that if made too much noise, whoever was on duty might spot him, and, and . . .

And *whatever*.

The fatigue crept up on him again on the drive back home, and Stephen had to grip the wheel tightly and concentrate as hard as he could on the road in front of him, just to keep the Fiesta from wandering off it. He cranked the window open a couple of inches, letting in a blast of cold air that stung him, punished him.

Punished him. Right.

By the time he reached his driveway, it was all he could do to tuck the paper and his mail under his arm, stagger into the house, dump everything on the kitchen table, and flop onto the sofa once more. It was becoming a home base of sorts, the sofa. He knew that these waves of fatigue and these retreats into sleep were nothing more than flight—his way of escaping a life that had suddenly become too difficult to bear. But even knowing that and understanding it didn't change things. He was still exhausted; he still couldn't keep his head up; he still couldn't help curling up on the sofa in a fetal position, his knees drawn up almost to his chest, his hands sandwiched between his thighs for warmth. His eyes burned, no doubt from the fumes of the Fiesta and the wind that had been hitting his face on the drive home. His eyelids felt as though they'd somehow developed these enormous, irresistible weights to them. He allowed them to shut—or rather they simply did so of their own accord, returning to their natural, intended position as though spring-loaded. And as they shut, they brought him darkness—sweet, blank, merciful darkness—sealing him off from all the terrible, chaotic things that lay out there.

In his dream, Stephen was holding the camera with both hands, peering through the viewfinder at Penny. For some reason he couldn't understand, she was wearing all black—black dress, black shoes, and a strange black hat. Her face, so pale it seemed almost white, wore a calm, resigned expression on it, as if she understood how things were going to turn out better than he did.

He went to snap the picture, but couldn't find the button on the camera. Not wanting to lose his daughter's image in the viewfinder, he held the camera focused on her with one hand while groping around blindly with the other one for the button. At last he found a device that felt like a trigger, and figured that had to be it. He squeezed it, gently at first, so as not to ruin the picture by jerking it, then harder, until finally he felt it give.

Suddenly there was a blinding flash and a deafening BANG! The explosion was so loud and so violent that it caused Stephen to shout out loud—

—and bolt upright on the sofa.

The room was dark, except for the front door—or at least where the front door was supposed to be. Beams of light, the same light that had blinded him a moment ago, reached toward him from there. It took him a while to grasp that the beams were coming from flashlights, powerful flashlights held by men in gray uniforms who lifted their feet awkwardly as they began to approach him. It took him even longer to realize that the reason they were lifting their feet was to step over or around the front door—*his* front door—which now lay flat on the floor, just inside the open frame, splintered and ripped from its hinges.

"*POLICE!*" one of them shouted. "We've got a search warrant!" And indeed, another one waved a piece of paper in his face, too fast and too close for him to make out a word of it.

For the next three hours, Stephen was shuttled from room to room as a half-dozen deputy sheriffs went through every cabinet, every closet, every drawer, every carton, every inch of his home.

His *home*.

He was told that as long as he sat still and kept his mouth shut, he wouldn't be handcuffed. No, he couldn't call his lawyer. Yes, he could go to the bathroom, but only if one of them stood by while he peed. Each time they moved him to another room, it was to get him out of the area they wanted to search. It wasn't hard to figure out that they didn't want him to be there to see what they were doing, what they were taking, what they were breaking.

Not that they were being intentionally destructive; they weren't, not so far as he could tell, not in the way *vandals* might have been. But the difference was largely academic: clothes still got yanked out of closets and dumped onto the floor, desk drawers got turned upside down and spilled out, mattresses were pulled off beds and flipped over, and books scooped up from shelves by the handful and left on the floor in random heaps. By the time they were finished, it would take him a full week just to put everything back in place.

He had no way of knowing exactly what they were taking, except for the larger items he could see them carrying out through the doorway. (They'd propped the door up in an attempt to keep out some of the cold, and one of them even suggested to Stephen that he might be able to get reimbursed for the damage they'd caused in kicking it down.) They took his computer, at least the part with the hard drive, as well as all his disks. They took his camera, and any photographs and film they found. They took his mail, including the letters he'd just picked up at the post office and hadn't even had a chance to open. They took all sorts of things from Penny's room—books, dolls, pictures she'd painted, stuffed animals, *underpants*. They went through the medicine chest in his bathroom, seizing ointments and salves and prescription drugs. And all the while, he was forced to sit silently, uncomplainingly, wherever they told him to, a powerless victim to a court-ordered invasion of his home. When finally they were done, they offered no apology, provided no explanation; they just marched out with whatever of his belongings they'd decided they felt like taking. Although one of them—the one who seemed the nicest, the one who'd told him about the possibility of getting reimbursed for the damage they'd done to his door—stopped in the doorway and turned around, just long enough to say something to him.

"Seeya in court, ya prick," is what he said.

NINE

By Wednesday, a mix of rain and wet snow had begun to fall. Theresa Mulholland knew that if there was going to be a follow-up story, she'd better get working on it. She phoned Flynt Adams, Stephen Barrow's lawyer, and offered him a chance to say something, anything that she could print that might be helpful to his client.

"I really can't comment," was all that Adams would say.

She called the state police headquarters down in Claverack. They put her on hold and shuttled her around for ten minutes. Finally a Sergeant Somebody told her that once a case was in the courts, they could no longer comment on it publicly. He referred her to Jim Hall at the district attorney's office. She thanked him and hung up.

She found Hall's number and dialed it. A woman put her through to Hall.

"Anything new on the Barrow case?" she asked him.

"Sure is," he said. "Going into the grand jury this morning. And Monday evening, we executed a search warrant at Mr. Barrow's residence."

"Find anything?"

"Yup, we sure did. All *sorts* of goodies."

"Like what?"

"Oh, I can't comment on that," said Hall. "We're still in the process of inventorying it."

"But it's incriminating stuff?"

"You could say that."

"Can I write it?"

Hall seemed to think a minute before answering. "Sure, why not?" he said. "Long as you don't say you heard it from me."

Great. A source close to the investigation, who insisted on remaining anonymous, stated that incriminating evidence was removed from the defendant's home, but declined to say what it was. Now *there's* a story for you.

Barrow's lawyer wouldn't comment; the state police *couldn't* comment, and the DA wouldn't give Theresa any details or allow her to use his name. So where did that leave her?

It left her with Stephen Barrow himself, is where it left her. And he'd already refused to talk to her. Still, it was worth another crack. Besides which, what did she have to lose?

Jim Hall, meanwhile, was ready to present the case against Stephen Barrow to a grand jury. The jurors, twenty-three strong, every one of them a standby volunteer who'd ignored the weather and jumped at the idea of earning forty bucks for an hour or two of work, were already seated in the courtroom, which on this Wednesday morning would serve as a grand jury room. They were laborers and mechanics, truck drivers and store clerks, homemakers and waitresses, as well as a number who, when asked to list their current employment, wrote down that they were "between jobs," "looking for employment," "receiving public assistance," or "unable to work" for one reason or another. The youngest was Stacy Coombs, a nineteen-year-old student at Columbia Greene Community College in need of a little cigarette money; the oldest was Vernon Lassiter, an eighty-three-year-old farmer, for whom a forty-dollar check in the middle of February was nothing less than a godsend. Of the twenty-three, sixteen were registered Republicans, four Democrats, two called themselves Independents, and one considered himself an "other." All twenty-three were white. About the only other things they had in common was that all were over eighteen and residents of Columbia County, and none had a felony record.

Although Jim Hall had spoken the truth when he'd told Theresa Mulholland that the sheriff's deputies had seized a bunch of *goodies* from Stephen Barrow's home, he'd nevertheless decided against using any of those goodies at the grand jury presentation. For one thing, the items were still being inventoried. For another, there was so much stuff in the computer—huge *manuscripts*, hundreds of pages long, among other things—that they'd been forced to hire an outside technician just to download the hard drive onto disks, and the guy was going to need a few more days to finish doing it. So far, he'd said there was no indication that Barrow had put any photos of his daughter out onto the Internet, or exchanged correspondence with other pornographers. But you never knew.

So at 11:15, when Hall marched into the courtroom—now the grand jury room—it was with what he liked to call a *bare-bones case*. But that was just fine with Hall, who knew that somewhere down the road the defense would be entitled to receive a transcript of whatever the witnesses said in the grand jury, at least those witnesses who also ended up testifying at trial. Therefore the rule was the less said, the better. Consequently, the jurors were only going to hear from Emma Priestley, as to how she'd come across the pornographic photos while developing them in the ColorMaster 3000, and Investigator Todd Stickley, who'd arrested Stephen Barrow in possession of them the following day. Then they'd get to look at the photos themselves. Well, not all of them: no use wasting their time with the twenty or so that didn't have anything to do with the case. Just the three or four of the kid naked, especially the one where he'd made her bend over and expose herself for all the world to see.

And that would be that.

No need for the girl herself to testify, one picture being worth a thousand words, just like they said. No need for some fancy expert to come in and say the photos were lewd—the good people of Columbia County would be more than able to judge that for themselves. And since Flynt Adams hadn't notified Jim Hall that he wanted his client to testify, there was no need to wait for him.

The entire presentation, from start to finish, took forty-one minutes. Given the opportunity to suggest questions of their own, the jurors declined, except for one man, who wanted to know if Mr. Barrow was locked up in jail, where he belonged.

"Not at the moment," Jim Hall replied. "But we aim to take care of that."

There was a ripple of approving laughter. Then Hall—who, in the absence of a judge, not only served as the prosecutor, but acted as the legal advisor to the grand jury as well—read the applicable law to the jurors, inviting them to consider four different charges, before excusing himself from the room, so they could vote in secret.

But he knew not to go far. He stood right outside the closed door for just over ninety seconds, at which point the sound of a buzzer summoned him back inside. The foreman of the grand jury promptly handed him four pieces of paper, each bearing a signature and a check mark in a box, right next to the words TRUE BILL. What the signatures and checks indicated was that the grand jury had formally returned an indictment against Stephen Barrow on each of the four counts submitted to them: Possessing a Sexual Performance by a Child, Promoting a Sexual Performance by a Child, Use of a Child in a Sexual Performance, and Endangering the Welfare of a Child. The first three of these charges were felonies, carrying maximum prison sentences of four, seven, and fifteen years, respectively. The fourth charge was a misdemeanor, punishable by up to a year in jail. And although New York law contains certain technical restrictions on when a defendant may be sentenced to consecutive terms, a lot of folks unfamiliar with those restrictions would fall back on simple mathematics and calculate that for what he'd done, Stephen Barrow was looking at twenty-seven years in the slammer. And as far as most of them were concerned, that sounded just about right.

Even though Stephen Barrow had no address listed in the phone book, and used a post office box instead of a street number, Theresa Mulholland had little trouble finding out where he lived. Theresa was, after all, a reporter, and all she had to do was drive through a light snow to the office of the town clerk in New Lebanon (New Lebanon being the township in which East Chatham was located), and look in the index book until she found the entry she was looking for.

> BARROW, STEPHEN. . . . . .14 HILLTOP DRIVE,
> EAST CHATHAM 12060

it said. People thought they had privacy, but they were wrong. It was all out there, everything you wanted to know about anybody—address, phone number (whether listed or not), Social Security number, bank balance, annual income, credit rating, party registration, arrest record, videos rented, cars owned, tickets received, library books overdue.

You name it, she could find it.

But when it came to Stephen Barrow, Theresa didn't need any of that stuff, just his address. Next she walked over to the far wall, where a large map of New Lebanon Township hung. From a street index, she located Hilltop Road in East Chatham. It was off Route 295, up the hill from Bristol Road.

The next question was whether to phone ahead or simply drop by unannounced. Phoning ahead was certainly the polite thing to do, particularly in light of Stephen Barrow's earlier reaction the moment he'd found out she was a reporter. But if she phoned him, asking his permission to meet with him, chances were pretty good he'd say no. He'd either refuse outright or insist on first calling his lawyer, who'd then refuse for him. She could try for a phone interview, but phone interviews were no substitute for face-to-face meetings; they never were. So it became a no-brainer: She had to go see him in person, without calling ahead.

That's all there was to it.

Except for one thing: Getting Stephen Barrow to actually talk to her was going to take some doing. It was going to require a plan, a *strategy*.

Shortly after noon on that same Wednesday, Flynt Adams was served with an order to show cause drawn up by the lawyers for Ada Barrow. It required him to appear in Supreme Court in Hudson on Friday, and to convince the court that certain temporary relief should not be granted to Stephen Barrow's ex-wife. Specifically, they were seeking an order that would grant Ada Barrow "sole and exclusive custody of the minor child" (Adams despised lawyers who deliberately used redundancies for no discernable purpose) "at least until the resolution of the felony charges currently pending" against Stephen (this came as no surprise, and was certain to be granted); an increase in the alimony and child-support payments Stephen was sending Ada each week (the surprise here was that Stephen had been paying her any child support at all, since he was the one who'd been taking care of Penny; still, now that Ada had her, the court was sure to agree she needed even more money); and additional money so that Penny could "receive psychotherapy to assist her in attempting to cope with the profound trauma caused her" by Stephen's actions (again, a sure bet).

Adams hated to call Stephen, to break the news to him. He'd been on the phone with him half a dozen times the day before, explaining that the sheriff's deputies who'd come to Stephen's home Monday night had indeed had a search warrant (Adams had checked with Jim Hall), didn't have to knock before kicking in the door, and might or might not be willing to pay for the damage they caused to it. No, he couldn't get his computer back right away, even if it meant he wouldn't be able to get back to his writing. Yes, they were allowed to take his mail, and that meant they could open it and read it, too. No, there was no indictment yet that he was aware of, but there was every reason to believe there'd be one in a day or two.

The conversations had not been fun.

Still, being a lawyer meant you had to say you were sorry sometimes, and Adams knew he had to call his client. He dialed the number, which he'd already committed to memory. He listened as it rang three times before an answering machine clicked on, signaling a reprieve from having to deliver the bad news in person.

"Sorry," said the voice of young girl, *"we're not home right now. But if you leave us a message, we'll call ya soon."*

"Cute message," said Adams, before realizing he probably shouldn't have commented on it. "Stephen, this is Flynt. Give me a call at the office when you get a chance, okay? Thanks."

The reason why Flynt Adams missed Stephen Barrow was that at the moment Adams called, Stephen was out shivering in his unheated garage, gathering up the tools he figured he was going to need to repair his front door and reattach it to its hinges. Walking back to the house, his boots left deep prints in the snow. Stephen's house was not only on Hilltop Drive, it was at the very *top* of Hilltop Drive, making it virtually the highest point in the county. And it was a *sudden* height, in the sense that the drop-off to Route 295, only three miles to the south, was a full fifteen hundred feet, making for an incline of nearly ten percent. The result was a phenomenon quite familiar to downhill skiers: It can be raining when you get onto a chairlift at the bottom of a mountain, and snowing by the time you reach the top. And if it happens to be sleet or wet snow that's just beginning to stick down below, up top it'll already be piling up.

With nothing but a thin storm door to keep the weather out, Stephen had decided he couldn't put off his repair job any longer. Flynt Adams had suggested he take photographs of the damage, or call in a contractor to fix the door so he'd have a receipt to show for it. But Stephen's camera had been taken in the search, and he knew better than to expect a contractor to come out in the snow for such a small job. So he'd decided to do it himself, the best he could, even if it meant doing a lot of the work out in the cold.

As soon as Theresa Mulholland made the turn off of Route 295 and began the climb up Bristol Road, she noticed that the snow suddenly seemed to be falling more heavily, and was *definitely* deeper. Still, her Honda was pretty good on snow—not as good as a four-wheeler, of course, but good. She downshifted to second gear in order to deal with not only the snow but the incline, which was a lot to contend with all by itself.

She'd been thinking about strategy on the way over, trying to come up with some ruse to get Stephen Barrow to talk to her. She'd considered offering him the opportunity of having his side of the story printed in her follow-up, without editorial change. She'd toyed with the idea of suggesting a trade, swapping her knowledge that the DA was presenting his case to the grand jury today in exchange for some comment from him. She'd even flirted with making up a mystery witness, an enticing source she couldn't reveal, except to hint that he or she could prove helpful, if only Stephen would grant Theresa an interview.

Now, however, all thoughts of tactics vanished as Theresa was forced to turn her full concentration to maintaining her speed in the deepening snow. According to the drawing she'd made from the township map, she was on the second of three dirt roads she'd have to climb simply to get to the beginning of Hilltop Drive.

It occurred to Theresa to give it up, to make a U-turn and head down the hill while she still could. But she was afraid if she even slowed down enough to look for a place where it was safe to turn around, she'd get stuck. So she plowed ahead stubbornly, the front wheels of the Honda slipping occasionally, but for the most part crunching through the snow. The road was narrower now, and bordered closely on both sides by tall trees that blocked some of the falling snow and made for a little better visibility. Still, she almost missed the turnoff onto Hilltop Drive, and the Honda skidded frighteningly before getting its head again and resuming the climb.

She made it the rest of the way up to the top, and had already pretty much decided on first gear for the downhill stretch that lay ahead of her, when she spotted a small number 14 on a birch tree at the beginning of a long driveway. Just her luck: Even the *driveway* went up. She gunned the engine as she made the turn, and the Honda valiantly plowed forward for another twenty feet before finally coming to a stop and stalling out.

"Jesus!" she muttered. "There must be three feet of snow up here."

Actually, there was less than half that much. Stephen Barrow knew, because he'd just walked through it, coming back toward the house from the garage. But with no place else to go, he was hardly in a hurry to begin shoveling. He'd listened to the radio, and they were predicting somewhere between eighteen and twenty-two inches, not so much that you had to shovel in stages just to keep up with it. No, he'd wait till it was over, whenever that might be, and do it once. Better to spend his time fixing the door. If he put that off until it started getting dark, not only wouldn't he be able to see what he was doing, but his fingers would grow so numb from the cold that he wouldn't be able to do what he was seeing, either.

He couldn't decide if the symmetry of that idea was extremely clever or just plain wordy. Normally, when he came up with something like that, he'd find paper and pen and jot it down, save it somewhere, and decide later on whether or not it was worth incorporating into whatever he was writing. But now *whatever he was writing* was gone, seized by the sheriff's deputies along with his computer and all his disks. And because he hadn't printed out the seventy pages, it looked as though he wasn't going to be writing anything for a while. So there was no use jotting anything down and saving it.

He jammed a couple of toothpicks into the top screw hole in the doorframe, then broke them off flush with the surface. He did the same with the three remaining holes for the first hinge. Next he filled the holes with wood glue. He was waiting a moment for the glue to begin to set when he thought he heard a car door slam.

Now the thing was, from Stephen Barrow's house, he couldn't *hear* a car door slam. Not unless it was parked on his own property, that was, or right down on the road at the bottom of his driveway.

His first thought was that it might be police of some sort, coming to pay him another visit. But that didn't seem likely: There was simply nothing left for them to take. He positioned the hinge, inserted the first screw, and tightened it down. With the toothpicks narrowing the hole, it held nicely. He repeated the process with the three other screws before stepping back to appraise his handiwork. Satisfied, he reached into his jacket pocket for his gloves, pulled up his collar, and headed down the driveway to see if someone down on the road needed help.

Because the snow was falling pretty heavily, he was about three quarters of the way down before he saw the car. It was red, and looked to be a Toyota, or maybe a Honda. And it seemed as though the driver had gotten stuck trying to turn around in Stephen's driveway. That was the trouble with front-wheel drive: As you went uphill, the car's weight shifted to the rear wheels, and the front ones lost traction. You were okay as long as you kept moving, but as soon as you slowed down, you got into trouble. Well, he could lend a hand. How hard could it be to push the thing back down to the road? Although, from the look of things, both right wheels seemed to be off the driveway, and more in the drainage ditch that ran alongside it.

So focused was Stephen on the car that he didn't see the man standing off to the side of it until he was almost on top of him.

"Hey buddy, can I give you a hand?"

"I guess so," said a voice too high to be coming from anybody's *buddy*.

"Sorry," said Stephen. "I'm afraid I couldn't see you too well." He waved one arm in the air by way of explanation.

"*Tell* me about it," said the woman. "It was barely snowing at all down below."

"I know. We seem to have our own weather system up here. I'm Stephen Barrow, by the way."

"I know who you are," said the woman. "I'm Terry Mulholland, and the thing is, I was stopping by hoping to apologize to you. And now I'm stuck, and I feel like an absolute *idiot*."

"Apologize to *me?*" He squinted to try to make out her face, but in the blowing snow, it was hard to see much of anything.

"Yes," she said. "I'm the reporter who tried to talk to you Saturday, over in South Chatham, right after you'd come out of court. You walked off when you found out who I was."

He remembered, sort of. "So you thought you'd give me another chance to refuse to talk to you?"

"I thought I'd apologize for being insensitive the first time."

Stephen said nothing.

"I apologize," she said.

"I accept your apology," said Stephen. "But I'm still not going to talk to you."

"Can you at least give me a push and help me get out of here?"

She was about the last person in the world Stephen wanted to help, but the thought of getting her out of there did have some appeal. He walked around to the right side of the car and kicked some of the snow away from the tires. Just as he'd suspected, she'd managed to find the ditch. With his Renegade, it would have been no problem. The four-wheel drive would have allowed him to push her out from above, or even pull her out from below, if he could have gotten around her. But with the Ford Fiesta, there was no way.

"We can try to shovel you out," he said, "but you seem to have done a pretty good job there."

"Sorry," she said. He could see she was shivering.

"Why don't you come inside, Miss—"

"Terry."

"—Terry. We can try to call a cab or a tow truck. Meanwhile, you can warm up."

She turned and looked at her car. "Will it be okay here?"

"Oh, it's not going to go anywhere," he assured her.

And neither was she, it seemed.

It turned out all the tow-truck operators in the area were busy hooking up their plows, hoping the snow down below was going to amount to something. Some of them plowed part-time for the county, others for the town, and most of the rest of them had standing arrangements with homeowners to do their driveways, at twenty-five to thirty-five dollars a pop, depending on the driveway. Stephen's—a nasty combination of long, winding, narrow, and steep—would have been a fifty-dollar job, at least. Which is why he'd gone out and bought a plow that fit the Renegade, so he could do it himself.

Used to do it himself, make that.

As for getting a cab driver crazy enough to try to make it up the hill, well, Stephen wasn't even going to waste his time calling.

"Here," he said, handing the phone book to Terry. "Knock your socks off." He remembered her now, the redhead with the green eyes. Flynt Adams had read him the article she'd written for her newspaper. According to her, the photo he'd taken of Penny was a *sexual performance*, and Stephen was a child pornographer. She was the enemy; she'd come here *hoping to apologize to him*. Bullshit. She was here to get something on him, so she could *really* bury him in her next story.

She took his spot at the kitchen wall phone and dialed the first number. The snow on her clothes and boots had melted and now was dripping off her. "I'm going to ruin your floor," she said.

"I think the brick can take it," said Stephen, heading back to finish his repair job on the front door. As much as he disliked her, he still found it an effort to be nasty to her: She was that pretty.

He went to work on the second hinge of the door, and was soon absorbed in the process. Stephen liked working with his hands, and he particularly liked solving little repair problems. The toothpicks, for example—using them to fill the screw holes, and seeing them work to perfection—that was the kind of thing that gave him pleasure.

"What happened to your door?"

He hadn't heard her come up behind him, and he jumped slightly at the sound of her voice.

"Sorry," she said when he didn't answer. "I've called every cab company listed in the directory. As soon as they hear where I am, they laugh."

He tightened down the last screw and wiped off the excess glue. "They kicked it down when they came to search my home," he said, surprised now to hear his own voice. He hadn't meant to answer her.

"Search for *what*?"

"Evidence, they said."

"Did they take anything?"

He laughed bitterly, at both the question and her seamless way of launching into an interview.

"My lawyer told me not to talk to anyone," he said, tapping the pins down into the hinges and closing the door. "I don't recall him saying, 'Except reporters.'"

"We're off the record," said Terry.

He managed another bitter laugh. "How do I know that?"

She seemed to think a moment. "You just took me into your home in the middle of a snowstorm," she said, "after I'd written a pretty nasty story about you. You tried to find a tow truck for me. You let me use your phone. The reason you know we're off the record is 'cause I said so. I'm a reporter, Mr. Barrow, not a *cunt*."

At that, he did a double-take. And then, in spite of himself, he laughed. Not a bitter laugh, the kind he'd been finding himself involuntarily spitting out lately, but a *real* laugh. The absurdity of it all: the sight of this timid little prude—*prude* because from the article she'd written she evidently believed (or at least was willing to embrace the belief) that any photo of a naked child could only be pornographic, and *timid* because only a moment ago she'd felt the need apologize for dripping water onto a brick floor you couldn't hurt with battery acid— had all of a sudden blurted out the C-word, just like that. It was the last thing in the world he'd expected from her.

So he'd laughed. Big deal.

Except that somewhere in the back of his mind, it occurred to Stephen that the laugh brought his total for the last four days to an even one.

"It's not *Mr. Barrow*," he told her now. "It's Stephen."

She hadn't meant to use the word; it certainly wasn't part of her everyday vocabulary. But once she'd said it, and he'd *laughed* in response to it, everything changed. All the *attitude* suddenly went out of him, and he dropped the protective cover of nastiness—which, as far as she was concerned, he hadn't seemed too comfortable wearing in the first place.

He made them tea, or at least something that might have passed for tea with someone who wasn't of Irish extraction. Sitting across from him at the kitchen table, she followed his cue and drank it with honey and lemon instead of asking for milk, which she would have preferred. He made her take off her wet coat and hung it on a peg—not to save his floor, but to help her dry out. He had this old, rusty stove in the middle of the room, and the thing seemed positively *alive* to her with its two glowing burners for eyes and a slotted grate at the bottom that looked like the teeth of a grinning mouth. Every once in a while he'd feed it a new log, and the thing would make these weird clanking and whooshing noises, as though it was *eating* them.

But it sure kept the place warm.

"They took my Jeep," he explained to her, "my computer, my camera, every photograph they could find in the house, a bunch of my daughter's toys —"

"Safari Barbie?"

"Excuse me?"

"Safari Barbie," she repeated.

He stared at her as though she might be some kind of Gypsy with magical powers. "How did you know about Safari Barbie?" he asked.

"I was in line right behind you at the Drug Mart the day you bought it. I tried to make a joke about it, asking if you were going to Africa."

A look of recognition slowly spread across his face. He *had* noticed her, after all. "And I, like a jerk, thought you were serious, and said no."

"Right. You told me it was for your daughter."

They both laughed. She could actually see him beginning to relax in front of her. She was good at this, thought Theresa the reporter. She decided to push a little. "And then you dropped off a roll of film," she said.

He nodded, but said nothing. Had she pushed too quickly?

The phone rang. He got up to answer it. She drank her teawater while he spoke, and from his end of the conversation she was able to figure out that he was talking to his lawyer, and that the news wasn't good. By the time he'd hung up the phone and rejoined her at the table, his face was pained, his whole body seemed tense, and he was having trouble making eye contact.

"That was my lawyer," he said.

"I know."

"We've got to go to court Friday," he explained. "My ex-wife's asking for permanent custody and increased child support."

"I'm sorry," said Theresa. It was hard not to be, so visible was his pain. "May I ask you a question?"

He looked up, as though he had one of his own.

"Don't worry," she said. "We're still off the record."

"I guess so," he said, with a shrug.

"Why were you giving your ex-wife child support in the first place? Wasn't your daughter living with *you*?"

He laughed, but it came out sounding more like a snort. "Technically, we've always had joint custody," he said. "And being Jewish, I felt guilty about the original separation and divorce. *No-fault guilt*, I call it. So paying child support seemed therapeutic. Then, even after my daughter started spending all her time here, I was so grateful I didn't want to rock the boat. So I kept on sending the support checks, along with the alimony ones. I suppose it was bribery, in a way: I was paying my ex-wife not to share custody."

"And now she wants more money."

"Lots more, apparently. And she wants to put our daughter in therapy."

"Does she need therapy?"

Stephen seemed to measure his words before speaking. "My daughter is the most terrific, normalest kid who ever lived," he said. "If she needs therapy, then so does everyone else on the planet."

"You sound like you're very antitherapy."

"I don't really think so," he said. "I've been in therapy myself. And before my wife and I separated, I was the one who suggested we go into marriage counseling."

"And?"

"And she insisted on having her own therapist, so there wouldn't be a *conflict of interest*. Of course, there was no conflict when it came to who was going to pay the therapy bills. Anyway, it took the therapist about a month to convince my wife she better move out before I murdered her in her sleep. So she did. She moved in with the therapist."

Coming from an Irish family, Theresa didn't know too much about therapy. The best she could offer was, "That happens a lot, they say."

"With *two women?*"

"You didn't mention that."

"It was just a stage. With Ada, everything's a stage. The militant feminism, the yoga, the drugs, the drinking. Marriage, motherhood."

"Then maybe spending all day with a six-year-old will turn out to be only a stage, too."

"*Spending all day with her?* You don't know Ada. First thing she'll do when she gets more child support is go out and hire a nanny, or drive to the nearest mall and find a dozen truants in need of baby-sitting money."

"Not exactly a *hands-on mom*, huh?"

"Thank God," said Stephen. "It's the only thing that'll save Penny."

It was the first time he'd mentioned her by name. "Penny," Theresa repeated. "Pretty name. Tell me about her," she said, not quite certain if it was Theresa the clever reporter who was asking, or some other Theresa altogether.

And so he did. For the next fifteen minutes, almost without interruption, Stephen Barrow talked about his daughter. Or at least he *thought* he was talking about his daughter. What he was really talking about, it was quite clear to Theresa, was his relationship with his daughter, and therefore himself. He told her about their breakfast routine, their drive to school each morning, the things they'd talk about on the way, how he looked forward to picking her up each afternoon, how she shared her school day with him, the chores they did together, their outings, her critiques of his writing, their cooking collaboration, their dinnertime, their bedtime stories. He talked about driving her to gymnastics, shopping with her for her new clothes, cutting her hair, meeting with her teachers, get-

ting to know her friends, or consoling her when she didn't
think she had any.

And by the time he was finished, Theresa the reporter knew
that her days on the crime beat were over. The story she'd
hoped to get, wasn't. There *was* no child pornography, because
there was no child pornographer. Whatever it was that had
happened that day between Stephen and his daughter that had
prompted him to reach for his camera and photograph her, it
couldn't possibly be what she'd thought it was, and what—
thanks in large part to *her*—her readers no doubt still thought
it was. She wanted to tell him that, to let him know she understood how wrong she'd been, and how she wished she hadn't
written the article in the first place.

"I'm so, so sorry," is how it came out.

He nodded. "I already accepted your apology," he said.

"But you didn't forgive me."

"Last I checked," he said, "that was somebody else's department."

"What happens now?"

She meant with his case, with his ex-wife, with his daughter,
with picking up the pieces of his life. But he misunderstood
her, whether inadvertently or deliberately. She decided it was
most likely the latter, that he'd simply reached a point where he
didn't feel like talking about those things anymore.

"What happens now," he said, "is we start thinking about
putting something together for dinner."

"Oh, no," said Theresa. "I've imposed on you too much
already."

"Suit yourself," he said, "but neither you nor your car is
going anywhere for a while. And you should look at it this
way: You've actually done me a favor. Except for my lawyer,
who calls me every time he's got some bad news, you're the
first person I've had a conversation with in four days. You've
also given me the first occasion to laugh out loud, something I
was beginning to think I was never going to do again. And

now you're going to give me an excuse to cook a meal, sit down at a table like an adult human being, and eat."

"Will that be another first?"

"Pretty much," he said.

Then again, if his tea was a preview of his cooking skills, she figured she might be in for a lot of trouble.

While she sat, he chopped thing up. He didn't believe in food processors, blenders, and other electronic gadgets. He rather enjoyed coring and dicing peppers, could slice an onion into wafers so thin you could see through them, and took pleasure from the simple act of making uniform wedges from a tomato. It took longer when you did it by hand, but when you were finished, all you had to do was wipe off a knife and rinse a cutting board. And you'd *created* something.

What he created this particular evening was a thick vegetable soup with slices of turkey sausage he found in the freezer and sliced (by hand, of course) while they were still hard, so they ended up thin as pepperoni, but without the fat.

They ate at the kitchen table. It was where Stephen and his daughter always ate: After Ada had moved out, he'd eliminated the dining room by moving the long harvest table against one wall and selling six of the eight chairs. The remaining two he'd placed side by side, creating a writing space for himself and a work surface for Penny. Sometimes, when she'd finished her homework—and she was *very* serious about her homework—she'd teach him to do things on the computer.

"Good soup."

"Huh?"

"Where were you?"

"Nowhere," he said. "I don't know."

He did know, of course; he just wasn't willing to tell her, this woman who'd already gotten him to open up much more than he'd wanted to, simply by listening. *She's a reporter*, he had to keep reminding himself. She'd come out here to *interview* him, to collect *dirt* on him, so she could put it in her newspaper.

He got up from the table and walked over to the window. Stood there for a moment, his back to her. Outside in the darkness, the snow seemed to be falling a little less heavily, but it was still coming down. He wanted her to go now; he was tired and ready to be alone again, ready to pull the covers up over his head and make the world disappear. But he knew she wasn't going to be able to go anywhere. He was stuck with her, and the thought of it made him angry.

He was aware that she was saying something now, speaking to him. He turned around. She was waiting for him to answer whatever it was she'd said.

"I'm sorry," he said. "I didn't hear you."

She smiled. "I said go to bed, Stephen. I'll do the dishes."

He gestured vaguely toward the living room. He didn't want her sleeping in Penny's room; he knew that much. But he didn't have the energy to find blankets for her, either, and towels and a pillow and whatever else she might need.

"Go ahead," she said. "I'll be fine."

"Good," he said. He knew it must have sounded stupid to her, but it was all he had left, that one syllable.

Somehow he made it to his room and onto his bed before collapsing. He would sleep for the next ten hours straight, the first time he'd done something like that since his college days. And when he'd awaken at first light, he'd discover that someone had covered him, after removing his boots and placing them neatly at the foot of his bed.

TEN

It was full light outside when Theresa awoke, and full light doesn't come to northern Columbia County in February until well after eight o'clock.

After doing the dishes and straightening up the night before, she'd found a spare blanket and made a bed of the living-room sofa, using a cushion for a pillow. Walking by Stephen's bedroom on the way to the bathroom, she'd seen him, still fully dressed, stretched out across his bed as though he'd fallen onto it. It had seemed cold in that end of the house, and she'd taken the comforter he was on and wrapped it around him as best she could. And when he'd given no sign of waking, she'd untied his boots and slipped them off.

He never budged.

Back in the living room, she took inventory of his library. It was a hodgepodge of contemporary fiction, Shakespeare, reference works, and children's books. And there, tucked over in the far corner, four novels authored by Stephen Barrow. She pulled out the first of them, or at least the one farthest to the left. *The Dying of the Light*, it was called. She thumbed the first couple of pages until she found the source of the title.

And you, my father, there on the sad height,
Curse, bless, me now with your fierce tears, I pray.
Do not go gentle into that good night.
Rage, rage, against the dying of the light.

She didn't need to look to know it was from Dylan Thomas. She turned the page, found a dedication.

> To my daughter, Penny, born the exact day I finished this manuscript:
> I'm afraid this story is a sad one, and I'm sorry for that. But from now on, thanks to you, the rest of them will be absolutely joyous.

She closed the book. Was she somehow invading his privacy, she wondered, reading a book of his in his own home, a book dedicated to his daughter? But that was absurd: It had been published, hadn't it? She could have walked into any bookstore and bought it, simply by plunking down . . . whatever. She turned it over, looking for the price. But she never saw it. Instead her eyes were drawn to his photo, a black-and-white glossy that almost filled the back of the jacket. He was standing by a woodpile of split birch logs, wearing jeans and a T-shirt and a suntan, and smiling back at her broadly. This wasn't the Stephen Barrow she knew—the pale, drained man collapsed on his bed down the hallway. This man looked younger by fifteen years, heavier by twenty pounds, and, what? *Alive,* that's what. This was the man she'd tried to flirt with in the Drug Mart that day long, long ago.

This was Wednesday. *Long, long ago* had been five days earlier.

The book, it turned out, was about a boxer, a semiprofessional middleweight. Apparently Stephen had written a *guy story.*

She took it to bed with her (or at least to the sofa, where she rolled herself in the blanket and propped her head against the cushion), figuring to skim the first few pages. She ended up reading for two hours, and she might have read more, but she wanted to get up in the morning before Stephen, so he wouldn't end up having to make breakfast for his uninvited guest as well as dinner. Still, it was hard putting the book down. Not only could the man write, but his characters talked the same way real people talk, and they did things that real people do, and from time to time they fucked up just like real people fuck up.

Like Stephen himself had fucked up?

Of course, he had a lot to learn about boxing. Like the difference in the rationales behind the mandatory eight-count and the three-knockdown rule, or the proper weight in ounces of training gloves versus sparring gloves.

It was well after midnight by the time she forced herself to put the book down and turn off the light. The sofa may not have made the most comfortable bed in the world, but it couldn't have been too bad, because the next thing she was aware of was that it was light outside. That and the aroma of brewing coffee—which, if it tasted half as good as it smelled, promised to be a good deal better than yesterday's tea.

She followed her nose into the kitchen, where Stephen was putting mugs on the table. "How long have you been up?" she asked him.

"An hour or so. Long enough to dig your car out."

"Thank you," she said. A polite invitation to leave? *Your car's dug out; you can go now.*

The coffee was hot and strong. She declined a second mug, explaining that she ought to get going. She noticed that he didn't argue.

"I'm afraid you never got your interview," he said.

"Maybe some other time," said Theresa. "And anyway, I got much more than an interview."

"Like what?"

"Like a good meal and a good night's sleep, for starters. On top of that, I got to meet a very special person, an extraordinary father, and a pretty good writer."

"Oh?"

"*The Dying of the Light?*"

"Why *that* one?" he asked. "I wrote it a long time ago. And I can't imagine you're into *boxing.*"

She shrugged. "I figured I might learn a thing or two," she said.

"And did you?" His smile struck her just a tiny bit condescending.

"Sure," she said. "Only I've gotta tell you: For my money, Everlast makes much better gloves than either Lee or Title."

Once Theresa had left, Stephen went back to work on the rest of his driveway. It took him nearly two hours to clear enough snow for the Fiesta to make it down to the road and have half a chance of getting back up. Two hours of serious, heart-attack labor. It made him understand why, when a snowstorm was predicted, some of his neighbors simply moved their cars as close to the road as they could.

Next time.

The roads themselves were in good shape, as he'd expected. The snow had stopped sometime during the night, giving the plowers a chance to get things cleared for the folks who had to get to work early, like the truckers and the school-bus drivers. Snow was a fact of life in Columbia County. The prosperity of the '90s may have fattened the traders down on Wall Street, but up on Main Street, things were still pretty much touch and go. A minor inconvenience like a couple of feet of snow was no reason to miss a day's work, which would mean a day's pay. So the roads got plowed, the trucks got through, the schoolkids got picked up, and their parents were able to go off to work.

Stephen Barrow went off to see his lawyer.

"We've got a double-header tomorrow," Flynt Adams told him. "You get arraigned on the indictment in the morning. And then, in the afternoon, we have to be at a hearing on your ex-wife's show-cause order."

"Jesus," said Stephen. "Not exactly what you'd call a *Good Friday*, huh?"

"Actually, the timing might just help us a bit."

"How's that?"

"Well," said Adams, "the way I see it, it's less likely that Judge Wainwright will put you in in the morning, knowing that if he does so, Judge McGee won't be able to squeeze more money out of you for your ex-wife."

"*Put me in?* Can he really *do* that?"

"Yes," said Adams. "The way he does it is to set bail."

"But I thought you convinced that other judge, whatshis-name—"

"That was then. This is a different judge and a different situation. You've been indicted now."

"What does that mean?"

"It means a grand jury has heard a little bit of the evidence against you and voted to formally charge you with a felony. Or felonies. On top of that, Everett Wainwright is much tougher on bail, as well as most other things, than Homer Quackenbush."

"Great," said Stephen. "Will I get a chance to say anything?"

"Yes. You'll say the words, 'Not guilty,' when they ask you how you plead."

"That's it?"

"That's it. I'll do the rest of the talking. It's what you're paying me the big bucks for."

"And suppose he does set bail?" Stephen asked.

"We'll do our best to deal with it. Do you own your home?"

"Me and the bank."

"What's your equity in it?" Adams wanted to know.

"What do you mean?"

"Market value less outstanding mortgage."

"I don't know," said Stephen. "About eleven dollars or so."

Adams laughed.

Stephen wished he were only kidding. "And in the afternoon? What happens then?"

"Any money you have left, Judge McGee orders you to turn it over to your wife."

"Ex-wife."

"Ex-wife, sorry."

"Unless they can make me marry her again."

"That's the one thing they can't do."

But everything else, they could.

Stephen showed up early for his arraignment, as Flynt Adams had instructed, and in the suit and tie Adams had strongly recommended. He felt as though he was going to a wedding or a bar mitzvah, or perhaps his own funeral.

He'd been to the county courthouse in Hudson only once before, when he'd needed to look up the deed on his home for some reason a couple of years ago. Now he climbed the flight of stairs to the courtroom, entered, and winced at the yellowest paint he'd ever seen. Flynt Adams was already there, frowning over a set of papers that comprised the indictment. The original charge of Possessing a Sexual Performance by a Child, Adams explained, had been retained, joined by three new charges: Promoting a Sexual Performance by a Child, Use of a Child in a Sexual Performance, and Endangering the Welfare of a Child.

The people who had taken his daughter from him and sent her to live with her neurotic mother were accusing *him* of endangering her welfare.

There were maybe twenty or thirty people in the room, not counting court personnel. Stephen recognized Theresa Mulholland, but not an older man who was with her. Theresa made a point of smiling at him, but kept her distance. Adams pointed at a large man who stood at one of the tables up front.

"That's Jim Hall," he said. "He's the district attorney, the one who'll be prosecuting you. He says he's got a couple of other arraignments on the calendar, which they're going to do first, in order to get them out of the way."

Evidently, Stephen was the main attraction.

The judge took the bench promptly at ten. Well over six feet tall, with sharp features and graying hair, he *looked* like an Everett Wainwright. "Good morning," he said, and those who knew the drill returned the greeting. Stephen took a seat next to his lawyer in the second row. He could hear his own heart beating.

The other two cases involved middle-aged black defendants, both accused of selling small amounts of crack cocaine to undercover officers, right there in Hudson. Both were led into the courtroom handcuffed, through a side door, by sheriff's deputies—Stephen recognized the gray uniforms only too well. Both pleaded not guilty. Jim Hall, speaking in an accent that sounded more Southern than upstate New York, requested that fifty-thousand-dollar bail be set on each of them, and Judge Wainwright complied. Both were led out through the same side door. One of them tried to wave at his family sitting in the rear of the courtroom, but the hand- cuffs made it difficult. The thought of either of them, or their families, raising fifty thousand dollars was simply beyond imagination.

"People versus Stephen Barrow," announced the clerk, and Stephen stood and stepped forward with his lawyer. "Are you Stephen Barrow?" asked the clerk, who was dressed in gray slacks and a blue blazer, and could have passed as a desk clerk at a fancy hotel.

"Yes," said Stephen.

"The grand jury of Columbia County has charged you as follows." As he listed the crimes, a hush fell over the court- room, and Stephen could feel the back of his neck redden. "How do you plead, guilty or not guilty?"

"Not guilty," Flynt Adams whispered to him.

"Not guilty," said Stephen.

"Are the People requesting bail?" the judge asked. Just in case Jim Hall might forget.

"Most certainly, your honor. These are serious charges,"

he intoned, sounding more Southern with each word, "involving a child of very tender years. The People ask that bail be set in the amount of thirty thousand dollars on each of the three felony charges, and ten thousand dollars on the misdemeanor, for a total of one hundred thousand dollars."

Judge Wainwright turned to Adams. "Counselor?"

"Your honor, my client is a longtime resident of the county. He has no prior record whatsoever. He took a couple of photos of his daughter that with better judgment and the gift of hindsight, perhaps he shouldn't have. But he's not going to suddenly abandon his daughter and his home, and flee the jurisdiction. He was released on his own recognizance by the town justice, and appeared today as directed. In fact, he got here a full half hour early. Finally, none of the charges are armed felonies, or violent ones. I'm asking you to continue his present status."

"Who R-O-R'd him?"

"Justice Quackenbush."

Judge Wainwright chuckled. "He'd R-O-R Attila the Hun," he said, to a ripple of laughter. "And you say these aren't armed or violent felonies?"

"That's correct, sir," said Adams. The Penal Law—"

"Never mind the *Penal Law*. As far as I'm concerned, this defendant was *armed with a camera* and did *serious violence to a child*. Still, he *did* show up today. Does he have a passport?"

Adams turned to Stephen, who shook his head from side to side. He had one, but he'd let it expire a couple of years earlier.

"No, your honor."

"Bail is set in the amount of fifty thousand dollars, cash or surety bond," said the judge.

Stephen gasped audibly.

"I understand your client has an appearance before Judge McGee this afternoon?"

"That's correct, your honor."

"See that he's there. I'll give him to the close of business Tuesday to post the bond."

"Might we have a few extra days, your honor? He's going to need—"

"Close of business Tuesday," Judge Wainwright repeated. "It'd be Monday, but that's a holiday, and I won't be here. Now, Mr.—"

"Adams."

"Right. How much time are you going to need to get your motions in?"

"I'd like three weeks, please."

"March third."

Adams studied his calendar book. "I think that's only *two* weeks, your honor."

"I know," said the judge. "I can count."

If the morning's arraignment was a qualified success—at least Stephen was permitted to leave the courtroom by the main door, rather than the side one in handcuffs—the afternoon's hearing was a different story.

They met in a conference room, with Judge McGee seated at the head of a long table. Stephen and Flynt took seats on one side, across from Ada and her lawyer, Jane Sparrow, a small, shrill woman with beady eyes that never stopped darting around the room. Two deputy sheriffs, a court reporter, and one of the hotel clerks completed the gathering. Stephen had wondered if Penny would be there, but she wasn't. It had been six days now since he'd seen her or spoken a word to her. He just wanted to see that she was okay, that was all—that she wasn't sick, that she was eating all right, that she was still the same Penny.

Priscilla McGee could have been a young sixty or an old fifty; she wore a lot of makeup, so it was hard to tell. She had a habit of glancing at her watch as soon as anyone else started speaking, as though she was timing their remarks and might interrupt at any moment, something she did constantly when it was Adams who happened to be speaking.

The hearing lasted thirty-five minutes. By the time it was over, Ada Barrow had been granted exclusive custody of Penny until "further order of this court," an event that seemed likely to occur sometime after the next ice age; Stephen's child-support payments had been increased from three hundred dollars a month to seven hundred and fifty; Penny would immediately be seen by a therapist who was a "qualified expert" in child abuse, and who would evaluate Penny and report directly to the court; and Stephen would bear the expense of the therapy, as well as all of Ada's legal bills.

When Adams had asked about the possibility of Stephen's having visitation rights, Judge McGee had shot him down. "Certainly not before I've heard from the therapist," she said, "and we find out just how much irreparable damage your client has already caused this poor child."

Irreparable damage, thought Stephen. This from a woman who had never *met* Penny, had never so much as set *eyes* on her, let alone heard her singing, *"Don't worry, be happy,"* at the top of her lungs, the day after Stephen had caused her *irreparable damage* by photographing her mooning him.

It was enough to make you appreciate Judge Wainwright.

That same Friday afternoon, Jim Hall finally got a copy of the search-warrant return, the inventory of property that had been seized from Stephen Barrow's home. As he looked down the list—which ran a full three pages of single-spaced typing—he placed little checkmarks by those items he considered particularly noteworthy. He ended up checking the following:

✓ Numerous photos of child complainant, some in underwear or bathing suits, some topless

✓ X-rated and sacrilegious video, "The Devil Made Me Do Him"

✓ 4 anatomically correct female dolls, all apparently named "Barbie"

✓ 1 Valentine's Day card from the child complainant to Stephen Barrow, containing a child's depiction of Barrow in some sort of undergarments, and signed "I love you"

✓ 3 Valentine's Day cards from Stephen Barrow to the child complainant, one of which is inscribed, "To the love of my life," and signed "Love, Stephen"

✓ 1 camera, Nikon brand;

✓ 8 pairs of child's underpants;

✓ 1 child's drawing depicting a small girl and a man embracing each other

The camera, Hall figured, could be the weapon—or *instrumentality* was probably the correct way to phrase it. The underdrawers would be submitted to the state police lab to test for semen stains. The porn movie Hall would have to take home, so he could examine it on his VCR. It was evidence, after all, even if the title didn't seem to suggest it was kiddie porn. But the item that intrigued him the most was the Valentine's Day card Barrow had mailed to his daughter, the one that said, "To the love of my life," and was signed, "Love, Stephen."

Now what kind of man sends a card to his six-year-old kid and signs his *name* to it? "Daddy," "Dad," "Pop," "your father," "the old man," whatever. But *Stephen*? What kind of a man wants to be called *Stephen* by his daughter? And what did that say about his relationship with her?

To Jim Hall, it said plenty.

He found Flynt Adams's phone number and dialed it. Adams picked up on the first ring and said, "Law office."

"That you, Flynt?"

"Yes."

"Jim Hall here. Just got the return on the Barrow search warrant, and the law says you're entitled to a copy. Going to mail it out to you, if that's okay."

"How long is it?" Adams asked.

"Looks to be about four or five pages."

"Think you could fax it over?"

"Sorry," said Hall. "I'm afraid our fax machine is out of paper."

"You're faxing it to *me*," Adams told him. "*I'm* the only one who needs paper, not you."

"Not *paper*," said Hall. "I said it's out of *order*."

There was a pause while Adams seemed to think over that little juke. "Anything significant in the return?" he asked. In other words, it seemed he'd already accepted the fact that he wasn't going to get to see it until next week.

By God, Hall thought, *I love lawyering.*

"Not really," he said. "A camera, a porno flick. I honestly can't remember seeing anything else in there that seemed interesting."

"I'll look for it in Monday's mail," said Adams.

"You do that," said Jim Hall.

Cathy Silverman was straightening up her office and getting ready to leave for the evening when her phone rang. It was already dark out and almost five o'clock, and she toyed with the idea of letting it ring, or at least allowing the answering machine to pick up. But Cathy Silverman was a dedicated professional, and letting a phone ring unanswered was all but impossible for her to do.

"Child Counseling Services," she said.

"Cathy?"

"Yes."

"Jane Sparrow here. I'm glad I caught you. Judge McGee agreed to appoint you to evaluate the Barrow child."

"The little girl we spoke about?"

"Right, the one in the child porn case. How do you want to set it up?"

"Why don't you have the mother give me a call," said Silverman. "I'll be in at eight-thirty Tuesday morning."

"I've got her here right now," said Sparrow.

"The girl?"

"No, the mother. I understand the girl's still too shook up to go out. Want me to put her on?"

Without removing her coat, Cathy Silverman sat down and reached for her appointment book. "Sure," she said, "put her on."

Cathy Silverman—her patients called her *Dr. Silverman*, even though she wasn't a physician, and it would be two full years before she'd earn her Ph.D.—had worked for the state for six years as a child protective services worker. A year and a half ago, she'd resigned and opened her own practice, a hybrid of clinical testing, counseling, and psychotherapy for what she liked to call *children at risk*. Her self-anointed specialty—and primary source of clients—was to serve the court system as an *evaluator*, an expert in substantiating claims of child sexual abuse. Until recently, the preferred term had actually been *validator*, but that term had fallen out of favor when critics began suggesting that the word itself implied a built-in bias on the part of a supposedly neutral professional.

"Hello, Dr. Silverman," said a woman's voice with just an edge of a whine to it. "I'm Ada Barrow."

"Hello, Mrs. Barrow. I understand I'll be making an evaluation of your daughter."

"That's right. When can we come see you?"

Silverman opened her appointment book and thumbed the pages until she came to next week. "How about Tuesday or Wednesday?" she asked.

"You can't see us Monday?"

"Monday's a holiday," said Silverman.

"What kind of a *holiday*?"

"It's President's Day." It said so right in her book.

"This is awfully important," said Mrs. Barrow.

"How about right after school Tuesday?" suggested Silverman.

"Oh, I'm not letting her go back to school yet, no way. At least not until I know if she's, you know, *okay*."

Silverman thumbed back a page. "I could see her tomorrow," she said, "Saturday. If you can have her here by nine, that is."

"How 'bout in the afternoon?"

"I only have hours in the morning," explained Silverman. "So it's nine o'clock, or else it'll have to wait till Tuesday."

"I guess we'll see you at nine. Oh, and wait a sec, my lawyer wants to talk to you again."

"Cathy?" It was Jane Sparrow, back on the line.

"Yes?"

"I saved the best news for last. Judge McGee ordered Daddy to pick up the tab."

Cathy Silverman smiled as she hung up the phone, glad she'd decided to pick it up in the first place. It was beginning to look as though she could go ahead and order that new side-by-side refrigerator, after all.

"*Of course* you've got to get off the story," Neil Witt told Theresa Mulholland over lunch. "And anyway, no one wants to read that a man who takes dirty pictures of his kid is really a nice guy. Besides which, you could be called as a *witness* if the case ever goes to trial."

"A *witness*?"

"You saw him drop off the photos to be developed. You said so yourself."

"How does that make me a witness?"

"You're in a position to testify that he was acting furtively, tried to hide his face, looked nervous, whatever. State of mind, consciousness of guilt, that kinda thing. Besides, Tom Grady'll be back Monday. He'll pick it up from here."

"From here to where?"

"Wherever it takes him. I hear they found some pretty weird stuff at his home when they went there with the search warrant."

"Like what?"

"Forget it, Terry, you're off it. And do yourself a favor. Stay away from the guy. He's going down."

At that particular moment, Stephen Barrow wasn't thinking about going down; he was far more worried about going *in*. Judge Wainwright had given him until Tuesday afternoon to either come up with fifty thousand dollars in cash, or convince a bail bondsman to accept as collateral a house that had virtually no equity in it. The chances of Stephen's being able to do either of those things were nonexistent. And from what he'd already seen of the judge's no-nonsense approach to things, Tuesday afternoon was beginning to look a lot like go-to-jail day for Stephen.

He dialed Flynt Adams's number and caught him, even though it was Friday and after five. "Don't you ever go home?" he asked him.

"Soon," said Adams, "soon. What's up?"

"Suppose I can't make the bail," Stephen said. "What happens then? I mean, what *jail* do they put me in?"

"The Columbia County Detention Facility, right over in beautiful downtown Hudson. You and those two crack dealers you saw this morning, and a dozen or so of their buddies. Why?"

"No reason," said Stephen. "I mean, I was just wondering, you know."

Adams had given him the phone numbers of two bail bondsmen to call. Now he asked Stephen if he'd done so.

"Yeah," said Stephen. "I left messages for both of them."

"Don't worry. They'll get back to you."

Don't worry, be happy.

Who was to say those crack dealers were such bad guys, anyway?

ELEVEN

Ada and Penny Barrow showed up at Cathy Silverman's office at 9:25 Saturday morning. "Sorry we're late," said Ada. "This one finally slept, for the first time in a week, would you believe, and I didn't want to wake her up. She's been through so much, you know. Right, sweetie?"

Penny shrugged. Silverman's first impression of the child was that she looked pale and drawn, seemed nervous, and was reluctant to speak. Hardly the textbook picture of a normal six-year-old girl. "Why don't we sit down," she suggested, "and get ourselves acquainted."

For the next twenty minutes, as Penny sat between the two women in near silence, Silverman had Ada Barrow describe her daughter's behavior over the course of the past week. A few of the doctor's questions were open-ended, such as, "How has she been acting in general?" But only a few. Most were specific to the point of being suggestive, what lawyers tend to object to as *leading* questions. "Have there been any episodes of bed-wetting?" the doctor wanted to know. "Is she having nightmares?" "Has she been sucking her thumb?" "Throwing temper tantrums?"

Ada answered yes to just about all of them.

There finally came a time when Silverman asked Ada to step outside and have a seat in the waiting area, so that she could speak with Penny alone.

"Is that really necessary?" Ada wanted to know. "I mean, she's so nervous. Even with me here."

Silverman explained that it really was necessary. "Suppose I'm asked at some point if I ever bothered to interview her without your being present," she pointed out. "It would look much better all around if I could say yes."

Ada complied reluctantly, but she complied. In a later written report describing the session, Silverman would make a point of commenting on the mother's obvious devotion to her daughter.

"So," she said, finally turning her full attention to the little girl seated in the adult-sized chair, "how are we feeling today?"

"Fine," said Penny.

In a gentle voice, Silverman asked her if she loved her mommy.

"Yes."

"How about your *daddy*?"

"I love him, too."

"I see. You and your daddy were living alone, is that right?"

"No."

"*No?*"

"We weren't living alone," Penny explained. "We were living with each other."

"I see," Silverman said again. "Tell me, did you ever used to get into your daddy's bed?"

"Yes, when it was cold."

Silverman made a written note of this. Personally, she considered it a taboo, parents allowing children of the opposite sex to get into bed with them. She couldn't understand why so many people did it. Pen poised in hand, she asked, "What happened on the times you got into bed with your daddy?"

Penny took a moment before answering, leading Silverman to suspect she was on to something. Finally Penny said, "I got warmer?"

"No. I mean, did your daddy *tickle* you?"

"In bed?"

"Yes, in bed."

"No."

"But he did tickle you?"

"Sometimes."

Silverman made another note. She considered tickling highly problematic. "How does it make you feel, when he tickles you?"

"I don't know. I laugh."

"Tell me, Penny. Do you like it when your daddy takes pictures of you with his camera?"

A shrug.

"How about when you have no clothes on?"

Another shrug.

"I need you to answer in words," the doctor explained. What she didn't explain was that she needed an answer to that question in particular. It was, to a social worker, what was called a *win-win question*. If the subject answered no, it demonstrated her discomfort with her father's behavior and indicated that the behavior was therefore forced upon her and abusive. On the other hand, if the subject said yes—meaning she *liked it* when her father took naked photographs of her—that would reveal a pathological relationship between the two, and would be even *more* suggestive of abuse.

"If you tell me," said Silverman, "I promise not to tell anyone else. Okay?"

Penny's thumb went into her mouth, prompting the doctor to make a written note of the fact. "I need my Baba," said the little girl.

"Who?"

"My Baba."

"Who's your Baba?"

But no explanation was forthcoming. "Tell me," said the doctor. "Does Daddy ever hurt you?"

"No."

"Are you ever afraid of him? Even a little bit?"

"No."

"Does he ever make you do things you don't like?"

No answer.

"What kind of things does he make you do, that you don't like to do?"

Still no answer. Penny's thumb was back in her mouth.

"I'll tell you what. If you can tell me just one of the things, that'll be enough, and we'll stop."

The thumb came out just long enough for Penny to answer. "Sometimes," she said, "he makes me eat *broccoli*."

Because she considered the response an obvious effort on the child's part to deflect a difficult question, Silverman didn't bother entering it in her notes.

Outside in the waiting area, Silverman drew Ada Barrow aside. "Who's *Baba*?" she asked in a whisper.

"That's what she used to call her blanket," Ada explained. "She carried it around with her all the time, when she was a baby. Why?"

"Well," said the doctor, "it might be a good idea for you to let her bring it next time."

"Next time?"

"Yes."

"I didn't know there'd *be* a next time."

"Oh, yes," said Silverman. "I'm pretty sure there's something *going on* here."

At noon on that same Saturday, a real estate appraiser showed up at Stephen Barrow's home. The appraiser had been recommended by Flynt Adams, and did a lot of grumbling about having to come out on such short notice. "You ought to fix this door better," he said, "and straighten up the inside a little, before you put this on the market."

"I'm not putting it on the market," Stephen explained. "I'm trying to put it up for collateral on a bail bond, and I was told I'd need an appraisal first."

"Oh," was all the appraiser had to say about that. For the next fifteen minutes, he poked around the place, making little *clucking* noises every time he came across something he didn't like. Finally he handed Stephen two pieces of paper. One was an appraisal form, declaring that the current market value of the property, structures included, was $145,000. The other was a bill for his services, which came to $350.

After he'd written out a check and said good-bye to the appraiser, Stephen called the bail bondsman, as Adams had instructed him to.

"Free at Last," answered a gravelly voiced man.

"Excuse me?"

"Free at Last Bail Bonds. Manny speaking. What can I do for ya?"

"My name is Stephen Barrow. My lawyer—"

"Yeah, yeah, Flynt tole me aboutchoo. Wha'd the appraisal come in at?"

Stephen glanced at the form. "A hundred and forty-five thousand," he said.

"And whaddaya owe?"

"Owe?"

"How much ya got left on the mawgage?"

Stephen found his latest statement and read from it. "One hundred and thirty-one thousand, five hundred and sixty-two dollars, and fourteen cents."

"Which means ya got less than fourteen thou clear, right?"

Manny's math was a lot faster than Stephen's. "I guess so," he said.

"And the bail is fifty, right?"

"Right."

"Sorry, pal. No can do."

"But Mr. Adams told me—"

"Pardon my French, but I don't give a flyin' fuck *what* Mr. Adams tole ya. I got a *bidness* to run heah, not some kinda *charity*. Whadelse ya got?"

"Excuse me?"

"Cash, bankbooks, jewelry, guns. That kinda stuff."

Stephen thought for a moment. "I've got a car," he said. "It's worth sixteen hundred dollars."

"I don't take cars."

"A lot of books, a snowplow, some tools."

"Forget about that shit—I ain't a friggin' *pawnshop*. Call Flynt, tell him he better go see the judge, get your bail cut. The way things are, I can't do nuthin' for ya. Fuckit, I'll save ya the trouble. I'll call him myself."

"Thanks," said Stephen. "In the meantime, what should I do with the appraisal?"

"That? Ya wanna roll that up real tight like. Then ya wanna bend over an' give it a good *shove*, all the good it's gonna do ya. Sorry to have to break the news to ya, pal. Ya seem like a nice enough guy. Don't take it personal."

As she sat at her desk typing her preliminary report on Penny Barrow, Cathy Silverman began to realize that she had a problem. She'd been called in by the court to make an evaluation of the child and determine if she could benefit from therapy. Silverman had already concluded that she could. (In fact, since she'd been in practice, Silverman had yet to conclude that someone could *not* benefit from therapy. This consistency was no doubt driven by her heartfelt confidence in her own powers to treat; but it may have also had a little something to do with the fact that she made her living from providing the continuing therapy, once she'd decided it was called for.)

What bothered Silverman at the moment was her strong suspicion that in addition to needing therapy, Penny Barrow had been sexually abused, and the abuser was most likely her own father.

All the classic signs were present: the nervousness, the withdrawn and self-protective body language, the reluctance to speak, the sleeplessness, the nightmares, the bed-wetting, the thumb-sucking, the temper tantrums, the sudden need of her blanket, the reversion to baby talk. (Never mind that all of these symptoms might easily have been attributed to the trauma of Penny's being wrenched from her father and placed with her mother, in surroundings that were at best strange and uncomfortable; to Silverman, they had abuse written all over them.) Equally telling to Silverman were Penny's transparent attempts at denial: her pitiful insistence that she was just fine, that she loved her daddy, and that the only thing he ever made her do that she didn't like was to tell her to eat her broccoli. How was *that* for a textbook case of denial? (It has long been one of the sacred axioms of child-abuse evaluators that denial of abuse is in itself often a telltale *sign* of abuse — in spite of the obvious catch-22 consequences of such thinking.)

To Cathy Silverman, it was all there. And when she added in the fact that Stephen Barrow had been caught with nude photos of his daughter, in which her private parts had not only been visible, but actually *displayed for the camera*, there was simply no room for doubt.

In 1973, a well-intentioned United States Congress had passed the Mondale Act, providing millions of dollars in federal matching funds to states that established programs to prevent, detect, and prosecute cases of child abuse. It took several years for the states to meet the compliance guidelines, but after a lag period, the results that began coming in were dramatic. In 1976, the number of child-abuse reports nationwide was 670,000; by 1993, it was 3 *million*. In terms of reports specifying child *sexual* abuse, the 1976 figure was 21,000; by 1993 it had soared to 320,000, *an increase of more than 1,500 percent*. One of the original requirements of the Mondale Act was that, in order to qualify for matching funds, states designate "mandated reporters"—physicians, therapists, teachers, and others—who would be required to report all instances of suspected abuse they came across. Their failure to report a case—whether that failure was willful or simply negligent—could subject them to criminal prosecution, a fact that put them under tremendous pressure to err on the side of reporting cases, even when they had little to go on other than a vague suspicion.

Cathy Silverman was a mandated reporter.

Priscilla McGee was a judge who didn't mind being disturbed on a weekend, providing it was a matter that needed her immediate attention. When the phone rang, it was her court clerk calling, who in turn had been chased down by someone in the sheriff's office.

"Judge, I've got a *doctor* on the line, says it's real important she speaks with you. Name's Silverman, Cathy Silverman. Want me to put her through?"

Judge McGee knew Cathy Silverman well, having appointed her on a half-dozen cases over the past year and a half. Silverman was a serious young woman who wouldn't be calling simply to waste the judge's time.

"Yes," she told her clerk, and waited while he performed whatever magic was required to splice one call onto another.

Eventually she heard a "Go ahead," followed by Silverman's "Hello?"

"Hello, Cathy."

"Hello, Judge. I'm sorry to bother you on a Saturday."

"That's all right."

"It's the Barrow child, the one you—"

"Yes, I know the case. The one whose father takes nude pictures of her."

"Right. Well, I'm pretty sure he's been doing more than that."

"Like what?"

"I don't know for sure yet, but she's showing all the symptoms of sexual abuse."

"Hmmmm," said the judge. "I'm not at all surprised."

"I just wanted to let you know right—"

"Yes, yes, you did the right thing."

"I'll get you my preliminary report right away," said Silverman. "And I think perhaps I ought to keep seeing her, at least until—"

"Oh, yes, you keep seeing her. And meanwhile, I'll decide what *I'm* going to do about it."

In the end, Priscilla McGee decided to do two things about it. First, she placed a call to Jane Sparrow, the lawyer for Penny Barrow's mother. This itself was an act of dubious judicial ethics, insofar as it amounted to an *ex parte* communication with counsel on a matter before the court. Judge McGee knew this, but she felt she had something of an emergency on her hand. She'd inform the other side later, and make a record of her actions explaining the reasons for them.

In judicial circles, a practice commonly referred to as *covering your butt.*

"Jane," she said. "Priscilla McGee."

"Hello, Judge."

"I just got an emergency call from Cathy Silverman, the therapist I appointed on the Barrow case."

"Yes?"

"She's found what she considers to be strong evidence of sexual abuse in the child's behavior. I want you to find a doctor, I guess it should be a pediatric gynecologist, to do an examination on the child, as soon as possible. It's been a week since the father's had contact, and these things can heal. The court will pay for it, so try to keep the cost down, okay?"

"Okay," said Jane Sparrow, doing her best to cover her exhilaration.

The second thing Judge McGee did was to call her colleague Everett Wainwright. It took a while for him to get her message and get back to her, but when he did, she confided in him what she'd done.

"You did the right thing," he told her. "And as soon as you get the results, you notify me, hear? If I find out this guy's been diddlin' his daughter, he'll *wish* he still had a fifty-thousand-dollar bail."

"*Diddlin' his daughter,* huh? You always *did* have a way with words, Ev."

They both chuckled.

Lleander Singh was between patients at the Albany Medical Center when his phone rang. A lot of the doctors refused to answer, figuring it was the receptionist's job, and if she didn't pick up, eventually one of the nurses would. But Dr. Singh didn't mind: In the hospital he'd trained at, in Pakistan, they didn't *have* telephones.

"Dr. Singh speaking," he said.

"Ah, Dr. Singh," said a woman whose voice he didn't recognize. "Just the person I'm looking for. My name is Jane Sparrow, and I'm calling on behalf of Judge McGee in Hudson."

"And how may I be of service?"

"We have a little girl, six years old. Her father's been sexually abusing her. The judge would like her examined as soon as possible."

"What would the purpose of the examination be?"

"What do you mean?"

"I mean," said Dr. Singh, "is she in great distress? Is she bleeding, torn, badly bruised, for example? The sort of thing that's going to require an emergency-room setting?"

"Oh, no," said the woman, "nothing like that. It's just that we're interested in, you know, *confirming the diagnosis.*"

"If it's not an emergency, might you not be better off with a female physician?" Dr. Singh asked. "An examination of this sort can be upsetting enough as it is."

"Well, the thing is, it *is* an emergency. The judge needs it done right away."

"Have you tried Edna Scherl, down at Vassar and Brothers, in Poughkeepsie, or Allison Guttmacher, over at the Berkshire Medical Center, in Pittsfield?"

"Yes," said the woman, "but neither of them can do it. It's a holiday weekend."

"How about Claire Jarvis, at Northern Dutchess?"

"She can't, either."

Which was interesting, because there was no Claire Jarvis at Northern Dutchess, and never had been. Lleander Singh had just made up the name in order to see if he was being told the truth or not. Nevertheless, he didn't like turning away patients, particularly young children. "I suppose I could manage to squeeze her in," he said. "Do you think you can arrange to have here a little before five?"

Flynt Adams got the bad news from Manny the bondsman Saturday afternoon. "Case like this, I need at least fifty percent collateral to write the paper," Manny told him. "Otherwise the surety company'll kick my ass. Your guy's got less than fourteen thou clear in his house. He's barely halfway there. Who you infronta, McGee or Wainwright?"

"Wainwright." The two judges took turns. One of them would sit on criminal cases for a three-month stretch, while the other handled civil matters. Then, just when lawyers and litigants were beginning to drive them totally crazy, they'd swap assignments.

"Whyntcha go inna cawt Monday morning, make an application," Manny suggested. "See if he'll drop it down to twenty-five. He ain't such a bad guy."

"He might not be a bad guy," said Adams, "but he doesn't particularly like sex cases—"

"Hey, who does?"

"—and as it is, he cut the DA's original request in half. But what the hell, we've got nothing to lose. I'll give it a shot."

Which meant he'd have to notify Jim Hall. But there was no use giving his adversary too much advance warning and a lot of extra time to come up with arguments against the bail being lowered. Better to wait until tomorrow night to call him, or even first thing Monday morning.

A few minutes after five, Ada Barrow and her lawyer, Jane Sparrow, arrived at the pediatric floor of the Albany Medical Center with Penny. Penny was carrying her Baba, but was otherwise behaving like a normal, if somewhat depressed, six-year-old. Of course, neither adult had bothered to inform her of the nature of the examination she was about to undergo, instead letting her believe that a second doctor simply wanted to talk to her, much the way Cathy Silverman had that morning. They'd decided to let Dr. Singh handle breaking the news to her.

He *was* the doctor, after all.

Technically, Dr. Singh was a pediatrician with a subspecialty in urology. Because his work required him to perform examinations on his patients that they invariably found unpleasant, if not downright traumatic, he'd developed a protocol over time to minimize the unpleasantness. Both hospital rules and medical ethics required that another adult be present during the examination. That adult could be a parent or guardian, or a nurse. It was Dr. Singh's experience that "the more the merrier" had no place in this equation, and if a parent *wanted* to be present (or if the child expressed a preference that the parent be present), that would suffice. On the other hand, recent studies had shown that an inanimate *parent substitute*—a favorite toy, a blanket, or a familiar pillow—served just as well as a parent, and sometimes better. The object could be held throughout the examination and, if need be, cuddled, squeezed, or even talked to. And the best thing was, the object itself never got nervous or squeamish or hysterical, and never imparted its own discomfort to the child.

"I see you've brought Penny's blanket along," Dr. Singh noted.

"It was *her* idea," said the mother, apparently eager to distance herself from it.

"Well, Penny, it was an *excellent* idea."

"Thank you," said Penny.

"Does it have a special name, by any chance?"

"Baba."

"Baba," Dr. Singh repeated. "I used to call mine 'Nookie.' Would you do me a big favor, Penny?"

"What?"

"You and Baba and I are going to walk down that hallway right there and look for *Elizabeth*. Elizabeth is my nurse, but I keep losing track of her. We'll know her when we see her, because she has red hair—I mean *very* red hair. She's very nice, and I understand she has a drawer full of lollipops, but since I'm not a kid, I'm not sure about that. Once we find Elizabeth—*if* we can find her, that is—I'm going to let you and Baba hang out with her for a few minutes while I come back and talk with your mom. Sound okay to you?"

Penny shrugged, and her mother opened her mouth to say something, but before she could get the words out, Dr. Singh had Penny's small hand in his and the three of them were walking down the hall—doctor, child, and blanket.

"She's just fine," he announced, when he returned to the room five minutes later. "She and Elizabeth are reading. Now, tell me what's been going on?"

Jane Sparrow took that as her cue. "According to the therapist she's been seeing, her father's been sexually abusing her."

"In what way?"

"We're not sure."

He turned to Ada. "What physical symptoms, if any, have you noticed?"

"Like what?"

Dr. Singh was leery of making it a multiple-choice or true-false test. "Like anything at all," he said.

"She won't undress in front of me," said Ada, "and she doesn't want me around when she bathes. I see her *touching herself* every once in a while, you know, *down there*. And I did notice a bruise on the inside of her thigh. Is that the kind of thing you mean?"

"Sure. Anything else?"

Ada looked at her lawyer. "You said she cries a lot," said Sparrow, "and refuses to eat."

"Okay," said Dr. Singh. "But I'm most interested in her *physical* complaints right now. Anything else you can think of?"

"She has a burn mark on the back of her hand," said Ada.

"Does she say how it got there?"

"I didn't ask her," said Ada. "She's very protective of her father, you understand, and she's afraid to say the least thing against him."

"I see," said Dr. Singh. "Has she ever had a gynecological exam before?"

It was Ada's turn to shrug.

"Does she use any particular word to describe her genitals?"

Another shrug.

"Or the act of urinating?"

Silence.

"Okay," said Dr. Singh. "I won't be long." And he was out of the room and walking down the hall before they could object.

Stephen Barrow spent the remainder of the weekend convinced it would be his last as a free man. He paid his bills, threw out some stuff that had begun to gather blue mold in the back of the refrigerator, and pretty much completed the process of putting things that had been moved around during the search back where they belonged. By Sunday evening, he had a strong urge to write, to commit to paper his thoughts on going to jail for having taken a photograph of his daughter. He felt strongly that there was a story in there somewhere, even if he didn't know quite what it was yet.

But writing, of course, had been made difficult for Stephen by the loss of his computer. He tried to remember how he'd managed to do it B.C.—before computers. There'd been a type-writer once, complete with messy ribbons, little bottles of Wite-Out, and perpetually stained fingers. But he'd thrown it out, or given it away, long ago. Then there'd been a tape recorder, a tiny thing he used to speak into and send the tapes off to a service, who'd type up whatever was on them and send it back to him. But that hadn't worked out too well. For one thing, it became expensive; for another, its microphone must have been too sensitive because it used to pick up everything in the room. He'd get manuscripts back with notations on them like "music in background," "telephone ringing," and "toilet flushing." He'd ended up giving the thing to Penny a year or two ago. Within ten minutes, she'd figured out what each of the buttons did and turned it into a perpetual *Barney* machine. Not long after, she'd lost or misplaced it, suggesting to Stephen that there might just be a God after all.

So in the end, he did it the old-fashioned way: He found a pad of paper and a pen. But by that time, he'd lost the urge to write. The notion of going to jail no longer seemed interesting and ironic to him, or even all that frightening. It was *depressing*, that was all.

He went to bed around ten, determined to get a good night's sleep. He figured it might be his last one for a while, what with all the crack dealers he'd soon have for cellmates.

TWELVE

When Priscilla McGee arrived at her chambers Tuesday morning, she found a fax waiting for her.

OFFICIAL AND CONFIDENTIAL

TO: The Honorable Priscilla McGee
        Justice of the Supreme Court
        Columbia County
FROM: Lleander Singh, M.D.
        Albany County Medical Center
RE: Penny Barrow

Background

On February 19, 2000, in the presence of Elizabeth McDowell, R. N., I performed an examination of the above child at the Albany County Medical Center. The child was referred to me by the court, and brought to the medical center by her mother, Ada Barrow, and Mrs. Barrow's attorney, Jane Sparrow, Esq.

Mrs. Barrow and Ms. Sparrow advised me that the child is suspected of having been sexually abused.

Clinical Findings

The child presents as a normally developed girl, consistent with her reported age of 6 years. During the examination she was somewhat nervous and withdrawn, but her behavior could be easily explained by the nature of the occasion.

External examination is essentially unremarkable. There is a burn mark, most likely 2 to 6 weeks old, on the superior portion of the right hand. The child attributes it to having accidentally touched the surface of a wood-burning stove in the middle of the kitchen of her father's home. (It might be a good idea to determine if there is such a stove; if there is not, this might provide a fertile avenue for follow-up questions.) There is a 1" circular bruise of indeterminate age on the child's left inner thigh, 8" above the knee. The child claims to be unable to recall how or when she got it. There is an old scar, .5" in length, running through the child's left eyebrow. She reports that she fell "about a year ago" while playing a game of "hide-and-seek" with her father.

Upon gynecological examination, the vagina appears somewhat sensitive to the touch, but not remarkably so. The hymen is intact. The vaginal os shows evidence of an old tear, less than .25" in length and almost fully healed. In addition, there is a slight amount of hyperpigmentation. (Note that these findings are not uncommon, even in children of this age who are *not* suspected of having been abused.) The anus appears unremarkable. There is no discharge visible from either orifice. When asked, the child reports that she occasionally experiences a slight itchiness or burning sensation when urinating, particularly "when I have to hold it in for a long time."

Vaginal and anal smears were taken for microscopic examination and submitted to the laboratory for analysis.

Impressions
Pending laboratory analysis of the smears for possible gonorrhea, chlamydia, etc., I am unable to determine to a

degree of medical certainty whether or not the child has been sexually abused.

Rape and anal penetration may be safely ruled out.

With respect to the old tear to the vagina and its hyper-pigmentation and tenderness, the bruise to the thigh, the burn mark, and the facial scar, while all of these findings are consistent with sexual abuse, none of them, alone or in combination with the others, is significant enough to justify an actual clinical diagnosis of sexual abuse.

Conclusion

While some of the findings are consistent with sexual abuse, and while sexual abuse therefore cannot be ruled out, no positive clinical diagnosis can be made at this time.

Lleander Singh, M.D.

Judge McGee read the report in its entirety, twice. The second time through, she took a yellow marker and highlighted the following portions: ". . . nervous and withdrawn . . . burn mark . . . bruise . . . left inner thigh . . . old scar . . . the vagina appears sensitive to the touch . . . vaginal os shows evidence of an old tear . . . hyperpigmentation . . . itchiness or burning sensation when urinating."

The following portions she not only highlighted, but circled: ". . . all of these findings are consistent with sexual abuse . . . sexual abuse therefore cannot be ruled out."

Then she picked up the phone and dialed Judge Wainwright's number. "Ev," she said, "you asked me to notify you if there were positive findings of abuse on that Barrow girl."

"Yes?"

"Well, listen to this."

And she proceeded to read him every single word. The ones she'd highlighted, that is.

"Thanks," said Judge Wainwright, before adding, "it's a hell of a world we live in, Priscilla."

"You said it."

"Well, I've already got word from Flynt Adams—that's the father's lawyer—that he and Jim Hall want to see me on a bail application this morning. I'm afraid Mr. Adams is going to wish he'd stayed in bed."

Tom Grady stayed in bed until a little after nine that morning. The first thing he did was to light a cigarette and go through his morning coughing ritual. The second thing he did was to check the calendar on his bedside table. Tuesday, it said, February 22. Which made it ten full days now that he hadn't had a drop.

The phone rang. He let it ring twice before picking up and saying "Grady" in a gravelly voice.

"Tom, Neil Witt."

"Don't worry, Neil, I'm fine. Be there in an hour."

"No, don't come here. Go straight over to the courthouse, Tom. Judge Wainwright's going to be hearing a bail application on the Barrow case this morning. I understand it could get interesting."

"How so?"

"Barrow's lawyer wants to knock the bail in half. Turns out he could be walking into a hornet's nest. Word is, there's evidence his client has not only been posing his kid for porn photos, he's been sexually abusing her all along, too."

"Beautiful," said Tom Grady. "I'll get right over there."

After lighting another cigarette, that was. At the twelve-step meetings, they always told you it was best to concentrate on one addiction at a time. You wanted to stop drinking, you were going to need your nicotine and your caffeine to get you through the day.

No sense arguing with advice like that, was there?

On that same Tuesday morning, Theresa Mulholland was already up in Albany covering a breakfast meeting of the regional chapter of Mothers Against Gun Violence. Inside the League of Women Voters Center, 137 women listened as the guest of honor and featured speaker, Hillary Clinton, called for stricter gun-control measures. Outside, in temperatures hovering around the 20-degree mark, thirty-eight other women and fifty-two men—every one of them a hunter and a dues-paying member of the National Rifle Association—carried signs condemning the women for violating their Second Amendment right to bear arms (or, as one hastily drawn sign put it, to arm bears).

Theresa picked at her cold scrambled eggs and limp bacon, rearranging them on her plate so it would look like she'd eaten something. Pretty soon, she told herself, she was going to have to do something about getting a life.

The bail application was heard a little after eleven. Stephen Barrow had gotten a call from Flynt Adams the night before, telling him to be there.

"Is there any chance he'll lower it?" he'd asked.

"There's a chance," Adams had told him. "Besides which, what do we have to lose?"

Jim Hall had heard from Adams at ten that morning. "Sure, I can make it," he said. "Wouldn't miss it for the world."

Unlike Adams, Hall already knew about the reports Judge McGee had received from the therapist and the pediatrician. He'd gotten a call first thing that morning from Judge McGee's law secretary, a bright young man fresh out of Albany Law School, who, as things would have it, was hoping to land a job with the Columbia County District Attorney's office. The way he figured things, there was no harm in getting on Jim Hall's good side.

Stephen looked around the courtroom, noticed there were no crack dealers or their families present this time. It was just him, his lawyer, the DA, and the court staff. And one old guy he hadn't seen before, who from time to time would break into a burst of coughing that threatened to be his last.

There was an "All rise!" as Judge Wainwright strode into the room and took his place. The clerk called the case, and Stephen and his lawyer stepped forward.

"Good morning," said the judge. "I understand we're on at the defense's request, on an application to reduce bail."

"That's correct," said Adams. "And I thank you for—"

"You're welcome. Before I hear you, I want to know if you're aware of these two reports Judge McGee has received, from Cathy Silverman and this, uh, Dr. Singh?" He held up some papers.

"Reports?"

To Stephen, the look on Flynt Adams's face said it all. He obviously had no clue.

"How about you, Mr. Hall?"

"First I'm hearing of it, your honor."

"Why don't we recess for a few minutes," the judge suggested, "while I have my clerk make copies of these for both sides."

For Stephen, the next half hour was an absolute blur. He read the reports over his lawyer's shoulder, phrases like "classic behavioral signs of sexual abuse," "consistent with sexual abuse," and "sexual abuse therefore cannot be ruled out" spinning wildly on the pages in front of him.

"What are they *saying*?" he asked Adams at one point.

"They're saying they think you've been sexually abusing your daughter."

"*Sexually abusing* her? *How?*"

"They don't say," Adams told him. "And they're not sure. But this is going to absolutely *kill* us."

And kill them it did. When they resumed, Adams made his bail application. He called the reports "nothing but speculation and innuendo," and asked the judge to disregard them. But it was clear that the wind had gone out of his sails; he knew he was done even before he'd begun.

Jim Hall conceded that the reports didn't quite rise to the level of establishing conclusively that Stephen had been abusing his daughter. "Still," he contended, "as the old saying goes, where there's smoke, there's fire. And I say there's enough smoke here, coming from two independent, court-appointed experts, to warrant raising this man's bail to two hundred and fifty thousand dollars. And that's the People's request."

Those *people* again, thought Stephen.

In the end, Judge Wainwright, to his credit, left the bail right where it was. He found the reports preliminary and "somewhat speculative." On the other hand, he was troubled enough by what was in them that he certainly wasn't going to *reduce* the bail.

"So, counselor," he asked Adams. "Is your client going be able to post the fifty thousand by the end of the day?"

"No, sir, he's not."

"Then why don't we spare him a difficult afternoon? Deputy, please take Mr. Barrow into custody."

And Stephen heard again the ratcheting sound of handcuffs opening, and saw a large man in a gray uniform walking toward him.

"Hands behind your back," the man said.

Then there was silence, broken only by the consumptive coughing fit of the older man who'd been taking notes while seated in the jury box, off to one side.

Downstairs in the building's basement level, they removed the handcuffs so Stephen could empty out his pockets. He was then searched up and down, the deputy apologizing as he patted Stephen's crotch area.

"You never know," he said.

Stephen nodded, not wanting to make trouble. Besides, he guessed there had to be a reason for it, like maybe he'd showed up for his bail application with a machine gun hidden in his undershorts. He was placed in a holding cell. The only other occupant was a black man, no doubt a crack dealer.

"Wha' they got *you* for, man?" he wanted to know.

"I took a picture of my daughter," Stephen said absently.

"Nekkid?"

"Excuse me?"

"Wit' no clothes on?"

Stephen nodded.

"Sheeeet," said the black man.

It dawned on Stephen that he probably shouldn't have answered the man, at least not truthfully. Weren't you always reading about other inmates *killing* people like him, or *castrating* them, as soon as the guards walked away? But the black man didn't say anything more, just shook his head slowly from side to side, and said "Sheeeet" again.

An hour later, Stephen was taken out of the holding cell by a deputy and led down a series of corridors. They stopped at a desk long enough for Stephen to be handed a blanket, an orange jumpsuit, and a pair of paper shoes. Then he was led down one last corridor, with barred cells on either side. The deputy used a huge key to unlock one of the cells, and Stephen stepped inside. It was square, maybe eight feet on each side. There was a cot on the far wall, a sink, and an exposed lidless toilet. In the middle of the ceiling was a bare lightbulb, protected by a wire cage. There was no window.

The door was slammed shut and locked behind him. The upper half of it had a cutout portion, with bars, so he could see the area of the corridor that was directly in front of him, but nothing else.

"Whatchoo in heah faw, Whitey?"

He couldn't see the man who was asking, and decided not to answer him.

"I said, *Whatchoo in heah faw?*"

"Murder," said Stephen.

It was a full two days before Theresa Mulholland learned that Stephen Barrow had been put in jail. She found out almost by accident, when she saw a note on the weekly assignment board saying that Tom Grady had been put back on the story, and that one of the things Neil Witt had suggested was for him to "try to get an interview with Barrow in jail."

Jail?

"What happened?" Theresa asked Grady.

"Couldn't make the bail," said Grady. "That, and it looks like he's been abusing his kid all along."

"*Abusing* her?"

"Yeah, as in *sexually* abusing her."

"Tom, that's *impossible*. It *can't* be true."

"You were there?"

"Yes, as a matter a fact. I drove up there to interview him, and I got snowed in and ended up having to spend the night. I'm telling you, Tom, this guy's a super parent. There's no way on *earth* he could have done anything to her."

"Well, there's a child therapist and an M.D. who think otherwise," said Grady. "But I'll be sure to bear in mind what you've told me."

It didn't take long for things to fall into a routine for Stephen. He'd expected jail to be like it was in the movies: hundreds of men banging spoons against the bars of their cells, arguing over which TV channel to watch, and gathering at mealtimes in a huge mess hall; race riots punctuating half-court basketball games in the exercise yard; mournful guitar strumming by a lone death-row prisoner late at night; and sadistic guards eager to mete out vicious beatings for the most trivial of infractions—all watched over by a stern but wise warden.

It was nothing like that.

Places like that they called *prisons*, Stephen soon learned, where you went to serve out your sentence. Columbia County was simply a *jail*—or more euphemistically, a *detention facility*—where you were kept while awaiting trial, if you weren't lucky enough to have the money to make bail. The total population fluctuated somewhere between a handful of inmates and a couple dozen. There was no mess hall; meals were slid through the bars of your door on a cardboard tray and picked up half an hour later. There were no fights over TV channels, because there was no TV; no half-court basketball games, because there was no exercise yard. There was no mournful guitar strumming by anyone on death row, because there was no death row, and because no musical instruments were permitted. The guards—who were actually deputy sheriffs—weren't sadistic. And there was no stern but wise warden, only a sheriff, who on the one appearance he made struck Stephen as neither stern nor particularly wise.

The cot was narrow and hard, the blanket thin and moth-eaten. The food was bland to the point of being tasteless, but was otherwise edible. The coffee—Stephen *assumed* it was coffee—was weak and lukewarm. Every third day, you were permitted a shower, three and a half minutes under a trickle of water that alternately froze and scalded you.

But by far the worst thing was that there was nothing to do, absolutely nothing. No books to read, no TV to watch, no radio to listen to. You could talk to the inmates you could see across the corridor, or those in the adjoining cells you *couldn't* see, so long as you were quiet about it. But for the most part, none of them had anything interesting to say, or cared much about what Stephen might have to say. So you sat and waited, and ate three times a day, and showered every third day. And you counted the days to your next court appearance. Stephen's was March third, a week and a half away from the time he first came in.

It might as well have been a year and a half.

On the seventh day, or maybe it was the eighth—in spite of the fact that he had nothing else to do, he still found it impossible to keep track of the days—Stephen was told he had a visitor. The only visitor he'd had up that point had been Flynt Adams, who'd dropped in to see him twice, to tell him he was working on his motions for the criminal case. Those visits had taken place in a special counsel room, where an inmate and his lawyer were permitted to sit at a table so they could go over court papers and stuff like that.

This was different.

This was what they called a *social visit*.

He was taken from his cell and led through the underground maze to a room that had tiny cubicles along one wall. Each cubicle had a chair, which faced a dirty, yellowish window. The windows had chicken wire in the glass. There was a phone, or at least the handset from a phone, which you picked up and used to talk to your visitor, who sat in another room, seated in an identical chair, holding an identical handset, on the other side of the chicken-wire window.

The visitor was an older man, thin and gray-haired. At first Stephen didn't recognize him, and figured there must be some mistake. Still, talking to someone else's visitor was better than talking to nobody at all. Stephen picked up the phone, and when the older man did the same, he said, "I'm Stephen Barrow. Who are you here to see?"

"You," said the man. And then he launched into a prolonged fit of coughing, which prompted Stephen to remember him. He'd been in the courtroom the day Judge Wainwright had put Stephen in.

"I'm Tom Grady," the man said, once his coughing had subsided. "I write for the *Hudson Valley Herald*." The phone connection, all two feet of it, was full of static, making it difficult to hear.

"What happened to Terry?" Stephen asked. He couldn't remember her last name.

"She got taken off the story."

"How come?"

"She only caught it in the first place 'cause I was out sick for a coupla days. I'm the regular crime reporter, see? So I'm the one who's going to do the follow-up, tell the readers your story."

"My story," Stephen echoed. There was something about this guy he didn't like. "What kind of a story *am* I?" he asked.

"That's entirely up to you."

Stephen had to wait through another coughing spasm for an explanation.

"The way I figure it," said Grady, "you're either a sick pervert, or you're just a dumb jerk locked up for what amounts to *felony stupidity.*"

Stephen managed a small smile.

"So what's it gonna be?" Grady asked. "You gonna let me help you, or not?"

"What is it you want to know?"

"Everything, start to finish."

"My lawyer told me that under no circumstances—"

"Kid, do yourself a favor, why don't you, and cut the crap. You been doing everything your lawyer told you to so far, right?"

"I guess so, pretty much."

"And look where it's got you."

He had a point. Still, Adams had been insistent. "He says we've got an excellent chance of beating this thing in court, and I should just be patient."

"*He says,*" Grady mimicked. "Lookit, willya? It's all the same to me. I get my paycheck at the enda the week either way. So to tell you the truth, I don't give a rat's ass one way or the other. I'm here to help you if you want me to. If you don't, hey, that's okay, too. But I got a deadline to meet and a story to write, and I'm going to write it, with or without your help. So it's your call, Barrow. Whaddaya say?"

"I guess," said Stephen, "it's going to have to be without me."

There'd been a reason Flynt Adams had told Stephen Barrow not to talk to anybody, especially now that he was in jail. Adams knew how inmates were always looking to get an edge.

Suppose one of them were to get in touch with the detective on his case, tell him that the guy accused of taking porno shots of his daughter had confided in him that he'd been doing it for years, and making money selling the photos? Next thing you knew, the guy was the DA's star witness at trial. And then, maybe six months later, after everyone had forgotten all about him, he'd quietly be released after serving two years of a fifteen-year sentence. So Adams knew how important it was for Stephen not to talk to anybody. And he'd let Stephen know, in no uncertain terms.

What's more, Flynt Adams had indeed told Stephen that, according to what he'd come up with while doing research for his motion papers on the criminal case, it was beginning to look like the law was on Stephen's side. The three felony charges had one thing in common: In order to win a conviction, the prosecution would have to prove "sexual conduct" by a child. The New York State Penal Law defined "sexual conduct" as "actual or simulated sexual intercourse, deviate sexual intercourse, sexual beastiality, masturbation, sadomasochistic abuse, or lewd exhibition of the genitals."

Since none of the other categories even began to fit the photograph, it was clear to Adams that Jim Hall would contend that it was the last category—*lewd exhibition of the genitals*—that the photo depicted. And since the genitals were obviously exhibited, the only question left—*in fact, the only question in the entire criminal case*—was whether or not that exhibition was *lewd*.

If it was, Stephen Barrow was guilty.

If it wasn't, he was innocent. Not just not guilty on some technicality, or some inability of the prosecution to prove its case. No, he'd be truly *innocent*.

Flynt Adams had *heard* of lawyers who'd had clients who were actually and truly one hundred percent innocent. He'd just never had one himself. Not till now, anyway.

Since the word *lewd* wasn't defined in the Penal Law, the

rule was that its normal meaning would control. Adams found his dictionary and looked it up.

lewd (lood), *adj.* **1.** Inclined to, characterized by, or inciting to lust or lechery. **2.** Obscene or indecent, as language, songs, etc. **3.** *Obs.* **a.** base or vile, esp. of a person. **b.** bad, worthless, or poor, esp. of a thing.

If the third meaning was obsolete, he figured he could safely forget about it. That left the first two. And of those, only the first made any sense, or took you anywhere in your analysis but in a never-ending circle. So could you look at the photo and conclude from it—and from it alone—that the child's genitals were displayed in such a way that they were "inclined to" (which to Adams had to mean *likely to*) "incite lust or lechery"? *Of course you couldn't.*

First, it was only a single photograph among many. (The one or two other partially nude shots were just that, the kind of photo any parent might take of a prepubescent child.) Next, there was no suggestion that his client had ever done anything like this before, no indication that he'd deliberately posed his daughter for the shot, compelled her to display herself that way, punished her if she refused, or rewarded her if she complied. As far as Adams knew, the DA had no evidence that Barrow had intended to exploit his daughter in any way—whether by selling the photo, sending it off to some pornographic magazine, posting it on the Internet, running off copies to share with friends or associates, or by any other method. Nor could the DA prove that Barrow had intended to gratify some strange sexual desire of his, or of anyone else's.

Quite to the contrary, Barrow's behavior after taking the photo demonstrated an *openness* he'd had about it, a matter-of-factness that belied any special interest in the subject matter. He'd taken the roll of exposed film to a local store for processing, had written his own name and phone number on the envelope, and had even brought his daughter along when he'd come to call for the prints the next day.

All it was was a photograph, plain and simple. And even though it might show bad taste, questionable judgment, and a lack of sensitivity on the part of the parent who'd taken it, none of those things made it *lewd*. Not to Flynt Adams, anyway. And, the way he saw it, not to anyone else who was willing to stop and think about it for a moment.

Like Justice Wainwright, for example.

All that was the good news.

The bad news was that at this stage of the proceedings, the prosecution didn't have to prove its case the way it would at trial, *beyond a reasonable doubt*. All Jim Hall would have to do to survive Flynt Adam's motion to dismiss would be to convince Judge Wainwright that the lewdness issue was a question for a jury to decide. Wainwright was a former district attorney himself, and his rulings in criminal cases tended to side with the prosecution. But he wasn't an *assassin*, a *hit man*—one of those judges whose greatest pleasure in life came from hurting defendants, and by extension, their lawyers.

He wasn't, for example, a Priscilla McGee.

The more he read, the more he thought about it, and the more he wrote, Flynt Adams was beginning to think that it was very possible—he didn't dare say *probable*—that Everett Wainwright might do the right thing. The judge knew how unpredictable a jury could be: they might convict Barrow, or they might not. But even if they did, there was a chance that some appellate court would reverse them. And whose fault would *that* be? The judge's, of course. Better to toss the thing out right now, save everybody the time, trouble, and expense.

At least that's the way things played out in Flynt Adams's little fantasy. And as he worked long into the night on his motion to dismiss the charges, his conscious goal was to make his argument so compelling that Wainwright would *have* to grant it, would have no choice *but* to toss the case out. Adams had once heard someone say, "If you think you can do some-thing, or you think you can't, you're probably right," and he'd adopted the saying as a sort of informal motto. Not that he'd made a sign of it and had it framed and hung on the wall above his desk, or anything corny like that. It was just something he liked, and thought about at times like this.

If Flynt Adams's optimism was of any consolation to Stephen Barrow, it would have been hard to tell from looking at him. Back in his cell after his brief visit with Tom Grady, Stephen sank onto his cot and draped a forearm across his eyes to block the glare of the lightbulb in the ceiling. By now he'd gotten into the habit of sleeping away most of the day. At first, he'd rebelled against what he recognized as an obvious symptom of depression, and had resisted the urge to sleep. But after a while, he stopped fighting and simply gave in to it. It came down to this: There was just nothing worth staying awake for.

He was in jail, and he was there for something he'd done. But it wasn't a crime, what he'd done, it couldn't possibly be. Yet here he was. And God only knew what was going on with Penny. He tried his best not to think about *that*. But it was impossible, of course.

So he slept.

On the tenth day of his confinement, the day before he was scheduled to go to court on his criminal case, he received a let-ter. It was the first piece of mail he'd gotten since he'd been in. It was a square white envelope, handed to him through the bars, and he took it to the back of his cell, where he sat down on his cot and turned it over and over again in his hands, as though it were some priceless piece of history. For he recog-nized the handwriting, even as he saw that the writer had tried to disguise it. It had no stamp or return address, and from the somewhat limited information provided on the front of it, he considered it nothing short of a miracle that it had found him.

MISTER STEPHEN BARROW
WHOSE IN THE JAIL THEY SEND YOU TOO
WHEN YOU LIVE IN EAST CHATHAM

He opened it up. Inside was a single lined sheet of composition paper. On it was a drawing, depicting the face of a child, its mouth a downward crescent, huge tears dripping from both eyes.

I LOVE YOU, DADDY

is all it said.
He cried for three hours.

THIRTEEN

JUDGE TO RULE FRIDAY ON SEX OFFENDER'S MOTION TO DISMISS

By Tom Grady
Special to the Hudson Valley Herald

Lawyers for Stephen Barrow, the East Chatham man accused of using his own 6-year-old daughter to star in pornographic photos, will go into Columbia County Supreme Court this Friday, March 3rd, and ask that the case against their client be dismissed on various technicalities, sources close to the investigation have advised the *Herald*.

Barrow, who is being held in the Hudson detention facility in lieu of $50,000 bail, faces 15 years in prison if convicted on the most serious of the charges. He will appear before Supreme Court Justice T. Everett Wainwright, a judge long known for being tough on sex offenders and protective of child victims. Justice Wainwright was originally appointed by Governor Cuomo and has been on the bench for nine and a half years. He is running for reelection this fall, and faces a primary challenge.

District Attorney Jim Hall, who is personally prosecuting Barrow, expressed confidence that all of the charges would withstand scrutiny. "This guy did what he did," he told this reporter, "and all you have to do to know that is to look at the evidence. The people of Columbia County deserve an oppor-

tunity to bring him to trial, and I have confidence
that Judge Wainwright understands that."

This reporter took the very unusual step of visit-
ing Barrow personally, in jail. Presented with an
opportunity to tell his side of the story in full, Barrow refused to comment.

The first thing that Everett Wainwright noticed, as he read
the article in chambers that Friday morning, was that they'd
got the story wrong, as they almost always did. The case
wasn't on today for him to decide the defense's motion to
dismiss; it was only on for the defense to *submit* its motion.
Once they did that, the case would be adjourned to give the
district attorney an opportunity to answer it, by putting in
papers of its own. And when that had happened, say a couple
of weeks from now, there'd be another adjournment, while
the court considered the issues and wrote a decision. So right
now, they were a good month away from an actual ruling.
Sure, all of those things could have been accomplished over
the span of one long adjournment. But in criminal cases,
especially where the defendant was incarcerated, Justice
Wainwright liked to put the case on his calendar every two
weeks or so—even if nothing much was going to happen in
court—just so the defendant would be brought up into the
courtroom, and the poor slob would know they hadn't forgotten about him.

The public didn't understand that, of course. And the
reporters, even though they knew better, would write that all
these court appearances were nothing but a waste of time and
taxpayers' money.

Still, the misstatement that there'd be a decision today was
hardly what bothered Everett Wainwright. No, what bothered
him was the thinly veiled threat contained in the article, the
reference to him as a Cuomo appointee. That was a back-
handed way of pointing out that he was a holdover liberal
Democrat in a predominantly conservative Republican county.

Then there was the reminder that he was not only up for reelection in the fall, but first faced a primary challenge from within his own party. And although the comment that he was known as tough on sex offenders and protective of children was accurate enough, to label a man accused of taking a couple of photos of his daughter a "sex offender" was a reach, and Tom Grady was smart enough to know that. So what the *Herald* was doing was setting Wainwright up, in a way. If he ruled in favor of the defendant and dismissed the case on the law (which was anything but a "technicality" to Justice Wainwright), the voters could conclude that he'd suddenly come out in favor of sex offenders and turned his back on children. Add to that Jim Hall's comment that a dismissal would have the effect of depriving the citizens of Columbia County an opportunity to try the defendant, and it was pretty easy to see how the *Herald* was doing its best to paint Wainwright into a corner.

Well, *fuck 'em*. Everett Wainwright was sixty-eight years old and nearing retirement age as it was. He'd be *damned* if he was going to knuckle under to the likes of a lush like Tom Grady. When the motion to dismiss and the DA's papers opposing it finally got to him, he'd decide it fair and square, just like he always did. As far as he was concerned, they could like it or lump it. And if it ended up costing him his seat on the bench, well, *fuck 'em all*, they could have that, too.

Stephen Barrow's court appearance lasted less than four minutes. Flynt Adams handed one copy of his motion papers to the DA, and another copy to the clerk. Jim Hall asked for two weeks to respond to them, and the judge adjourned the case to March 17.

"That's St. Patrick's Day," the clerk said.

"So?" said the judge. "You the grand marshal of some parade I don't know about?"

"No, sir," said the clerk.

"Then it's March seventeen," the judge repeated.

And that was that.

Justice Wainwright wasn't the only one who saw Tom Grady's article that morning. Theresa Mulholland read it over coffee, and couldn't believe her eyes. To begin with, the headline itself—and that had to be Neil Witt's touch—was totally uncalled for. Stephen Barrow was no *sex offender*; all he was accused of doing was taking a photo of his daughter, a photograph that might or might not turn out to be "lewd" under the law. And to characterize that as *using her to star in pornographic photos*—what had they done, taken the *Herald* and turned it overnight into the *New York Post*, or the *National Enquirer*?

She dialed the paper's number and tried to speak with Grady, but he wasn't in. Of course he wasn't; it wasn't eleven yet. She asked for Neil Witt, and launched into him as soon as he picked up.

"What are you *doing* with this story?" she demanded to know. "All of a sudden, the guy's a *convicted sex offender*?"

"Calm down, Terry. It doesn't say anything about *convicted*."

"How about *using her to star in pornographic photos*? Where do you get *that shit* from?"

"That's precisely the allegation," said Witt. "And that's exactly how we've portrayed it. The East Chatham man 'accused of using his own six-year-old daughter—' "

"I know what it says, Neil. I've got it right in front of me. And it *stinks*, every last word of it. And you *know* it."

"I know nothing of the sort."

"Will you let me write an editorial on the case, to at least provide some balance?"

"No."

"How about a letter to the editor?"

"From one of our own staff reporters?"

"I'll sign it 'Anonymous.' "

"Remember when I said you had a conflict on this case, Terry?"

Theresa remembered.

"Well, it's showing. You're off the case. *Stay* off the case. And while I've got you on the phone, I'd like you to do a piece on the animal shelter over in—"

"*Fuck* the animal shelter!" Theresa shouted, and slammed down the phone as hard as she could.

Another week went by, more or less. It became increasingly difficult for Stephen to keep track of the days. With no window in his cell, he was never quite certain if it was day or night. The lightbulb in his ceiling was no help—it stayed on twenty-four hours a day. Something about suicide prevention, one of the deputies had explained to him. Although it was hard to see how he could kill himself: They'd taken away his belt and his shoelaces, and except for court appearances, he was required to wear his orange jumpsuit and paper slippers at all times. Then again, maybe they were afraid he'd fashion an orange noose out of his jumpsuit, or stuff his slippers down his throat until he suffocated.

On the seventeenth day of his confinement (then again, it might have been the sixteenth or the eighteenth; he couldn't be sure), one of the deputies, a decent man whose nameplate had REYNOLDS printed on it, pushed a newspaper through the bars and said, "Check it out, Barrow. Page twenty-one."

He took the paper. It was an issue of the *Columbia County Advertiser*. He wasn't sure, but he didn't think that was the one Terry worked for, or Tom Grady, either. It didn't seem to be much of a paper. The big news on page 1 was the unseasonably warm weather. Page 21 was way at the end, the inside of the back page.

It took him a while to find the article, and when he found it, he realized it wasn't an article at all that the deputy named Reynolds had meant to point out to him, but one of those letters people were always writing to newspapers or magazines.

Dear Advertiser:

I am a reporter for the *Hudson County Herald*, or perhaps I should say a former reporter, in the event you decide to print this letter. I'm writing to protest the *Herald*'s unfair treatment of Stephen Barrow, the East Chatham man accused of taking several nude photos of his daughter.

In a February 22 story, run under the misleading (not to mention factually incorrect) headline, "JUDGE TO RULE FRIDAY ON SEX OFFENDER'S MOTION TO DISMISS," the *Herald* accuses Mr. Barrow of having used his own daughter "to star in pornographic photos." Nothing could be further from the truth.

As a staff reporter for the *Herald* who was originally assigned to the story, I had occasion to interview Stephen Barrow at great length. I came away convinced that he is a law-abiding citizen who is guilty, at very most, of having exercised bad judgment in photographing his child undressed. More important, I found him to be a wonderful father who is absolutely devoted to his daughter in only the healthiest way imaginable.

The people of this county owe it to Mr. Barrow to refrain from labeling him and prejudging his case. He is entitled to the same presumption of innocence you or I would be, were one of us accused of wrongdoing. The *Herald* does a grave disservice not only to Mr. Barrow, but to its readers, and to our system of justice as well.

Theresa Mulholland
Canaan, New York

He read the letter a dozen times before returning the paper to Reynolds.

"Nice letter," said the deputy. "Wonder what the *Herald*'ll have to say about it."

Stephen could only nod. There was a lump in his throat at the moment, and he was afraid if he said anything, his voice might break and give him away. You weren't supposed to cry in jail, he knew. You were supposed to be tough, like you could handle whatever came your way—good, bad, or indifferent.

But the letter was something else.

The letter was special.

Over the next four days, Stephen became more friendly with the deputy named Reynolds. That is, if you could call exchanging twenty words a day with someone *friendly*. But it was a lot more of a relationship than he had with any of the other deputies, who uniformly eyed him with that special measure of distaste reserved for the lowest of the low, the pedophile. Still, none of them actually mistreated him in any way. They didn't beat him, spit at him, cite him for imagined infractions of the rules, or poison his food.

In jail, Stephen had come to realize, you became grateful when people didn't beat you or poison you. And if somebody actually went out of his way to have a *conversation* with you, however brief or insignificant, you found yourself almost overwhelmed with gratitude. Which was pretty much how Stephen responded when, on the fifth day after reading Theresa's letter, Reynolds handed him the latest edition of the *Herald*.

"Thank you so much," said Stephen.

"You won't be thanking me after you've read it," the deputy warned him.

And he was right, of course.

HERALD REPORTER
TERMINATED OVER BIAS IN
SEX CASE

By Tom Grady
Special to the Hudson Valley Herald

The *Herald* has terminated the employment of
Theresa Mulholland, a staff reporter for the past
four years, following an internal investigation into
alleged improprieties committed by Ms. Mulholland while she was covering the story of Stephen
Barrow, the East Chatham man accused of sexually
abusing his 6-year-old daughter by forcing her to
pose naked so he could take pornographic photographs of her.

The investigation was touched off when Ms.
Mulholland took the unprecedented step of writing a letter to the *Columbia County Advertiser*, in
which she protested the *Herald*'s coverage of the
case as being biased against Barrow.

Although the tone of Ms. Mulholland's letter
portrayed her as someone whose only concern was
for the defendant's right to receive a fair trial (a
right the *Herald* certainly endorses), an internal
investigation spearheaded by Neil Witt, the managing editor of the *Herald*, revealed that Ms. Mulholland herself was a witness to certain aspects of
the case, and had been removed from covering the
story solely for that reason.

Even more significantly, it has been learned that
shortly after Barrow's arrest in South Chatham on
February 12, Ms. Mulholland, without the knowledge or permission of her supervisors, drove to
Barrow's home on Hilltop Drive and spent the
night with him.

"We have a reputation to uphold," said Witt,
"and a duty to report the news to our readers, free
from bias. While I regret having to terminate the

employment of any staff member, this sort of behavior cannot be tolerated."

Barrow, who is currently incarcerated awaiting trial, next appears in Columbia County Supreme court on March 17. He faces 15 years in prison if convicted.

Stephen was stunned.

Not only had he screwed up his own life, and that of his daughter; now he'd gone and gotten Terry fired as well. To say nothing of what he'd done to her reputation, by allowing her to *spend the night with him.*

What was he *supposed* to have done? Thrown her out into the *blizzard,* so she could *freeze to death?* The paper didn't bother to mention the foot and a half of snow, or the fact that her car was stuck in the ditch alongside his driveway, did it? Or the fact that she'd slept fully clothed on a sofa in the living room, while he was behind a closed door in his bedroom. No, they didn't care about *that.* All they cared about was that she'd *spent the night with him.*

That, and the fact that he was likely to spend the next fifteen years of his life in prison. They always managed to get *that* in, too. Just in case there was somebody out there who thought what he'd done wasn't such a big deal.

Well, it *was* a big deal. He knew that now. He'd been finding out the hard way.

"Some development, huh?" It was Reynolds.

"Yeah," said Stephen, "some development." He wasn't afraid to speak this time; there was no lump in his throat, no tears welled up behind his eyes.

What there was, was *anger.*

As for Theresa Mulholland, she was *way* beyond anger. The job? They could *have* the damn job. She'd given up on that the day she'd written the letter to the *Advertiser.* Even before that, when she thought about it. Back when Neil Witt had taken her off the story because of what he called a *conflict of interest*. Or when he'd sent her up to Albany to eat breakfast and listen to *Hillary Clinton*. Or when he'd told her no, she couldn't do an editorial piece, he needed her for a story on the *humane society*. Whatever the final straw had been, her parting company from the *Herald* had been a long time coming. And she had only one thing to say about that.

Good riddance.

It had only begun to dawn on her that the unique circumstances of her firing might mean she'd never work for another newspaper. But she didn't have any time to worry about that. Not right now, anyway. There were some other things she had to do first.

Stephen was back in court that Friday. Again, however, it was a non-event. One of Jim Hall's assistants showed up in Hall's place and submitted a written response to the defense's motions. Justice Wainwright looked it over and said, "I'm going to need a couple of weeks to decide this. How's April third, gentlemen?"

April 3 was apparently fine with both sides. To Stephen, it no longer made a difference: Dates had lost all meaning to him. He could no longer remember the order of the months. Every once in a while, it would occur to him that he hadn't made his mortgage payment, or paid this bill or that. He would experience a moment of intense panic, but it would soon pass. He was in jail, after all; he couldn't do those things; someone else would have to take care of them. The rational part of him knew that no one else would, but it was his way of overcoming the panic: He simply blotted the problem out, pretended it wasn't his to worry about.

The latest adjournment of two and a half weeks was the longest yet. As Stephen and his lawyer left the courtroom— Adams by the front door, Stephen by the side one—Adams had tried to tell Stephen it was an encouraging sign, and could mean that Justice Wainwright needed the extra time because he intended to write an opinion dismissing the charges. "I don't want to get your hopes up too high," he said, "but this could be our best chance ever. Because if this case ever goes before a jury, there's no telling what *they'll* do."

Stephen had always thought a jury was his best chance. Now he was being told it was nothing but a crapshoot, and that his best hope lay with the judge, the same judge who'd put him in jail.

The deputy named Reynolds, the closest thing to a friend Stephen had made in jail, was transferred to another location. The deputy who replaced him, a large, mustached man who seemed to spend most of his shift discussing his personal business on the telephone, hinted that Reynolds's undoing had been his habit of befriending the inmates. He made it clear that he intended to avoid that temptation, and he kept his word. As a result, Stephen's access to the outside world, as limited as it had been before, now became nonexistent. No letters arrived for him; no newspapers found their way between the bars of his cell; no small talk was offered. He was reduced to spending virtually all his time lying on his cot, waiting. Waiting for the next meal, the next change of shift, the next shower day, the next court appearance.

Physically, he knew he was deteriorating. Even without a mirror to look into or belt notches to measure his waist, he could tell that he was losing weight. Yet he found himself increasingly repulsed by the food, which he now picked at and rearranged on the cardboard tray, and left uneaten. He was aware that his body had lost much of its muscle tone, and knew he should be doing exercises of some sort. But he didn't; he simply couldn't muster the resolve to force himself. Once he'd been able to do fifty push-ups in a single set; now he collapsed before reaching ten. The rest of his body was doing no better:

His teeth ached and his gums would bleed if he so much as ran his tongue over them. He had a foul taste in his mouth that wouldn't go away. His hair needed cutting, and his face needed shaving. He was a mess.

Worse yet, he didn't care.

Lying on his back, his forearm across his eyes in what had become his standard position, he came to realize that as happy as he'd been over the past couple of years, his entire existence had been totally focused on just two things, to which he'd been completely devoted—his daughter and his writing. And now that they'd taken both of those away from him, he was left with nothing to live for. He began to think of his life as a failure, and of himself as a pathetic creature, in some way fully deserving of everything that had happened to him.

In spite of the fact that his case was all he had to think about—he steadfastly refused to think about his daughter, for fear he'd go truly insane if he allowed himself to—he now found himself thinking less and less about it. For a time, he'd pinned his hopes on the outcome of the criminal trial. If only he could win that, he'd reasoned, everything else would fall into place. Seeing that he'd done nothing wrong to his daughter, the judge in the civil case would have no choice but to restore Penny's custody to him. Everything would return to the way it had been before.

But the more he thought about it, the more he realized that wasn't so. That other judge, the woman—he could no longer remember her name—hated him, had it in for him for some reason he didn't understand. So even if he somehow managed to win the criminal case, she was going to do everything in her power to see to it that Penny stayed with Ada. And she was the judge. She could do whatever she wanted to.

So in the end, it made no difference *what* happened. It simply didn't matter.

Nothing mattered anymore.

———

A week went by. March 22 came and went, making it a month since they'd first put Stephen in jail. He wouldn't have known it, though, had it not been for the fact that a doctor came by to check him, explaining that state law required a monthly examination. He was an older man who wore a rumpled suit and spoke with an Eastern European accent Stephen couldn't quite place. Hungarian, maybe, or Czech. He took Stephen's pulse and blood pressure, and pointed a flashlight down his throat and into his ears.

"Fine," he said. "You're doing just fine."

Flynt Adams came to see him, to remind him they'd be going to court Monday to get Justice Wainwright's decision on the dismissal motion. He seemed hopeful.

"What's today?" Stephen asked.

"Saturday."

"No, I mean the date."

Adams looked at his watch. "The first," he said. "April first."

Something came back to Stephen, as though from far away. April first. April first. *April Fools' Day,* that was it. He and Penny loved to play April Fools' jokes on each other. He'd had to tell her it was April Fools' Day, of course; she was still too young to keep track of such things herself. But as soon as he'd told her, she got into it. One year, she'd hidden the keys to the Jeep. He'd retaliated by telling her she had dirt all over her forehead, and made her go into the bathroom to see. Another time, she'd pretended she had a terrible stomachache. He'd believed her, and they'd been in the Jeep, all ready to race to the emergency room (he was terrified it was her appendix, about to burst and kill her), when she'd burst into laughter and—

"Where are you?"

"Huh?"

It was Flynt Adams's face in front of him, and they were sitting at a table in the counsel room. "Are you okay?" Adams was asking him.

"Me? I'm fine," said Stephen. "It's April Fools' Day."

"And?"

And nothing. The old lump was suddenly back in Stephen's throat, and he knew better than to try to explain.

"You might want to think about shaving," said Adams, running his hand over his own chin, as if to remind Stephen what shaving was. "And combing your hair. You know, before we go to court?"

Stephen nodded. But he was having trouble concentrating, and following what Adams was saying. His thoughts kept wandering all over the place. Right now, he was trying to come up with a good trick to play on Penny this year, something that would really fool her and make her laugh.

FOURTEEN

Even as Flynt Adams clung to his hopes for a dismissal, and Stephen Barrow had abandoned all hope, T. Everett Wainwright (he seldom used the T., and never what it stood for, figuring his name already sounded pompous enough without the addition of *Tillinghast* to it) sat by a fire that Saturday night, wrestling with the case.

He'd read Adams's motion to dismiss a dozen times, and Jim Hall's response almost as many. He'd been to the library, and he'd done the research. In his gut, he agreed with the defense's position. The photograph that exhibited the child's genitals (and you could forget the other photos, the one or two nude ones; they were *nothing*) wasn't "lewd" *per se*, in and of itself. Adams was right. There had to be some additional showing—for example, that the father had deliberately posed her like that, or had intended to make some sexual or commercial use of the photo, either for his own gratification or someone else's.

Wainwright had to keep reminding himself that the case wasn't at the trial stage. He wasn't being asked to find Barrow guilty or not guilty, or even to rule on whether a jury's convicting him could stand up on appeal. If he were, the appropriate standard would be whether the prosecution had succeeded in proving that the photo was lewd, and doing so beyond a reasonable doubt. And they hadn't.

But they didn't have to—not yet, anyway. All they had to do

at this stage of the proceedings was to show that there was a triable issue of fact, a question that a reasonable jury might decide either way. If you looked at it that way, the prosecution was entitled to an opportunity to bring in witnesses who could shed light on the defendant's state of mind. Did Barrow have a drawer full of similar photos, for example? Did he post them on the Internet, share them with others, send them off to magazines? Had he forced his daughter to pose like that, threatened her if she refused, or rewarded her if she complied?

Jim Hall hadn't proved anything of the sort at the grand jury; a reading of the transcript made that clear. Hall had simply relied on Barrow's possession of the photo and his admission to the investigator that he'd been the one who'd taken it. Then he'd passed the photo around. Was that enough?

"Dear, it's after midnight." The judge's wife worried about him when he worked too hard. He'd already had two heart attacks over the past ten years, and his doctor had warned him to take it easy.

"I'll be up soon," he said.

"You can't still be thinking of dismissing that case, can you?" His wife was a lawyer, though she no longer practiced. She knew the question her husband was wrestling with, and shared his view (he having been persuaded by Flynt Adams's motion papers) that the case turned on the issue of whether the prosecution had established that the display of the child's genitals was lewd. Personally, she thought that was for the jury to decide. Carla Wainwright was active in politics, a Democrat on the local school board, which gave her and her husband something in common: They were both endangered species. Only she'd been a quicker study when it came to adapting.

"Yes," he said. "I'm still thinking about it."

"They'll *crucify* you."

"*They?*"

"The party."

"The *party*," he repeated, giving the ashes in the fireplace a poke. "You make it sound like we're living in the old Soviet Union," he said.

"Well, we are, in a way. You dismiss that indictment, you'll see how long they let you keep wearing that robe."

"There's more to life than that robe, you know."

"Yes," she said. "There's bills and taxes and medical coverage, and things like that. You're sixty-eight years old. What are you going to do, start looking for a *job* at your age?"

"Yes," he said. "I might just do that. You go on to bed. I'll be up in a little while."

She shook her head and gave him a kiss on the forehead before walking out of the room. As soon as she was gone, he put another log on the fire.

The way Jim Hall saw it, it was a no-brainer. If Wainwright dismissed the indictment, the voters would eat him alive. In rural upstate New York, *soft on crime* was about as bad a label as you could hang on a candidate, right up there with *opposes the NRA, favors higher taxes,* and *supports partial-birth abortions.*

No, when it came down to it, T. Everett had no choice. He might hem and haw a bit, but eventually he'd do the right thing and let the case go to trial. And a trial was all Jim Hall needed. Convincing a Columbia County jury that they knew a lewd photo when they saw one? Shit, he could do that with one hand tied behind his back an' the other playin' pocket pool.

As he lathered his face to shave for the morning's court appearance, Flynt Adams could already feel the butterflies beginning to stir. Not that there was anything he'd actually have to *do* in court, in terms of performing. While his presence—like that of the defendant and the DA—was required, his role would be pretty much limited to that of an observer, albeit a keenly interested one. Today was Justice Wainwright's day: He'd either have the balls to throw the case out, or cave in to all the political pressure he must be feeling, and say he couldn't.

And if he couldn't, it would mean a trial. Not today or tomorrow, but within the next few weeks or months. And it would be a trial Flynt Adams might well be able to win, a trial that would mean significantly more money for him, with maybe even a little media exposure thrown in. But at the same time, a trial he was afraid of. Because Flynt Adams knew this about trials: They could go either way. When it came right down to it, they were the criminal justice system's equivalent of saying a prayer, closing your eyes, and rolling the dice.

He felt the nick, and waited for the blood to appear. If he'd been going to the office to spend the day doing paperwork, he could have shaved with his left hand. But on court days, no matter how careful he was, he always managed to cut himself.

Always.

Of all the players, only Stephen Barrow wasn't nervous. It wasn't that he was feeling more confident than the others; by this time he'd lost every shred of confidence he'd ever had. No, Stephen's lack of nerves was simply a reflection of the fact that he'd reached a point that was beyond worrying, beyond understanding, and dangerously close to beyond caring.

Sitting in the holding pen behind the courtroom, Stephen looked like a beaten man. In the six weeks he'd now been in jail, he'd lost nearly twenty pounds. His clothes—and for court they'd brought him his *street clothes* to put on, the ones he happened to be wearing the day they put him in—had become several sizes too large for him. When he stood, he had to use one hand to hold the waist of his pants closed: Without a belt, they'd fall off otherwise. His laceless shoes felt too big, and in order to keep them from slipping off when he walked, he had to slide his feet along in a shuffle, instead of lifting one after the other.

Dark circles surrounded his eyes, and although he'd shaved that morning, his face looked gray. His skin seemed to have lost all its elasticity: It hung from his face slackly, as though somebody had ordered it in a size too large for his features. His whole body sagged, even his mouth hung slightly open, and a tiny spittle of drool would drip from it when he forgot—or simply didn't bother—to swallow.

"Barrow!" called a deputy. "Let's go!"

They unlocked the gate to the holding pen, and Stephen stepped out. They handcuffed him behind his back, the immediate result being that his pants slipped down to his hipbones and threatened to fall to his ankles. Noticing, one of the deputies rolled up the waist, yanking the crotch up painfully as he did it. Stephen followed them out into the courtroom, doing his little shuffle, and took his place next to Flynt Adams, facing the judge.

"Good morning," said the judge. It was the same one.

"Good morning," said the lawyers.

"With respect to the defense's motion to dismiss," said the judge, "I confess I'm quite troubled by the apparent lack of evidence offered by the People at the grand jury on the issue of whether the photograph, in and of itself, rises to the level of constituting a 'sexual performance.' Were this a trial without a jury, and Mr. Hall could make no stronger a showing on this point, I would be compelled to find the defendant not guilty. That said, it is *not* a trial, and the law applicable to this stage of the proceedings requires me to give Mr. Hall an opportunity to go forward and see what additional evidence, if any, he can come up with. The defense's motion to dismiss is therefore denied. This being a jail case, I'm giving it a preference. Both sides are given two weeks to get ready for trial. We'll set this down for April seventeenth, for jury selection. *If* the defense wants a jury, that is. Next case."

Flynt Adams followed Stephen and the deputies back to the holding pen. "We may have lost the motion," he said, "but did you hear what Wainwright said at the end there?"

Stephen confessed that he'd heard little and understood less.

"He's telling us to waive a jury," said Adams, his eyes bright with excitement. "He's saying, if the DA can't come up with some more evidence, he'll acquit you. And there *is* no more evidence. So what do you say? Should we put it in Wainwright's hands, and sign a jury waiver?"

Stephen shrugged. He had no idea what his lawyer was talking about. Why would they want to wave at a jury? Was that even proper? "It's up to you," he said.

"Then let's do it," said Flynt Adams.

Jim Hall understood the implications of Justice Wainwright's ruling every bit as well as Flynt Adams did. Immediately after court, he gathered his staff around him in his office. And if any of them thought they'd been invited to celebrate the morning's victory, he set them straight pretty quickly.

"Okay," he told them, "we won that battle, but we're in danger of losing the war. You heard the judge. He all but came right out and told Adams to try the case nonjury in front of him. And unless we can come up with something else, he's going to go ahead and *acquit* that pervert."

"How about the stuff from the search warrant?" suggested Hall's investigator, Ed Sprague. "Like that 'Love, Stephen' card?"

"That's a nice touch," said Hall. "But it doesn't really zero in on the photo."

"What about the gynecologist's report?" asked Hank Bournagan, pronouncing the word *jynecologist*. "You know, that his findings were 'consistent with sexual abuse'? Couldn't that help?"

"Prob'ly not," said Hall. "Knowing Wainwright, he wouldn't even let that in. He'd consider it evidence of an uncharged crime. But you may be on the right track. How 'bout that *other* doctor, the therapist?"

"Silverman?"

"Yeah. Maybe *she* can help us out. Give her a call, why don't you. Find out if she's still seeing the kid. See what she can come up with."

Cathy Silverman was most definitely still seeing the kid. Aside from her own her own heartfelt certainty that Penny Barrow had been sexually abused by her father and needed ongoing therapy to deal with the trauma she'd suffered as a result, Silverman was continuing to see the child for two additional reasons. First, referrals from judges and lawyers made up a significant portion of her practice, and she sensed (rightly or wrongly) that those who made the referrals to her *wanted* her to find abuse. After all, she almost always found it, and they kept referring her more cases. Beyond that, there was the practical aspect of it: The bottom line was that Cathy Silverman's livelihood depended upon her finding abuse. She'd been seeing the Barrow child for six weeks now, twice a week, at the rate of $250 a visit. That added up to the tidy sum of three thousand dollars. And the longer she saw the child, the more she'd make. Throw in some extra hours for preparing her reports, meeting with the lawyers, talking on the telephone, and testifying in court, and pretty soon Cathy would be able to buy that Subaru Forester she'd had her eye on. And the best part of it was that she didn't even have to feel guilty about billing the county for her services. Her fee was being paid by Stephen Barrow—the very man who she believed was responsible for his daughter's needing therapy in the first place.

Now *there* was justice for you!

She picked up her phone on the first ring and answered, "Cathy Silverman."

"Hi, Dr. Silverman," said a young man. "This is Hank Bournagan, over at the DA's office in Hudson. I'm calling you about Penny Barrow."

"Yes, that poor child."

"How's she doing?"

"I think we're making a little progress," said Silverman. "But it takes time, you know. They're slow to open up."

"Yes, I understand. The thing is, Mr. Hall was wondering if you'd come up with anything new yet."

"*New*. Like what?"

"Oh, anything at all. Like if there'd been other photo sessions, videos, other kids involved, any *props* used. What her father had had to do in order to get her to pose like that. You know, that sort of stuff."

"Well," said Silverman, "nothing along those lines yet. But I've got her scheduled for this afternoon. I'll see what I can do."

"Good," said Hank Bournagan. "In the meantime, why don't you write down my phone number? Just so you have it handy."

It was Friday of that week when Stephen was called out of his cell. Though by that time, Stephen had lost all track of time. It had been almost seven weeks now that he'd been in jail, and he'd lost the ability to estimate the time of day, name the day or date, or even say with any degree of certainty what month it was. He knew Flynt Adams came to see him once a week at least, sometimes more, but only because Adams himself had told him so. He knew he was supposed to have a trial on April 17, and remembered signing a paper for Adams, saying he was giving up his right to a jury, and would instead be having a something called a bench trial. Yet he had no real idea of how far off in the future that would be, at least not in any meaningful terms.

So when they'd handed him his street clothes through the bars and told him to change into them, he'd guessed his trial was about to start. That was the only time they had him take off his orange jumpsuit, after all: for court appearances.

"What day is today?" he asked the deputy, expecting to hear that it was indeed the 17.

"Friday."

"No, the number," said Stephen. "The date."

"The seventh."

To Stephen, it sounded enough like the seventeenth to confirm his suspicion. Either he'd misheard the deputy, or he'd misheard the judge last time they'd been in court. Either way, it seemed the moment had finally come. He ran his hand over his face, and wished he'd thought to shave. He did his best to smooth his hair into place. He didn't want his lawyer to be angry with him.

He followed the deputy down the corridor as instructed, only vaguely aware that they were taking a different route to the courtroom this time. They stopped at a small desk, where another deputy sat, just inside a large gate.

"You got Barrow's papers?" the first one asked.

"Yeah, right here."

He was handed a pen and told to sign his name beneath a lot of fine print. Evidently it was different when you were on trial, more formal. When he went to sign his name, he found it difficult, not having written anything for so long a time, but he did his best.

The deputy at the desk looked at Stephen's signature for a long time, comparing it with something on another piece of paper, before nodding to the first deputy. Then he stood up and unlocked the gate, motioning Stephen to step through.

"Hold it," he said, and Stephen stopped, certain he'd done something wrong. But the deputy only wanted to hand him a slip of paper. Stephen looked at it. All it said was, "April 17, 9:30 A.M."

"What's this?" Stephen asked.

"A reminder," said the deputy.

"Of what?"

"Your next court date."

"Isn't it today?"

"No."

Stephen frowned. He had no idea what was going on. It was as if the two deputies were speaking in some dialect he didn't quite understand.

"You still don't get it, do you?" the first deputy asked him. And when Stephen just looked at him blankly, he said, "Follow me."

They walked down another corridor, a long one Stephen couldn't remember having ever been in. At the end was another gate, where someone stood just on the other side of the bars. But because it was bright down at that end, behind the person, he couldn't see who it was.

It wasn't until they were nearly at the very end of the corridor that the deputy turned to Stephen and said, almost matter-of-factly, "Your bond has been posted. You're going home." By that time, they'd drawn close enough to the person waiting on the other side of the gate for Stephen to see that she had red hair and very green eyes.

FIFTEEN

It had taken Theresa Mulholland three full weeks to post the fifty-thousand-dollar bond required to get Stephen Barrow out of jail. She'd persuaded her brother to put up the deed of his home, which still left her almost fifteen thousand short. She'd emptied her own savings account, which had just under eight thousand in it. Then, over the next two weeks, she'd borrowed from anyone she could—other family members, friends, acquaintances—until she'd made up the difference.

Why had she done that?

In trying to explain her actions much later, Theresa would put it this way: "Look, I know it didn't make sense, like there was nothing rational about it. I mean, I barely knew this guy. But I did know a couple of things about him. I knew he loved his little girl, and could never have done anything to take advantage of her. That was plain to see. And I knew he wasn't going to run away and abandon her. So as crazy as it was for me to do it, at least I was pretty sure the money would be safe."

At this point, Theresa would stop for a moment. "But there's more to it than that," she'd admit. "First I get myself stuck in the snow trying to sneak an exclusive out of this guy. He probably could have had me arrested for trespassing if he'd wanted to. Instead what does he do? He ends up taking *care* of me, seeing to it that I don't *freeze* to death. Next thing, I go and lose my job over it. Now I've suddenly got all this free time on my hands, and nothing to do with it but obsess about the guy and his problem. I got to the point where I convinced myself that it was meant to be, that it was my own personal *destiny* to help him.

"Sure, there were times I knew I should back off, when I realized posting his bail wasn't my responsibility. So I'd put things on hold for a day or two, tell myself to mind my own business. Then I'd see him in court—I kept going to court each time the case was on, I couldn't help it—and each time he looked worse and worse. What finally drove me over the edge was that last time, when the judge said he wanted to dismiss the case but couldn't. By that time Stephen looked so thin, and—and *beaten*. He could barely hold his head up. The thought even occurred to me that he might not *live* through this, that he really might die in jail. Not from being killed by somebody else, or anything like that, but from just wasting away. You know, like you hear about some animal that gets put in a zoo, and it won't eat, and after a while it just dies. At that point, I knew I had no choice, I *had* to get him out. There was simply no way I could have lived with myself if I hadn't done it, and he'd died in there. And after all, the more I thought about it, the more I realized it was only *money* I was talking about, right?"

Wrong.

Theresa had been operating under the assumption that she could post the bond, pick up Stephen at the jail, and give him a ride home. Sure, she'd seen how bad he'd looked in court at the beginning of the week, but she figured that the simple act of getting out would snap him out of his funk. A hot bath, some good food, a sound night's sleep, and he'd be well on the road to recovery.

What she hadn't counted on was just how close to the bottom Stephen had sunk. When she'd finished making all the arrangements, signing all the papers, bringing the release order around to the entrance of the jail, and waiting there for an hour while they did whatever it was they had to do inside, there finally came a time when one of the guards had walked

Stephen toward her. He'd looked up and had to have seen her standing there, just outside the front gate. Even once they'd opened the gate and let him walk through it, she wasn't sure he'd recognized her, or grasped what was happening. On the way to her car, he'd walked—*shuffled* was more like it—all stooped over, like her grandfather used to. He smelled. He mumbled to himself. In the car, he took turns squinting and blinking, even though the day was overcast.

"Your place or mine?" she asked, intending it as a joke, trying to pry a smile out of him.

"Mine," he said, straight-faced. "Penny . . ." But the thought drifted off, unfinished.

So she took him home, to his place. But when they got there, and she helped him up the steps, it all seemed strange and frightening to him. He didn't seem to know how to turn the lights on, or where the matches were to light the wood-burning stove. He kept looking around, as if he couldn't quite place his surroundings, didn't quite remember this place he was sitting in.

His own home.

By this time, Theresa knew there was no way she could leave him alone like that. Her earlier thought, that she could simply give him a ride home, now struck her as foolishly naïve. He was simply in no shape to take care of himself. Left alone, it was only a question of whether he'd freeze to death, starve, or burn the house down first. So she looked at it this way: She'd already been his surety and his chauffeur; now, it seemed, she was about to become his nurse.

But if taking that next step seemed even more bizarre than the earlier ones, Theresa's later explanation would at least have the virtue of consistency.

"I had no choice," she would say.

Word of Stephen Barrow's release spread quickly. Flynt Adams found out that very afternoon, when he drove to the jail to check on his client only to learn he was no longer there. Tom Grady wrote a follow-up piece for the *Hudson Valley Herald*, in which he questioned the wisdom of allowing bail for those accused of sexual crimes against children. Stephen's ex-wife, Ada, phoned her lawyer, Jane Sparrow, demanding that an order of protection be issued, prohibiting Stephen from going anywhere within a ten-mile radius of their daughter. Sparrow told her there was already an order in force (though one slightly less restrictive in its terms), and if Stephen violated it, all she had to do was notify the sheriff's office, and they'd arrest him on the spot for contempt.

Both of the judges were surprised, but both were also pleased on one level—Everett Wainwright because he never really thought Stephen Barrow belonged in jail in the first place and had been surprised it took him so long to get out, and Priscilla McGee because Barrow's release would give her additional leverage to force him to catch up on back alimony and child support he owed his ex-wife, and pay the bills from the physician and the therapist, which had begun to pile up. When a defendant was in jail, after all, there wasn't all that much you could force him to do.

But of all the parties touched by the case in one way or another, the one most heartened by the news was, surprisingly enough, the man whose job it would be to send Stephen Barrow *back* to jail. Reached by the sheriff only moments after Barrow had walked out the main gate, District Attorney Jim Hall turned to his assistant, Hank Bournagan, and smiled broadly.

"Guess who just made bail?" he asked. And then, without waiting for an answer, he said, "Our friend Stephen Barrow."

"Bummer," said Bournagan.

"Au contrairy," said Hall, whose French was pretty much on a par with his Spanish. "This is gonna turn out to be exactly the break we were looking for."

"How's that?"

"You just stay tuned," said Hall, winking mischievously, "and you'll see how the game is played."

When, sometime around noon on Sunday, Stephen Barrow turned to Theresa Mulholland and said, "I can't believe I'm home," it wasn't just a figure of speech. In fact, it took Stephen the entire weekend to fully comprehend that he was indeed home—that his bedroom wasn't his jail cell; that it was okay for him not to be wearing his orange jumpsuit; that no one had sneaked in while he wasn't looking and added a fixture to the bare lightbulb in his ceiling, or forgotten to pass him his meals on a cardboard tray; and that this woman who kept taking care of him was not some deputy sheriff in civilian clothes, sent into his cell to spy on him.

People react in different ways to being locked up. Some rail at their captors; some vent their anger on their fellow inmates. There are inmates who embrace religion, study law, or "turn snitch," becoming informants in order to earn early release or receive some other form of leniency. Still others bide their time, obsessing over the possibility of escape, no matter how remote the odds.

Stephen Barrow hadn't followed any of those models. His particular method of adjustment had been to surrender, to give up, to accept his confinement as something he himself had not only brought on, but on some level had even deserved. And his surrender had been so complete and so effective that it had almost cost him his life. He'd reached the point, in those final days of his confinement, that he'd stopped eating altogether, and all but stopped drinking. He'd lost so much weight by the time of his release that one wonders if he could have survived another week.

Worse yet, he hadn't seemed to care.

As a result, Stephen's postincarceration recovery wasn't simply a matter of restoring his body with food, fluids, and sleep, and then making it presentable with a shower, a shave, and a haircut. He needed much more than that. He needed, among other things, to *find himself* again, to locate that part of him that he'd abandoned at some point while he'd been in jail.

And Terry (for now he remembered *exactly* who she was—the reporter who'd gotten her car stuck in the snowstorm and been forced to spend the night in Stephen's living room), Terry seemed to understand this. So each time he'd eaten and drank and slept and cleaned himself up, she'd talk to him. She'd tell him what had been going on while he was, well, *away*. She'd bring him up to date on his case—how close the judge had come to dismissing it before chickening out at the last minute; how Stephen had to go back to court on the seventeenth, and what was likely to happen when he did; and, even though he was no longer in jail, how much trouble he was still in. She'd tell him about his daughter, how Penny was still living with her mother, but was apparently not attending school; how several experts had suggested that not only had Stephen photographed her naked, but he'd done other things, *sexual* things, to her as well.

And bit by bit, day by day, it all began to sink in—the things he'd never known, or had known but forgotten, or had simply chosen to ignore. And the more he learned or remembered, the more difficult it became for him not to care.

They had his daughter. They were saying he'd done terrible things to her. They intended to keep her from him for as long as they possibly could, maybe even forever. They had no interest in helping her; their interest in her was limited to how they could use her to hurt *him*.

It took the entire weekend and half the next week. Terry stayed with him the entire time, except toward the end, when she began to trust him enough to leave him for an hour or two while she went out to buy food, pick up the mail, or run some other errand. And as Stephen came to realize what her presence had done for him—that it had very possibly been *lifesaving,* in the most literal sense of the word; he took to thanking her over and over again, until she finally tired of it, and snapped at him.

"Just keep getting better," she'd tell him. "That's all the thanks I want."

So he got better. Not just physically, but emotionally as well. And on the sixth day, a Wednesday, it was—he was keeping track of time by then—as she was telling him for the umpteenth time that Penny still wasn't back in school, Stephen rose from the chair he'd been sitting in and started screaming at the top of his lungs. And Terry? Terry only smiled. For in that instant, from that screaming, Theresa knew that Stephen was back at last. He'd somehow managed to rediscover that part of him he'd left behind in his cell, or more likely misplaced even before he'd got there in the first place. That part of him he was going to need so desperately now.

His *anger*.

Ever since Cathy Silverman had been asked by Assistant District Attorney Hank Bournagan to come up with something new from Penny Barrow, she'd been trying her best. She'd already asked the child in a dozen ways if her father had ever abused her, only to receive the expected (but no doubt false) denial each time. She'd handed Penny a box of sixty-four crayons and instructed her to draw a picture of her family. Penny had drawn a man and a child, walking through the woods, holding hands. Silverman had not only considered the subject matter of the portrayal troubling, she'd also noted Penny's selection of a red crayon when it had come time to draw herself. Abused children invariably chose red. No one knew exactly why, but it was right there in all the textbooks. And what had the odds been of Penny's picking red? One in sixty-four, that's what. Or maybe a little less, if you wanted to get technical and count magenta and maroon, and a few others like that. Still, Silverman knew she couldn't ascribe it to mere coincidence.

She'd had Penny study inkblots, draw pictures, arrange anatomically correct dolls, play word-association games, and share secrets (Silverman went first at that, and the secret she revealed was that her daddy had liked to rub her back). Now she graduated to more suggestive methods (though Silverman would never call them that, preferring to use the term *directed*).

"Penny," she said one afternoon, "I know you keep telling me that your father didn't do anything else bad to you. Right?"

And Penny, sitting with her Baba in her lap and her thumb never far from her mouth, said, "Right."

"Well, Penny, suppose we play a little game. Why don't we close our eyes—go ahead and close them—and just for a moment, let's just *pretend* your father *did* do something else bad. Okay?"

"I don't *want* to play that game."

"Come on, just give it a try," said Silverman.

Penny's thumb went into her mouth.

"I'll tell you what. You do this for me, and I'll give you a *special surprise*."

"What kind of surprise?"

"I can't tell you. It wouldn't be a *surprise* if I told you, would it be?"

Still nothing. Whatever it was her father had done to her, he'd obviously done a pretty good job of buying her silence about it. But Cathy Silverman was a professional, and she was determined to get to the bottom of it, no matter what it took.

"How about this, Penny? You tell me a story about some *other* father, and what he did to *his* little girl. We'll call the father 'Sam,' and the little girl will be 'Patty.' "

Still nothing.

"How about I start it for you?" Silverman suggested. "That way, we can take turns, and it'll be over very quickly. All right. Once upon a time, there was a little girl named Patty. She lived alone in a big house with her daddy, whose name was Sam. She loved her daddy, but one day . . . Okay," she said. "Your turn."

Gently, she pried Penny's thumb from her mouth. "But one day . . ." Silverman repeated.

"One day they took her away from her father."

"Good," said Silverman. At least it was a start. "And the reason they took her away from her father was because her father . . ."

"Loved her."

"All right, he loved her. In fact, he loved her *too much*. It turned out he loved her *so much* that one time he . . ."

"Got mad that people were trying to make things up about him."

"And when he got mad, he . . ."

"Killed them."

Well, if the response wasn't quite what Silverman had been hoping for, it certainly was a textbook symptom of homicidal ideation. Silverman made a written note of it. "Why is it," she asked, "that your daddy wants to kill somebody?"

"It's not my daddy we're talking about," said Penny. "It's Sam. Remember?"

Silverman smiled. *Smart-ass kid.* Fortunately, she wasn't smart enough to understand the concept of *transference*, and to realize she really *was* talking about herself and her own father. "Right," she said, "*Sam.* Why does *Sam* want to kill somebody?"

"Because," said Penny, "he hates stupid people."

They were interrupted, perhaps mercifully, by the telephone. Silverman picked it up after the first ring, something she always tried to do. "Cathy Silverman," she said.

"Hello, Dr. Silverman. "This is Hank Bournagan, from the Columbia County DA's—"

"Yes, Mr. Bournagan. As a matter of fact, I have the subject in front of me right now."

"The subject," Bournagan repeated. He wasn't accustomed to thinking of people as *subjects*. Defendants, witnesses, victims, yes. But *subjects*?

"The Barrow child," he heard Silverman whispering into the phone.

"Oh, right."

"And I'm doing my best," said Silverman. "But you have to understand how difficult these cases are. There's often a tremendous amount of fear, and a reluctance to open—"

"Yes, yes, I do understand. You take as much time as you need, Dr. Silverman. In fact, Mr. Hall—he's my boss—he says he'd be especially appreciative if you were to say that the, uh, *subject* won't be ready to testify in court until sometime next month."

"Well, I suppose I could say that."

"Why don't you go ahead and tell me that right now, so I can go in to my boss and tell him you just said it. What do you say?"

What Cathy Silverman *didn't* say was that all of a sudden this eerie feeling came over her, as though she was one of her own patients, being told to mouth words that weren't quite her own. But mouth them she did. "The subject won't be ready to testify until next month," she said. And the eerie feeling passed, as quickly as it had come.

"See how easy that is?" she told Penny Barrow.

Stephen Barrow's newfound anger didn't suffer from any lack of targets. He was angry at the stupid store clerk who'd started the whole thing in the first place; angry at the troopers who'd arrested him, the grand jurors who'd indicted him, and the DA who was prosecuting him; angry at the doctors who were accusing him of abusing his daughter, without having even met him; angry at the judges—the one who'd been too timid to dismiss the case, and the one who'd taken his daughter away from him; angry at his ex-wife, who was no doubt doing her best to make Penny's life completely miserable; and angry at her lawyer, who was behind her every step of the way.

The problem was that as angry as Stephen was at all these people, he couldn't *get* at any of them, at least not without getting *himself* thrown back in jail. So over the course of the next day and a half, he simmered, he cursed, he shouted, and he even snapped once or twice at Theresa—who quickly put him in his place and assured him she'd leave the next time he did it.

The fact is, some people are good at anger, and some are not. Stephen had always been in the second camp. On the rare occasion when he'd been moved to true anger, he'd found it absolutely *consumed* him. It preoccupied his every thought, made functioning on a normal level all but impossible, and ended up draining him of all his energy. He actually admired people who could sustain anger and feed off it. To his way of thinking, there was something truly noble about a man driven by rage to get even, whatever the odds, whatever the price, whatever the penalty.

That man simply wasn't Stephen Barrow.

So he continued to simmer, but it was an unproductive, unsatisfying simmer that left him wandering around the house looking for someone or something to kick, but never quite fixing on a suitable target.

On the Friday before his trial was scheduled to start, Stephen and Theresa drove over to Flynt Adams's office in Chatham. At first Theresa had balked at the idea of coming along, questioning whether it was smart for her to be present.

"C'mon," Stephen had said, "I need some moral support. Besides which, you could be a *witness*. You said so yourself." Theresa had in fact mentioned to Stephen that she still had a distinct recollection from the day she'd first seen him at the Drug Mart, and could say with certainty that he'd almost forgotten to drop the roll of film off for developing. To Stephen, that helped prove how unimportant the photos were to him, and how he couldn't possibly have had a special interest in them.

Flynt Adams wasn't so sure about the idea.

"For one thing," he was quick to point out, "the fact that you're sleeping together is going to undermine your credibility. Jim Hall will want to go into it, and Wainwright'll have to permit him. It shows bias."

"Who says we're *sleeping* together?" Stephen demanded to know. Apparently not all of his anger had simmered away.

"That reporter guy, he's been writing all about it in his newspaper stories," said Adams. "Weren't you *fired* because of it?" he asked Theresa.

"Does that mean it's *true*?" she countered. "Any more than Stephen's a criminal, just because people are *saying* he is?"

"That's different," Adams told her. "The judge will presume he's innocent; the law requires him to. But the two of you sleeping together—"

"We're not," said Stephen.

"Not what?"

"Not sleeping together. Terry sleeps on the sofa, in the living room. I sleep in my bedroom."

"So you haven't—"

"Had sex? No," said Stephen, "as a matter of fact, we haven't."

Adams shook his head at the two people sitting across the desk from him. They were both extraordinarily good-looking. Stephen was older, but by how much? Five years? Ten, tops? She'd gone into debt to bail him out, and then lost her job over him. They'd been living alone, under the same roof, for a week now. They'd come together to his office. Adams had simply made what he considered a logical assumption. And if *he* had . . .

"Nobody's going to believe that," he said.

There was an awkward silence. To Stephen, it was a revealing moment, a painful lesson the three of them had collectively stumbled upon. At trial, the truth didn't matter. It was other people's *perception* of what the truth was that mattered.

They spent the next hour preparing Stephen's testimony. Adams felt strongly that however weak the prosecution's case turned out to be, unless they got a clear signal from Justice Wainwright that it wouldn't be necessary, Stephen had to be ready to take the stand and talk about his healthy relationship with his daughter, the spontaneity with which she'd mooned him, and his lack of any sexual or commercial interest in the photos he'd taken of her.

"How does he send us a *signal?*" Stephen asked.

"Easy," said Adams. "At the end of the DA's case, before we've had our turn, I move to dismiss the charges. The judge says something like, 'I'll deny *that* motion, counselor.' That's his way of telling me to rest, without putting you on the stand, and make my next motion, which would be for an acquittal."

"And you think he'll do that?" Theresa asked.

"He just might," said Adams. "Or he might want to hear Stephen's side before finding him not guilty. It all comes down to whether or not Hall has anything up his sleeve besides the photo itself."

Jim Hall, of course, had plenty up his sleeve. Hall was a firm believer in the theory that cases weren't won or lost by court-room theatrics. They were decided long beforehand, by the pre-trial maneuverings and countermaneuverings of the lawyers. *Infighting,* Hall liked to call it. He considered himself a master at it, and few who'd been up against him cared to argue the point.

Take the Barrow case, for example. Jim Hall was determined to win this case. A year or two ago, he'd prosecuted a case against a sex offender, a Peeping Tom who liked to hang out in neighbors' backyards at night. The various shrinks who'd

examined the guy concluded he didn't pose a danger to the
community. So Hall had gone easy on him, allowed him to
plead guilty to a reduced charge and get five years' probation.
Six months later, the guy goes and kills a nine-year-old boy.
Cut his *privates* off, he did, although they kept that little detail
out of the papers.

So much for leniency.

This time there'd be no sympathy, no lesser charges, no probation. This case was going to go to trial, and Jim Hall was
going to win it. Not with some dramatic opening statement or
brilliant last-minute summation; not with a bunch of Ivy
League experts with fancy degrees; and not with a lot of
legalese and case citations.

If it took pulling out those Valentine's Day cards the
deputies had seized when they executed the search warrant,
then Hall would pull them out, especially the one that said
"To the love of my life" and was signed "Love, Stephen."
None of the rest of the stuff seized had panned out as well as
Hall had hoped. The eight pairs of child's underpants, for
example, had tested negative for semen stains, human hairs,
and traces of DNA. The porno film, *The Devil Made Me Do
Him,* had turned out to be mismarked; it was actually a copy
of an Al Pacino movie, *The Devil's Advocate*, and pretty boring
at that.

Or maybe it would take reaching into Stephen Barrow's
past. While his print sheet had showed no priors, Hall knew
from experience that that simply meant there had been no con-
victions of crimes. So he'd had his investigator, Ed Sprague,
run an FBI check, and Sprague had come up with an old arrest
from New York City, way back when Barrow was eighteen.
The original charge had been indecent exposure—Public
Lewdness, they called it—and even though some liberal judge
down there had let Barrow cop out to an Administrative Code
violation for urinating in public, getting the word *lewdness* into
the record, wouldn't hurt too much, would it?

That would have to wait. But one way or another, Jim Hall

was going to win this case, because he was a master at infighting. In fact, he was going to try to win it first thing Monday morning, by saying five little words.

By Sunday night, Stephen was too nervous to sit still. Theresa had made soup, something thick and good-smelling, but he couldn't get more than a mouthful down.

"It's a *nonjury* trial," Theresa had reminded him. "Your lawyer says you're going to be acquitted. Try to *relax* a little, will you?"

"*Relax?*" Stephen snapped. "I lose this case, and they're going to make Penny stay with her *mother* for the rest of her life. Do you know what that'll *do* to her?"

"You're not going to lose it, Stephen, unless maybe you fall asleep on the witness stand, in the middle of your testimony. *Look* at you."

He didn't have to. He hadn't slept at all Saturday night, and had managed only an hour or two the night before. He'd barely eaten all weekend. He knew what he must look like.

"Well, it's after midnight," she said. "I'm going to bed so at least one of us'll be able to drive to court in the morning."

"Go ahead," he said. "I'm going to take a shower."

They both chuckled. It would be his third shower of the day. He claimed they calmed him down, the way baths calmed Penny. Theresa was yet to be convinced.

He left her to make up the sofa, and closed the door of his bedroom behind him. He checked the outfit she'd laid out for him on his bed: a blue blazer, gray slacks, a white shirt, a subdued tie. Brown loafers and belt. "You want to look nice," Flynt Adams had told him, "but not *too* nice. A sport jacket and tie is respectful. A suit starts getting too dressy."

The water felt good. He turned it up a notch, and inched the dial a little farther over toward the "H." He let it hit his back and shoulders full blast, trying his best to relax. Steam rose around him. *Twelve hours,* he figured. *Twelve hours and this whole thing'll be over. We win the criminal case, everything else'll fall into place, it'll have to. So hold on, Penny. Hold on one more night, Sweetie.*

Drying off, he caught sight of his face in the mirror. *Jesus,* he thought. *I really do look scary. If I didn't know me, I'd think I was, what? A sex maniac?* He tried to smile at his little joke, but the muscles in his face refused to cooperate. He knew how tired he was. But the mere thought of it brought on a whole new wave of anxiety: The more he needed to sleep, the more he knew he wouldn't be able to.

Back in his bedroom, he was surprised to find he'd already hung up his clothes for the morning and dimmed the lights. That kind of stuff had been happening to him a lot lately—he'd do something, and then ten minutes later he'd completely forgotten he'd done it. Two days ago, the morning after a light snow, he'd gotten all bundled up and gone outside to shovel the walk, only to discover that he'd done it the night before. *This must be what it's like to lose your mind,* he decided.

He tightened the towel around his waist and wandered over to the bedside table. Out of habit, he set the alarm clock, a precaution he knew was unnecessary: He knew that no matter what time it went off, he'd be awake to hear it.

He sat on the edge of the bed, and in the near darkness, felt something there. He must have left something on the bed, he realized, though he couldn't remember having done so. He reached out and felt a lump, but it was beneath the covers and too large to be clothes.

"Hello," it said.

Flynt Adams didn't expect to get much sleep, either.

A trial—even one where the judge had all but told him to waive a jury—was a roll of the dice, a game of chance you played when all your efforts to resolve a case had failed. Sometimes it was a matter of a prosecutor being unreasonable; more often it was when your own client was too stubborn and too self-destructive to understand that a guilty plea was in his own best interest.

But neither seemed to be the situation here. Adams knew Jim Hall couldn't plea-bargain the case; he was in a bind, politically. He'd been burned once on a sex case, and the voters wouldn't forgive him a second time. As for Justice Wainwright, he, too, was in a tough spot. By refusing to dismiss the case, he was simply covering his own butt. And you could hardly say Stephen Barrow was being unreasonable by going to trial. With custody of his daughter at stake, there was no charge on the books he could plead guilty to, even if Hall had been inclined to offer one.

So a trial it would be. And Flynt Adams would toss and turn for a while, think about his opening statement, check the clock, plan his direct examination of his client, listen to the furnace turn off and on, rehearse his summation, and finally watch the sky begin to lighten in the east. In between, if he was lucky, he'd catch three hours of sleep.

Jim Hall slept like a baby.

For him, the worst thing about Monday morning was that Wainwright would give him a little grief. But when it came right down to it, there'd be nothing the judge could do.

To Hall, the wonderful thing about the American system of justice was the delicate balance of power built into it. You had a judge and a prosecutor. (You could forget about the defense attorney: He had no power at all in the equation.) The judge got a fancy title that went in front of his name, a special license plate to stick on his car, a nice black robe to wear, an expensive leather chair to lean back in, a great big desk to sit behind, and even a little wooden hammer to bang on it when things got out of hand.

All the trappings of power.

But the *real* power, as Hall and everyone else in the system knew, belonged to the prosecutor. The power to indict or refrain from indicting; the power to plea-bargain or be hard-nosed; the power to fast-track cases or let them languish; and even much of the power to control who went free, who went to prison, and—now that capital punishment had finally been restored—who lived and who died.

Tomorrow would be a good test of that balance of power. Wainwright could wear his robe, sit in his chair, and bang his hammer on his desk all he wanted. When he was finished doing all that, he'd finally get around to giving Hall exactly what the DA wanted.

He'd have no other choice.

When whatever it was that was under the covers said "Hello," Stephen jumped up as though he'd been catapulted from the bed.

Police officers, emergency medical technicians, and others whose business it is to respond to serious motor vehicle accidents share a macabre little piece of information unknown to the general public. A pedestrian struck by a moving car tends to be launched—and *launched* is the operative word here; no other expression accurately describes the phenomenon—an astounding distance. So suddenly does the victim take off, and with such incredible force, that his shoes are invariably left behind on the pavement, in the precise place and position they'd been just prior to the victim's departure. In fact, for that very reason they're often used as a reference mark for the point of impact in the ensuing investigation.

At the moment before he was catapulted upward from the bed, Stephen Barrow hadn't been wearing shoes. Had he been, they undoubtedly would have been left behind on the floor, one beside the other, right by the edge of his bed.

He had, however, been wearing a towel.

Another thing: While Stephen's vision had still been in the process of accommodating to the semidarkness of the room at the moment of his liftoff, the utterer of the "Hello" had been lying there long enough to be able to observe the event in considerable detail, particularly the dramatic separation of the booster towel. And, seldom at a loss for words, she now summed up her impression.

"From the look of things," she said, "that must have been a very hot shower."

Stephen, who tended to be more at ease with the written word than the spoken one, could do no better than, *"Terry?"*

"Yes?"

"What are *you* doing here?"

"Were you expecting someone *else?*" she asked.

"I mean, what are you *doing* here?"

"I decided," she said, "that one way or another, you needed to get a good night's sleep."

"And you think *this* is going to do it?"

"Actually," she said, "I already *know* this is going to do it." And, lifting herself up onto one elbow and simultaneously revealing one bare breast, she reached out for him.

"But you heard what Mr. Adams said," Stephen reminded her. "People are going to assume we're—"

"The *hell* with people. They already assume we're sleeping together. So the way I see it, we might as well be." And she reached out farther until she succeeded in grabbing onto the nearest part of him, not to mention the most prominent.

No thruster ever reacted more dramatically.

SIXTEEN

People versus Stephen Barrow," announced Justice Wainwright, who had a habit of calling his own calendar, rather than waiting for his clerk to do it. "I understand that Mr. Barrow has executed a waiver of trial by jury, and wants a bench trial. Is that correct, Mr. Adams?"

"Yes, sir, it is."

"Are both sides ready?"

"The defendant is ready," said Adams.

Jim Hall rose slowly from the prosecution table, as though what he was about to say caused him great pain. "The People are not ready," he said. "We intend to call the child victim as a witness. We believe her testimony is absolutely essential to our case. Unfortunately, we're advised by Dr. Silverman, the therapist who's been treating the child, that she's still much too upset to testify, and won't be able to for another month."

Adams jumped to his feet. "Your honor—"

Wainwright cut him off with an outstretched hand. "It seems to me, Mr. Hall, that this case is about the nature of a photograph allegedly possessed by the defendant. Perhaps you'd like to give me an offer of proof as to how the child's testimony will bear on that."

"Certainly, your honor. We expect the child to testify to a number of things, including the fact that the defendant deliberately posed her for the pictures, had taken a number of similar pictures of her in the past, punished her when she refused to comply, rewarded her when she agreed to—"

Flynt Adams was on his feet again, his face red with anger. What Hall had done was to take Adams's motion papers, the part where Adams had argued that the case had to be dismissed because the prosecution couldn't prove any of these things. Now Hall was taking every item Adams had listed and saying he *could* prove them, by calling Penny as a witness, but he just wasn't ready to do it yet.

But again, the judge silenced Adams and continued to direct his attention to Hall. "What leads you to believe that she'll say these things?"

Hall bent down and huddled with Hank Bournagan before answering. "My associate here tells me he's been in constant contact with Dr. Silverman. He says she says that the child has told her all these things, at one time or another."

" '*He says she says,*' " mimicked the judge. "So then why can't the child come in here and tell *me* these things today?"

Again Hall conferred with Bournagan. "According to the doctor, she's still too, uh, too *traumatized.*"

"I'll give you one week, Mr. Hall, one week. The trial will take place April twenty-fourth, with or without the child. Do I make myself clear?"

"I'll do my best, your honor."

Flynt Adams never got a word in. Like Hall and Wainwright, he understood all too well that he was nothing but a bit player in this power struggle, a minor character with no speaking lines.

"*Too traumatized?*" said Stephen afterward.

"I know, I know," said Adams. "That's all nonsense. But you see what's really going on here, don't you? Hall's trying to get the case away from Wainwright. He figured he could get it knocked over to May, when Justice McGee comes into the part. But Wainwright saw right through it and outfoxed him."

"Suppose he does it again next time?" Theresa asked.

"You heard the judge," said Adams. "This case is going to start a week from today, with or without the child."

But if Flynt Adams did his best to sound certain, neither Stephen Barrow nor Theresa Mulholland walked away fully convinced. They'd seen too much already. Stephen shook his head slowly. "All that sleep for nothing," he said.

Theresa shot him a look, letting him know he'd get his later. Or more likely not.

Tom Grady was hunched over his typewriter in a small cubicle at the office of the *Hudson Valley Herald*, working on the day's fifth cup of coffee. Cigarettes he'd lost count of, and had some time ago begun reckoning his consumption of them not in numbers smoked or even packs purchased, but in occasions he was compelled to empty his ashtray.

"What's new with the Barrow case?"

Grady hadn't sensed anyone at the entrance of his cubicle. Now he looked up and saw Neil Witt, clipboard in hand.

"Nothing much," said Grady. "Put off a week."

"You going to have something for the issue?"

"Like what?" Grady asked. " 'Barrow Trial Adjourned'?"

"I was thinking more along the lines of human interest," said Witt. "You know, how the kid's doing at school—"

"She's not in school."

"—or at home."

Grady said nothing. Kids tended to annoy him under the best of circumstances.

"Or how Barrow's so upset at losing her that he's replaced her with a certain former reporter."

Grady leaned back slowly in his chair. "You mean a sorta *Carl Coppolino piece*?" he asked. Carl Coppolino had been a physician and a murder defendant, what, a quarter of a century ago? He'd been accused of using an exotic poison to kill off not one but *two* wives. Or maybe a wife and a girlfriend, whatever. He'd hired F. Lee Bailey to represent him, at a time when Bailey was on top of his game. They'd won the first trial, in New Jersey. The second one was down in Florida. Just before it began, some photographer snapped a shot of Coppolino, romping on the beach with his latest girlfriend, a big smile on his face, like he didn't have a care in the world.

A Florida jury wiped the smile off his face.

"Yeah," said Neil Witt, whose reading at the time had pretty much been confined to the Hardy Boys, but had later studied the Coppolino case at the Cornell School of Journalism in a course about how reporting could shape events. "Sorta like that."

Jim Hall assembled his staff in his office that same afternoon. "Okay, folks," he told them. "Wainwright wants to play hard-ball with us, we'll teach him a thing or two. Hank, you take a look at Article Sixty-five of the CPL, see what it takes to have the kid declared a 'vulnerable witness,' authorizing the use of closed-circuit TV for her testimony at trial. That oughta take a full week to litigate right there. Meanwhile, Wendy, you draw up a motion to recuse Wainwright on the ground that he's pre-judged the case."

"How'm I going to do *that*?" she asked. "He really hasn't done anything yet."

"You just draw it up in general terms," Hall told her, "and let me fill in the blanks. And even if we come up a little short, the beauty of it is that by the time we lose the battle, we'll have won the war. See, you kids gotta learn to keep your eyes on the big picture. So just do as I say, okay? Then sit back, relax, and leave the rest to me. You'll see how it works."

Actually, it wasn't working all that well, at least as far as Cathy Silverman was concerned. She was making a little headway with the Barrow child, to be sure, but it was awfully slow going. Each time she'd managed to extract some concession or other from the subject, the next thing out of the child's mouth would be a retraction of some sort, or a qualifier. There was, for example, the time when Silverman had finally gotten Penny to admit that it had been her father who'd posed her for the mooning photograph.

"So he had you undress," she said. "Right?"

Silence. Blanket on lap, as always.

"Right?"

"It was bath time."

"Okay, it was bath time, and he had you undress."

Thumb to mouth.

"Right?"

"I guess so."

"How often did he do this?"

"Do what?"

"Have you undress?"

"Once a day, I guess."

"Good. And did he come into the room when you were undressed?"

"I guess so. To check on me."

"When you were *completely* undressed?"

A nod, thumb in mouth.

"And that one time, when you bent over, and he took your picture. He was there in the room with you, right?"

"*Duh.*"

"What?"

"Nothing."

"Did you *like it* when he took the picture?"

A shrug.

"Did you say anything?"

"I said, 'Daddy!' "

"So you didn't like it, did you?"

Silence.

"Did you?"

"I guess not."

"But he took it anyway."

A barely perceptible nod.

"How did it make you feel?"

"I don't know. I remember I laughed."

"You were happy it was over?"

"No. It was *funny*."

"It was *funny* that he made you bend over naked so he could take your picture?"

"He didn't *make* me. I bended over all by myself."

"But it was his idea, right?"

"What was?"

"Come on, Penny. Why do you always have to make this so hard?"

" 'Cause you keep confusing me."

"It's a simple question, and I need a simple answer. Then we'll be finished for today. Whose idea was it? Yours or his?"

"To take the picture?"

"I give up. Whatever."

"His."

"Thank you. Now that wasn't so hard, was it?"

"But it was *my* idea to—"

"I said we're finished."

In her write-up of the session, Silverman described how Penny Barrow was still much too upset to come to court. (Hank Bournagan had asked her to be sure to include that fact in each of her reports.) Then she noted the following:

Wednesday, April 12, 2000

Subject appears as before, accompanied by her baby blanket, and constantly sucking her thumb. When pressed, subject states that her father would direct her to undress completely, on an average of once a day. Subject further states that her father would constantly enter the room when she was naked, under the guise of "checking on her."

Subject spoke reluctantly about the photo her father took of her bending over with her genitals and anus exposed. She said she didn't like it when her father took the photo, and complained to him at the time, but he took it anyway, over her objection. After some hesitation, subject admitted that the entire incident was her father's idea.

Tom Grady's idea was to catch Stephen Barrow and Theresa Mulholland in a compromising position, as the saying went, and document it with a photograph that would reveal the exact nature of their relationship. That oughta knock Theresa off her high horse of concern for Barrow's rights and the American System of Truth and Justice, and expose the two of them for what they were—a pair of self-absorbed lovers every bit as smug as Carl Coppolino and his floozy had been, romping on the beach like they owned the world.

The problem, of course, was in the catching.

Grady didn't have a car, or a driver's license, for that matter. He'd had both at one time, but three accidents and four DWI arrests had pretty much broken him of the driving habit. As a result, Grady wasn't in a position to follow either Stephen or Theresa around, hoping to catch them smooching over lunch at the Cottage Restaurant, or holding hands at the bar of Fresca's Pizzeria. Besides which, Grady was lazy. Unlike his boss, Neil Witt, he was an old-fashioned, seat-of-the-pants reporter. He hadn't attended the Cornell School of Journalism or even finished college. He didn't believe in painstaking research, time-consuming investigation, or bothersome fact-checking. All that beating around the bush might be fine for someone else. For Tom Grady, it was nothing but a bunch of crap.

You wanted a story, you went to the source.

Which is why, when it came time to catch Stephen and Theresa together, Grady got a hold of Danny LaFontaine, one of the paper's two staff photographers.

"Danny, you got your car?"

"Yeah, I got my car." Danny always had his car; along with his Leica, it was the reason he'd been hired in the first place. The *Herald* reimbursed him at the rate of twelve cents a mile. When gas had cost eighty-nine cents a gallon, it had been a pretty good deal; at $1.69, it had lost some of its cachet.

"Good," said Grady. "Why don't you meet me at Poppy's about eleven-fifteen tonight, okay?"

"Eleven-fifteen?"

"Yeah, and make sure your flash is working this time." Last time out, they'd tried to surprise a group of poachers using floodlights to hunt deer over at the dump. But the poachers heard them drive up and killed the lights, and when Danny tried to catch them in the dark, the flash on his camera misfired. End of story.

"What are we working on this time?" Danny wanted to know. "Coyotes?"

"Coppolinos," said Grady.

"Say what?"

Grady didn't bother explaining. Danny was twenty-two years old.

They drove in silence up the dirt road from Route 295, the headlights on Danny's Plymouth surprising raccoons, possum, and a pretty good-sized doe. They left the car on Beacon Hill Road, right before the turnoff to Hilltop Drive, and hiked the last quarter mile. It was mid-April, and spring may have been coming to the rest of the world, but in Columbia County there was still a hard frost underfoot, and as the two men walked, every breath they exhaled hung in the air in front of them, lit up by the moonlight.

They stopped at the base of the driveway so that Grady could rest, his six-ashtray habit taking its toll. "When we get up there," he told Danny, his words punctuated by short gasps, "you get right up close behind me. I'll knock on the door. Whichever one of 'em answers it, I'll ask for the other one. Soon as they're both standin' there in front of us, I'll step aside, and you fire away. Got it?"

"Got it," said Danny.

Ever since Theresa's surprise appearance in his bed, Stephen Barrow had been sleeping considerably better. If Theresa could do little during the day to help him overcome his anxieties, at least she could be there beside him at night, to help him fight off the terrors that tended to grow and multiply and visit him in the dark.

Not that this particular night was an unusually dark one. The moon had been full just two nights earlier, and had risen over the treetops in the eastern sky only slightly bent out of shape, and as they lay under the covers of his bed, Stephen and Theresa, if not quite bathed in white reflection, were at least fully visible to each other from the neck up. They'd shared a half-bottle of wine with dinner, he to celebrate Passover, she to usher in Good Friday. If their different faiths made for some slightly schizophrenic toasting, including a brief but determined attempt to come up with a suitable name for an equal-opportunity wine (neither Mogendavi nor Manichablis seemed to do it), their efforts at least left them in good spirits, in every sense of the phrase.

Which is why they were still very much awake around midnight when they heard footsteps outside, a muffled coughing, and finally a knocking on the front door. Stephen, who didn't own a bathrobe—like umbrellas and hats with brims, bathrobes were strictly for city folk and old men—had to retrieve his jeans from the floor, climb into them, and remember to take care in zipping them up (a decidedly hazardous procedure in the absence of undershorts). He pulled a sweatshirt over his head as he walked to the door, the floor cold under his still bare feet.

It was at times like this that Stephen wondered if it might not be a bad idea to keep a rifle or a shotgun handy, loaded or not, or even one of those pellet guns that *looked* like the real thing. All his neighbors were armed, at least all the year-rounders. Trapper Jeff down the road had a veritable arsenal at his disposal, with everything from pistols to antitank guns and medium-range missiles. Even old Martin André who was now well into his eighties and blind in one eye, got his deer each fall and filled his freezer with steaks to get him through the winter.

But Stephen didn't live with Trapper Jeff or Martin André; he lived with his daughter, Penny. To her, guns were not just dangerous tools possessed by hunters; guns were weapons of destruction. Guns were what killed small, furry animals, dropped beautiful songbirds out of the sky, and blew away innocent schoolchildren in faraway places with names like Colorado and Florida. If three years after having seen the movie, she still wasn't prepared to forgive the cold-blooded murderers of Bambi's mother, what chance would her father possibly have in pleading his Second Amendment rights?

Which is why Stephen had no gun in his hand, real or fake, loaded or unloaded, when he unlocked the front door and confronted the two men who'd been knocking on it. The first man—because there was definitely a first, and a second hiding behind him—was older and not particularly threatening in appearance, and even looked familiar to Stephen.

"Sorry to bother you so late at night," he said, holding his hat in both hands as though to demonstrate how truly sorry he was. "But we've been looking for Miss Theresa Mulholland. I'm afraid we have some bad news for her."

"What kind of news?" Stephen asked, not quite ready to invite them in.

"There's been a death in the family," said the older man.

Which of course disarmed the unarmed Stephen even more. "Why don't you come in," he said, opening the door wider and stepping back to let them enter.

"No, no," said the older man. "We'll just tell her and then be on our way, if that's all right."

So Stephen, not knowing quite what else to do, turned from them and called Theresa's name. But he needn't have; she'd already slipped on her robe (evidently not sharing Stephen's concern about being mistaken for either a city folk or an old man) and made her way from the bedroom. As soon as she came into view, Stephen reached a hand out to her.

"There's been a death," he said, taking her hand in his own, readying himself to be there for her as much as she'd been there for him.

Only when she was alongside him did Theresa seem to recognize the older man, too. But unlike Stephen, she was able to put a name on his face.

"Tom?" she said.

What happened next happened very fast. The older man, the one Theresa had addressed as Tom, shouted "Now!" and jumped to one side. The younger one left standing in the door-way raised something to his face, and there was a sudden explosion of white light, accompanied by a popping sound. Stephen was completely blinded, and might have thought he'd gone deaf, as well, except that he heard something coming from the older man, or at least from where the older man had been the instant before everything went white.

"Gotcha!" is what he heard.

Theresa heard *Gotcha*, too. But unlike Stephen, Theresa hadn't been fooled for a moment by Tom Grady's standing there in the doorway with his hat in his hands and Danny LaFontaine hiding behind him, or by Stephen's announcement that there'd been a death. Like Stephen, Theresa had been blinded by the flashbulb; but unlike Stephen, she needed no time to piece together the events that had occurred in order to make sense out of them.

At one point in her exercise routine at the gym, Tony the Trainer had lost all patience with Theresa's inability to get any kind of a rhythm going on the speed bag. "Stop *lookin'* at it, Red! The thing ain't gonna *bite* you, fer Chrissakes. *Feel* for it. Close yer pretty green eyes and *feel* for it. That way you'll be able to tell which way it's goin', insteada tryna remember where it was last time you seen it. The hand is quicker than the eye, see?" So she'd done as she'd been told. She'd closed her eyes and tried to work the bag by feeling for where it would be next, rather than by watching it where it had been before. And it had worked, up to a point. Later on, when she'd finally gotten good at the routine, she found she could comfortably glance away from the bag from time to time, even take her eyes off it alto-gether for short stretches, without losing track of where it would be, where its arc would position it for her next right or left.

Now she waded in, sightless, hands held high, jabbing at where Tom Grady's head had been when last she'd seen it, until finally she felt contact with a left, then a right, then another left. She remembered what Tony always told her, that there was no need to hit the thing hard, it was the *rhythm* that counted. And she had a *rhythm* going now, a sweet, pleasing *rat-tat-tat, rat-tat-tat* of lefts and rights, lefts and rights, and she kept hitting it, kept it going, back and forth, nothing able to stop her. . . .

By April of each year, winter begins to loosen her icy grip on Columbia County. In the woods surrounding Stephen Barrow's home, deer have foaled and black bear awakened from hibernation. The thickets teem with red fox and their newborn kits, raccoon, fisher, martin, and even an occasional bobcat. With dens full of tiny hungry mouths to feed, nighttime means hunting time.

This April night was no different. It was alive with the crunch of dry leaves underfoot, the yips and barks and wails of the chase, the eight-note cry of the barred owl, the distant piercing howl of the coyote.

But on this night the symphony was suddenly silenced, as though the raised hand of some unseen conductor had stopped it midnote. In the brush, a thousand pairs of glowing eyes widened, a thousand pairs of ears alerted, trying to identify a strange new sound coming from the place on top of the hill, where lights sometimes shone in the evening and tiny red sparks flew up into the night sky.

Rat-tat-tat, it went, *rat-tat-tat, rat-tat-tat, rat-tat-tat.* A muffled groan, then silence. And, tentatively at first, but soon with abandon, the hunters returned to the hunt.

It took all three of them to stop Theresa, and even then it wasn't easy. By the time she was finished using his head for a speed bag, she'd given Tom Grady a bloody nose, a matching

pair of black eyes, a fat lip, and a lesson he wouldn't soon forget. Danny LaFontaine fared better: He got off with a broken
Leica and an overexposed roll of film. Theresa herself ended up
with cuts and bruises on both hands, but enough satisfaction
to make the pain a small price to pay.

For a while, they worried that Grady and LaFontaine
might file criminal charges or bring a lawsuit, but in the end
they did neither. They must have figured they were on pretty
shaky grounds, considering that their death-in-the-family
ruse was likely to expose them to trespassing charges. Not to
mention the considerable embarrassment of having been
taken to the woodshed by a skinny, unarmed woman who
couldn't see.

Stephen went back to court on April 24. Flynt Adams again
answered ready for trial. To no one's surprise, Jim Hall did not.

"Your honor," he said, "the People are submitting two
motions today. Naturally, we've already served copies upon
the defense. Our first motion is to have the child victim in this
case declared 'vulnerable' within the meaning of Article Sixty-
five of the Criminal Procedure Law. As you can see from my
affirmation and the attached extracts of reports from Dr. Silverman, we contend that having to be in the same room as the
defendant would intimidate the child to the point where she'd
be unable to testify truthfully."

There was a brief interruption in the proceedings as Flynt
Adams had to restrain Stephen Barrow from jumping out of
his seat and physically attacking Jim Hall.

"See what I mean?" said Hall, once order had been restored.
"Our second motion, if I might move on, is made very reluctantly. But as the elected district attorney of the citizens of this
county, I feel it is nonetheless my duty to make it, and therefore I—"

"Cut the crap and get to the point," said Justice Wainwright. "What's the motion?"

"The motion, your honor, if you'll just allow me," said Hall, who was good at many things, but *cutting the crap* and *getting to the point* were decidedly not among them, "is to recuse you from further involvement in the case."

"On what basis?"

"On the basis that you've prejudged the facts, or at very least created an *appearance* that you've done so. Either way—"

"Mr. Adams, do you wish to be heard?"

Adams rose. "Your honor, this puts the defense in a very difficult position," he began. "Mr. Hall did indeed serve me with copies of these motion papers, but he neglected to mention that he did so about three minutes ago. I haven't even had time to *read* them, much less respond to his arguments."

Wainwright looked up at the clock. "It's ten after ten," he noted. "We'll be in recess until eleven o'clock. I suggest you read Mr. Hall's papers, Mr. Adams. I'll be doing the same. And in the event I rule against you on both issues, Mr. Hall, are you ready to proceed?"

"No, your honor, I'm afraid not."

Stephen Barrow couldn't be sure, but he thought he detected just a hint of a smile on Hall's face as he spoke the words. "Give me five minutes with him," he told Flynt Adams, "five minutes."

"Careful," Adams warned him. "Jim Hall's a pretty big guy."

"My thinking," said Stephen, "is to hit him between the eyes with a pretty big sledgehammer."

Everett Wainwright was sitting in his chambers, reading through Jim Hall's motion papers and writing sarcastic comments in the margins, when the phone rang. Rather than waiting for his secretary to answer it at her desk, he picked up himself and said, "Chambers."

"That you, Everett?"

"It's me. Who's this?"

"Clay Underwood, from the Third Department."

Wainwright sat up. Clarence Underwood was a fellow

Supreme Court justice, but he was assigned to the Appellate Division up in Albany, the court that handled appeals for all of eastern New York State except for the greater New York City area. As such, he was one of Wainwright's superiors, if not quite technically his boss.

"Hello, Clay. What can I do for you?"

"I hear you've been asked to step aside on a child-abuse case."

"Word sure travels fast," said Wainwright. "How'd you hear that?"

"Oh, my staff tries to keep me posted," said Underwood. "How's your wife, by the way?"

"She's well, thank you."

"Now I understand there's probably not much to this recusal motion."

"Not much? There's *nothing* to it."

"I'm sure you're right," said Underwood, "I'm sure you're right. Still and all, they tell me it's a bench trial."

"They." Wainwright was pretty certain *they* were Jim Hall. It was widely known that Underwood and Hall played golf together, and that each had helped the other out by raising money in past elections.

"My staff."

"Right."

"The thing is, Everett, sometimes the *appearance* of bias can be just as harmful to the system as *actual* bias."

"What makes you think," Wainwright asked, "that there's even the *appearance* of bias here?"

"May I speak frankly?"

"Please do."

"The rumor we're picking up is that there's talk of a contract on the case. You know, that you gave some sort of a signal to the defense attorney that he should waive a jury and try the case before you."

"That's *bullshit*," said Wainwright.

"I'm sure it is, I'm sure it is. These things always are. Still, the point is, there *is* this rumor, and a waiver *was* executed, and now there's all this *talk*." He left it at that.

"So you're telling me to recuse myself."

"No, no," said Underwood, "of course not. I'd never do *that*. All I'm suggesting is, perhaps you ought to just knock the case over a week or two for a response or a decision. By the time it comes back on, you'll be out of the part, and it won't be your problem anymore. End of crisis."

"Are you saying this is a *crisis*?"

"No, Everett. I'm saying we don't *want* a crisis, and that it's part of my job to see to it that we don't *have* one. That's all. So tell me, how's everything else going?"

"Everything else is just fine."

"They tell me you might be in for a little primary battle this time around."

"Might be."

"Well," said Underwood, "maybe we can be of some help there. We've got some friends down in Columbia County, you know."

I bet we do, thought Everett Wainwright.

"The motion to recuse me is denied," announced Justice Wainwright, much to the relief of Flynt Adams and Stephen Barrow, who couldn't help smiling in Jim Hall's direction. "As for the motion pursuant for closed-circuit television testimony by the child witness, decision is reserved until May first. Mr. Adams, if you want to submit papers in opposition to the motion, have them in by this Thursday."

Adams was already on his feet. "I assume, your honor, that you'll be keeping this case before you, even after the end of the month."

"You assume incorrectly. We'll operate as we always do. When Judge McGee comes into the part, it'll become her case."

It was Jim Hall's turn to smile.

SEVENTEEN

With Priscilla McGee scheduled to replace Everett Wainwright as the judge on the criminal case, spirits in the defense camp darkened. The thought of trying the case without a jury suddenly became unthinkable. Beyond that, McGee was all but certain to grant the prosecution's motion to permit Penny Barrow to testify over closed-circuit television. The result of such a ruling, Flynt Adams knew, could be disastrous for the defense. Penny was Jim Hall's witness; even though Hall would be in the courtroom, his people would be the ones setting up the equipment and working the cameras at some remote location. They'd be in a position to coach Penny and suggest answers to her. Their mere presence in the room with her would have an effect on her, just as would the absence of anyone connected with her father. So even as Flynt Adams submitted papers in opposition to the motion—arguing first that a six-year-old child was too young to testify under oath in the first place, and second that even if she could testify, she should do so in open court like any other witness—he was forced to take the fallback position that if closed-circuit TV *was* used, the defense should be allowed to have somebody present at the remote sight to observe what went on there.

The thought even occurred to Adams that Justice McGee might raise Stephen Barrow's bail. But, very much aware of his client's fragile emotional status, he kept that concern to himself.

As it turned out, Adams need not have worried about the bail. He should have worried more about other things. The first thing McGee did when the parties appeared before her on the first day of May was to announce that she was granting Jim Hall's motion to permit the use of closed-circuit television for Penny Barrow's testimony.

"I find," she said, "that the child is indeed a 'vulnerable witness' within the meaning of the law. As to the defense's wish to have somebody present where she testifies, that's precisely what the statute is designed to avoid. Anyway, no one's going to coach the child, are they, Mr. Hall?"

"Of course not, your honor."

"Very well. How soon can you have the necessary equipment set up, Mr. Hall?"

"I figure it should take my staff a day or two, at most."

"A day or two? This is a nonjury case, Mr. Hall. I was hoping to try it this afternoon."

Adams jumped to his feet; it was becoming something of a routine with him. "Your honor," he said.

"Yes, Mr. Adams?"

"My client has had a change of heart. He's decided he wants a jury trial after all."

"Well, isn't that nice. What do you have to say about the defendant's change of heart, Mr. Hall?"

"It's my understanding," said Hall, "that Mr. Barrow executed a written waiver. It should be right there in front of you, your honor, in the court papers."

"And so it is," said the judge. "Isn't this your client's signature, Mr. Adams?"

"I'm sure it is. But—"

"And yours, as his attorney."

"Yes."

"Is this the first mention you've made of this, this *change of heart?*"

"Yes, but—"

"Well, it seems to me that you've been engaging in *judge-*

shopping, and I'm not going to tolerate it. I find that the defendant's jury waiver, having been voluntarily and intelligently made, stands. If it was good enough for Justice Wainwright, it's good enough for me. Mr. Adams, your motion to withdraw it is denied. When can both sides be ready to try this case?"

"Two days," said Hall.

Adams couldn't believe what he was hearing. "Your honor," he said, "the defendant has a constitutional right to a trial by a jury of his peers."

"And I've already ruled that he waived that right, as the law permits him to do. This case will begin, and hopefully end, May twenty-second. That's three weeks from today. And that's all, gentlemen."

"Can she *do* that?" Stephen asked once they were outside.

"No," said Adams, "not really. But she just did."

"So what do we do about it?"

"There's nothing much we *can* do. Then again, it might turn out to be a blessing in disguise."

"How's that?" Stephen wanted to know.

"I'm pretty sure she's wrong on the law," Adams said. "I think the cases say you can insist on a jury, up until the time the trial actually begins. So if she goes ahead and makes us go nonjury, over our objection, and finds you guilty, all she's done is to give us a great issue for appeal."

"And how long would an appeal take?"

"Oh, a year, maybe. Less if you're in prison."

"Great. So in the meantime, I go to prison, and Penny stays with her mother."

Adams could do no better than to nod in agreement.

"I don't want an *appeal*!" Stephen shouted. "I want this *over*. I want my *daughter* back! Don't you understand that?"

"Of course I do. And I'm doing all I can, you know that."

"I *don't* know that. I don't know *anything*."

"There are rules," said Adams, "and I have to play by those rules, whether I like them or not. You know that as well as I do."

"Yeah, yeah," said Stephen, who wanted to ask why the rules never seemed to apply to the Jim Halls of the world, or the Priscilla McGees. But he knew he'd only be wasting his breath. "So what do we do now?" he asked.

Adams looked at his watch. "In exactly twenty minutes," he said, "we go up to Justice Wainwright's court."

"I thought he was off the case."

"Yes and no," said Adams. "He's off the criminal case, but that means he's now on the civil case. I've brought on an order to show cause, to see if I can't get you visitation rights with your daughter."

"When were you going to tell me?"

"Frankly, I was afraid to. I didn't want to get your hopes up."

"If there's anything you don't have to worry about," said Stephen, "it's getting my hopes up too high." They shared a chuckle; it was about as close to a laugh as either of them was going to get.

"Why *shouldn't* Mr. Barrow have visitation?" Justice Wainwright asked Jane Sparrow. "After all, he hasn't been convicted of any crime, and as far as abusing or neglecting his daughter, he hasn't even been *accused* of anything like that."

Sparrow rose from the table where she and Ada Barrow had been sitting. *Sparrow and Barrow*, thought Stephen; they made quite a pair.

"Dr. Silverman's reports are *replete* with evidence that Mr. Barrow has been abusing his daughter all along, in a variety of ways," said the lawyer, waving a sheaf of papers in the judge's direction. "Not only that, but Dr. Singh discovered all sorts of findings consistent with sexual abuse."

"I just love that phrase," said Judge Wainwright, "and I've

read all those reports. And I have to tell you I think most of what's in there is pure hogwash. What happened on the criminal case this morning?"

"It was adjourned three weeks," someone said.

"Very well," said the judge. "Effective immediately, the father shall be permitted one visit per week with his daughter. The visits will be on neutral ground—in other words, at neither the father's home nor the mother's. Each visit will be one hour in duration, and will be supervised by a certified social worker, whose fee shall be the responsibility of the father. Any questions?"

"Yes," said Jane Sparrow, her beady eyes narrowed to pinpoints. "Why on earth are you subjecting the poor child to this?"

"Fair question," said Justice Wainwright. "Only it's one you folks should have asked yourselves a long time ago."

Stephen was elated.

It was going on three months since he'd last seen his daughter. In that time, he'd been arrested, freed, indicted, and locked up again; he'd spent a month and a half in jail, barely surviving the experience; he'd been nursed back to health and led to believe things were almost over, only to have the carrot pulled away from him once again. And in all that time, the only contact he'd had with his daughter had been a single card from her.

Now he was about to *see* her.

Flynt Adams made the arrangements, locating an agency in Albany to supervise the visits. When Ada Barrow refused either to deliver Penny to the agency or to permit Stephen to pick her up at her home, Adams saw to it that one of the agency's social workers would double as a chauffeur, driving the child the thirty miles to and from the visit site. The additional expense, of course, was to be borne by Stephen, but he couldn't have cared less.

He was going to see his daughter.

The first visit took place three days after Justice Wainwright's order. Stephen spent the morning worrying about what jeans to wear, whether he'd shaved closely enough, the length of his hair, the smell of his breath. He thought of stopping off to buy a gift for Penny, but decided that might be interpreted as an attempt to buy her affection. He cleaned his car, both inside and out. He tried his best not to leave home too early, but still arrived half an hour ahead of schedule.

He felt like he was going on a first date—then quickly banished the thought, fearful that someone might read his thoughts and attach sexual significance to the analogy. Still, he had no idea how his daughter was going to react to him, especially after so long. Would she fling herself into his arms? Or would she cower in the corner? Was she still the same old Penny, or after all this time away from him had she bought into the notion that her father was the ogre some were painting him as?

The social worker/chauffeur was a young graduate student named William (Stephen missed his last name, and never did learn it). William came into the waiting room alone in order to prepare Stephen for the visit. He was tall, thin, had bad skin, and wore glasses that were much too big for his face.

"Here are the rules, Mr. Barrow. No leaving the room with your daughter, for any reason. No intimate contact, no discussing any aspect of your case or your daughter's upcoming testimony. No passing of notes, whispering, communicating by gesturing, or speaking in a foreign language."

As if he and his six-year-old might suddenly lapse into American Sign Language. Or Japanese, perhaps.

"And remember this. Your daughter's been through a lot lately. Give her a chance to get used to you, okay? Sometimes these things take a while."

"Okay," said Stephen. There was no way he was going to question anything, not when some kid who looked barely seventeen had the power to yank his daughter away from him at any given moment for some perceived violation of the rules. "Okay," he repeated.

William nodded thoughtfully and departed. When he returned a moment later, he was leading Penny by the hand.

Stephen was struck immediately by how *tall* she looked. Here he'd been away from her for only a couple of months, and yet it seemed she'd shot up during that time. Other than that, she looked thin, and maybe a little tired. And she was carrying her old baby blanket. What had she called it? Her *Baba*.

"Hi, Daddy," she said, with what struck him as a nervous smile. Not fearful, but not exactly flinging herself into his arms, either.

Sometimes these things take a while.

They sat at a tiny table, Stephen's butt stuffed into a chair meant for someone half his size. "I'm fine," Penny kept telling him. "I'm *not* too thin. I miss you, too. I *am* eating, I *promise*."

While she seemed genuinely happy to see him, it was as though there was a part of her that wasn't quite there, that had been left behind somewhere.

"Are you going to school?" he asked her.

"Mommy says soon. Right after things are over."

"Does Mommy read to you, at least?"

"Sometimes. She's not such a good reader."

"Are you warm enough?"

"Uh-huh."

"Do you need anything? Like for next time?"

"Some books. Ones I can read by myself. A couple 'Junie B. Jones' would be nice."

"Anything else?"

"A pen. Mommy only gives me crayons."

"Okay."

"That's it?"

"My orange sneakers. The ones with the purple laces."

And before he knew it, the hour was up.

The second visit, a week later, went about the same. Again
Penny seemed happy enough to see her father, but to Stephen
there was still something missing. His daughter lacked the
spark he'd been so used to, the mischievous quality he loved
about her. She smiled, she even laughed once or twice, but
generally she seemed subdued, flat. The thought even occurred
to him that they might have her on some sort of medication.

"Are you eating okay?" he asked her.

"Yes, Daddy."

"Taking your Flintstones?" Those were her vitamins.

"Yes."

"Taking any other medicine?"

A look from William, who always sat nearby, told Stephen
the question was off-limits. But if Stephen was concerned with
Penny's listlessness, William was impressed with the interac-
tion between father and daughter. At the end of the meeting,
before driving Penny back to her mother, he let Stephen look
over his shoulder as he filled out an evaluation form. Stephen
couldn't read the entire thing, but he was able to make out part
of it.

> Father and daughter seem quite comfortable together.
> Daughter exhibits no fear of father, and is relaxed in his
> presence. There is no evidence of any intimidation or
> other improper behavior, and it is the opinion of the
> undersigned that the visits should continue and perhaps
> even be extended in length.

If William was simply looking to increase his hours and the
pay that went with them, that was quite all right with Stephen.
"Who does this go to?" he asked.

"To the court," William told him. "Do you happen to know
the judge's name?"

"McGee," said Stephen. "Priscilla McGee."

It was only on the drive home that Stephen realized he'd misspoken. McGee was now the judge on the criminal case. (How could he have forgotten?) It had been Wainwright who'd ordered the visits and should therefore be getting the evaluations. So that afternoon, Stephen phoned William to report his mistake.

"Too late," William said. "I already faxed it to Judge McGee."

"Well," suggested Stephen, "maybe you better fax a copy to Judge Wainwright, too."

"Good idea."

The result was that both judges ended up reading the evaluation. And just as Priscilla McGee was about to toss hers into the trash can beneath her desk (she never would have allowed visits in the first place, and wasn't particularly moved by the fact that they were going well), in walked her colleague, waving his own copy of the report, a smug I-told-you-so look on his face.

"So much for the DA's need for closed-circuit TV to protect the Barrow child," he said.

And for one of those rare moments in her professional life, Justice McGee found herself cornered by the facts, and forced to acknowledge that she'd have to reverse one of her rulings. "Hilda," she said to her secretary, "send a letter to the parties on the Barrow case. Tell them we won't need television for the child's testimony after all."

She looked back at Wainwright, as if to say, *Satisfied?* But he wasn't finished with her.

"While we're on the subject," he said, "somebody told me you wouldn't let the defendant withdraw his waiver of a jury trial. I told my source he must be mistaken, that you'd never do a thing like that."

McGee said nothing. Instead, she broke off eye contact and suddenly seemed distracted.

"You know they'll reverse you in a minute for that," Wainwright told her. "It's a *Constitutional right,* Priscilla, with a capital C."

"Constitutional rights get waived all the time," snapped McGee. "People waive their Miranda rights, they consent to having their cars searched, they plead guilty instead of going to trial. How's waiving a jury any different?"

"It's different," said Wainwright, "because the appellate decisions say so. Barrow's changed his mind, and he's done so before it's too late to do anything about it. Read the cases."

Again McGee was silent. *Reading the cases* was something no one had ever accused her of doing to excess. To be sure, there were judges who made their reputations by being legal scholars. Priscilla McGee just didn't happen to be one of them.

And so it was that in the space of five minutes, and without even knowing about it, the prosecution was dealt two setbacks, and the defense finally caught a couple of breaks. The only problem was that Hilda, Justice McGee's secretary, was every bit as inefficient as her boss was unscholarly. Told to send the letters that Thursday, she put off writing them until Friday (when the copy machine happened to be undergoing repairs, and was out of service), and didn't get them into the mail until late Monday. The carrier picked them up Tuesday morning. Delivery being somewhat unpredictable in rural New York state, Jim Hall's copy arrived at his office the following afternoon (though Hall himself had left for the day without seeing it). Flynt Adams didn't receive his copy until Thursday morning. He tried to reach Stephen Barrow right away with the good news. But Stephen, early as always, had by that time left for his next visit with Penny.

They say airplane disasters invariably result not from any single cause, but from an almost impossible confluence of events. Not only does a previously undetected worn part suddenly overheat and break, but the alarm that should alert the crew has been disconnected because it kept coming on even when there was no problem. At the same time, a backup system fails to kick in for some unfathomable reason, and the pilot (experienced, but fatigued by a long wait prior to takeoff, and distracted by unusual weather conditions) fails to notice the drop on the oil pressure gauge. Eventually the broken part, the extra weight the plane took off with, and the additional drag of ice accumulated on the wings, are just enough to render the craft vulnerable to a sudden, unexpected burst of wind shear, extremely rare for that particular time of year.

So, too, did that Thursday's disaster have many contributing causes.

Not only had Justice McGee's secretary been derelict in getting the letters out to the lawyers, the Postal Service less than diligent in its appointed rounds, and Stephen Barrow neurotically early in leaving for his visit with his daughter, but William was having a very bad day.

William, of course, was the young man chosen to supervise the visits and to serve the secondary function of Penny's chauffeur. Unlike the rest of William's life, which was for the most part vague and uncentered, the problem William was having that day was extremely focused. The site of its focus was the rear molar of the lower left quadrant of his mouth. William had what is generally referred to in dental parlance as an abscess, or a second-degree, fully impacted infection.

Or, in laymen's terms, one hell of a fucking toothache.

William was, to begin with, not too good at pain. Hangnails bothered him; paper cuts caused him to cry out; blisters brought him to his knees. He'd gone to bed Wednesday night with a dull, throbbing ache in his mouth, only to awaken sometime around 3:30 with searing pain. His dentist couldn't see him until late in the afternoon. In the meantime, he advised William to gargle with warm salt water and take a couple of aspirin.

William had taken eight so far, and it wasn't yet noon.

Somehow he toughed it out. He picked up Penny Barrow and managed to drive her to the center. (Luckily, the kid was quiet; conversation was something William simply couldn't have handled.) At the center, he tried to find someone to sit in for him and supervise the Barrow visit. At a hundred dollars an hour, that was rarely a problem, and often he could get someone to do it for sixty or seventy, pocketing the change. Today, no one would do it for the full hundred. Fillmore was busy with a client, Mazeroski was in Syracuse attending some crisis intervention seminar, and Balzitch was out sick. That left Utstein, who immediately started giving William an argument about individual responsibility.

In the end, William did it himself. Or tried to. Downing two Tylenol and two ibuprofen on top of the eight aspirin, he found a chair in the corner of the room, covered his eyes with a damp washcloth, and prayed for death.

At the same time, across the room, Stephen was thinking he noticed a distinct change in his daughter. On the first two visits, she'd seemed happy to see him. Reserved, to be sure, but the circumstances could have more than accounted for that. Today, however, she was downright apprehensive. Her hug was unenthusiastic. She was unusually quiet, answering his inquiries with monosyllables. At the same time, she seemed to have something she wanted to say. Her eyes darted around the room, never quite meeting his. She kept glancing over toward William.

Meanwhile, over in the corner, the aspirin-Tylenol-ibuprofen combination was beginning to work. Halfway into the visit, William's prayers were finally answered, at least to the extent that a distinct snoring noise began resonating from beneath the washcloth. The sound was magnified several-fold by William's alternately inhaling and then exhaling the water with which he'd soaked the thing.

If Stephen found the sound amusing, Penny seemed to take it as a cue to open up a bit.

"Daddy," she said, "can I ask you something?"

"Sure," he said without thinking. "Anything."

"Did you ever *hurt* me? You know, do something *really bad* to me?"

Stephen hesitated. By nature, he was a follower of rules, and didn't want to risk jeopardizing his visits with his daughter. "You know I'm not allowed to talk to you about the case," he told her.

Her eyes darted from him to the snoring William, and back to him. As so often happened, his daughter had been quicker to grasp the significance of things than he'd been. Now she sat waiting for his answer.

"Of *course* not," Stephen said. "You know I could never hurt you, Cookie."

"Then why do they keep telling me you did? And trying to get me to remember things I can't remember?"

"Who's doing that?" he asked.

"Everybody."

"Who's *everybody*?"

"Mommy. Mommy's lawyer. Cathy. Mr. Hall. Mr. Hall's assistant. *All* of them. They keep trying to *wash my brain*, Daddy."

As if by their own volition, Stephen's arms opened, and his daughter came up out of her chair and into them. He hugged her as tightly as he could without breaking her tiny bones. She was so thin, he thought, so terribly thin.

This wasn't fair. When it came to him, they could do anything they wanted to. They could arrest him, they could take away his car, they could invade his home, they could put him in jail. He was an adult; he could handle it. But this was different. This was a *child*. *His* child. This they couldn't do. He could feel her tears running down his face, mixing with his own, pooling in the hollow of his collarbone.

He heard her voice now, breathless between sobs. "Do you love me, Daddy?"

It hit him like a sucker punch in the gut delivered by some schoolyard bully, and it took him a beat to recover. "Of *course* I love you, Sweetie." But even to himself, the words sounded silly, ineffective, detached. Here his only child—the love of his life, the stuff of his dreams, the single person in all of the universe he'd unflinchingly throw himself in front of a locomotive to save—was pleading for some proof that he loved her. And what did he have to answer her with? Words.

"*Really* love me?"

"More than anything," he told her. "You know that."

"Then take me away."

Jim Hall slit open the envelope with a silver letter opener, a gift from some campaign contributor whose name he could no longer recall. Hall was used to getting mail from judges, and seeing Priscilla McGee's name in the upper left-hand corner of the envelope didn't surprise him.

But her letter sure did.

"*Can you believe this shit?*" he said to no one in particular.

Wendy Garafolo, the assistant who'd recently returned from maternity leave, rose from her chair, wandered over, and took a look. But she read too slowly for Hall.

"She's changed her mind on the TV thing," he said. "*And she's going to let Barrow have a jury trial.*"

"Well, *that* she had to do," said Garafolo.

"Yeah," said Hall. "But she could have at least let him squirm a while."

"You still going to put the kid on?"

"Fuck, yes," said Hall. "And I'm still gonna get me a conviction, too."

As much as he believed in rules, Stephen Barrow believed even more that life was a series of tests. From the moment you came into the world, naked and helpless, you were tested. You took that first breath, or you died. It was that simple. You learned to suck at the breast, to crawl, to walk, to speak. It was an endless string of tests, one after another. Play, school, sports, work, all of it. You succeeded and went on to the next level, or you failed. Love was a test. Marriage was a test, one he'd failed badly at.

Fatherhood was a test.

So when his daughter, clinging to his chest, tears streaming down her face, begged him to take her away from the people who were doing these terrible things (interestingly enough, the word Stephen actually came up with in his mind, to describe what it was they were doing to her, was *abusing*), that, too, was a test.

And in that fraction of a second, that blink of the cosmos that was all the time Stephen had to decide what to do, he chose to think this: *If I say no, I pass this test for William, snoring over there in the corner. I pass it for the evaluation, for the lawyers, for the judges, for the court case. I pass it for me. The only one I fail is my child. Years from now, she won't remember the reasons I gave her, the explanations I made. For the rest of her life, all she'll remember is that I said no.*

It was at that moment that he rose from his chair and, with his daughter still wrapped tightly in his arms, walked out the door.

"Go find Hank," Jim Hall told Wendy Garafolo.

In the two minutes it took for Hank Bournagan to appear in the doorway, Hall reread Justice McGee's letter three times.

"Gutless wonder," he muttered, along with a couple of other choice thoughts.

"What's up, boss?" asked Bournagan.

"Nothing good. Get a hold of that Cathy Silverstein, and—"

"Silverman."

"Silverstein, Silverman, whatever. Just get a hold of her, will you, for Chrissakes?"

"Yessir."

"And tell her we need something *good* from that Barrow kid. Something that'll stand up in open court, in front of a jury. Do you think you can do that?"

"You bet."

———

"What happened to our Jeep?" was the first thing Penny asked as Stephen strapped her into the passenger seat of the Ford Fiesta.

"They took it away," he said.

"This sure is a funny little car."

"It sure is."

He made a right turn out of the parking lot, and found Route 20. "Where would you like to go?" he asked her.

"McDonald's?"

"McDonald's it is."

At the drive-thru window, he ordered Big Macs, fries, and Cokes. They found a parking spot and ate in the front seat, Penny dismantling her Big Mac into its component parts so that she could dip each bite first into ketchup, then into special sauce. They ate slowly, savoring every mouthful. To Stephen, no steak, no lobster, no key lime pie ever tasted so good.

He felt like Steve McQueen. He figured if they drove all day and all night, they could reach the Mexican border before dark tomorrow. He was practicing his Spanish and thinking he'd look pretty good with a mustache when he heard his daughter's voice from alongside him.

"You have to take me back now, don't you?"

He looked down at her. The tears had dried, leaving barely perceptible vertical lines on her cheeks. There was a tiny drop of special sauce at one corner of her mouth. She was smiling.

If he spent the next fifteen years in prison, every day of it in solitary confinement, she would always know he loved her. If they chained him to the wall of some dungeon and beat him unmercifully, she would never have to ask him again. And in time, when she was old enough, she'd come to visit him, bringing along books and cookies, and maybe even a Big Mac, if they permitted that sort of thing.

He placed a hand on either side of her face, bent down, and

kissed her on the forehead. "Yes," he said, "I have to take you back now."

Hank Bournagan decided against talking to Cathy Silverman on the phone. Hank had been a state trooper for two years before he'd gone to law school. He didn't trust phones all that much. Besides which, the drive to Albany would get him out of the office for a couple of hours and away from a smoldering Jim Hall.

He found Silverman at her computer.

"My boss is concerned about the Barrow kid," he told her. "The judge is going to allow her to testify in open court, in front of a jury. The trial's going to start Monday. We need to know if we can trust her."

"To do what?"

"You know," said Bournagan. They'd been through it before, five or six times. Without ever saying so in as many words, Bournagan had made it abundantly clear that if Silverman expected to continue getting referrals from the Columbia County courts, she'd have to deliver on this one. And *delivering* meant getting Penny Barrow to testify that her father had posed her, had done so on earlier occasions as well, had rewarded her each time she'd complied, and punished her each time she'd refused. And it also meant getting her to stick to her story and hold up under cross-examination.

"I'm seeing her tomorrow," said Silverman. "I think she'll do okay. I just wish that other judge hadn't permitted her to have visits with her father. You never know what *that* could lead to."

"Yeah," Bournagan agreed. "Wainwright's a real pain in the ass."

"Maybe," said Silverman, "I ought to give that social worker guy a call. You know, the one who monitors the visits?"

"Might be worth a try."

Silverman flipped through her file until she found the number of the center. She dialed it and waited for an answer. "It's Thursday," she told Bournagan. "They've got a visit scheduled for today. C'mon, pick up."

The aspirin, Tylenol, and ibuprofen that William had taken that morning had done more for him than at last bringing on the relief of sleep. They'd also produced a case of acute tinnitis, a constant, loud ringing sensation in his ears. Now, in the midst of his dream (he would forget the dream as soon as he awoke, except for the fact that he'd been inappropriately naked in it), the ringing suddenly changed from steady to intermittent, and got even louder. William opened his eyes on the third ring, but for some reason he still couldn't see. He wondered momentarily if he'd finally gone blind from excessive masturbation. On the fourth ring, he discovered a wet washcloth on his face and removed it, trying to remember how it had gotten there in the first place. On the fifth ring, the pain returned, reminding him.

It wasn't until the sixth ring that William spotted the phone, somehow connected the ringing sound to it, and picked up.

"Hello," he said.

"Hi," said a woman. William wondered briefly if she was naked. "This is Cathy Silverman, the therapist for Penny Barrow. Are you the one who supervises her visits with her father?"

William sat up straight. "Uh, yes," he said, "I am."

It was right about then that he noticed the two empty chairs across the room.

"Well," the woman was saying, "I was wondering if you could tell me how the visits are going. I'm concerned that the child might be regressing as a result of them."

Regressing? How about *disappearing?*

William rose to his feet, as though that might give him a better view of the room. But even from his improved vantage point, there was still no sign of either Stephen Barrow or his daughter.

Even in his state, William knew he was in big trouble. "Uh," he said, "I'm afraid I'm going to have to get back to you on that."

Stephen and Penny Barrow spoke very little on the drive back from McDonald's. As far as Stephen was concerned, he'd done what he'd had to do, and was prepared to suffer the consequences. As for his daughter, she seemed at peace with things. After all, it had been her idea that they go back to the center.

Which was probably just as well. The thirty dollars and change in Stephen's pocket probably would have run out before they'd made it to the Mexican border. Besides which, what else was there to say? He'd already shown her how much he loved her, and she in turn had obviously gotten the message, as well as some food in her stomach. In the great scheme of things, those seemed like two pretty important developments, at least to Stephen.

After a quick check of the waiting room, the rest rooms, and the cafeteria, William ran down the steps and out into the parking lot. Because Stephen always showed up absurdly early for his visits with his daughter, sitting in his car until William and Penny arrived, William had come to recognize Stephen's car. It helped that it was easy to spot with its mismatched doors, dented hood, and cracked windshield.

Right now, it was nowhere in sight.

Had William only waited five minutes—four, in fact—Stephen and Penny would have driven right up to where he was standing, and he might have been able to overlook their departure. But William was an employee, and like most employees, he feared for his job. After one last look around the parking lot, he went back into the building and reported to his director.

"Whaddaya mean, *they went AWOL?*"

And to cover for his own supervisory lapse, William was compelled to make things sound just a little better for himself, and just a little worse for Stephen Barrow. The director thereupon demanded the file, located the original court order, and phoned the courthouse in Hudson.

"Judge Wainwright's on the bench," somebody told him. "Would you like me to transfer you over to Judge McGee?"

"Sure," said the director.

Which explains how lunch at McDonald's ended up costing Stephen Barrow $8.73, his visits with Penny, and his freedom.

EIGHTEEN

TRIAL BEGINS TODAY IN CHILD PORN CASE

By Tom Grady
Special to the Hudson Valley Herald

The trial of Stephen Barrow, the East Chatham man accused of taking pornographic photos of his 6-year-old daughter, begins Monday in Hudson before Judge Priscilla McGee.

Barrow is being held without bail after briefly kidnapping his daughter Thursday from the center where he had been permitted to visit with her. But District Attorney Jim Hall is not expected to seek additional charges against him.

"He brought the child back shortly after he took her," said Hall. "Besides, we have such a strong case against him already, we don't need to worry."

In a surprise move recently revealed exclusively to this reporter, Judge McGee has ordered that the daughter, whose name is being withheld because of her age, will testify on behalf of the prosecution in open court, rather than via closed-circuit television, as had previously been expected. Judge McGee is also expected to announce that, in spite of the fact that Barrow had earlier expressly waived his right to a jury trial, she will nevertheless permit him to withdraw the waiver.

While declining to confirm that it would now definitely be a jury trial, Judge McGee did tell the *Herald*, "I believe in being fair, and if the defendant wants to change his mind now and take his chances with a jury, my inclination would be to allow him, no matter how late the date or what the law says. These are very serious charges, after all, and I wouldn't want to hear him complain afterward that he wasn't treated fairly."

The trial is expected to last a week to 10 days. If convicted of the top count in the indictment, Barrow faces 15 years in prison.

A trial, Stephen Barrow had often heard, was a search for the truth. Wasn't that what the lawyer for that football player had said, before getting his client acquitted of two murders that everyone in America knew he'd committed?

Stephen had also heard it said that no system was perfect.

A trial, Flynt Adams reminded himself, was a roll of the dice, a court of last resort for those cases you'd been unable to resolve by civilized means.

It was a time when your relationship with your client tended to stretch to the breaking point, especially when he pulled some stupid stunt like running off with his daughter so he could get himself thrown in jail, making his lawyer's job twice as difficult as it already had been.

It was also a time when your practice went to hell, you fought with your wife and kids, you became seriously sleep deprived, and your intestines more or less turned inside out.

A trial, Jim Hall knew, was a game. If you were better at it than your opponent, you won, nine times out of ten. The idea, of course, was to play as hard as you could, even if meant throwing an elbow or two along the way. As in most games, you were *expected* to step over the line now and then. Why else did they allow you five or six fouls in basketball before throwing you out, pace off a couple of yards against you in football, or banish you to a penalty box for two minutes in hockey?

It was all part of the game, that's why.

A trial, Priscilla McGee had long felt, was a pain in the rear. It lasted forever, took you away from the rest of your work, destroyed your personal life, messed up your case disposition statistics, required your undivided attention, could get you reversed if you weren't careful, and (in spite of your best efforts to shape the outcome) it didn't always turn out the way you wanted it to.

Worst of all, you didn't get paid one cent more than you would have if the defendant had only had the good sense to plead guilty in the first place and stop wasting your time.

A trial, Theresa Mulholland figured, was the only fitting way for the story to end. With her strict Catholic upbringing, Theresa had always tended to regard life as something of a morality play. For Stephen Barrow and his daughter, Penny, the trial would simply be the final act. So Theresa kept telling herself that, as unthinkable as it might seem to her, if a jury decided Stephen was guilty, he'd be convicted and sent off to prison, and his chances of ever being reunited with his daughter would come to an end. On the other hand, if he was found innocent (not being a lawyer herself, Theresa made the layman's mistake of thinking that the opposite of being found guilty was being found innocent), he'd be acquitted and would regain custody of his daughter, and he and Penny would live happily ever after.

But either way, there'd be no place in Stephen's life for Theresa. If he did go off to prison, as fond as she'd grown of him, she wasn't about to spend the next ten years, or whatever, as his pen pal. The day after the McDonald's fiasco, when Stephen had been remanded to the Columbia County Detention Facility, Theresa had moved her things out of his place and back into her own. She'd driven home in tears, telling herself that if things went well, she could always move back in with him.

But even then, she'd known better.

Even if Stephen were somehow to win and get his daughter back—as unlikely as those things now seemed—he'd need a long period of healing with Penny. It wouldn't be fair to any of the three of them to have Penny return home to find that during her absence, a woman had moved in and was sharing her father's bed. Penny would feel horribly threatened, Stephen would be torn between the two of them just when his daughter needed his undivided love, and Theresa would be left with the guilt of having driven a wedge between them.

It simply wouldn't work. It *couldn't* work.

And yet she came to the trial, and took a seat in the second row, her hands carefully folded to hide the Band-Aids across her knuckles.

Where else, after all, was she supposed to go?

"All rise! Part One of the Supreme Court, in and for the county of Columbia, is now in session. The Honorable Priscilla McGee, Justice of the Supreme Court, presiding. Please be seated. For trial, the People of the State of New York versus Stephen Barrow."

Sitting alongside his lawyer at the defense table, Stephen tried to smooth the wrinkles out of his sweater. It was an old sweater, worn and badly moth-eaten in spots. Together with faded jeans and an old pair of work boots, it comprised his latest edition of street clothes, the things he'd happened to be wearing the day of the McDonald's incident—which, depending upon your particular orientation, had come to be referred to as either the *kidnapping* or the *lunch break*.

"I assume," said Justice McGee, "that both sides are ready for trial."

"The defendant is ready," said Adams.

"The People are ready," said Jim Hall.

How weird, thought Stephen, *that with those two little responses, the balance of my life is about to be decided.*

"As you already know," said the judge, "I've revisited the issue of the child's testimony. There will be no television used. If you want to call the child, Mr. Hall, she'll have to testify like any other witness, in open court."

"Exception," said Hall.

A hundred years ago, trial lawyers were required to voice their disagreement with a judge's ruling by uttering the word "exception." This was so even when the lawyer had already made his position known—either by raising the point in the first instance with the word "objection," or by arguing the issue, orally or in writing. Although the requirement has long gone the way of the court crier and the powdered wig, the expression continues to survive in some areas, particularly among older professionals and in the Deep South. Jim Hall was neither old nor Southern. His use of the word in this instance was motivated by a bit of frustration, and was intended to convey his personal disapproval to Justice McGee. He said, "Exception" because he wanted to get under her skin just a little bit. He knew she was still on his side; he just wanted to make sure she remembered.

"Your exception is noted," said the judge, who wasn't above playing games. Which in this case meant responding to a meaningless comment with an equally meaningless comment of her own.

"I've also given additional thought to Mr. Barrow's waiver of a jury trial. What's your position on that now, Mr. Adams?"

"My client would like a jury," said Adams. Having read the judge's letter, he saw no need to argue the point further.

"Then a jury he shall have."

"Exception," said Jim Hall again.

"Noted," said McGee. "Bring in the panel."

A hundred and six white people filed into the courtroom. For the rest of the day, they would be questioned by the judge and the lawyers on every imaginable subject, from what they did for a living to which magazines they read to how they felt about creationism. Stephen's only previous experience with the jury system had been a dozen years ago, when he'd been living in Manhattan's Greenwich Village and had been summoned to serve on a drug case. "The defense lawyer looks familiar to me," he'd been compelled to tell the judge. "I may have seen him in my neighborhood." He was thanked for his candor and promptly excused.

Almost all of these jurors, it seemed, knew Jim Hall, or one of his assistants, or somebody in the sheriff's office or the state police. A couple of them shopped at the Drug Mart in South Chatham. Most had heard of the case, either by reading Tom Grady's articles in the *Herald* or by hearing mention of it from those who had. At first Stephen thought the judge might have to excuse them all. Instead she simply asked them, "Can you assure me you'll be fair in spite of that?"

"Oh, yes," they all told her.

It was much the same story when it came to the subject matter of the case. Although they visibly squirmed in their seats at the mere mention of child pornography, few of the jurors admitted to having strong feelings on the matter. Those that did were asked if they could set those feelings aside and give the defendant a fair trial anyway.

"Absolutely," they said.

By late afternoon, it seemed Flynt Adams had exhausted his challenges on those jurors who were first cousins of Jim Hall, had campaigned for him in more than one of his elections, or were currently married to state troopers. Hall, in turn, had knocked off anyone who had facial hair (including one unfortunate housewife from Ghent), had ever opened a copy of *Playboy*, or appeared to be a day under fifty.

They were left with a jury of smooth-faced, middle-aged folks who—while they themselves had certainly never set eyes on a centerfold—promised they were ready to forgive anyone who had.

Justice McGee broke for the day.

"So what do you think?" Stephen asked his lawyer.

Adams looked up from his notes and shrugged. "They look okay to me," he said.

What planet was he *living on?*

Cathy Silverman was elated. On Friday she'd had what she considered a breakthrough session with Penny Barrow. Not that it had started off well, what with the child's familiar insistence that her father hadn't posed her, had never taken similar photos in the past, and had neither rewarded her nor punished her to gain her compliance.

Exasperated, Silverman finally lost it. "Look," she said, "You're lying to me. I *know* your father abused you."

Penny, as she did whenever things got stressful, rearranged her baby blanket with one hand and raised the other to her mouth. Thumb-sucking would be next; it always was. Only this time, Penny surprised Silverman.

"How do you know?" she asked.

The manuals were quite clear on this point. The idea was to give the subject the impression that you knew *everything*. That way, she'd come to realize that you could see right through her attempts at deception, and that she was going to have to tell you the truth sooner or later.

"It's my *job* to know," said Silverman. "I went to school for many, many years, just so I'd be able to know all there is to know about things like this. I'm an *expert*."

"Well," said Penny, "if you know all the right answers, why don't you just *tell* them to me? That way, I'll know them, too."

Silverman paused to think about that. Was the child being sarcastic with her, trying to manipulate the interview? Such things happened, she knew, but usually with older subjects. Six was pretty young for that. And then Silverman recalled what she'd been taught was Rule Number One in behavioral science: Always look for the simplest, most obvious explanation.

To Silverman, the simplest explanation behind what Penny had just said was this: Penny finally was ready to drop her denials and confirm what Silverman had strongly suspected all along, and had now come right out and said she *knew to be true*—that Penny's father had indeed abused her. At the same time, however, Penny needed to make it look as though she was simply going along with Silverman. That way, it wouldn't seem as though she was turning on her own father.

And in that moment, Cathy Silverman realized that all this poor child was asking her for was a way to tell the truth that she could somehow live with. After all she'd been through, she deserved no less.

"Did your father make you bend over naked like that?" she asked, immediately followed up with a whispered, *"Yes, he did."*

"Yes, he did," said Penny.

"Had he made you do things like that before? *Yes, he had.*"

"Yes, he had."

"How many times? *Three or four.*"

"Three or four."

"Did he punish you if you refused? *Yes, he did.*"

"Yes, he did."

"How? *He'd spank me.*"

"He'd spank me."

"Did he reward you if you did as he told you to? *Yes, he did.*"

"Yes, he did."

"How? *He'd give me treats.*"

"He'd give me treats."

"What kind of treats? *Candy, ice cream, strawberries.*"

"Candy, ice cream, strawberries."

"*Excellent,*" said Silverman. No matter that the child's affect was slightly flat; that was to be expected in sex-abuse cases. "Now, here's what I'm going to do. I'm going to ask you the same questions, but this time I'm not going to tell you the right answers. Do you think you can remember them yourself?"

"I'll try," said Penny.

They ran through the exercise again, this time without Silverman supplying the answers. Except for not being able to list the treats, Penny did fine. *"Wonderful,"* said Silverman. "One last time, and then we'll be finished for the day, okay?"

"Okay."

And they did it a third time. Only this time, just prior to asking the questions, Silverman quietly flipped a little switch under her desk. The switch activated a hidden video camera across the room. The microphone that worked in conjunction with the camera was taped to the underside of the chair in which Penny was sitting.

"Did your father make you bend over naked like that?" asked Silverman.

"Yes, he did," said Penny . . .

When he heard the news of Cathy Silverman's breakthrough with Penny Barrow, Jim Hall was every bit as elated as Silverman. Personally, Hall had had his doubts about the child, and had decided to put off calling her until the very end of his case. By doing that, he'd be able to see how things were going, and make a last-minute decision as to whether he needed her testimony at all.

But this changed everything.

"Tell you what," Hall told Hank Bournagan, who'd delivered not only the good news but the videotape to back it up. "We're gonna do this thing *chronologically*, just like the events themselves unfolded. We'll let those jurors relive it for themselves. I'm gonna lead off with the kid, have her describe how her daddy forced her to pose."

"Want to put her on before she changes her mind, huh?"

Hall smiled. "She can't change her mind, Hank. That's the beauty of the videotape."

"Right," Bournagan agreed. You tended to do that a lot when you worked for Jim Hall.

"Then I'll call the three Drug Mart witnesses—first, the one he dropped the film off with; next, that Priestley woman, who saw they were kiddie porn and called nine-one-one; and last, the clerk he picked them up from. From there we'll shift to the troopers, get in the arrest and the confession."

"Sure works for *me*," said Bournagan.

"And *goddamn* if it won't work for the *jury*, too. Roll that tape one more time, why don't you?"

Flynt Adams, of course, knew nothing of Penny Barrow's conversion, or the videotape that documented it. As far as Adams was concerned, this case was still winnable, as long as he could either keep Penny off the stand altogether, or somehow contain her testimony so that she added nothing significant to the prosecution's case. If he could do either of those things, the case would come down to the photograph itself. And Adams believed that any group of reasonable people—including those twelve jurors they'd picked earlier in the day—would be unable to agree that the photo, standing by itself, was "lewd" enough to constitute a "sexual performance."

Adams worked characteristically late that Monday night, preparing his opening statement and reading through a hundred pages of witness statements Jim Hall had dumped on him at the close of the day's court session. Hall hadn't done so out of any sense of fair play; the law required him to turn the stuff over, and even then he'd waited till the last possible moment to do so.

Then, when he was finished reading the statements, Adams spent another hour researching the law on how old a child had to be in order to be sworn in as a witness. It was after 2:00 when he finally went upstairs to bed. And even then, he lay awake in the dark for another forty-five minutes, listening to the regular breathing of his wife and thinking of questions to ask, issues to raise, and arguments to make.

Trials were like that for Flynt Adams.

————

Stephen Barrow had trouble falling asleep that night, too. But in Stephen's case, the problem was that he was still having difficulty adjusting to life back in jail. He'd grown accustomed to sleeping with Theresa, with having her warmth beside him, her reassuring voice when he awoke in the middle of the night and remembered his daughter was under a different roof.

In place of that, he had his bare lightbulb back, the eternal flame burning in the middle of his ceiling. Stephen had always noticed those ads in the backs of magazines for energy-saving bulbs that lasted for thousands of hours and were guaranteed to work for ten years before giving out, or your money back. He'd always thought about sending away for a couple of them, just to see if they really worked, but he'd never gotten around to it. They were probably bogus, he'd decided, a total rip-off. After all, had he ever heard of *anyone* who'd ever bought one?

Now he had.

He put his forearm across his face, closed his eyes, and prayed for sleep. He knew it wouldn't be right to pray for an acquittal; for someone who wasn't accustomed to praying (and was far from convinced there was anyone up there listening to you in the first place), it struck him as an *unseemly* thing to do. Kind of like praying for his daughter's return. It was simply too much to ask, right out of the blue like that.

But *sleep*? Surely it was okay to pray for *sleep*.

NINETEEN

"Are we ready to bring in the jury and proceed with opening statements?" asked Justice McGee.

"Yes, your honor," said Flynt Adams.

Instead of answering, Jim Hall rose slowly from his chair. From his own seat, Adams could see that his adversary was holding something in his hands, but he couldn't make out what it was.

"Your honor, yesterday afternoon, pursuant to the *Rosario* requirement, I turned over to defense counsel copies of all statements of witnesses the People intend to call at this trial. Late last evening, quite unexpectedly, I came into possession of a videotape of one of my witnesses. It was only made this past Friday, and I didn't even know of its existence until it was delivered to my office. I've had a copy made for the defense, and one for the court, as well, and I'd like to turn them over at this time."

"Please do so," said the judge. "Mr. Adams?"

Adams had jumped to his feet midway through Hall's speech. "May we know who the witness is," he asked, "and when Mr. Hall intends to call him?"

"Certainly," said Hall, who appeared to be enjoying every minute of this. "Though it's not a *him,* it's a *her.* The name of the witness is Penny Barrow, and—"

"This is *outrageous*!" Adams shouted. "This is nothing but an *ambush*! We haven't had a chance to look at this. And I don't believe his story for a moment, that he didn't know it existed until it suddenly *fell into his lap* yesterday evening."

For once in his life, Flynt Adams was wrong about Jim Hall. Which only goes to show that not all snakes bite all the time.

They found a VCR and allowed Adams and his client to view the videotape in the sheriff's office. It didn't take long: The whole thing lasted less than three minutes. There was Penny, sitting in a chair, her Baba draped over her lap. And there was Cathy Silverman, sitting maybe five feet away from her, asking her questions in a relaxed, conversational tone.

"Did your father make you bend over naked like that?" Silverman asked.

"Yes, he did," Penny answered.

Twice Adams rewound the tape and played it through again in its entirety. Penny's answers were the same each time. She was even able to describe what sort of *treats* her father had given in order to get her to perform for him.

"This is *devastating*," said Adams.

Stephen could only nod weakly. He'd seen and heard his daughter's responses three times now, and he still didn't know what to make of them.

"I've got to know," he heard Adams saying to him. "Is she telling the truth or not?"

She was his daughter. For all intents and purposes, he'd raised her, made her what she was. He'd taught her above all to be nice to living things, to take responsibility for her own actions, and to tell the truth. What was he going to say now, that she was a *liar*?

Which prompted Stephen to ask himself the unthinkable, the one question it had never before occurred to him to ask. Was it possible that she was telling the truth? Could he have done those things to her, after all, and then somehow managed to *forget*? It didn't seem likely. And yet, here was his daughter. . . .

"I'm your lawyer," Adams was saying. "I need to know."

Stephen looked at him. He wanted to scream out, *"NO! NO! NO! Can't you see she's* lying? *How can you even* think *I could have done something like that?"* But the scream wouldn't come; the words wouldn't form. He was left to sit there helplessly, and shrug.

"I don't think so," he said, finally. "I don't think so."

There are bad moments in every trial, Flynt Adams knew. Jurors who seemed perfect for the defense disqualified themselves, surprise witnesses crawled out of the woodwork to bite you, cops remembered damaging things they'd neglected to put in their reports, alibis dissolved, or the defendant took the witness stand and destroyed himself.

But this was worse.

The defendant's own daughter was about to walk into the courtroom and blow them away. A six-year-old, cute as a button. The jury would eat up everything she told them. And what was she going to tell them? That her father was guilty, with a capital G. And if that wasn't bad enough, here was the father, all but admitting it by saying, "I don't think so."

Flynt Adams was no dummy. He knew full well that Stephen's "I don't think so" could mean only one thing. And he *hated* Stephen for it, wanted to *strangle* him. Not just because of what he'd done to his daughter. *That* he could forgive him for. He was one sick bastard, to be sure, but when you made your living defending criminals, you tended to meet people who'd done very bad things, and you learned to get past it.

No, he hated Stephen for another reason altogether, one that only a trial lawyer could even begin to comprehend. He hated him because he now knew that what Stephen had done to his daughter was going to cause Flynt Adams to lose this case. So he did what every conscientious lawyer does when he realizes he's about to go down in flames.

He looked for a way out.

"Suppose I could get you five years' probation with psychiatric counseling," he said, having no idea whether Jim Hall would go for it, or Justice McGee, either, for that matter. But he wasn't above *begging*. Begging was part of being a criminal defense lawyer, too.

"What would I have to do?" asked Stephen.

"Plead guilty," said Adams. "Admit you did those things your daughter says you did."

Stephen tried to think about that, but thinking about anything was becoming increasingly difficult. He'd reached the point where he was no longer certain what the truth was. He couldn't remember doing those things. Surely he would have remembered: *You couldn't possibly do stuff like that, and then not remember, could you?* But then again, here was Penny, saying he'd done them. And Penny didn't lie—not even that time she'd broken the thermometer, causing all the *Jupiter* to spill out.

Maybe Penny wasn't sure, either. Maybe they'd *washed her brain* so much that *she* no longer knew what was true and what wasn't. Maybe she was looking to *him* for her answer. But if that was so, and he were to stand up in court now and say, "Yes, God help me, I did those things," then it would *become* the truth for her, and she'd have to live the rest of her life believing that her father had in fact abused her, and that there must have been something terrible about her that had caused him to do it.

How could he do that to her?

He turned to Adams. "No," he said, "I can't do that."

And Flynt Adams thought he understood. There were certain clients who, no matter what they'd done and how overwhelming the evidence against them might be, simply couldn't bring themselves to admit their guilt. Not to the judge, not to their own lawyer, not to members of their own family, not even, sometimes, to themselves. And given the nature of what Stephen Barrow had done, it wasn't hard to see why he was having trouble admitting it.

And another thing. Adams had found over the years that the one thing his criminal clients had most in common was their infinite capacity to act in self-destructive ways. They robbed the convenience store they'd once worked at, so they'd be sure to be recognized by employees who knew them. They got caught full-face on the security camera, left perfect fingerprints on the cash register, and drove off in a car they'd rented under their own name the day before. Arrested, they either confessed or claimed a demonstrably false alibi. Offered a five-year plea bargain, they invariably turned it down, went to trial, and ended up with twenty. Finally up for parole consideration after ten years, they continued to insist they were innocent, earning an additional five for failure to accept responsibility.

At every step—from the planning to the parole board—they acted as their own worst enemy. Stephen Barrow was smarter than most of them, and certainly more educated. But obviously he was no less self-destructive. All Adams had to do to remind himself was to think back to the McDonald's episode, the *kidnapping*. You couldn't get much more self-destructive than that.

"Okay," Adams told Stephen, patting him on the arm. "Okay."

He wanted to kill him.

"The People call Penny Barrow," announced Jim Hall as soon as opening statements had been completed. Having alerted the defense that he intended to call Penny at some point, and having made the same promise to the jury, Hall had failed to reveal that she would in fact be his very first witness. His announcement now not only caught the defense by surprise (making it two for two that morning), but produced a collective gasp from the jury box.

Adams bounced to his feet. "May we approach the sidebar?" he asked.

"Yes," said the judge, "come on up." Her voice had a weary quality to it, as though to convey the impression to the jury that it might have been the twentieth time Adams had made such an interruption, when it was actually the first. But inflections of that sort don't show up on court transcripts, as judges well know.

Both lawyers, the court reporter, and the clerk gathered around the judge in a sort of football huddle. From where he sat Stephen wasn't able to hear the conversation, but he could see that Adams was doing most of the talking and Hall most of the smiling, with the judge throwing in an exaggerated eye-roll now and then. Then they broke the huddle, and the players returned to their positions.

"We'll take a brief recess," said Justice McGee. Everyone waited while the jurors were led out of the room. What a way for a trial to begin, thought Stephen. The first witness gets called, and doesn't even make it into the courtroom before they announce a time-out. Hollywood would never put up with a wasted scene like that.

"Bring in the child," said Justice McGee. At a nod from Jim Hall, Hank Bournagan rose from the prosecution table and left the room by a side door.

A hush fell over the courtroom as all eyes remained glued to the door. A minute went by, maybe more. Then it swung open, and in walked Bournagan, followed by an entourage consisting of Ada Barrow, Jane Sparrow, and Cathy Silverman. Only when the adults in front of her got out of the way was Stephen able to see that Silverman was leading his daughter by one hand. Wrapped over Penny's other arm was her Baba.

The sight caused Stephen to rise to his feet involuntarily, and Flynt Adams had to place a hand on his shoulder and lower him back down into his chair. What was it Stephen had been going to do or say? He hadn't the slightest idea.

Penny was led to the witness stand and told to sit. It was a full-sized chair, evidently intended to be ample enough for the widest of witnesses, and she seemed tiny in it, *lost*. Bournagan resumed his spot next to Hall at the prosecution table. Stephen's ex-wife and her lawyer were directed to take seats in the front row. Only Cathy Silverman was allowed to stay next to Penny, taking up a position beside her like some foreign-language interpreter.

Justice McGee put on her best imitation of a smile. "Hello, Penny," she said. "My name is Priscilla McGee. I'm the judge."

"Hello, Priscilla." Penny's voice seemed small and far away. She glanced at Stephen, caught his eyes, and looked away.

"I want you to relax," said the judge. "Everything's going to be just fine. Okay?" From the way she spoke, Stephen could tell she'd never had children of her own.

"Okay," said Penny, arranging her blanket on her lap.

"How old are you?"

"Seven."

McGee looked up. "I thought you said she was *six*."

"Saturday was my birthday," explained Penny.

Stephen felt a stabbing sensation in his chest. May 20, of course. *He'd forgotten his daughter's birthday.* No matter that he'd been in jail, unable to be with her to celebrate it. He'd *forgotten* it. How could he have been so wrapped up in his own problems to have let that happen?

"Penny," asked the judge, "do you believe in God?"

She seemed to consider that for a moment, before answering, "I don't know."

"Do you know what it means when you promise you're going to do something, and then *swear* to do it?"

"Yes."

"What does it mean?"

"It means you're really going to do it, no matter what."

"And do you know what it means to tell the truth?"

"Yes."

"What does it mean?"

"To not tell a lie."

"Right. And what's a *lie*?"

"When you make something up."

"Very good," said the judge, as though she were talking to a three-year-old. "Now is it better to tell the truth or to lie?"

"It's better to tell the truth."

As he sat listening, Stephen remembered what his lawyer had told him—that without his daughter's testimony, they probably couldn't convict him, but with it (at least the version depicted on the videotape) they most surely would. He knew, therefore, that he should be rooting *against* Penny, hoping she couldn't come up with the right answers that would qualify her to be a witness. And yet he found he couldn't do that, that quite the opposite was true. She was his daughter. She was smart as a whip. And with each correct answer she gave, all he could feel was pride. He knew that was totally crazy, but still he couldn't help it.

"Why is it better to tell the truth?" the judge wanted to know.

Penny shrugged. "It just is," she said.

"What happens to you if you tell a lie?"

"Nothing."

"Don't you get punished?"

"I don't know."

Of course she doesn't know, Stephen wanted to shout. His daughter didn't tell lies, and he didn't punish her. Was that so difficult to understand?

Apparently so, for the judge. "So if you don't get punished, why is it better to tell the truth?"

Again Penny's eyes sought Stephen's, and he tried to nod at her, to let her know in some small way that it was okay, that she was doing just fine. That he loved her.

She looked up at the judge and said, "It's just one of those things that's right to do, that's all."

And to Stephen, Penny suddenly appeared to go blurry, as though she'd somehow slipped out of focus, and it took him a moment to realize it wasn't her at all; it was the tears in his eyes.

"Have her step outside," said the judge, and Penny was escorted from the room. "Mr. Adams, I take it you still object to her being sworn?"

"Yes, your honor. The law sets *twelve* as the presumptive age at which a child may give sworn testimony. This child isn't twelve. She's not eleven or ten or nine, or even eight. She's *seven years and three days old*. And no matter how cute she may look and how smart she may sound, she's not even *close* to the age the legislature had in mind when they wrote the statute."

As Adams sat, Jim Hall rose.

"No need, Mr. Hall," said the judge. "I find that the child is extraordinarily intelligent and wise beyond her years. Even better than saying you should tell the truth to avoid being punished, she seems to comprehend that truth-telling is *intrinsically* better than lying. I can't imagine where she picked that notion up, but it's more than most of our *adult* witnesses know. I find that she understands the nature of an oath, and can be sworn as a witness. Put her back on the stand and bring in the jury."

Adams slumped visibly in his chair. Stephen felt his loyalties divided. He was proud of his daughter, but felt bad for his lawyer. His own survival skills had all but abandoned him; he no longer knew what was best for him. In his mind, the outcome of the trial no longer depended on his own testimony, as he'd once been told it would. It depended instead on his daughter's, and whether his lawyer would be clever enough to discredit her when it came time for him to cross-examine her. But *discredit* was the wrong word; the word you always heard them use was *destroy*.

How on earth could he hope for *that*?

The jurors hadn't expected Penny to be on the witness stand when they returned to the courtroom, and as they filed in and took their seats in the jury box, every one of them stared at her intently. One or two smiled at the sight of her, only to quickly remember the dreadful things she'd come there to tell them.

"In the matter of the People of the State of New York versus Stephen Barrow, do you swear to tell the truth, the whole truth, and nothing but the truth, so help you God?"

"Yes."

"Would you tell us your name, please."

"Penny Barrow."

"And how old you are?"

"Seven."

"Mr. Hall, you may inquire."

Hall rose slowly—Stephen thought even overdramatically—from his chair, stepped to the podium, and arranged his notes. "Good morning, young lady," he said to Penny.

"Good morning," she replied, adjusting her blanket protectively.

"What's your Daddy's name?"

"Stephen Barrow."

"Do you by any chance see him in the courtroom?"

"Yes."

"Could you point him out for us?"

Penny dutifully pointed in Stephen's direction.

"May the record reflect," said Hall, "that the witness has correctly indicated the defend-*ant*." He stressed the last syllable of the word, as though to suggest that Stephen was not so much a human being as an *insect* of some sort.

"Back in February, right before Valentine's Day, were you living with your daddy?"

"Yes."

"Was anyone else living with you, or was it just the two of you?"

"Just the two of us."

"By the way, do you love your daddy?"

"Yes."

"You wouldn't say anything to hurt him, would you? Unless it was the truth, that is. Would you?"

"Objection," said Flynt Adams.

"Overruled," said the judge.

"Would you?" Hall repeated.

"No."

"Do you remember one day, toward the end of the time you were living alone with your daddy, that he took some pictures of you with a camera?"

"Yes."

"Do you remember him taking several pictures of you when you had no clothes on?"

Penny hesitated. "How many is *several*?" she asked.

"Three or four."

"Yes."

"Do you remember one picture in particular, in which you were bending way over, facing away from your daddy, and your rear end was pointed toward him?"

The courtroom, already hushed, went stone quiet. No one had expected Jim Hall to move in for the kill quite this quickly.

"Do you remember that picture?" Hall asked.

"Yes," said Penny.

"Very good," said Hall. "Now do you by any chance remember whose idea it was that you bend over like that?"

Just to his right, Stephen thought he could hear Flynt Adams mumble, "Just say no."

But Penny was too far away to hear. "Yes," she said.

"Do you think you could point out that person for us?"

Slowly, Penny uncurled one tiny fist, and extended one slender index finger.

To Stephen, it suddenly seemed as though he were watching the trial from somewhere else, and that things had somehow shifted into very slow motion. And the thought that dawned on him was this: *How strange to witness the precise moment when my life ends. Not when I* took *the photo—I had no idea then that I was doing anything that would ever turn out to be important. But this moment now, this is what I'll always look back on, as the single moment in my life when being a father came to an end for me.*

Slowly, tantalizingly slowly, as though teasing some unseen playmate in a game of eeny-meeny-miney-mo, Penny swung her finger in a wide arc, aiming it closer and closer to Stephen. And then, at the very last moment, just before settling on him for good, she redirected it, until her fingertip came to rest against her own chest.

In the jury box, twelve pairs of eyes widened and swung from the witness to the prosecutor.

"I don't think she understood what you wanted her to do," said the judge. "I think she's asking you, 'Who's supposed to do the pointing?'"

"My mistake," said Jim Hall. "Why don't you just *tell* us, young lady, like you told Cathy. Whose idea was it for you to bend over like that?"

And Penny looked straight at him and said, "It was *my* idea."

Hall cleared his throat. "Are you *sure*?" he asked her.

"Sure, I'm sure. I *mooned* my father. I saw them do it in *Grease*. I thought it would be funny."

Even as Stephen fought back his tears, even as Flynt Adams came to life and straightened up in his chair, even as the jurors whispered among themselves, even as Priscilla McGee banged her gavel to restore order—even then, Jim Hall wasn't finished.

"*Do you remember,*" he boomed, "answering some questions for Cathy here, just four days ago?"

"Yes," said Penny.

"And did Cathy ask you if your daddy made you bend over like that?"

"I guess so."

"And did you say, 'Yes, he did'?"

"Yes, but—"

"And did Cathy ask you if he'd made you do things like that before?"

"Yes."

"And you said, 'Yes, he had'?"

"Yes."

"And Cathy asked you, 'How many times'?"

"Yes."

"And you said, 'Three or four'?"

"Yes."

"Well, young lady, were those things true when you said them to Cathy?"

"No."

"No? Then why did you tell her they were?"

If there is one cardinal rule to cross-examination, it is to never ask a question unless you know in advance what the witness's answer will be. But right after that comes a second rule, almost as important, but far too often forgotten.

Never ask a *why* question.

Jim Hall would explain later on that he felt he had no choice, that given Penny Barrow's acknowledgment that she'd told Cathy Silverman the truth (or at least what Hall still considered to be the truth), he had no choice now but to demand an explanation for her sudden claim that it hadn't been.

"Why?" he asked a second time.

"Because," said Penny, "she told me to say those things."

If Penny's answer amounted to yet another setback for Hall, he showed no sign of defeat. A good trial lawyer is someone capable of maintaining a smile while in the throes of a heart attack. Beyond that, Hall knew he had Cathy Silverman to call to the stand later on. Silverman would flatly deny that she'd told Penny what to say, and given the choice between a confused child and an adult professional, the jury would be forced to believe Silverman. But even better, Hall had the videotape, literally sitting right in front of him at this very moment. And if ever there was a time to bring out your ace, Jim Hall knew this was it.

"Your honor," he said, "the People most respectfully request the right to play the videotape for the witness."

"Objection," said Flynt Adams. "He can't do that."

"Overruled," said the judge.

Apparently, he *could*.

A recess was declared so that Hall and his staff could set up the video equipment. Monitors were positioned in such a way that the tape would be able to be seen from every angle of the courtroom—the witness stand, the jury box, the judge's bench, the two counsel tables, even the spectator section. After a test run to make sure everything was in working order, Penny resumed the stand, and the jury reentered the courtroom.

"Now Penny," Hall began, "I believe you told us a little while ago that the only reason you said your daddy made you bend over was because Cathy told you to say so. Is that right?"

"Yes."

"And did she tell you to say so this past Friday, which was the last time you were at her office?"

"Yes."

"Penny, I'm going to show you a *videotape*. Do you know what a *videotape* is?"

From the look Penny gave to Hall, Stephen was afraid she was about to come out with one of her *duhs*. But she managed to confine herself to a "Yes."

"Good," said Hall. "Now you just watch that screen in front of you, okay?"

"Okay."

Hall started the tape, and Stephen watched the monitor on the defense table. As before, there was Penny, her blanket draped across her lap just as it was today, sitting across from Cathy Silverman.

"Did your father make you bend over like that?" Silverman asked.

"Yes, he did," said Penny.

Hall played the tape straight through, from beginning to end. By the time he was finished, it was Penny the jurors were staring at.

"Were you able to see that on your screen?" Hall asked Penny.

"Yes."

"Were you able to hear everything?"

"Yes."

"Tell me," said Hall, his tone turning thoughtful. "At any point on that videotape, did you see or hear Cathy telling you what to say?"

"No," Penny admitted.

"Even once?"

"No."

Penny's thumb went to her mouth. She looked smaller and thinner than ever. And it looked as though Jim Hall had managed to snatch victory from the jaws of defeat. There was no way, Hall knew, that she could possibly explain the tape. He therefore decided to risk asking another *why* question. The difference was, this time there really *was* no risk: Hall couldn't lose. It was what lawyers like to think of as a win-win situation, where whatever the witness does simply gets them into deeper trouble.

"Why isn't it on the tape, Penny?"

Penny shrugged.

"You have to answer," the judge told her.

"She gave me the answers," Penny insisted, her voice barely audible. "She really did. I don't know why they're not there."

"Maybe they disappeared," Hall suggested.

Her thumb in her mouth now, Penny whispered something Stephen couldn't make out.

"Maybe they're hiding. Or *maybe*," said Hall, "they were never there in the first place."

Again Stephen was unable to hear. Either, apparently, was Justice McGee. "Speak up," she said. "And will somebody please do me a favor, and take that *blanket* away from her. Maybe that'll help."

A sheriff's deputy rose and approached the witness stand. But when he reached for the blanket, Penny pulled it back and clung to it more tightly than ever. Gently but firmly, the deputy gave it a tug. Try as she might, Penny was simply no match for him. As the blanket came free, something slipped from her lap and fell to the floor in front of her. It was made of black plastic, and was the size and shape of a deck of playing cards. For a moment, no one seemed to know what it was. No one, that is, except for Penny.

And Stephen.

"My tape recorder," he whispered to Flynt Adams. "That's my old tape recorder."

But if Adams had been sitting close enough to Stephen to hear, the judge had been unable to. "What *is* that, child?" she asked.

Penny seemed to think for a moment. Then she looked directly up at the judge. And when she gave her answer, this time it was in a steady voice, loud enough for all in the courtroom to hear without difficulty.

"That," she said, "is where the rest of Cathy's words are hiding."

TWENTY

Anyone who has ever lined up a row of dominos and then knocked the first one into the second understands what a chain reaction is.

When Penny Barrow looked up at the judge and said, "That's where the rest of Cathy's words are hiding," her statement set into motion a sequence of events that was almost nuclear in its proportions.

Flynt Adams, who had the advantage of having learned seconds earlier from Stephen Barrow that the object that had fallen to the floor was a tape recorder, jumped to his feet and demanded that whatever it contained be immediately played for the jury. Jim Hall pounded his fist on the podium and loudly demanded a recess. Samuel Ethridge, the sheriff's deputy who had precipitated the commotion by pulling Penny's blanket from her lap—having initially dived for cover, certain the object was a miniature bomb of some sort—now lowered himself carefully to the floor to inspect the item. And all the while, the jurors looked on in wide-eyed, open-mouthed disbelief at this latest turn of events.

The deputy, apparently reassured by the absence of any ticking sound emanating from the device, extended a finger and touched it tentatively, then quickly drew back. Stephen had once seen a chimpanzee reacting in identical fashion to the presence of a toy giraffe placed in his habitat. After several tries, each progressively bolder, the creature had finally summoned up the courage to pick it up.

Samuel Ethridge did the same now. Then he stood and looked at the judge for guidance.

Priscilla McGee had no idea what to do. With all the commotion, she'd missed hearing the fact that the thing was a tape recorder. The defense was demanding that it be *played,* whatever that meant. The prosecution wanted a recess, but she'd already declared two of those, and they were still on direct examination of the first witness. If there was one thing she hated, it was constant interruptions. Besides which, the jurors seemed anxious to have the mystery resolved. So Justice McGee figured they might as well find out what the damned thing was, without further delay. Turning in the direction of Samuel Ethridge, she announced her decision.

"Play it, Sam."

It took the deputy a while to figure out how to work the contraption—far longer, as a matter of fact, than it had taken Penny. Of course, Ethridge was at something of a disadvantage: He hadn't had a father to show him how the thing worked in the first place, and he hadn't had two weeks' worth of practice to reach the point where he could work the buttons, sight unseen, beneath a baby blanket. But he finally got the hang of it.

To say that the tape was revealing would be somewhat akin to saying the Hindenburg experienced a rough landing, or Edmund Hillary took a hike. There was some static, but then there was Cathy Silverman's voice, supplying Penny the answers to each of her questions, right down to the treats her father had given her as rewards. Even strawberries, which—as both father and daughter well knew—Penny was seriously allergic to. But there was more. There was Penny's mother, telling her how much her father secretly hated her and how glad he'd been to get rid of her. There was Jane Sparrow, warning Penny she'd better do as she was told, or else she'd end up with *no* parents. And there was even Jim Hall at one point, assuring Penny that the truth could wait until later, and that her only job on the witness stand was to make sure she answered the questions the same way as she had for Cathy Silverman.

Penny Barrow's tape recordings did more than bring an end to the trial. By nightfall, Priscilla McGee had dismissed all charges against Stephen Barrow and ordered his release. Everett Wainwright had permanently restored Penny's custody to her father. Theresa Mulholland had a lengthy article published by her new employer, the *Albany Times Union*, in which she argued forcefully that the trial indeed had been about a case of abuse, only this time there'd been an unusual twist: The victim had turned out to be the accused himself, and the abusers those entrusted with the reins of power.

For a while, it looked very much as though heads would roll. Cathy Silverman's objectivity and methodology were questioned, Jane Sparrow had to answer a complaint before the disciplinary committee, and Jim Hall was subjected to the embarrassment of a recall petition.

But in the legal world, as in so many others, the system has a way of protecting its own. Silverman was issued a mild reprimand, but permitted to continue accepting court assignments; Sparrow apologized for her "vigorous advocacy," and was exonerated of any wrongdoing; and Hall not only survived the recall petition, but won reelection in the fall by a wider margin than ever. It seemed the good people of Columbia County understood that Hall had acted only out of the best of intentions, believing in his heart that the end had justified the means.

By the year 2002, the annual number of reports of child sexual abuse in this country will have surpassed the one-hundred-thousand mark. Of those, at least 70 percent will prove to be incapable of substantiation. In cases involving disputes over the custody of children, knowledgeable experts estimate that *as many as eighty-five percent of the allegations are completely false.*

Today, Stephen Barrow writes and lives with his daughter outside a small town in the shadows cast by the Rocky Mountains. He speaks with Theresa Mulholland on a regular basis, and she's promised to come out and visit during ski season. The Ford Fiesta died on the trip west, somewhere in the middle of Kansas. Unable to locate a suitable Jeep Renegade to replace it, Stephen and Penny settled instead on a Wrangler. But its windshield wipers stick, its horn works only occasionally, and it reminds them of old times. Anyway, the price was right. For even though Stephen has been relieved of the requirement that he send child support to his ex-wife, it will be many years before he recovers from the debt he incurred during the course of the court proceedings against him.

Still, he considers himself lucky.

For even now, there are other Stephens out there. And while some of them are surely guilty of serious crimes and fully deserving of punishment, others are just as surely innocent. Yet they, too, find themselves at the mercy of righteous police officers, well-meaning child-care workers, zealous legal advocates, and prosecutors with nothing but the very best of intentions in their hearts.

ACKNOWLEDGMENTS

I am indebted to my editor, Ruth Cavin, her assistant, Julie Sullivan, and my copy editor, Naomi Shulman, all of whom must surely wince on a regular basis, but ultimately allow me to treat the rules of grammar and style as mere suggestions.

I thank my literary agent, Bob Diforio, and my Man-on-the-West-Coast, John Ufland, who's still determined to see something of mine climb off the printed page and onto the screen. From your mouth to God's ear, John.

Closer to home, I thank my wife, Sandy, my children, Wendy, Ron, and Tracy, my sister Tillie, and my uncle Joe for once again serving as early readers and encouragers.

Finally, my thanks go out to the good people of northeast Columbia County, a few of whom may even find themselves in these pages, for allowing an old city dweller like me to run from the law and begin the process of becoming one of them.